Henry Bascom Ridgaway

The Life of Edmund S. Janes

Henry Bascom Ridgaway

The Life of Edmund S. Janes

ISBN/EAN: 9783337333324

Printed in Europe, USA, Canada, Australia, Japan

Cover: Foto ©Raphael Reischuk / pixelio.de

More available books at **www.hansebooks.com**

OF

EDMUND S. JANES, D.D., LL.D.,

Late Senior Bishop of the Methodist Episcopal Church.

BY

HENRY B. RIDGAWAY, D.D.

NEW YORK:

PHILLIPS & HUNT.

CINCINNATI:

WALDEN & STOWE.

1882.

CONTENTS.

CHAPTER V.—1844.

CHAPTER VI.—1844-1848.

CHAPTER VII.—1848-1850.

CHAPTER VIII.—1850-1852.

CHAPTER IX.—1852, 1853.

CHAPTER XVI.—1865–1868.

1*

CHAPTER XXI.

Illustrations.

TO

THE METHODISTS OF ALL LANDS;

OF WHOM

BISHOP JANES REJOICED TO BE ONE, AND WITH WHOM IN LOVING

FELLOWSHIP HE LIVED AND DIED,

THIS MEMORIAL

OF HIS LIFE AND SERVICES IS AFFECTIONATELY INSCRIBED

BY THE AUTHOR.

The Christian man is a most free lord of all, subject to none. The Christian man is a most dutiful servant of all, subject to all.

Luther on Christian Liberty.

THE LIFE

OF

EDMUND STORER JANES, D.D., LL.D.

CHAPTER I.

1807–1829.

Birth—Ancestry—Early Manhood—Conversion.

FOR full forty years there moved a man through the land, touching well-nigh every part of it with a personal force which was recognized and felt by all whom he met. The impulse which his presence imparted gently quickened the best sentiments in his fellow-beings, and left lingering in their hearts purposes and plans for nobler things. As to and from the great commercial metropolis he passed every-where, answering incessant claims, his course was not marked by the noise of the politician, the clatter of trade, or the parade of the warrior; simply and quietly, as a man and a minister of the Prince of peace, he came and went.

His work lay in the sphere of morals and religion. His zeal was for the highest good of the race. While possessed of a certain ascendency over men, he used its privileges only that he might bear witness to the truth, and be servant of all.

It shall be my aim in these pages to give some account of this man. The Church at large, as well as his own denomination, knew Bishop Janes in his official work. Beneath the high and useful public career there was a heart the full insight of which but few had while he lived, and the revealing of which, even very partially, cannot fail to lead to a higher estimate of his worth.

There is an instinctive desire in mankind to come near to a benefactor, to ascertain whence the streams of influence which have so refreshed them flowed, and to see how far the man whom they have looked at in the distance is like themselves in those things in which a nature common to their own shows itself. If much of the privacy of the life I shall seek to portray be presented, this, then, is my apology: "We know the Bishop; let us also know the man."

Edmund Storer Janes was born in the town of Sheffield, Berkshire County, Massachusetts, on the 27th of April, 1807. He was the son of Benjamin and Sally Janes, respectable and industrious people, who raised to maturity a family of eight children, five sons and three daughters. The Janes family trace their origin, in this country, as far as to William Janes, who was born in Essex, England, during the reign of James I., about the year 1610. The family name, Janes, is evidently the same as De Janes or De Jeanes, and is of Norman or French origin. It is still found in Kirtling, county of Cambridge, connected with the estates once belonging to Geoffrey de Janes about 1200 or 1204. This Geoffrey de Janes was a crusader, and helped to make Baldwin, count of Flanders, king of Jerusalem. While the genealogical links between the noted crusader and William Janes cannot be traced, it is well ascertained that William was of the Kirtling family, and that with the John Davenport colony he came out to this country. The colony at first landed in Massachusetts, in or near Boston, remained there eight months, and then, sailing for New Haven, Conn., their chosen abode, they there made their final settlement in 1637. These colonists, in common with many others, had fled from the persecutions of Archbishop Laud, to seek religious freedom in the American wilderness.

In the colony at New Haven William Janes was a prominent person. For about seventeen years he was a teacher of the rudiments of education and of the doctrines of the Bible, imparting to the children of the colonists the best intellectual and religious culture which their limited facilities allowed. " Vigorous, systematic, resolute, and true to every instinct of manhood, he was beloved and respected by all who knew him." *

* " The Janes Family. A Genealogy and Brief History of the Descendants of William Janes, the Emigrant Ancestor of 1637," by the Rev. Frederic Janes. New York : John H. Dingman. 1868. From this work these family references are taken.

William Janes subsequently, about 1656, removed, in company with other "pioneers of liberty," to Northampton, Mass., in the Connecticut valley. Here he was recorder of deeds and a teaching elder, and, in the absence of the minister, conducted the religious service of the Sabbath. "Some seventeen years later, when another new colony was started by the people of Northampton and Hadley, for some untried section farther up the valley, they proposed to William Janes to go, with his influence, his talents, and his property, and to be their religious teacher and counselor in their expected perils. He consented, as he loved his mission of doing good and planting religion in every part of the new country so soon to be settled." When they had reached the spot, *Squawkeague*, afterward known as Northfield, "he preached his first sermon on the Sabbath after their arrival under the spreading branches of a large oak-tree."

The colonists, however, on the outbreak of Philip's War, were driven away by the Indians, and, after losing some of their number, fell back to the settlement at Northampton. Among those slain were Ebenezer and Jonathan Janes, sons of William, lads of about seventeen and eighteen years of age. Another attempt was made at the settlement of this spot about ten years afterward which was even more disastrous. From this time until his death William lived at Northampton. He died

September 20, 1690, "leaving behind a name revered, untarnished, and imperishable."

This original William Janes was the great-great-great-grandfather of Edmund Storer. Of the intervening paternal ancestors, the great-great-grandfather William, and the great-grandfather Michael, little is known. Thomas Janes, the grandfather, was a soldier in the War of the Revolution, his name being found upon the roll of a Connecticut regiment of infantry, under Colonel Moses Thayer, from January 1, 1777, to January, 1782. After escaping all the perils of the war he was accidentally killed by the overturning of a loaded cart while he was engaged at work on his farm in Wallingford, Conn. He left a widow with a young family, the oldest of whom, Benjamin, was but twelve years of age. Thus the father of Edmund Storer was obliged, when only a lad, to become the main-stay of his mother and younger brothers and sisters. He learned the trade of carpenter and joiner, and early formed industrious habits. Benjamin Janes married Miss Sally Wood, of Chatham, N. Y., and removed when quite young to Sheffield, Mass. Here, as I have stated, Edmund Storer was born, being the seventh generation from the great emigrant and pioneer.

It will thus be seen that our subject was well descended. He was born of a religious and heroic race. He was heir to the grandest ideas and tradi-

tions which ever fell to a human being. His direct
ancestry stood not alone, but were of the company
of noble confessors who contended for the maintenance of the political and religious principles which
have since shaped American institutions, and are
now molding the character and directing the destinies of all civilized nations. The two forces of
civilization, Guizot tells us, are what the individual gets from the thoughts and spirit of society,
and what society derives from the discoveries and
enterprise of the individual. It is consequently of
advantage to a person to be born in a community
which is fraught with great and good principles and
which is controlled by just and wise laws.

"There is a country accent," says La Roche-
foucauld, "not in speech only, but in thought, conduct, character, and manner of existing, which never
forsakes a man. . . . A country where the entire
people is, or even once has been, laid hold of—
filled to the heart—with an infinite religious idea,
has 'made a step from which it cannot retrograde.'
Thought, conscience, the sense that man is denizen
of a universe, creature of an eternity, has penetrated to the remotest cottage, to the simplest
heart. . . . There is an inspiration in such a people :
one may say in a more special sense, the inspiration of the Almighty giveth them understanding.
Honor to all the brave and true ; everlasting honor
to brave old Knox, (one of the truest of the true !)

that in the moment while he and his cause, amid civil broils, in convulsion and confusion, were still but struggling for life, he sent the school-master forth to all corners, and said, 'Let the people be taught:' . . . His message, in its true compass, was, ' Let men know that they are men ; created by God, responsible to God ; who work in any merest moment of time what will last through eternity!' "

What the great seer of Chelsea, whose last wail over the falseness of the world has only so recently fallen upon our ear, wrote of Presbyterian Scotland, may be with equal truth written of Calvinistic New England. In this New Scotland of religious faith and practice, of political liberty and order, of public schools and colleges, of thrift and enterprise, young Janes had his first and forming years. As naturally as the air from the Berkshire hills streamed into his lungs did the moral life of his native State insinuate itself into his soul. Nor can I overlook nor lessen, for the mere uses of illustration, the physical surroundings upon which he first gazed and in the midst of which he was reared.

Berkshire County is noted for its picturesque scenery. There is not to be found in any land a more beautiful valley than that of the Housatonic, stretching from the town of Lenox, Mass., on the north, to that of Salisbury, Conn., on the south. In the distance northward can be seen the Saddle-back Mountains, reaching their highest point in old Gray Lock,

whence they fall away in all directions in gentle un-
dulations. Near by the hills rise in sufficiently varying heights to impart a sense of grandeur, while the
river winds and rushes in its gravelly bed through
meadows studded with the graceful elm, and of glossy
smoothness. This valley has ever been the favorite
resort and home of poets and orators, and of people
of culture and leisure. Here Miss Catherine Sedgwick was born and lived; here also William Cullen
Bryant spent his early manhood; here Orville Dewey,
the famous Unitarian preacher, whose lectures on
" Beauty" were rapturously received, loved to linger
through the long summer days; here, too, the intellectual T. F. R. Mercein, of the Methodist Episcopal Church, whose marvelous promise as theologian and preacher was cut short by death in the very
town where young Janes was born, conceived some
of his most suggestive theories.

Mr. Bryant, referring to his reminiscences of this
region, says: "It was on the third of October,
in the year I have mentioned, (1816,) that I made
the journey thither from Cummington. The woods
were in all the glory of autumn, and I well remember,
as I passed through Stockbridge, how much I was
struck by the beauty of the smooth green meadows
on the banks of a lovely river which winds near
the Sedgwick mansion, the Housatonic, and whose
gently-flowing waters seemed tinged with the gold
and crimson of the trees that overhung them.

I admired no less the contrast between this soft scene and the steep, craggy hills that overlooked them, clothed with their many-colored forests. I had never before seen the southern part of Berkshire, and congratulated myself on becoming an inhabitant of so picturesque a region."

Amid these scenes of natural beauty the boy Edmund grew up. While he was quite young his father moved a little way down the valley to the town of Salisbury, Conn., where he added to his trade of carpenter the peaceful pursuit of farmer. Here Edmund's youth was spent, alternating in attendance upon the district school and in wholesome work upon the farm. In the one he laid the foundation of his after mental culture, and on the other, in tough encounter with the soil, the foundation of the sinewy and elastic body which became subsequently the physical basis of well-nigh superhuman tasks. Long years subsequently, when on a visit to the scenes of his boyhood, he wrote to his own son: "I saw the stone-wall (fence) which I helped to build when I was a lad." In these rough, homely pursuits the physical culture received, while important, was not the highest benefit arising; he was trained in habits of self-help. He learned to wait on himself, to be mindful of others, and thoughtful in little things. There is no evidence at hand that his schooling went further than was afforded by the facilities of the neighborhood.

But to have had the education of a godly, frugal, and industrious New England home, associated and interwoven with his knowledge of plain English, was a good starting-point for a youth of those days. He needed only the mastership of a district school to put him forward on the high road to professional studies; and that, too, soon came.

During all these days of spelling-book and grammar there was at work upon young Janes's heart the genial and plastic influence of a wise and devout mother. Of her we know but little, yet her character is easy to learn, not only from what he became, but also from his private references to her piety and the high estimate and tender regard he ever manifested for woman's nurture and a mother's influence. In an old manuscript on " Female Education " — one of his very earliest, judging from the rough, yellow, torn paper and the neat chirography—speaking of the mother, he says: " The empire of the mind is equally subject to her sway. The mother is the first book the child ever reads. Her loving smile, her actions, her accents, compose the first alphabet the child ever learns. It is an alphabet of hieroglyphics — every sign stands for a separate idea. Corresponding to their nature and influence will be the character and direction of the shooting ideas. How important, then, that this first book be a good one. . . . The peculiar character of the mother gives her great fitness to attain and maintain ascendency over the child. In her tenderness the child always finds sympathy; in her goodness the child always finds a disposition to relieve and bless; and in her maternal affection one who is interested in its happiness. Her versatility of character enables her to accommodate herself to all the calls and circumstances of her offspring, and her patience enables her to bear with all its perverseness and weakness and wants." Such language shows he was speaking from experience, and that likely the original of the picture was his own mother.

It appears that Mr. Janes began his first efforts at teaching when about seventeen years of age. Mr. Ludlow E. Lapham, of Penn Yan, N. Y., says in a letter of March 5, 1878:

In the summer of 1824 Mr. Janes taught a district school at Ancram Furnace, in Livingston's Manor, Columbia County, N. Y. It was my fortune to succeed him the following winter. He was then a youth just budding into manhood. He was very successful in the calling, and in gaining the good-will and esteem of scholars and patrons. He infused the sweet and lovely charm among scholars, patrons, and the neighborhood that I have ever found following him in his subsequent history. Later in life we met at the Conference in this place, where we talked of the old school district and the families, namely, Judge Tremain's, John S. Harris's, J. A. Coon's, and Allen Sheldon's. . . . I think he told me he was converted at that school-house, but I am not sure. Revs. Miller and Lovejoy were the circuit preachers, and held their meetings there. Again I met him in the streets of New York,

2

and our conversation would revert to the early school-house;
he seemed to fix it as the beginning of his Christian life.

Mr. Janes continued to teach in different districts in his native region for about five years.   One
of the schools was near Dover Plains, in Dutchess
County, N. Y.   The Rev. Elbert Osborn, late of
the New York Conference, speaking of the dedication of the church in this village, which occurred
in 1854 or 1855, says: " Our host was a young convert who had been once a pupil of Mr. Janes's before he entered the ministry and when he was
teaching a district school in that vicinity.   It was
very pleasant to both of them to call up the incidents of former days.   The good brother took us in
his conveyance to the school-house where the
Bishop had formerly taught, and there we looked
at the place where he used to study his Bible in
the intervals of teaching."

The date of Mr. Janes's conversion cannot be
definitely fixed.   It was evidently at some time during the five years that he was engaged in teaching in
some one of these district schools.   Previous to his
conversion he had been somewhat skeptical, and
when converted he did not unite with the Church
until careful inquiry into its doctrines and discipline.
As the itinerant preachers passed his school-house
door in their rounds upon the circuit, he would
stop them and ply them with questions, thus early
showing his desire for knowledge and his love

of accuracy. The Rev. Phineas Cook, an aged preacher, is said to have mentioned the incident that when on one occasion he was going by the school-house Mr. Janes came out with the Methodist Discipline in hand, with his finger upon the word "preventing," in the Eighth Article, (on Free-will,) and asked its meaning in that relation. The preacher requested him to bring his dictionary, and then showed him the different senses in which the term was used, and explained its fitness in the relation in which it appeared in the Discipline.

The Rev. J. K. Peck, of Wyoming Conference, in a paper on Bishop Janes, read at a district meeting in Guilford, N. Y., November, 1876, states, upon the authority of Mrs. George Devine, residing in, Susquehanna County, Pa., who was a companion of Mr. Janes in his early life, that during most of those years in which he taught school "he was known by his intimate friends as an unbeliever in the Christian religion, and that he regarded himself as somewhat of a poet." Mr. Peck further states: "I have in my possession two manuscript poems written by him in the year 1827. They are written upon coarse paper, the size of foolscap, without any sign of ruling either stamped or with pencil, yet the lines are remarkably regular and straight, and of uniform distance apart. . . . I received them from Mrs. George Devine. . . . She had preserved them very carefully through all these years. They, of course, became the more valued after her former young friend became a D. D. and a Bishop."

These manuscripts lie before me. The longer one is headed thus: " Lines composed extempore at a youth's ———— (carried on exclusively by young converts,) June 10, 1827, Canaan," in which the author aimed at nothing more than to express in poetic form their sentiments as advanced, and as nearly as practicable in the speakers' own language, merely to aid his memory in retaining them and their influence on his own mind.

Mr. Peck also says: " The young man who was able to reason away the truths that came from learned ministers and to ward off conviction, was compelled to own ' religion true ' while viewing such a scene." I incline to the opinion that it was soon after this time his conversion took place. It is quite clear from the testimony of Mrs. Devine, and also from the fact that Mr. Phineas Cook traveled Salisbury Circuit in 1826 and 1827, that it was in 1827 that he united with the Methodist Episcopal Church, though he may have been the subject of religious conviction before this. When about twenty years of age, and he was anticipating entering upon the practice of the law, for which he had been preparing, " God's solemn providence struck down suddenly his intended partner in business." Like Luther, whose companion was smitten by lightning by his side when on a journey, he was greatly alarmed. "This note of conscious warning turned his attention from secular to spiritual things, and determined his future plans for life." *

The manuscripts of these verses are of importance simply as showing his mental aptitudes and habits. Of the longer one Mr. Peck states: "There is one blot on the paper about the size of the letter *o* in writing, showing that a drop of ink had fallen from his pen upon the paper while he was writing, and an effort made to brush it off had only enlarged it. But how any one could write extempore verses in such a noisy meeting with pen and ink, and have every thing so perfect and correct, is a mystery. There is not a word or letter scratched, and only one word left out, and that is the word ' meeting ' in the heading. The commas and periods and semicolons are all in their proper places, and the i's are dotted and the t's crossed, and the lines are as straight as most of us write when our paper is ruled. The faculty that he there displayed of being composed and correct in confusion and excitement has been of great help to him, especially when presiding in stormy Conferences."

Thus it appears that, like most young people of a studious turn of mind, Mr. Janes tried his wing at poesy. Afterward, also, in maturer years he occasionally composed verses. Some of these possess

* "The Janes Family."

the merit of a smooth and an easy rhythm, and
contain just and devout sentiments, but none can
properly claim to be entitled poetry. Though from
youth rich in fancy and endowed with a keen sus-
ceptibility to beauty, yet he seems to have lacked
the original power of interpreting the poetical element of nature. Wisely, therefore, it will be seen,
he confined himself to prose. He was born an orator, not a poet; and he was so sagacious as to recognize and cultivate his true gift, and not to waste
his efforts upon an art in which he could never have
excelled. Nothing was more characteristic of him
than a sound and sober estimate of his own talents,
and the good sense with which he applied himself
in the direction of his natural genius must certainly
be commended.

CHAPTER II.

1829 – 1836.

Teacher—Itinerant Preacher—College Agent—Marriage.

THE years during which Mr. Janes taught in the district schools were eventful years to him. While he was training youth in the rudiments of an English education, he was training himself, not only in the art of instruction, but also in the elements of law and theology. Like many another before and since, he found *his* university in the simple, rude district school. There, in the intervals of hard work, he snatched moments for the side studies which prepared him for speedy and solid advancement. In these later times he would likely have gone from rudimentary teaching to the seminary and college; but then colleges were few, and among the Methodists there were none. There was scarcely a seminary of a high grade. He could only do the next best thing. Having formed his purpose to become a lawyer, he procured books and advice from a neighboring attorney, and commenced the study of the law in connection with his employment as teacher. Just how long he read law, or when he finally abandoned the purpose of adopting it as a profession, does not appear. Undoubtedly he would have made an able lawyer, and might have risen to the highest attainments and honors in the profession : still the time spent in this study, and the discipline and knowledge acquired, failed not to stamp his mind with an eminently judicial character, and thus he was all the more thoroughly fitted for the responsible career which afterward opened to him.

In 1829 he was led to make a change of residence. The following letter indicates his direction. It is addressed to Israel Crane, Esq., Bloomfield, Essex County, N. J.:

"SALISBURY, *April* 20, 1829.

DEAR SIR: The bearer, Mr. Edmund S. Janes, has expressed to me a wish to be employed as an instructor of an English school in some part of your State. I have taken the liberty to mention to him yourself, as a gentleman to whom I would advise him to apply for assistance should he happen to visit your neighborhood. Mr. Janes is a young gentleman with whom I have been much acquainted ; he has for many seasons been employed in this town and vicinity as an instructor of youth with very great credit to himself and advantage to his employers. He sustains a moral and religious character which has endeared him to his friends here, and should he find employment in his profession in your vicinity, I am confident he would not disappoint the hopes of his friends.

To this is added a note from Mr. Crane :

MR. SAMUEL I. RIKER :

SIR : Samuel Church, Esq., is a respectable gentleman of my acquaintance in the State of Connecticut. I should confide in his recommendation of the bearer, Mr. Janes. If there be any vacancy in the school in your neighborhood, and you should introduce this gentleman as teacher I doubt not he would meet your expectations.

"*April* 22, 1829."

While Mr. Janes was teaching in New Jersey he became convinced of his duty to preach the Gospel, and he was accordingly licensed as a local preacher by the Quarterly Conference of Belleville Circuit, of which the Rev. Isaac Winner was preacher in charge and the Rev. Joseph Lybrand presiding elder. By the same Quarterly Conference he was recommended to the Philadelphia Annual Conference for the regular ministry, and was received "on trial" by that body, April, 1830, in the city of Philadelphia. His name in the General Minutes stands eleventh in a class of fifteen. Among his classmates was the brilliant James Nicols, of the Eastern Shore of Maryland. The Rev. John Leonard Gilder is the only classmate who survives. The Philadelphia Conference at that time included a large portion of eastern Pennsylvania; the peninsula lying between the Chesapeake and Delaware Bays, comprising the State of Delaware, the Eastern Shore of Maryland, and the Eastern Shore of Virginia; and also the whole of the State of New Jersey. In the same territory there are now the Philadelphia, Wilmington, New Jersey, and Newark Conferences. Among the young preachers of the Conference were Charles

2*

Pitman, John Kennaday, John S. Porter, R. M.
Greenbank, Levi Scott, George G. Cookman, Francis
Hodgson, and Joseph Holdich. I doubt if any
Conference in the land possessed a nobler corps of
young men, and yet even among these Mr. Janes
almost immediately became distinguished.

The year in which Mr. Janes was admitted on
trial in the " traveling connection," the Church with
which he was henceforth to be so closely identified
had but 18 Annual Conferences, 4 Bishops, 476,153
members, and 1,900 traveling preachers. He was to
live to see it greatly extended and to have no small
share in its extension.

The first appointment of Mr. Janes was Elizabethtown, N. J., with Rev. Thomas Morrell, supernumer-
ary, in charge. Mr. Morrell was one of the wisest
and most highly esteemed ministers of the Conference. It was fortunate for the young inexperienced
preacher to have so devout and judicious a guide
in his first beginning. The well-nigh universal arrangement of earlier Methodism, whereby a novitiate
in the ministry was associated with an older and
more experienced person, contributed not a little to
its rapid success and thorough conservation. Zeal
and sagacity were happily united, the dash and enterprise of youth being tempered by the modera-
tion and caution of age.

Mr. Janes entered upon his ministerial duties with
promptness, and prosecuted them with much ear-

nestness. He not only preached in the principal churches, but entered every open door, occupying on week days and evenings all the school-houses and private dwellings that were offered for devotional services. He was incessant in work, and high in his aspirations. Naught but an inward fire which was kindled of a lofty purpose could have borne him along, despite some marked physical disabilities, to the eminence which he attained. He was made for command, and to reach command through the force of action. Temperament is the natural ground of character, and in itself must be regarded as innocent. It is only as temperaments differ that determinate types of character are possible, and it is within the sphere of temperament that divine grace works, modifying and directing to the highest and most useful ends.

The Rev. Thomas B. Sargent, D.D., then a very young man, had been transferred from the Philadelphia to the Baltimore Conference in the spring of 1830. He had been the preacher at Elizabethtown for 1826 and 1827. He made a visit to his former parishioners soon after Mr. Janes had been appointed to them, and he gives in 1876 this pleasant reminiscence : " My acquaintance with him began June 13, 1830, when I preached for him in the old forty-feet-square shingle-boarded church at Elizabethtown, in which I, as his predecessor, had ministered for two whole years—Dr. Holdich

having been between us. . . . I was led to urge
our little flock in Elizabethtown to enlarge, and
was seconded by Brother Janes. He and I on
Monday made a round of our fold, and I was deeply impressed with the modesty, sweetness, and spirituality of the man and minister, and said, ' Behold,
how they love him — both sheep and lambs.' "
The acquaintance which then began between these
two promising young ministers was soon afterward
ripened into a close friendship, which continued
without alloy or abatement during their whole
lives. Of this there will be further proofs.

Mr. Janes was re-appointed to Elizabethtown in
1831. The following letter to him, from the Rev.
John J. Matthias, Newark, November 28, 1831,
shows he was already attracting some attention as
a speaker beyond his own charge:

Our Sunday-school celebration will be on Wednesday evening, December 7, at six o'clock. We depend on you to give a
speech on the occasion, and you will please not disappoint us ;
for the meeting will be generally advertised, and we hope it
will pass off well. We are still going on here after the same
old sort, and need a great deal of grace—pray for us. I wish
you would come up in the morning stage and come to my
house.

If the young preacher began as he finished his
ministry, he was at Newark on time and spoke.

Thus early was his voice raised in the Sunday-
school cause, a department of Church work which

was just then rising to importance, and of which he was to be so efficient an advocate.

He attended the session of the Philadelphia Conference at Wilmington, Delaware, in the spring of 1832, and was then ordained a deacon, and admitted into full membership in the Conference.

The Rev. John S. Porter, D.D., in a communication, says:

My knowledge of Mr. Janes commenced in 1832, when he preached in Wilmington, Delaware, before a large number of the members of the Philadelphia Conference, to which he had been admitted into full membership the day before. It was a surprise to many that he should be appointed to preach on such an occasion, but when he had performed the duty assigned, the surprise was that he had given such proof that the appointment was every way justified by the ability displayed. Taking for his text, "Show thyself a man," he proceeded to give the programme of his own admirable life, which he filled out fully in all the years allotted to him.

At this session Mr. Janes had the pleasure of seeing his twin brother, the Rev. E. L. Janes, admitted on trial by the Conference. Thus the two brothers were to be united for life in the work of the Christian ministry, having their natural relationship re-enforced and cemented by a calling wholly congenial to their convictions and tastes. And a pair of loving brothers and fellow-helpers they proved.

Mr. Janes was assigned to Orange, New Jersey. His name stands alone in the Minutes. The only

item which I have in my possession that throws
any light on this year, is an old scrap of paper with
a vote of thanks on it:

REVEREND SIR: The Young Men's Temperance Association of Orange, at its last anniversary meeting, passed the following resolution, and instructed the president and secretary
of said society to forward you a copy of the same.

"*Resolved*, That the thanks of this association be presented
to the Rev. E. S. Janes for the very appropriate and excellent
address with which he favored the society on this occasion."

ORANGE, *Nov.* 9, 1832.

So we find the young evangelist laying hold of
all the side issues which pertained to the work of
saving the souls and bodies of men. Nothing was
foreign to his ministry by which he hoped to render
it more useful to the masses, and especially to
young people. From this day onward he was the
steadfast friend and supporter of the Temperance
Reform.

During this year he made a visit to his friend,
Mr. Sargent, who had been transferred to the Baltimore Conference, and was stationed in Baltimore city. Of this visit Dr. Sargent says, "He
preached with great acceptance and usefulness in
all our then best churches, for white and colored, the
latter offering a new and agreeable audience to him.
In conformity with a usage then and now prevailing
as distinctive of Methodism, he preached short,
seldom exceeding forty-five minutes, and prayed

long, over twenty-five or thirty minutes. One of
the preachers who had followed him over the city
ventured to say to him, 'Brother Janes, why do
you pray *so long?*' He answered with great softness, sweetness, and simplicity, 'Because I love to
pray.'"

The following year his name stands on the Minutes for Bloomfield and Orange, with James V. Potts
in charge. The Rev. S. S. Potter, D.D., of Cincinnati, says of this period: "It was some years
before his true worth was known even by his own
denomination. I think it was in a school-house
where I learned my A B C, that I first heard him
preach. It was at a time when my mind was first
exercised in regard to the ministry, and his preaching so favorably impressed me that it drew forth
the utterance, 'I would not mind being a preacher
if I could preach as well as that man.'"

It was at about this period that the youthful
preacher chanced to be in the company of some
older ministers and to hear a conversation which
made a deep impression upon him. John M. Howe,
M.D.—a life-long friend—received this account of it
from his lips: "When I was a young man, having
just entered the Conference, I was in company with
three aged ministers, to whose conversation I listened with marked interest. They were relating
their experience as Methodist preachers, and the
course that they had pursued in reference to their

intercourse with church members and persons generally. 'I,' said one, 'have got along without any
difficulties and have been governed by these three
rules: 1. Never to take offense ; 2. Never to ask any
explanations; 3. Treat every one as though nothing had ever happened.' 'By these rules,' said the
Bishop, 'I have been governed all along through
my ministry;' and he added, 'No words outside of
inspiration have been of so much real value to me.' "

At the Conference which met at Philadelphia,
April 9, 1834, Mr. Janes was elected and ordained
an elder, and appointed agent for Dickinson College.

The Methodists of the Philadelphia and Baltimore Conferences had long felt the need of a
school of high grade, and within the bounds of
the Baltimore Conference two unsuccessful attempts had been made to establish such an institution.   Dickinson College had been located at
Carlisle, Pa., in 1783, and was under the control and
patronage of the Presbyterians of the State of Pennsylvania.   It had maintained an honored but rather
precarious existence for a half century, when its
managers, despairing of any adequate support, proposed to transfer it to the Methodists.   The only
condition of the transfer with its entire accumula-
tion of appliances, was a pledge on the part of the
Baltimore and Philadelphia Conferences to raise
such an endowment as would reasonably guarantee

that the object of the founders would be realized in perpetuity. Accordingly in 1833 trustees were provisionally appointed by the Conferences, and the transfer was made. Three agents were immediately appointed to raise funds for the endowment: The Revs. S. G. Roszell and J. A. Collins, within the bounds of the Baltimore, and the Rev. E. S. Janes within the territory of the Philadelphia Conference.

Mr. Janes was selected because of his already approved ability as a speaker, and for his financial skill and unwearied industry. It was a trying time in which to raise money for such a purpose. The buildings of the two initial colleges, at Cokesbury and at Light Lane, Baltimore, had both been burned, and this circumstance, appealing to communities only meagerly educated, and with whom there was no slight prejudice against an educated ministry, induced a serious doubt as to whether the Methodists were providentially called to the work of higher education; it was, therefore, of no use to put into the field for this work a dull, spiritless speaker, or a man destitute of nerve and energy. Courage had to be inspired, doubts to be removed, liberality had to be called forth; indeed, a new era was to be created in the history of a people rapidly growing both in numbers and resources, and to do this required a man of method, fire, and persistence. Mr. Janes proved sufficient for the occasion. With Philadelphia as a base of operations he went from one end of the

Conference to the other, preaching sermons, making addresses, meeting committees, interviewing and soliciting private persons, taking collections, receiving pledges, selling scholarships, until he had everywhere aroused an enthusiasm for education and made Dickinson College a household word among the people. For two whole years he was thus engaged—the last year being associated with the eloquent Charles Pitman—in which time enough money was raised by the Conferences to create a respectable endowment, which, when supplemented by annual collections in the various charges, proved adequate to the support of what for those times was a full faculty of professors.

Dr. Porter, in the communication already quoted, speaking of this period, says :

I was stationed in Philadelphia, where he was frequently called in the discharge of his duties as agent. We were thus thrown together, and formed a mutual attachment, which was continued and strengthened during his natural life. The agency required all his energies, and he did not disappoint those who had chosen him for that important work. His serious earnestness, his tact, his persistence, and his intelligent, pious appeals, connected with his superior ministrations in preaching the word of God in our pulpits wherever he went, made him a successful agent in soliciting funds for the college at a time when the people had to be awakened to the importance of Christian education under Methodist auspices.

While agent of Dickinson College he had occasion to address the Pennsylvania Legislature in its interests. The circumstances were such that he

could make little or no written preparation. He
was obliged to depend upon such materials as he
could command at the moment. The effect upon
the gentlemen was very marked. His clear presentation of facts and principles, his unaffected and
forcible eloquence, completely captivated them. He
himself was taught a valuable lesson, one that followed him through life—with a mastering of his subject, always to depend, especially in platform addresses, upon the inspiration of the occasion. The
Rev. Dr. Potter, before quoted, referring to this address, remarks : "A neighbor of mine, a man of keen
intellectual discernment, by some means obtained a
copy of the address, and put it into my hands, saying as he did so, ' I don't know Mr. Janes, but, mark
my words, there is true worth and greatness in that
man, and we shall hear from him again.' "

The earliest letter from Mr. Janes which has
come into my possession is one addressed to John
M. Howe, M.D., then of New York city, dated
September 16, 1835. It was in answer to a request
from Mr. Howe for a copy of a sermon which he had
heard Mr. Janes preach in that city :

I last evening received your note of the 14th inst., containing
a request for a sketch of my sermon on Sunday morning. It
would afford me much pleasure to comply with your wishes
could I do so. I had no sketch of the sermon written before
preaching it, and it would be difficult for me to write one now.
I am disposed, however, to comply with your wishes as far as
time and the circumstances under which I preached it will allow.

The sketch in full given to his friend illustrates his habits of mind and the character of his preaching in the forming period of his ministry. It shows how fully he was imbued with the evangelical spirit, and how successfully he had acquired intellectual discipline, traits which ever afterward so eminently distinguished him. Such a sermon, delivered with all the fervor of youth, could not have failed to impress the thoughtful young Christians of his audience.

It was about the time of the delivery of this sermon—possibly on this very visit—that Mr. Janes addressed a missionary anniversary at Greene-street Church, New York. Dr. Howe had invited, with some warmth of expression, a certain young lady to attend this anniversary to hear a young man who was to speak. The young lady who accompanied Dr. Howe to the meeting was Miss Charlotte Thibou of that city. Miss Thibou's parents were members of the Protestant Episcopal Church; she herself had been reared in that communion, and had only recently left it and united with the Methodist Episcopal Church. All her traditions and associations were also in the Episcopal Church; her mother's brother, Bishop Croes, having been the predecessor of Bishop Doane, of the diocese of New Jersey. There was, however, a charm about the simplicity and spirituality of the Methodists that won her thoughtful, devout, and earnest nature. There was something in the plainness of their manners and in their love to one another, but more especially in the doctrine of perfect love, as set forth and exemplified in their teaching and practice, which drew her to their meetings and attached her to their company. She said substantially: "These people are God's people. They live after the New Testament pattern. They are filled with faith and the Holy Ghost. I find among them what meets my highest spiritual wants. I am at home and happy with them. These people shall be my people." Her decision met with some opposition from her friends; but the Huguenot blood in her veins and the Spirit of Christ in her heart rendered her firm and immovable in the choice she had once made.

Miss Thibou's first association with the Methodists was at Newark, N. J. After her removal to New York city she became a frequent attendant upon the meetings for the promotion of holiness, conducted by Mrs. John Harper. At these meetings she found that which was congenial to her religious experience. It was about this time that Mr. Janes was introduced to Miss Thibou. She was young and beautiful, highly intelligent and cultivated, already betokening that *spirituelle* of expression which became such a peculiar charm. The acquaintance rapidly ripened into a mutual affection, and in the month of May, 1835, they were married. I doubt if a truer and happier marriage was ever rati-

fied in heaven. Long years afterward the bride-
groom, then in the fullness of his power and fame,
said good-humoredly to some of his brethren who
were conversing on eligible marriage : " Well, I got
a fortune in my wife." She, too, as many years
after, in one of her sportive moods—for she had
them—when talking to a pastor, the Rev. William
Day, of her earlier recollections, thus alluded to this
eventful period : " When Mr. Janes was making his
earlier visits to me, and the great question of my
social life was under consideration, incidentally one
evening he said, in speaking of his circumstances,
' It has been my honor for some time to help support my parents.' Those incidental words *decided
my choice*, for I felt that my interests would be safe
in the hands of a young man who regarded it an
honor to support his aged parents." Mr. Day well
remarks : " I will not presume to say which most
claims our admiration ; the candor and filial devotion of Mr. Janes, or the character of her whose
choice was so controlled by that devotion."

As showing the devout spirit which animated
Miss Thibou in the period immediately preceding
her marriage, I give extracts from two letters written
to her life-long friend, Mrs. Joseph A. Wright, then
Mrs. Caroline R. Browne :

December 30, 1834.

. . . To-day I unite with you in praising the Lord. He imparts to me those inward delights that flow from communion

with himself. He causes streams of grace and salvation to water and replenish my soul. Peace, love, and joy are inmates of my breast, while the bright felicity of the saints in light stands revealed to the eye of my faith, enrapturing my soul. To my Jesus I continually aspire, striving to live to him every moment.

The fervent desires of your heart after inward purity and entire devotedness are to me delightful. How much more pleasing must they be to the eyes of your Prince. He will abundantly grant your most enlarged petitions by uniting you closely to him, and while you suffer him to reign without a rival, he will pour the full tide of light and love upon you from his sacred throne. . . . Praise his name! the precious pearl of perfect love is just before you. Reach after it—receive it as the free gift of Him who loves you.

I receive you, my friend, as my dear sister in Christ, and shall rejoice to have you love and treat me as such. The dearest bond that can unite sympathetic hearts is the mutual love that binds us to the Cross. Be this the strong connecting link that shall unite us in the closest friendship, never to be dissolved, but matured and perfected in heaven. . . .

Very affectionately yours, in the sweetest and best of bonds,

C. THIBOU.

Under date of Jan. 20, 1835, after a brief illness, she again writes to the same friend :

I am now quite comfortable, and only waiting to be fully restored that I may again be about my Master's business. I did not know but that the slight indisposition might be the messenger employed by the Prince of pilgrims to take me up to the celestial city. On some accounts I should have welcomed the call ; and yet I felt a desire, if consistent with His will, to tarry below awhile longer to be of some little use—to do something before the season of doing is passed forever. Why, my love, to wipe away one tear, to bind up one broken heart, to soothe one troubled breast, to warn a sinner, to pray for a backslider, .

or to point one penitent to the Lamb of God this, this is worth living for many long, wearisome years.

. . . To-day I have been solemnly renewing my covenant before the Lord to be *wholly* and *forever his.* O for the humility, the docility, the purity of a primitive disciple! O for the meek and lowly mind of Jesus himself! Nothing but this can suffice. Come, holy Saviour, and sit upon this heart; melt it thoroughly, and cause it to take fully the signature divine, and to shine forth after thy lovely likeness—*all praise, all meekness, and all love.*

. . . O the depth of love divine! And an'overflowing fountain, too, for some of its sacred streams reach even to my heart, refreshing and fertilizing, and, I trust, making it fruitful. . . . Now I ask of God the grace to improve to the *utmost* the rich privileges to which, as believers, we are entitled. O yes, we must have the fullness of God—the heaven of love!

Such was the spirit of the bride of Mr. Janes. Both had already been married to the Church, and in choosing one another each had an eye distinctly to the glory of God and the spread of that form of Christianity called Methodism, which was as dear to them as life itself. In full view of a career of self-sacrifice they joined their fortunes, and through long years of toil they mutually sustained each other, steadying and staying one another's steps, cheering one another's fainting spirit, rejoicing and weeping together, until their pilgrimage closed.

CHAPTER III.

1836–1841.

The City Pastor—Elected Secretary to the American Bible Society.

THE first appointment of Mr. Janes after marriage was to the Fifth-street charge, Philadelphia. It comprised 556 members. The church edifice was large, and the work of the pastor, both in pastoral visiting and preaching, was necessarily arduous. Mr. Janes suffered during the latter part of the year from an acute inflammation of the throat, so that by his own expressed wish he was changed in 1837 to the Nazareth charge, where the building was smaller. The number of members, however, was equally large—582. The care of so many members, together with the numerous persons to whom they were more or less allied, must have taxed the young minister to the utmost of his strength. His rather feeble body would undoubtedly have failed under it but for the system with which he did all his work, and the admirable skill with which he learned from this time—largely because compelled to do so—to manage all his powers, especially his voice, in speaking. His voice, feminine in tone and never strong, was somewhat im-

8

paired by disease and over-exertion, but, henceforth, under the perfect control to which he subjected it, he found continuous public speaking not only practicable and healthful, but the weak and unpromising voice became the facile instrument of his commanding thoughts.

In 1838 Mr. Janes was re-appointed to Nazareth charge, and spent another year. The General Minutes show a net gain for the two years of 100 members.

Two brief letters, during this period, from Mrs. Janes to the friend previously mentioned, shed a little light on the household and the pastor's doings :

I feel stronger desires than ever to be wholly devoted to God, and for him to live and die. I find him a present Saviour—a most loving friend. In his service is my supreme delight. I am surrounded with temporal and spiritual blessings. My husband is one of the very best. My little son, Lewis Thibou, is a sprightly, hearty boy of eighteen months. We live in Montgomery-street, No. 9, very near Nazareth Church, which we consider one of the most beautiful, pleasant, and commodious in the country. Our congregation is crowded. We receive several new members every Sunday. Mr. Janes's health is much improved.

Again, under date of May 8, 1838:

With much pleasure I acknowledge the receipt of your letter, and thank you for the satisfaction its contents imparted to my mind. It seemed like the return of former days, when we enjoyed the sweet delights of Christian friendship, and together tasted that the Lord is gracious. . . . I feel now more sensibly than ever, that the increase of the divine life in the soul is

the only thing that is worth being *anxious* about. . . . Then
let us mount up on the wings of holy contemplation, and be
much engaged with God for the full measure of the Holy Spirit
—for then only can the perfect union of the blessed Redeemer
be impressed upon our souls. . . . Mr. Janes will bring this to
New York, having been invited to deliver an address before
the American Bible Society on Thursday.

Dr. J. S. Porter gives us this glimpse :

While he was stationed in Philadelphia, and I was in Burlington, New Jersey, long continued revival work had well-
nigh exhausted me, and I went to Philadelphia to seek help.
At the preachers' meeting I saw a number of brethren, and
labored in vain to secure the services of some one or more, and
left for the boat which was to carry me back with feelings of
discomfort, when I met Brother Janes in the market-place.
Having made known the state of the case, which he heard patiently, he at once stated his own case—what he had been doing for the last week, and his appointments for that week ; but
it was apparent that there was one night of that week which
was not occupied with any appointment, concerning which he
said, " I think I should rest that night, and recuperate a little,
but if you say I must go to Burlington and preach for you, I
will go." As a matter of course I said, You must go, and he
came and rendered us great assistance. He did this at some
sacrifice, and made an impression on my mind of his gracious
goodness which was never effaced.

As showing the early kindling of Mr. Janes's zeal
for the closely related causes of Christian missions
and African colonization, I give two short letters
addressed to the Rev. Nathan Bangs, D.D., then
Corresponding Secretary of the Missionary Society
of the Methodist Episcopal Church. The first is
dated at Philadelphia, October 12, 1837:

I received your letter of the 7th inst. last evening. This morning I have made inquiries concerning the business upon which you wrote. I find that there will no vessel sail from this port for Africa soon. The Pennsylvania Colonization Society unite with the New York Society in fitting out the ship "Emperor," to sail from your port.

It would give me pleasure, at any time, to render yourself or the missionary cause any service that it may be in my power to confer.

The second is dated, Philadelphia, May 24, 1838:

I have understood that there is some probability that Brother Seys * will visit this country this summer. If so, I very much desire that he should come to this city. I think if he could do so, and give us the statistics of affairs in Africa, it would cure our people here of their opposition to our African missions and to colonization. I hope you will bear this matter in mind, and, should he visit this country, endeavor to make arrangements with him to spend a week or more, if practicable, in this city.

Should Brother Seys visit our city, try and make it convenient to come with him.

It may not be amiss to insert just here a short specimen sketch, showing how Mr. Janes's youthful missionary spirit found expression. It was the day of small things, of first beginnings in the mighty movement which was afterward to engage so much of his thought, and which he was to see encircling the globe:

Perhaps the influence of example is as powerful an influence as any that is brought to bear upon human feelings and conduct. It is the influence of fact. In the history of the missionary enterprise we are furnished with many soul-stirring inci-

* The Rev. John Seys, appointed missionary to Liberia, 1834.

dents. There is on the page of missionary history an account of a missionary meeting which, probably, you have all read and felt. It was a large and august assembly. It was held in a place amid the magnificence and splendor of royalty. A king presided at this meeting, and his only Son was present, and not only shared in the discourses, but presented the most priceless offering given on the occasion. The whole assembly, although accustomed to deliberate upon the interests of government and of empire, are serious and anxious when the great cause of missionary operations is presented for their deliberations. The restoration of a depraved and fallen world to holiness and to God was a subject transcending their comprehension and their hopes. But while all were contemplating this momentous subject, and were silent in view of its impossibility, the President, with majesty and benignity becoming a Sovereign and a President, arose and solemnly announced that his wisdom had found a plan ; that to his mind a scheme had presented itself by which the whole design might be accomplished. "But O the expense, the sacrifice, the suffering necessary to effect it! But it is the only plan ; it must be carried out ; and I have decided to give myself to the cause. The riches of my wisdom—the treasures of my love—the energies of my omnipotence—the fullness of my compassion—all, all, I lay upon the altar. There is no enterprise more stupendous or glorious, more worthy or becoming. I give myself to effect it."

Scarcely had he made this consecrating vow and ceased to speak, when his only Son, his well-beloved Son, addressed him thus : "Father, I give myself. I give this uncreated glory which I had with you before the world began. I will veil my dignity and my divinity. I will go to that benighted and perishing world. I will become their servant, and will bear their sins in my body on the tree. I will give my blood and my groans, my life and my death, to effect this great object, and fulfill your plan of mercy. Here, Father, I give myself." Scarcely had he done speaking when the impatient assembly, constituting the hierarchy of the celestial world, arose, and with united voice said, "Great Father of our being, we give ourselves. When

thy well-beloved Son descends into the abodes of wretched-
ness our songs shall celebrate and announce his mission.
When he treads the wine-press of the wrath of God and pours
forth the sweat of blood we will be with him to minister unto
him, to strengthen him.   When he has finished his work of
mercy and is to return we will let down his cloudy chariot,
and receive him up to thy right hand again.   We also will
minister to all them who become the heirs of salvation."
Here was the best missionary meeting ever held, and not breaking up until every one had consecrated himself to this great
work.

While a pastor in Philadelphia Mr. Janes studied
medicine.   That city has always been noted for the
number and excellence of its medical institutions,
and the professors of the various faculties have
uniformly courteously extended to the clergymen
of the city invitations to attend upon their lectures.
Mr. Janes, with the desire to know how properly to
treat his own health, and also with the purpose to
make himself useful among the poor, by being
able, when necessary, to render them medical help,
availed himself of this opportunity.   He subsequently received the degree of Doctor of Medicine
from the Vermont University.   He thus united
with a knowledge of the law some knowledge of
medicine, and was all the more thoroughly furnished
for his life-work.   He seems early to have felt that
all knowledge was important to a minister of the
Gospel.   While there is no evidence that he ever
after was in the least drawn aside by either of these

professions—for no man was by conviction and habit more a man of one work—still the discipline of mind and the technical information these studies afforded largely contributed to the width and accuracy of view which marked his opinions and his general intercourse with society. He was prepared to meet men of affairs on their own ground, and to converse with them in a manner which at once awakened their interest. In his public addresses the knowledge that he possessed of the three professions gave him an advantage which he seldom, though without ostentation, failed to use that he might render his sacred vocation more efficient. Already the grand ideal of his life, the ministry of the word, was crystallizing about it all the materials which it touched; all the resources available to him were entering into and augmenting the faculty of the preacher.

I have before alluded to his casual speaking and preaching in New York city. These exercises, in addition to the fame he had acquired in his more immediate work, brought him to the attention of the Methodists of New York. In the spring of 1839 he was, by request, transferred and appointed to the Mulberry-street charge in that city. The Mulberry-street Church had had but two pastors preceding his advent, the Revs. Robert Seney and Francis Hodgson. It was one of the two pewed Methodist Episcopal Churches of the city,

and in it were gathered a large number of the
wealthier and more intelligent Methodist families.
It was proof of the high estimate in which
Mr. Janes was held, both by the Bishops and the
people, that he should, while so young, be appointed to what was regarded as the leading
metropolitan pulpit.   He was just thirty-two years
of age, and his small stature and delicate, frail health
made him appear even more youthful than he was.
His ministrations at once attracted attention, and
he uniformly preached to large congregations.   To
pulpit ability he added rare executive talents, and
his organizing power was soon shown in the general
direction which was given to all the details of
Church work.   To the children and youth he was
very attentive, frequently preaching to them, and
mingling with them, especially in the sessisons of
the Sunday-school.   His sermons and addresses to
children were appropriate, pleasing, and instructive,
invariably gaining and holding their attention.   He
would unfold a subject in simple language, with
home-like and, as far as practicable, scriptural illus-
trations, pausing now and then as he proceeded to
question his young audience upon the points
which he had brought out, and he would never fail
in the end to impress upon their minds a useful
moral and religious lesson.   His habit was not only
to preach often distinctively to the young, but never
to preach a sermon which should be without some-

thing suited to their capacities. His opinion was, that the pastor who neglected the children lost his arm of greatest strength.

I give an extract from a manuscript sketch of a sermon on " Forgetfulness of God," which affords an example of the matter and style of his preaching at this time :

I know men have offered and urged excuses, but they are all fallacious. This forgetfulness of God has been ascribed to the invisibility of his person. There is no embodied, incarnate image before the eye ; no audible voice breaking upon the ear ; no physical impression upon our senses ; and this is pleaded in excuse of our forgetfulness of God. But is it so, that we cannot love an invisible object? The husbandman thinks of the seed that he has cast into the earth. The merchantman thinks of his ship that is far off upon the deep. The maid does not forget her ornaments, nor the bride her attire, though they are locked in the wardrobe and unseen. Why is it that at times you are indifferent to, and almost unconscious of, every object of sense around you? Something unseen hath engrossed the mind, an object of interest far off over the vast deep hath absorbed it. The form of a loved one comes up in the thoughts. But how is this? This object is unseen. He hath not even left his footsteps upon the intervening ocean. And yet he is in all thy thoughts, engrossing more of thy mind than when present with thee. Why is it that you go to the grave to weep there? It has hidden the beauteous form of thy friend deep in its dark and dreary bosom. Even if the disembodied spirit should linger above its green surface, still it would be invisible. And yet the bare remembrance of thy invisible friend hallows with undying interest even the place where the body lies. O tell me not that you cannot recollect an unseen object. The excuse is baseless, and altogether invalid.

3*

There was no sort of pastoral work which escaped the notice of this many-sided young minister. There were no themes which related to the
edification of the body of Christ which he did not
discuss and enforce. The duty of Christian beneficence engaged much of his thoughts, and he contributed not a little to lay the foundations of those
habits of systematic giving which became subsequently the main dependence of the benevolent
institutions of American Methodism. How could
the members of his congregation fail to appreciate
the subject when presented by their youthful pastor in the attractive garb with which he must have
clothed the following thoughts? Discoursing on
the "*greater blessedness of giving,*" he says:

This arises, 1, From the consciousness that we are fulfilling
the design of the gracious Giver. We receive as stewards ; as
such are we faithful ? Do we misapply none of our Master's
treasures ?

2. In giving, we exercise the noblest feelings of our nature—
sympathy for the necessities of others . . . generosity overcomes
the inherent selfishness of our fallen natures, and we feel that
we are not living to ourselves . . . all the kind and tender and
amiable affections of the soul. . . . This is the way to be
happy.

3. We harmonize with the universe of which we are an integral part. This is a useful world. Though the curse of sin
is upon it, yet we can clearly see that, like the mechanism of a
watch, every part was made for an important relative interest.

Survey the face of the earth. . . .
The heavens above. . . .
All fallen beings . . . angels . . . God. . . .

So that in giving we move in harmony with the physical and spiritual universe. The act of giving is divine.

4. It is inspiring, enlarging our hearts, expanding our minds, ennobling our characters.

5. Religious giving is surely and abundantly rewarded. . . . The pleasure of the time. . . . The pleasure that follows. . . . In after life, in death, in the judgment, in heaven. These are the natural results. Then, in addition, the positive reward of God.

> Here in this life a hundred fold. . . .
> Special glory in the life to come. . . .
> O, the contrast !"

In May, 1838, Mr. Janes, then residing in Philadelphia, had been invited to deliver one of the addresses at the Anniversary of the American Bible Society in New York. The impression made by his address on this occasion, together with his accredited success as agent of Dickinson College and his well-understood popularity as a pulpit and platform orator, led the managers of the Bible Society to elect him, in 1840, its Financial Secretary. About the same time he was re-appointed to the Mulberry-street charge. He felt constrained to accept the secretaryship, and accordingly resigned his charge, but the official members were not willing to part with his ministry, and they invited him to remain as their pastor for the year while retaining the secretaryship and dividing his services. This he consented to do, and thus became responsible for two most important trusts. In one of his earlier speeches he makes the following allusion to his appointment :

My position is not one of my own choosing. My allotments in life have been providential. My early circumstances accustomed me to labor and self-denial, and my study of the law made me acquainted with the forms of business. These things were known to the Board of Managers of the American Bible Society, and, in their judgment, gave me a degree of competency to manage the financial department of that institution. They accordingly elected me, and the constituted authorities of the Church appointed me. I admire the Methodist Episcopal Church economy, because it does not leave a man to choose his own work, but assigns to him that for which it judges him most competent. . . . My daily prayer is, that if there is one place in which I can be more useful than in another, or save one more soul, I may be there. The Church generally judges right.

This brief introduction strikes the key-note of Mr. Janes's life. The ground of his choice of one place over another was, that he might be more useful, that he might, if possible, save one more soul, and the only medium of choice which he knew was the voice of the Church. He chose not for himself. And so he was by conviction a member and minister of the Methodist Episcopal Church. He ever bowed without hesitation to its behests. His mind was in full sympathy with the aims and methods of the American Bible Society; but good as the object was, and broad as the scope which its operations would open to his energies, he would not select nor go until the Church, to whose form of government he had given his allegiance, should command him. He first learned obedience in the ranks, and, like all good soldiers, was thus qualified when attaining command, simply to expect of others what he himself had been glad to render, unquestioning loyalty.

Mr. Janes now entered upon that wider sphere. of activity for which his talents were so eminently fitted. The General Conference of the Methodist Episcopal Church in 1836 had agreed to disband their denominational Bible Society and to unite with the American Bible Society, and he had been chosen under this union to represent Methodism, with special reference to traveling at large through the country and advocating the claims of the society before the Methodist Annual Conferences.

Judging from a few *memoranda* on detached slips of paper, he must have confined his operations for the first year largely to the Middle States, within easy reaching distance of his pastoral charge.

Feb. 5, 1841. Left New York to attend a meeting of the Maryland State Bible Society, in Baltimore. Spent the Sabbath in Philadelphia. Attended the meeting on Monday evening. Not a large but a good meeting. On Tuesday evening attended the Missionary Anniversary of the Methodist Episcopal Church, which paid my expenses, so that my trip was without cost.

Feb. 17. Went to Newark to arrange an appointment to preach and take a collection. Expense, fifty cents.

Feb. 27. Left New York for Trenton. On Sabbath, the 28th, preached in Presbyterian and Methodist Churches. Found the cause in a very low state. Took a collection of $35 in the Methodist Church.

March 7. Preached in the Second Wesleyan Chapel, New York, and took a collection for the Bible cause.

March 14. Preached in the Second Avenue Presbyterian Church, and took a collection for the Bible cause.

March 21. Preached in the Methodist Episcopal Church in Williamsburgh, and took a collection for the Bible cause. Expenses of filling my pulpit and going, etc., $1.

March 30. Went to Freehold, Monmouth County, N. J., to attend the annual meeting of County Society on 31st. Had a small but useful meeting. Expenses, $4.

April 28. Visited the New Jersey Conference on the Society's business, also on the 30th. Expenses, $1 12½.

This meager record shows the industry and painstaking with which he worked in the cause while still the pastor of an influential Church.

CHAPTER IV.

1841–1844.

Secretary of the American Bible Society.

IN the month of May, 1841, emancipated from a pastoral charge, Mr. Janes was at liberty to give his whole time to the secretaryship. He threw himself with *abandon* into the work. The cause was entirely congenial with his feelings. The thought of giving to all people the sacred Scriptures, that every man might hear, in the same tongue in which he first heard the whispers of a mother's love, the glad evangel of a Saviour's love, aroused his whole nature, set him all aglow with holy zeal, and he rushed from point to point over the land, setting all hearts on fire with enthusiasm for the circulation of the Bible.

June 23, 1841. Left New York to visit the New Hampshire Conference of the Methodist Episcopal Church. The Conference entertained the Bible question, manifested a strong interest in it, and resolved to preach on the subject and take a collection in all their churches. On Sunday, 26th, preached on the Bible cause in the Congregational Church.

June 27. Went from Dover, the seat of the New Hampshire Conference, to Worcester, Mass., the seat of the New England Conference. This Conference also cordially entertained the subject of my mission, and passed resolutions not only approving the objects and operations of the American Bible Society, but also pledging themselves to preach on the subject and take up collections for our treasury.

July 12. Left New York to attend the annual meeting of the Delaware County Bible Society at Delhi. The meeting was held on the 14th, and was well attended by delegates from the different towns in the county. It was a spirited meeting. The Society resolved to ascertain the destitution, and to supply the people in their bounds; also to use all proper means to introduce the Bible into their common schools. The next day I went to Cooperstown, in Otsego County; saw the officers of that county, and urged them to enlist in an effort to supply the destitute in the county. They assured me it should be done so far as practicable.

The next day I went to Utica. On Sabbath, the 18th, preached in the morning in the Congregational Church, in the afternoon in the Dutch Reformed Church, and in the evening had a general meeting of all the congregations in the First Presbyterian Church. The County Society has an agent who will go through the city and make applications for donations. They preferred this way of doing business. If they do not do their duty now, the sin and guilt are their own. Tuesday went to Rome, where the Black River Conference of the Methodist Episcopal Church was in session. This Conference also entertained the Bible question very cordially. They also passed a resolution pledging themselves to take up collections for the Society. On Sunday evening I preached in the Methodist Episcopal Church, and obtained a collection of $170. I believe this to have been a useful tour.

While on this tour, or possibly one somewhat later, an incident occurred given by an eye witness which illustrates his marvelous power of appeal. It was a matter of record in the religious papers at the time: " When Secretary of the American

Bible Society, and addressing a Western New York
Conference in its behalf, he was arguing the necessity of personal consecration in order to liberal and
acceptable offerings unto God, and as he proceeded
with fervid and impassioned eloquence he threw
himself upon his knees, and in prayer led the body
of the Conference before they were aware, in the
very act of consecration; the effect was most thrilling, and was one of those life-time acts the memory
of which endures through generations."

In the winter of 1841–42 Mr. Janes made a
"Southern tour," going as far as the State of Georgia. None of his letters of the period have been
preserved, but fortunately scraps of a diary trans-
mit to us some account of his doings. Bishop
Waugh, of the Methodist Episcopal Church, whose
manuscript journal was temporarily in my possession, makes mention of hearing Mr. Janes on this
tour. He says of his preaching before the Conferences, in one instance, "it was excellent," and in another, "it was fine." They journeyed together in
their route northward. At this time Mr. Janes writes:

Dec. 29, 1841. Left New York to visit the States of North
and South Carolina and Georgia. Traveled in the mail line,
and reached Wilmington, N. C., on Saturday evening. Preached
in the morning, and had an appointment of a Bible meeting
given out in the different churches for the evening. The
evening, however, proved a very stormy one, and the congregation was quite small. I addressed those who were present,
and obtained a promise of future effort in the Bible cause.

Monday, Jan. 3, 1842. Went in steam packet from Wilmington to Charleston, S. C. Arrived in the latter city early next morning after a very pleasant sail.

Tuesday, 4. Spent this day and the following in·calling upon the officers of the Charleston Bible Society, consulting with them about my own and their operations. On Wednesday the Board were together, and I addressed them. They fixed the time of their annual meeting to suit my convenience, resolved to employ a local agent, etc.

Thursday, 6. Went to Augusta, Ga., by railroad. The next day started for Milledgeville, at which place I arrived in the afternoon of the following day, after a very fatiguing ride all night, being once upset and somewhat lamed. I found the Georgia Annual Conference of the Methodist Episcopal Church in session, to whom I was introduced, and by whom I was courteously received. The next day being Sabbath, I preached a missionary sermon in the evening. On Monday I attended Conference ; had a Bible committee appointed. On Tuesday the before-named committee reported, and I was permitted to address the Conference. Several expressive and important resolutions were passed by the Conference. In the afternoon visited the Oglethorpe University, where we have an auxiliary society among the students and professors. This society has been efficient. The term having only just commenced, but few of the students were present. Good promises were given. In the evening the Milledgeville and Baldwin County Bible Society held a public meeting, which I addressed at length. A good feeling was manifested. A liberal collection was taken. A collection of about $100 was also taken in the Conference in the morning. At the missionary meeting the evening before a very liberal collection was taken, (which meeting I also addressed,) which rendered the collection for the Bible cause the more acceptable.

Jan. 12. Returned to Augusta.

Thursday, 13. This evening attended the annual meeting of the Georgia Bible Society. Notice not having been properly given, the attendance was small. I, however, addressed those who were present. The next day the Board met, and resolved to hold another meeting the following Tuesday evening.

Friday, 14. I left in the evening for Savannah, traveled all night, though staging and the road rough. In the morning reached the railroad, and arrived at Savannah about five o'clock in the afternoon. Waited on Dr. Preston, who invited me to preach in his church on the following morning, and I agreed to address the Methodist Church in the evening. Sunday preached as before mentioned. The morning congregation was large and attentive. I am sure good will result from the sermons. In the evening we had a good meeting in the Methodist Church. Here a liberal collection was taken.

Monday, 17. Returned to Augusta by the same fatiguing route. On the 18th the meeting of the Georgia Bible Society was held. The attendance better than before. The meeting was quite a spirited one. Addressed by myself, Professor Means, and the president, Professor Ford. A liberal collection was taken up for the cause.

Wednesday, 19. Rode from Augusta to Charleston. The evening of Thursday, 20th, was fixed as the anniversary of the Charleston Bible Society. The evening proved stormy, and the meeting was postponed until the following Monday evening. Contrary to my calculations, I had to remain until that time. On Sabbath I preached in two of the Methodist churches, and in the church of Mr. Smyth, Presbyterian. Monday evening the meeting was well attended, and was addressed by the pastor of the First Presbyterian Church, Dr. Stevens, of Savannah, Ga.; Rev. William M. Wightman, of Charleston; and myself. It was certainly a good meeting, and good will result from it.

Tuesday, 25. I started for Charlotte, N. C., the seat of the South Carolina Conference, to attend its sittings. I passed through Columbia and Camden. At Camden I stopped and delivered a Bible discourse. The friends of the cause here seem quite spirited, especially in the matter of their county supply. Dr. George Reynolds is very much interested, and is an active, influential citizen. I arrived at Charlotte on the 28th, after a very fatiguing ride of nearly two hundred miles in a two-horse stage over almost impassable roads. The Conference was in session. Committee was appointed who considered and reported upon the Bible cause. On Tuesday I was permitted to address the Conference on the subject, when appropriate resolutions were passed, etc. On Monday evening we had a public Bible meeting, which I addressed, as did also the Rev. W. A. Smith. A very liberal collection was taken for the Bible cause. On Tuesday evening I started on my homeward journey. About two hundred miles of the distance I had to travel by stage over the worst road I ever traveled in my life. Some of the way we were obliged, on account of the badness of the roads, to travel in an open wagon all night through the rain. Sometimes we stuck fast in the mud, and were delayed until we could send for men and horses to get us out. Once upset, but mercifully preserved from serious injury. I arrived at home February 8, having been gone six weeks, and traveled two thousand eight hundred miles. Thankful to God for his care and kindness.

Mr. Janes is so lenient as not to state, as Bishop Waugh does, that the upset which they had was due to a drunken driver.

During this absence he preached and spoke about twenty-five times. Whenever he was not traveling he was either conferring with boards or agents, or engaged in addressing meetings, so that he was constantly employed. He would pass the night on well-nigh impassable stage-roads, and the next day speak with as much power and freshness as if the night had been spent in soothing sleep on a sumptuous couch. Ministers and people were carried away with his zeal and eloquence, and the

cause of Bible distribution received an impetus it
had never before known.

He thus concludes his observations:

> On the whole, though I found some indifference to the high
> claims of the blessed Bible cause in the South, yet I think it
> has a strong hold on the affections of the people, and is pros-
> pering. When the financial condition of the country shall im-
> prove, I think the contributions will be greatly enlarged. In
> my tour I labored to do all the good in my power. How
> much good was done I do not expect to know until the judg-
> ment-day.

Seldom did any other reference to his deeds escape him than what is here so modestly expressed—
that he had labored to do what good he could, and
was content to await the results until the judgment.
He worked and "endured as seeing Him who is
invisible."

On his return to the office at New York, a brief
record—a line or two—for each day shows the same
incessant activity. One example is sufficient.

> *Feb.* 13. Preached in the Methodist Protestant Church, At-
> torney-street, New York, and took up a collection for the
> Bible cause.

In the summer and autumn of 1842 he visited the
Western conferences. His advocacy of the Bible
cause was here equally effective as in the South.
Some of the older preachers of the Ohio Conference
still refer in warm terms to an address which he
delivered before that conference, at its session in

Hamilton, Ohio, in September of this year. There were present such men as William H. Raper, James B. Finley, George W. Walker, John F. Wright, C. Elliott, L. L. Hamline, Michael Marley, Joseph Trimble, William Nast, and others, whose names, for pulpit power, have become familiar throughout the State of Ohio. These men, who were accustomed to move the masses as a storm bends the forests, found themselves entirely at the will of the youthful secretary. At first, instructed and entertained, they were at length captured, and amid tears and shouts his address was concluded, and by a unanimous vote they stood ready to sustain his cause.

His address before the Indiana Conference, held at Centreville, Indiana, in the same autumn, was equally successful. As proof of the abiding impression produced by it, we insert a letter written to him by Mr. William Young, a venerable Christian, many years after, from Painesville, Ohio.

.Some twenty years or more ago, when you were agent for the American Bible Society, I had the pleasure of hearing you address the Indiana Conference, at Centreville, Bishop Morris presiding. I shall never forget the effect of the appeal you made in behalf of God's Bible. I was brought under conviction that I had not done my whole duty to this glorious cause, though I had done something every year. In making my will I left $1,000 to the cause, if it could be spared. But, as God has given me the means, I wish to execute this part of my will before I go hence, as I owe every thing I have that is good or comfortable for soul and body, for time and eternity, to God's Bible. I recollect some Christians of Philadelphia gave Bishop Asbury some Bibles to distribute among the poor. On his return next year he remarked from the pulpit, " There may be some errors in my preaching, but when I was distributing the word of God, without note or comment, then I knew I was sowing the pure seed of the kingdom." Will you permit me, through you, to present to the American Bible Society a bond, payable in New York, for $1,000, drawing 7 per cent. interest. . . . I am an old man, past seventy, much afflicted, but I have no cause to complain, for the lines have fallen to me in pleasant places, and I have a goodly heritage.

In the winter of 1843–44 Mr. Janes made another tour of the South as Bible Secretary. A communication from Mr. C. C. North, a Methodist layman of New York, who was then residing in Alabama, gives a brief account of his visit to the Alabama Conference, and will illustrate the uniform effects which attended his ministrations. Mr. North says:

In the winter of 1843 we were residing in Columbus, Miss. The same winter the Alabama Conference held its session in the town, the venerable Bishop Soule presiding. During the Conference Rev. E. S. Janes, recently chosen Financial Secretary of the American Bible Society, arrived, and made his home at our house. This was his last tour through the Southern States, in which he visited the Conferences as representative of that great society. He was small in stature, quick in action, gentle in manner, while his countenance wore that quiet, placid expression for which he was remarkable in after years. His pleasing manner and strong speeches gave him a place at once in the hearts of the preachers.

His sermon before the Conference, on Sunday morning, preached to a crowded house, was one of the most impressive of the many that I have heard from his lips. His theme was " Heaven," and during the delivery he seemed rapt with its glory. His countenance shone like that of Moses. The whole congregation were deeply moved by the wonderful power of his words, and responses were heard from all parts of the house. The preacher and the sermon formed a life-picture on the minds of all present. Similar sermons and speeches before the Southern Conferences during that and a former tour brought him to the attention of the Southern ministers as a suitable person for the episcopacy, and no doubt had much to do with his election at the memorable General Conference of 1844.

It was an unspeakable pleasure to have him for our guest. We were also privileged at the same time with the company of the Rev. James Collord, who represented the Book Concern before the Conference. To us, far away from our New York home, it was a great joy to have at our table these friends of our youth. Being young housekeepers, Mr. Janes took an affectionate interest in our domestic concerns, remarking, "Things are so home-like." During his stay we were favored with the presence (at dinner) of the venerable Bishop Soule and his wife. Being an inexperienced carver, and Mr. Janes noticing my embarrassment, he kindly offered his aid, took the knife in his hand, and soon skillfully disjointed the turkey. Ours was then an undivided Church. None of that company perceived a cloud of disorder in the clear sky. A universal calm rested upon the people, and no one, at least at that table, dreamed of the storm that burst upon the Church the following year, and in which all of them were to be participants.

His addresses before promiscuous audiences were equally effective with those before ministers. Indeed, it was not so much the audience or the occasion, as the subject, which filled him. Dr. J. S. Porter, writes:

When Secretary of the American Bible Society he was down for a speech at a Bible meeting in New Brunswick, where I was then stationed. By some means the cars were detained, and he did not reach the place till we had heard two good, but rather dull, speakers, when he came, and almost instantly began to speak, and he had but just entered upon the delivery of his speech when a great change came over the audience. From apparent drowsiness there was a lively interest awakened, and all seemed as if a new spirit had taken possession of them.

The secretary who could thus stir Conferences and conventions of ministers and the cultured congregations of the cities, was equally at home in the backwoods, and was not indifferent to the claims of the frontiersman. An incident is related that at one time he had an engagement to meet a Conference on a certain Sabbath. His route led him through a rough, mountainous and thinly settled section. A break in the railroad prevented him from reaching the place at the appointed day, though he made strenuous exertions to do so by stage or otherwise. . . . Sabbath morning found him in a neighborhood where a few cabins surrounded a court-house, but there was no church. By inquiring he learned that a religious meeting was to be held that morning in the court-house. He went, took his seat, no one knowing him. An unlettered man opened the meeting, reading the hymns as well as he could. After some devotional exercises there was a pause, when the leader hitched along on the bench on

4

which he sat, till he came near enough to Mr. Janes
to whisper in his ear, "Are you not a Church member?" An affirmative answer being given, he asked
him to speak to the people. He immediately did
so. A request was then made that he would preach
in the afternoon. The information being circulated, a large number assembled, and among them,
men in their hunting shirts, with their dogs and
guns, came to the place and listened attentively to
the word.

No mere sketch written as a preparation for
speaking, not even a *verbatim* report of a speech,
could convey an adequate idea of the impression
produced by his living utterance, yet I cannot
withhold one or two extracts from a manuscript, as
indicating his mode of treating the great subject
with which he was intrusted.

The Bible is an observatory so elevated, and furnished with
instruments so perfect, as to enable the careful, patient, and
devout student to survey the universe of truth in all its proportions and perfections.

Thank God for this perfect library ; this dictionary in which
infinite, unerring wisdom has defined all subjects of human
concernment ; this gazetteer of the moral world, giving the
topography, population, and condition of its important places ;
this history, giving an account of the works and ways of God
—of the dispensations of his providence and grace, including
the history of man, his creation, fall, and redemption ; this body
of divinity—stating and explaining the theological sentiments
of the infinite Mind—the divine teachings of the Deity. The
morality of the Bible does that which no other code of morals

attempts: it governs the heart; it not only forbids all criminal practices, as murder, adultery, theft, bearing false witness, lying, etc., but it also forbids all hatred, wrath, malice, envy, and all evil passions. It not only enjoins the performance of all virtuous actions, as feeding the hungry, clothing the naked, doing good unto all men, being ready for every good work, abstaining from all appearance of evil, and the like; but it also requires us to cultivate all pure and noble sentiments, chaste and magnanimous affections, justice, mercy, and truth, love, gratitude, patience, charity, and whatsoever is lovely and of good report. Furthermore, in order to secure the happiness and harmony of community, the morality of the Bible demands a rigid and jealous conformity in conduct to the institutions of society. No man can meet his obligations to his fellow-men without carefully complying with their requirements. Whoever abrogates the holy Sabbath, thereby robs the laboring classes of that portion of time which they need, and to which they are entitled, for bodily rest and moral improvement. Hence Bible morality remembers the Sabbath-day to keep it holy. To annihilate the family compact, to vitiate or discard the domestic relations, would be to visit with the frosts of death every flower of earth that delights with its beauty or regales with its fragrance; to contaminate the fresh blood of infancy, to poison the red current in the veins of age, to make leprous the whole mass of humanity, and to convert the sanctuary of the affections into the mad-house of the passions.

Civil government is also absolutely essential to the well-being of any people. Without it, society would resemble the ocean when the fury of the tempest is troubling its waters, exposing to the most disastrous shipwreck every vessel of State, and placing in awful jeopardy the many precious interests with which they are so richly freighted. The man who would break down the institutions of civil government, who would destroy the authority of the magistrate, the judge, and the rulers of the land, is so incendiary in his spirit, that, if he could do it with impunity, he would set fire to the temple of virtue, and exult to see her loveliest altars in flames. . . . Such character and conduct are strongly reprobated in the oracles of God. Civil as well as domestic government is therein most authoritatively established and most solemnly sanctioned. The superiority of the morality derived from the oracles of God is seen in the absoluteness of its authority. No doubt, in the estimate of their disciples the names of many moralists have given a degree of authority to their precepts : yet the wisest and most excellent among them have deeply felt, that in order to clothe their teachings with authority, they must also give to them an apparent fitness, and clearly establish their expediency and propriety.

That there is a perfect fitness in all the precepts and principles of scripture-morality is unquestionable. It is not necessary, however, that this fitness should appear in order to invest these precepts with the highest authority. The source from which they emanate endows them with this attribute. . . . Therefore, though there are some things in the divine requirements above our understanding, there is nothing unreasonable. When we cannot explain, we can consistently confide. The sanctions of Scripture morality are vastly more impressive and efficient than those of any other code. . . . But the Bible brings to us a religion of truth and praise and purity, a religion of light and love and joy. . . . The Christian system derives exceeding glory from the competent Saviour which it provides and presents.

That man is wicked in character and ruined in condition is a fact universally felt and generally confessed. His utter inability to retrieve his condition and regain his lost character is self-evident. Therefore if relief and restoration are obtained it must be at the hands of another. But in whom can help be found? To this engrossing question the oracles of earth are silent, but the oracles of God distinctly announce his name—it is Jesus! They also fully describe his character, and clearly set forth the manner of his mediation. "God so loved the world that he gave his only begotten Son, that whosoever believeth in him might not perish, but have everlasting life."

As showing the high appreciation of Mr. Janes's services to the Bible Socicty, I insert a copy of the resolutions passed by the Board of Managers when the voice of his Church in its highest council had called him to another sphere of action :

Resolved, That the resignation of Rev. Dr. Janes be accepted in accordance with his wishes.

Resolved, That in so doing the managers would express their unqualified satisfaction as to the efficient and impartial manner in which he has here discharged his official duties, and would fervently invoke the divine blessing upon him in the new station to which he is called.

Resolved, That while they regret the loss of his entire services in connection with this Society, they anticipate still, from his known attachment to the Bible cause as well as from his present letter, his occasional aid, and would therefore authorize and invite him to present its claims on such occasions and in such portions of the country as in his judgment may seem proper and useful.

Many years afterward, when this eminent servant of God had been called to that higher and wider sphere which is above and beyond the calls and appointments of the militant Church, the same board, in an extended minute with regard to him, made the following reference to this period of his services :

In the year 1838 he appeared as one of the anniversary speakers. Two years later he was made the Financial Secretary of the Society. The duties of this office, which he discharged for four years, awakened the rich enthusiasm of his soul. Impressions were made by his thrilling appeals, especially in the West and South, of which mention is made in glowing terms after a lapse of more than thirty years.

Almost immediately upon Mr. Janes's resignation as Secretary, he was elected a member of the Board of Managers, and thus through all his subsequent life he was intimately associated with the good and honored men who have brought this benign institution to its present marvelous proportions and usefulness.

CHAPTER V.

1844.

The Methodist Episcopal Church — The General Conference —
Elected to the Episcopacy.

THUS far I have said but little about the Church
of which Mr. Janes was an accredited and useful minister. Historically and geographically it
might be regarded at this period, 1844, as more
truly the national Church of America than any other
one denomination of Christians. While not as old
as some in its organization, it exceeded any other
in the number of its members, and in the univer-
sality of its spread. While other Churches were
strong in the North or the South, in the East or
the West, in the central East or central West, in
the larger cities or the rural districts, Methodism
obtained every-where, and had attained, by a remarkably equal growth, a firm footing in the whole
land. It stood side by side with the oldest and
richly endowed Churches of the great cities: entering the Southern States when they were colo-
nies, it became quite generally the Church of the
South: in New England, though late in the field,
it fought its way amid strongly intrenched Congre-
gationalism, and soon conquered recognition: and

in the great West it began with the first white set-
tlers of the soil, and moving abreast with the ever-
advancing population, it planted itself on every
frontier. The Methodist Episcopal Church was
pre-eminently the Church of the people.

This growth, at once solid and diffused, was due
to no one human agency so much as to its organized and organizing *itinerant* ministry. The regular ministers are a body of traveling preachers, all
under direct supervision, controlling and being controlled. Theoretically—and the theory is the result of experiment rather than of *a priori* speculation
—nothing can be more complete than the Methodist system. The class-meeting, composed of private members, as the unit, is in charge of one who
is the leader; the classes and leaders are in charge
of the pastor; the pastors and leaders are under
the oversight of presiding elders; and the presiding
elders, pastors, and all official members are under
the supervision of Bishops or General Superintendents; and all officers of every grade act under the
authority of the General Conference, the highest
legislative and judicial body known to the Church,
and are amenable to the rules and regulations which
it, under certain restrictions, may enact.

Too much credit cannot be awarded to the rank
and file of the earlier Methodist ministry. Their
practical intelligence, their deep piety, and their self-
sacrificing zeal have not been excelled in any age

of Christianity: yet I am persuaded that they owed their efficiency in large measure to the Episcopal supervision to which they were so strictly, and, at the same time, so loyally subject. The one-man power, legally and morally authorized, to touch, inspire, and move at will, hither and thither through the whole Church, according to its needs, the individuals of the great body of the ministry, was a chief cause of the grand achievements of the itinerancy. The general superintendency imparted to the itinerancy a sagacious adaptation, a flexibility, uniformity, and compactness of movement, which rendered it not only a conquering army, but an army of occupation; not only a corps of evangelists who penetrated the waste places and converted the people to God; but a body of pastors as well, who fed the flock of Christ, and nurtured and established a Church in the wilderness. The Episcopacy, like the pastorate, is itself an itinerant ministry—the Bishops having no diocese, but being required to travel at large in the work—so that when its functions are exercised upon any one measure or in any one place, it concentrates for the time the wisdom which is based upon the widest observation.

This feature of itinerant general superintendency in the Episcopacy had the additional advantage of promoting uniformity of doctrine and discipline in the Methodist Episcopal Church. The history of Episcopacy in the primitive Church shows that the

4*

doctrines and usages of the Churches at different prominent centers—such as Carthage, Rome, Antioch, Alexandria, and Constantinople—varied with the opinions and habits of the Bishops who occupied the several sees, and thus variations in creed and custom arose, and gradually hardened into obstinate and irreconcilable differences.

The Methodist Episcopalians were fortunate in a provision tending to guard against the recurrence of such an evil in their own constitution and history. It could not be otherwise than that their system should be tested in its first beginning, and that, like all other systems depending upon the assent of free people, it should be liable to ruptures and losses; yet it is remarkable to what extent it composed differences, resisted fundamental changes, survived transient secessions, retained its integrity, and pushed its way through all difficulties, and became numerically the foremost religious body of the nation. It requires but a glance to see the agency of a simple, pure, unworldly traveling superintendency in it all. And when a general rupture of the Church came, the issue was not a doctrinal one, nor was it a question of the polity relating to the general workings of ecclesiastical administration, but it was a *politico-religious* issue. African slavery was legalized by many of the States of the Union; it was recognized and protected by the General Government; and it

was not possible for any ecclesiastical foresight in
the leaders of the Church—which was co-extensive
with the nation, and which had ever felt that it was
its mission to save men irrespective of their social
and political conditions—to provide against the di-
visive results of an evil which had so insinuated itself into the body politic as to temporarily endanger
the nation before the evil could be ejected and de-
stroyed.

But I must not too far anticipate my theme.
The four years immediately preceding 1844 were
years of unprecedented prosperity. Revivals of religion had extensively prevailed, and converts by
thousands had been added to the Methodist Epis
copal Church. It was filling the country from the
Aroostook to the Rio Grande, from the Atlantic
slopes to the Mississippi valley, with its adherents,
its churches, schools, colleges, and publications.
But it was in this high prosperity fast approaching
its greatest trial. A crisis was at hand. Already
the evil angel which was to confuse the counsels
of its wise men was hovering in the air. .

On May 1, 1844, the ninth delegated General
Conference of the Methodist Episcopal Church as-
sembled in the Greene-street Church, New York.
Bishops Soule, Hedding, Andrew, Waugh, and
Morris were present, and 149 delegates of the whole
number (180) elected answered to their names.

As the Conference proceeded it became apparent

that the exciting question of slavery would obtrude itself upon the members and become the all-absorbing topic of the session. The appeal of the Rev. Francis A. Harding from the action of the Baltimore Conference, suspending him from the ministry for slave-holding, brought the subject very early in the proceedings directly to the attention of the body; and then very soon it was rumored that the Rev. James O. Andrew, one of the Bishops of the Church, had become involved in the ownership of slaves. The case of Mr. Harding was fully argued, and the action of the Baltimore Conference was sustained.

The Conference approached with the utmost caution and delicacy the case of Bishop Andrew. It was not until that of Mr. Harding had been disposed of, and a committee on pacification had been appointed to confer with the Bishops, and had reported their inability to agree upon any measures, and many of the members of the Conference felt themselves so far embarrassed by the rumor touching the Bishop as that the further business of the Conference was obstructed, that a motion of inquiry into the matter was finally ordered. A report from the Committee on Episcopacy, to which the motion of inquiry had been referred, brought the subject before the Conference on May 22, in the statement, confirmed by letter from Bishop Andrew himself, that he had become connected with slavery.

A preamble and resolution were at once offered by
Revs. A. Griffith and J. Davis, of the Baltimore
Conference, briefly reciting the facts, and the in-
compatibility of slave-holding by a general superintendent with the duties which he owed to the
whole Church, and affectionately requesting him to
resign his office.   The Rev. J. B. Finley and J. M.
Trimble, of the Ohio Conference, offered a substitute, which, after reciting substantially the same
facts and arguments, concluded as follows :

Resolved, That it is the sense of this General Conference that
he desist from the exercise of this office so long as this impedi-
ment remains.

It was soon made to appear from the declarations
of Southern delegates, and of Bishop Andrew himself, that he would not resign, even at the request
of the Conference; so that the whole ground of
action was shifted to an acceptance or rejection of
the substitute.   The Bishops presented an address,
signed at first by all but Bishop Andrew, from
which, however, Bishop Hedding afterward withdrew his name, advising, in the interest of union
and peace, the postponement of action for four
years.   This address was made the order of the
day for June 1, and, on motion, was laid on the
table, so that the Conference declined to consider,
much less to adopt, its recommendation.   Mr. Collins, of Baltimore, then moved to take up Mr. Finley's substitute, upon which the previous question

being called and sustained, the vote was taken by
yeas and nays, and the substitute was adopted by
a vote of 111 to 69.

This vote was decisive of the whole issue; it vir-
tually divided the Methodist Episcopal Church.
Efforts were made to break its force by explanatory
and modifying resolutions; but all in vain. It was
clear that those who voted with the majority thought
and meant to say that a slave-holding Bishop could
not be, and should not be, an acceptable Bishop
of the Church; and it was equally clear that those
who voted with the minority—most of them, at any
rate—meant that they could not and would not
yield the point, that what was admissible in themselves was a disqualification in a Bishop. A protest
was presented by fifty-one of the minority, from
thirteen Annual Conferences in the slave-holding
States. In this they rehearsed their grievances,
and concluded with the declaration that they did
not believe that the objects and purposes of the
Christian ministry and Church organization could
be. successfully accomplished by them under the
jurisdiction of the General Conference as then
constituted.

On the strength of this declaration, and to meet
the possibilities which it involved, a committee of
nine, of which the Rev. R. Paine, D.D., was chairman, reported a Plan of Separation for the Church,
in the event that the Southern delegates should find

it necessary for the preservation of their work to
form a distinct organization.   This Plan provided
for fixing the territorial line of division, and also the
partition of the chartered properties of the Church,
and it was adopted by an overwhelming majority.
It was claimed at the time by the leaders of the
Northern delegates that this action did not divide the
Church, and was not meant to do so; that the Plan
was a peace measure, to conciliate the South and
prevent division.   There certainly could have been
no stronger evidence of the magnanimity of the
Northern delegates than the concession here made.
As much cannot be said of their worldly wisdom.
Their assertion that the Plan did not divide the
Church, was subsequently overruled by the Supreme
Court of the United States, in the litigation after-
ward entailed by an attempt to draw back from the
fulfillment of its conditions.

Whatever was the intent of the Plan, whatever
should have been its final legal effect, it must be
recorded, to the credit of the representatives of a
great Church, tossed and torn as they were by as
fearful an agitation as ever vexed a legislative body,
that its adoption was one of the most beautiful ex-
hibitions of equity and self-surrender the history of
Christendom has known.   It certainly proved on
the part of those who felt constrained to vote that
Bishop Andrew should desist, etc., from his office,
that they were controlled by none other than the

highest and purest motives. Nor should it be assumed that the leaders of the South meditated all the consequences which afterward followed, and adroitly secured the Plan with a full determination to separate and reap its benefits. " Like *people* like priest." It may be that they only yielded at the last to a popular demand which they found it difficult if not impossible to resist. Looked at now in the light of history, that Plan, with all the parties . to it, were parts only of another greater and higher plan, which an unseen Hand was shaping and guiding for the speedy and final extirpation of the cause of all their troubles, in the extinction of American slavery, and, as may be devoutly hoped, for the ultimate re-union of their children, and children's children, on the broad and indestructible basis of the freedom and equality of the human race, and the scriptural character of Episcopal Methodism.

I have recalled this painful crisis of American Methodism as a necessary introduction to the most eventful epoch in the career of Mr. Janes. He was a silent but a close and deeply interested observer of the scenes which have been narrated. He was well acquainted with the men who were actors in them, and, as a sincere lover of the Church, he watched with the utmost jealousy every measure which was adopted. Although not a member of the General Conference, yet being at home in New York, and a prominent officer of the great Society

of which the Church was a patron, he attended
constantly upon its sessions and mingled freely with
the delegates.

On June 7, in accordance with a previous resolution, the Conference proceeded to the election of
two additional Bishops. The whole number of votes
cast was 176; necessary to a choice, 89. On the
first ballot Edmund S. Janes received 86, Leonidas
L. Hamline 75, George Peck 81, and the rest were
scattering. On the second ballot Edmund S. Janes
received 102, Leonidas L. Hamline 90, and George
Peck 80. On this ballot it was ascertained there
were more ballots cast than there were voters, and
the ballot was declared void. A third ballot was
taken and 177 votes cast, of which L. L. Hamline
received 102 and E. S. Janes 99, and each having
received a majority of the whole, they were declared
duly elected Bishops in the Methodist Episcopal
Church. On Monday, June 10, they were solemnly
consecrated to the office and work of a Bishop.

The attention of the members of the General
Conference was first decidedly turned to Dr. Hamline as a suitable person for a Bishop by his argu-
ment of the case of Bishop Andrew. The Rev.
F. G. Hibbard, D.D., his latest biographer, says:

The office had sought him, not he the office. The thought
of his fitness for the Episcopacy had burst upon the Conference
like the sudden blaze of a meteor when he stood before them,
fourteen days before the final adjournment, and delivered his

incomparable speech on the case of Bishop Andrew. In private intercourse and in committees he had already been felt
and appreciated, and his name was getting into leading circles.
But it was on that day and in that speech that he first stood
before the public in his full proportions.*

With Mr. Janes it was quite different. He had
had no opportunity of impressing the Conference,
either in open session or in Committee, and his
election seems to have been wholly due to the
opinion which the members had formed of his
character and work. He had impressed the whole
Church with his eloquence, piety, and wisdom; but
as he was not a member of the General Conference,
and was only thirty-seven years of age, it likely
would not have occurred to that body to elect him
to so high and responsible a position if the delegates
from the South had not adopted him as their candidate.

The Rev. Dr. T. B. Sargent, of Baltimore, who
was a member of the General Conference, and who
had voted with the Southern delegates in the action upon Bishop Andrew's case, in the communication previously quoted thus alludes to the can-
didacy of Mr. Janes:

To return to 1844: when the Baltimore delegation met to
confer in regard to men to "strengthen the Episcopacy," each
one was called on to name a man. When my turn came I

---

* "Biography of Leonidas L. Hamline, D.D.," pp. 148, 149.
Walden & Stowe, Cincinnati, O. 1881.

nominated Edmund Storer Janes, with a remark touching his fitness for the office. "They laughed me to scorn." Fifteen or twenty years afterward, when he had shown himself to be *primus inter pares*, and I had been associated with him for ten years as a presiding elder—and more than once spent the live-long night, and in one case two consecutive nights, in the cabinet work—I ventured, in our confidential talk, to tell this incident, without designating any one but our two selves. His observation was like himself : "Considering who your nominee was, I do not wonder they laughed you to scorn."

The Rev. Dr. Charles F. Deems, now of New York, who in his early manhood became acquainted with Mr. Janes at Dickinson College, and afterward knew him more intimately in New York, and then acted under his supervision as General Agent for the Bible Society for the State of North Carolina, writes of this period :

Three years thereafter occurred the famous General Conference of 1844. I went South with the impression that of all the men I had met during the six years I had spent North at college and in residence Edmund S. Janes was the fittest man to be made a Bishop. I imparted my impressions to influential Southern ministers ; and Dr. Janes's visits to Synods, Conferences, and Conventions in the South, had confirmed the impression I had labored to make. . . . When that stormy Conference came which resulted in the disruption of the Church the Southern men voted, I believe almost in a body, for Dr. Janes.

In the summer of 1842 I had occasion to come North, and traveled with Dr. Janes a week or two, in which we visited the Maine Conference. He was not carried away by the tide of Abolitionism then overflowing the Church. In arguments which arose upon the subject he discreetly corrected wrong impressions which many had received in regard to the South. This was in my presence, and I did not fail to use it in his behalf.

Bishop Waugh, in his unpublished journal, speaking of the course of the Bishops in arranging the Plan of Episcopal Visitation immediately on the adjournment of Conference, says:

Bishops Soule, Hedding, Morris, Hamline, Janes, and myself met to arrange the Plan of Episcopal Visitation for the ensuing four years. Bishop Andrew, although aware of such an arrangement in conformity with long-established usage, had left for Georgia without expressing his wish or purpose in regard to the plan. When the question arose in regard to the division of the work, whether we should include him in the oversight, Bishops Hedding, Morris, and myself thought, as the General Conference had by the answer to our questions as above stated * clearly intended to throw the whole responsibility of acting in his official character on Bishop Andrew alone, and as he was not present to speak for himself, and had not signified his desire or intention in relation thereto, we could not see our way clear to put his name on our plan, or to apportion any part of the work to him. In this opinion, I think, Bishop Hamline concurred; but as well as I recollect, Bishop Janes did not express an opinion, for as he was avowed by the Southern delegates to be of their nomination, I was desirous that he should not express himself on any question which might involve him with the South.

This last remark, while affording an illustration of the considerateness of Bishop Waugh, that prince of Christian gentlemen, is the more in point as con-

---

* "3. *Resolved,* That whether in any, and if any, in what work, Bishop Andrew be employed, is to be determined by his own decision and action, in relation to the previous action of this Conference in his case."—*Journal of the General Conference of* 1844, pp. 118, 120.

firming the view that the election of Mr. Janes was
largely attributable to the unanimity with which the
delegates from the South supported him.   Their
support was undoubtedly due, in the first place, to
the conviction they entertained of his personal fitness for the office, and then to the consideration
that they believed him to be conservative on the
slavery question.   Mr. Janes simply shared moderate views in common with most of the leading
men of the North and many of the foremost men of
the South.   There is no evidence that his convictions were not unequivocally with the Methodist
Discipline and traditions on the subject.   But he
was a man of action rather than of controversy,
Then, as always, he was no agitator in the politico-
ecclesiastical sense, but, accepting the condition of
things about him where beyond his control, he
sought to usher in universal righteousness by bringing all men to the knowledge of God and his salvation.

With the meekness becoming his position as junior Bishop, and so far the junior in years of his colleagues in the office, he began his work.   There were
some tears shed at the home on Lispenard-street on
the announcement of his election.   But the devout
wife, on whom the care of the little children was
more than ever to devolve, bravely accepted the
situation.   Henceforth, for thirty-two years, he was
to be a wanderer over the earth, traveling longer

distances, enduring longer absences from home, and performing more official work than had then fallen to the lot of any one of his calling since the apostolic age. Whatever may have been the controlling motives of the Southern men in preferring him for a Bishop, certainly, in securing his election ere they left the Methodist Episcopal Church, they bestowed the richest possible boon on the mother Church in giving her a man to preside over her destinies who became the historical link which bound the old *régime* to the new, transmitted in himself the wisdom of the fathers of the Episcopacy to their sons in the office, and so by his long, laborious, and wise guidance conserved the staunchest and fairest ecclesiastical fabric of modern times. His selection was at once a provision and a prophecy. God's bleeding Church was to have a healing hand in the present; and in the future this honored servant, more than any other one man, was to be the messenger of peace who was to speak the first words of reconciliation between its dissevered members.

CHAPTER VI.

1844-1848.

Earlier Work as Bishop—Division of the Church—Home Letters—
Recuperation of the Methodist Episcopal Church.

THE first Episcopal work of Bishop Janes lay in New England. A fragment of a diary has been found recording his very first work as General Superintendent. He began the diary, evidently with the intention of keeping a continuous record; but, alas! his work outran his words; pen and pencil could not keep pace with his flight. As Dr. Abel Stevens once playfully said, "Death itself could not catch up with him."

1844. *July* 24. This morning commenced the duties of a presiding Bishop by opening the session of the New England Conference. My feelings can be better imagined than expressed. The Conference received me with great courtesy and marked affection. The morning session was a pleasant one. In the afternoon, in meeting the council of elders, I found my duties even more solemn and difficult. The business in changing the pastoral relations of Christian ministers is truly serious and responsible. If an itinerant ministry is kept up, however, some one must be intrusted with this prerogative. I am so sensible of the immense superiority of an itinerant over a settled ministry, that I am willing to do the very best I can, in the capacity of a General Superintendent, to save such a ministry.

August 1. The New England Conference closed its session this evening. It has been a very harmonious and pleasant Conference. A more than ordinary measure of divine influence rested upon the preachers and was manifest in the public meetings. God has very graciously aided and sustained me. I pray that his blessing may rest upon the appointments !

August 28. This morning started for the Kentucky Conference and the others in the South-western district. Parting with my family, with the expectation of being absent six months, was certainly very painful. My affliction was much increased by the illness of my wife and the tears and sobs of my dear children. A sacrifice for Christ, therefore made cheerfully.

August 30. Reached Marietta, Ohio, and stopped to spend the Sabbath, etc.

Sept. 1. Sunday, preached twice. I trust some good was done. This is the seat of the Ohio Conference, which meets here on the 4th inst. I shall wait until that time that I may see Bishops Waugh and Soule, who are expected here by or before that time.

"Bishop Janes," writes Dr. Elliott to the "Western Christian Advocate," "was present on the opening of Conference and presided a few hours. He filled the chair with as much ease as if he had been an old practitioner. We pledge for him that he will go through his duties with great Methodistic accuracy and general satisfaction."

On his way to the Kentucky Conference he stopped in Cincinnati and preached in Morris Chapel, which had recently been opened, and was then the most beautiful Methodist Episcopal church in the city. A venerable Christian lady, who is still a member of that Church, (now St. Paul,) remembers the occasion, and was especially struck with the impressive manner in which he read the hymn, of which one of the stanzas is,

> "Thee will I love, my joy, my crown ;
> Thee will I love, my Lord, my God ;
> Thee will I love, beneath thy frown
> Or smile, thy scepter or thy rod.
> What though my flesh and heart decay ?
> Thee shall I love in endless day."

The Kentucky Conference met at Bowling Green, Ky., Sept. 11. The session was an exciting one. In the late General Conference the delegates of this Conference had voted as a unit against the action in the case of Bishop Andrew. The chairman of the delegation, the eloquent Dr. Bascom, President of Transylvania University, had written the protest against this action, and as this was the first Southern Conference sitting after the recent action, it was matter of great moment as to the measures the members would adopt. Bishop Janes was cordially received, and although the questions acted upon involved the sharpest debates, and he was obliged, at least in one instance—the ordination of slave-holding local preachers—to deny the wishes of the Conference, yet his presidency was highly commended. A correspondent of the " Nashville Advocate " writes :

Our newly elected Bishop, the Rev. Edmund S. Janes, who presided at the Kentucky Conference, gave general satisfaction. His expedition in the dispatch of business, his firmness,

5

modesty, affability, and unaffected piety, are very important qualifications for the high office to which he has been called. We trust he will find his visit to the South-west pleasant to himself; and we pray that it may be profitable to the Churches.

Since writing the above we have received the following resolution, which was adopted while the Bishop was absent from the conference room:

Resolved, By the Kentucky Annual Conference, that it affords us great pleasure to bear testimony to the ability, energy, and impartiality with which Bishop Janes has presided over the deliberations of this body during its present arduous and protracted session, and that we most cheerfully commend him to the kind and approving regards of the ministry and membership of the Church, wherever he may appear, as one of the Bishops of the Methodist Episcopal Church.

H. B. BASCOM,
E. STEVENSON.

If there had been the least misgiving in the minds of his northern friends as to the leanings of Bishop Janes in the event of a division of the Church, they were set at rest by his course at this Conference.

Dr. J. S. Porter, his early and long-tried friend, writes:

At the time he was elected by the General Conference of 1844, to be á Bishop of the Methodist Episcopal Church, there was some fear among the delegates of northern Conferences that he might be induced to cast his lot with the South, as the southern delegates were the first to mention his name in connection with the office, and regularly nominated him. To counteract any such influence as might be brought to bear upon the newly elected Bishop, he was reminded that the South had not votes enough to elect a Bishop at that Conference, and that we, of the North, who had cast our votes for him, did it most cordially and conscientiously because we wished his services in that position. It soon appeared in his administration of the office that there was no ground to fear his fidelity. When he presided at the Kentucky Conference, and found the brethren disposed to depart from their well-understood rule, and elect to orders in the local ministry some who were slave-holders, which they had up to that time declined to do, he informed them that he could not put to vote such a case, as it would, in his judgment, violate the Discipline of the Church; all, both North and South, who were informed of his action, became fully satisfied that the Methodist Episcopal Church in the United States had a Superintendent in Bishop Janes that could not be used to subvert the Discipline, or to ignore it, even under a powerful pressure. Though like his divine Master, he was meek and lowly in heart, he was as firm as a rock in adhering to his convictions.

The Kentucky Conference at this session appointed delegates to meet in convention at Louisville, Ky., May 1, 1845. The call for this convention had been made by the delegates from the Conferences in the slave-holding States, immediately at the close of the General Conference of 1844. So far, however, did a conservative feeling prevail in the Kentucky Conference, that delegates to the Convention were instructed "to prevent separation at present."

I am not able to follow the Bishop—in the absence of any records or letters—throughout his Southwestern tour. He presided over the Tennessee Conference, which began its session at Columbia, Maury County, Tenn., Nov. 2. There is a refer-

ence to his preaching in the correspondence of the
" Nashville Advocate : " " At ten o'clock A.M.
Bishop Janes filled the pulpit. He preached to a
crowded and highly interested audience. His sermon was plain, neat, chaste, breathing an ardent spirit
of piety, and attended with a peculiar unction."

It is probable that he went as far as Texas,
presiding over all the South-western Conferences,
accomplishing a tour in this, the first year of
his Episcopal service, remarkable not only for the
extent of traveling compassed, but for the hardships
of travel, caused by the rough roads and swollen
streams, and the mental strain which the crisis in
the Church imposed. Here is a specimen of his
adventures. Rev. E. Osborn says:

Soon after he was elected Bishop, in 1844, he was appointed
to attend some of the South-western Conferences. While on
this tour he was solicited to make an appointment to preach
at a place about forty miles, I think, to one side of his direct
route from one Conference to another. He rode all that distance on horseback, without seeing a house. About 3 P. M.
he saw an Indian roasting some venison, and being quite
hungry, he took out a silver piece, showed it to the hunter,
then pointed to the roasting meat, thus indicating to the man,
who understood no English, that he wanted to buy a piece.
A slice was soon cut off, rolled in white ashes as a substitute for salt, and the Bishop said that hunger made it taste
very good. Going on, he at length reached the old brother's
house, where he was to stop. The log meeting-house was
about two miles distant, and several rode on horseback to
the place. The windows were simply openings in the sides
of the building, and one of them was directly behind him.

The wind being very strong, he fastened his cloak up behind the pulpit, as a partial protection. Soon after the sermon was commenced a heavy gust, passing through the house, blew out all the lights, which were pine-knots fastened to the sides of the building. He then said to the people, " The Gospel is a light shining in a dark place, and if you will remain I will go on with my sermon." They assented to this, he continued his discourse, and he said they had a good time. But when they went out to find and mount the horses on which they rode, such was the darkness (accompanied with rain, I think) that they had no small difficulty in getting on their way, for the Bishop said it seemed to him to be the darkest place he was ever in. When they had finally succeeded in getting mounted, his host told them that his horse knew the road and he would lead the way while the others followed.

It was, I think, on this same tour the Bishop had occasion to cross the Cumberland Mountains. On the route he had to leave the ordinary stage-coach and take a wagon without springs. At a certain point the wagon must cross a bridge over a torrent which the swollen waters had rendered dangerous, and he was warned, when he had reached it, to get out of the wagon and walk across on a foot-bridge. He accordingly said to the driver as he got into the wagon—it was about nightfall—to let him know when they got to the stream : if he was asleep to wake him up, not to fail. Away went the wagon, on and on, over one of the roughest mountain passes in the land. The Bishop, exhausted by his travels and loss of rest, soon fell asleep. He knew nothing more until the driver reined up at his destination and hallooed to him to get out.

His episcopal dignity was down among the straw on the floor of the wagon, the treacherous bridge had been crossed, the journey ended, while he had been oblivious to all toils and dangers.

In March of the following spring (1845) he was present at the session of the Baltimore Conference, which was held in the Caroline-street Church, Baltimore. Dr. Sargent, alluding to his presence, says : " He came to Baltimore from his first episcopal tour, in 1845, (March,) and in Bishop Soule's room he recounted to us some of his painful and pleasant experiences, especially in Mississippi."

The event of the spring of 1845 was the holding of a convention at Louisville, Ky., composed of delegates (one to eleven) from the ministers of the Conferences lying wholly in slave-holding States. Bishops Soule and Andrew attended upon the convention. All the Bishops were invited to preside over its deliberations, but they alone accepted the invitation. And when this body formally organized the Conferences which it represented into the Methodist Episcopal Church, South, they gave in their adhesion, and became officially identified with it. The course of the convention and of these Bishops was regarded by the Bishops of the Methodist Episcopal Church as a withdrawal from the body. They accordingly, at a meeting held in New York, July 3, 1845, after rehearsing substantially the action of the convention, passed the following resolution :*

Resolved, That acting as we do, under the authority of the General Conference of the Methodist Episcopal Church, and amenable to said General Conference, we should not consider ourselves justified in presiding in said Conferences, conformably to the plan of visitation agreed upon at the close of the late General Conference, and published in the journals of the Church.

This resolution recognized " separation " as an accomplished fact. Whether the Bishops changed their plan of visitation, in declining to preside over the Southern Conferences, out of respect to the legality of the so-called Plan of Separation, or as a measure tending to peace, does not appear. They may have had both considerations in mind. In the *interim* of the General Conference they could not have done otherwise. If, as some at the North maintained, they ought to have gone forward and held, or attempted to hold, the Southern Conferences all the same, and thus if rejected by all except the barest minorities of the ministers, kept up the organization of the Methodist Episcopal Church, even in the very heart of the South, such persons ought to remember that the report of the Committee on Pacification, while it may not have been meant as an encouragement to division, certainly held out the possibility of it under given conditions, of which conditions the Southern min-

* The "Great Secession," by Charles Elliott, D.D., pp. 492, 493.

isters were to be the sole judges. And the probability is, that but for the bitter strifes engendered
and aggravated by the "Border War" along the
line where the division was most keenly felt, and
also the growing bitterness of the slavery controversy in both sections of the country, the plan
would have been quietly accepted, and the vested
properties of the Church amicably distributed.
Then, let those who may now say what the Bishops
ought to have done remember that in the state of
the country at the time, with the ministers and
people—all citizens in common—solidly with the
action of the Louisville Convention, it would have
been physically impossible for them to have done
otherwise than to pursue a policy of abstention.
Mob law would have summarily visited them, civil
war would have been precipitated, and the war, instead of freeing the slaves, would have tightened
their chains. The antislavery sentiment of the
country was not yet strong enough for a successful
conflict with the slave power. God's time, which
events were hastening on, was not come. The
Bishops, controlled by the highest wisdom of the
hour, could go no faster than that wisdom allowed.

Bishops Morris and Janes, who had been assigned
to some of the Southern Conferences, in harmony
with the resolution of the Bishops, withdrew their
appointments. Bishop Soule wrote to Bishop Morris, requesting him to take charge of the Illinois,

Iowa, and Rock River Conferences, to which he had been assigned, and proposing to take Bishop Morris's Southern Conferences, and to this Bishop Morris acceded.

I see no more at present of Bishop Janes's official action. It fell to his lot, likely, to hold the Maine Conference, which met this year (July 15, 1845) at Portland, Me., and from that point he wrote to his little daughter Elizabeth :

I am pretty well. I hope our heavenly Father and his good angels have taken care of you and your sister. I hope also that you have been such good girls that your heavenly Father will love you and the blessed angels will love to stay with you. I have received uncle's letter, which was written last Thursday. I am much pleased that my little girls behave themselves so nicely. I shall love them very much for their good behavior. I expect to be home the last of this week—perhaps on Saturday. I hope I shall find you well and happy. Can you give sister a kiss for papa, and tell her papa sends his love to her? Don't forget to say your prayers.

In the winter of 1845-46 Bishop Janes made a visit to the Eastern shore of Maryland. It was a visit of much social pleasure, but also of incessant travel and preaching. He fain would have rested in the intervals of the autumn and spring Conferences in the quiet of his own home, and amid the scenes and duties adjacent to it, but no; he must heed the calls from afar. For the present we get glimpses of the paternal heart, as from this and other distant points it turns to the wife and children

5*

at home.   His correspondence with his family was prompt and constant.   He thus sought in some degree to compensate both them and himself for the privations suffered by his frequent and long absences.   His son Lewis, the first-born, was now nine years of age.

To Lewis T. Janes, from Easton, Md., Dec. 27:

I arrived here last evening.   I go this afternoon to the Royal Oak, the place where I am to dedicate the church to-morrow. I this morning met here the Rev. James Nichols, an old friend of mine.

I hope you are all well and have had a happy Christmas.   I wish very much that I could be with you on New-Years' day to help to make you all happy.   But I think it was my duty to take this tour of official services, and so I am reconciled to my absence from you on the holidays, and, indeed, on most other days too.   When we feel that we are doing right we can be happy under any privations.   The way of duty is the only path of safety and delight.   We cannot be happy while we are doing any thing that is wrong, or neglecting to do any thing that it is right for us to do.

I hope you are a good boy and are trying in every way you can to make your mother and dear sisters happy.   I was greatly delighted before I left to find you could read so well and that you loved so much to read.   I hope you still love to read. I will buy you all the good books with good print that you need, if you will only read them.   I now begin to hope that your heavenly Father will give you sight enough to enable you to be a minister.   O, how glad I shall be if my dear Lewis is ever good enough and wise enough to become a minister!   I have prayed for it a great deal.   I hope you will pray for it.   You must become very religious before you can be a minister. You must do nothing that is wicked and do every thing that the Bible points out to us as our duty . . .

To Lewis T. Janes, from Snow Hill, Md., Jan. 17:

In her last letter your mother states that you are improving in your reading and in your deportment. I am so much pleased to hear this that I determined to sit right down and write you a letter, and tell you how happy it makes me to hear that you are becoming a better boy. It is not your turn to receive a letter, and it is late, and I am tired, but I determined to write to you before I go to sleep. I am very much pleased indeed. It makes me very happy to learn that you are trying to be good I hope you will keep trying. You will not only make your father and mother happy, but you will also be much happier yourself. Naughty persons are never happy. It is only good persons that are happy. . . . Now, my dear, be a good boy, fear God, obey and love your mother, be kind to your sisters, say your prayers, read your Bible, and may your heavenly Father bless you in all things!

The Bishop met the Troy Conference, at Keeseville, N. Y., on May 27, 1846. From Albany, on his way, he wrote to Lewis:

I had quite a pleasant sail up the Hudson river on Saturday, though we had some hard showers. . . I expect to leave now in a little while for Troy, and go on to-night in a packet-boat to White Hall, where I expect to take a steamboat across Lake Champlain to Keeseville.

I did not preach yesterday, but I addressed the Sabbath-school in the afternoon. The school was in the church, and there was quite a large congregation, so it was much the same as preaching. They have a good school in Garrettson Station in this city. . . .

Do you try to make mamma and sisters happy? Do you say your prayers and try to love your heavenly Father and your dear Saviour? Are you trying to get a new heart, so that you can go to heaven? Think of all these things. . . .

To his daughter Charlotte he writes, from Keese-ville, May 28:

Our Conference opened yesterday and has progressed pleas-antly. I have not had time to survey the town yet. I think, however, there is not much beauty about it, though it is a pros-perous business village. It is about four miles west of Lake Champlain. My sail across the lake on Tuesday was a very pleasant one. It was a beautiful day; we had a beautiful boat and good company and splendid scenery, which, in combination, made a very pleasant sail of it. The night before on the packet-boat I had a miserable time.

I am putting up with the minister stationed here. He has two daughters and one son. The youngest daughter is waiting to take your letter to the post-office. Committees are coming in upon me and I can write no more. Be a good girl and make all happy around you. Kiss mamma, and tell her papa sends his best love to her. Kiss brother and sister and tell them father sends much love to them. In a very pleasant manner tell Miss Rohn and Rebecca papa sends his kindest remembrance to them.

From Lowville, N. Y., the seat of the Black River Conference, to Lewis, June 18:

I write now to show you that I think of you, and also be-cause I think it will give you pleasure to receive a line from your father. I love to make you happy. And when Lewis is good and pleasant he is happy. He is a very cheerful, pleasant boy generally. He is also generally very kind and very gener-ous. . . . Now I have told you what I think is right and good in your character. . . . Well, now, Lewis has improved very much in some things within a few months, will he not try to improve more? To be more manly? To try to make his lit-tle sisters and all others happy? Come, now, what does Lewis say? I think he says, Yes. I think he will try. Well, we will try to help you and encourage you. We will tell you when we think you are improving. You can be very good and pleasant if you will. You know how if you will only try.

I want Lewis to become so gentle and pleasant in his manners and so trustworthy in his character that I can take him with me anywhere. And so I can always feel when I go away from home that his mother has a little man to wait on her, to keep her company, and make her happy. . . .

In the early autumn of this year he held the Genesee Conference, at Lyons, N. Y. Thence he writes, September 9, to his youngest daughter, Elizabeth:

Well, pet, how do you do this morning? I am pretty well, and hope you are also. How is mamma? Have you kissed her this morning? How are brother and sister? Have you kissed them this morning? I wonder if my little children are all affectionate and gentle and happy this morning. I should love to see them very much and have a sweet kiss from each of them. Well, I expect I shall have some sweet kisses from them when I get home. They may give all their sweet kisses to mamma until I get home, and then they will give me a few of them.

Have you prayed this morning? Did you pray with your heart? Remember we must pray with our hearts to obtain the blessing of our heavenly Father. You need his blessing. No one else can forgive your sins. No one else can give you a new heart. No one else can make you happy. No one else can take you to heaven. So you must pray to him with your heart. . . . We had a missionary meeting last night. I made a speech, and Dr. Bond also. It was a good meeting, only the people did not give money very freely. I hope the time will soon come when people will understand and do their duty to their poor heathen brethren. How does your missionary box come on? I must now bid you adieu. Now see how prettily you can tell mamma, brother, and sister that papa sends love to them. . . .

The Bishop's face was now set to the North-west. Incidentally a letter from Mrs. Janes to Lewis, Sept. 25, mentions him as in the State of Michigan:

It is a pleasure to me to write to you. We are all well and comfortable. The little girls are more quiet in their plays now than when their brother was with them. There is no more playing horse, and no more stages, etc. Charlotte tries to take your place all she can. She goes of errands, and goes to the post-office. You would be amused to see her with the little hatchet splitting wood, and yesterday she took the saw. She is a dear little girl. She sends a great deal of love, and so does Lizzie.

I received a letter from your dear papa yesterday. He was well. He was at Detroit. He has now gone to Marshall, Michigan, where the Conference opened on Wednesday. . . . It is evening. Little Lizzie has just gone to sleep. She prays for her brother. Charlotte is sitting by the stand knitting. . . . Don't forget your little hymns: "In the green fields of Paradise," "A poor way-faring man of grief," "Sparkling and bright," "The day is past and gone," "Come, thou Fount."

The years 1846–47 passed with Bishop Janes in the usual routine of episcopal work. It was a period of great danger to the peace of the Church and to the efficient working of all its methods and institutions. Never did its chief pastors need more to be men of piety and equanimity. In addition to the vast numbers which had gone off bodily into the Southern Methodist organization, the irritations incident to such a rupture, and a very general reaction from the excitement caused by the Second Adventism of the times, had induced a general decline of religious revivals and of accessions to the Church. A process of sifting and settling was going on.

The minds of the thoughtful were now turning upon the internal life of the Church—the conservation of its morals, experience, and various benevolent organizations. The last General Conference had restored Mr. Wesley's original rule on temperance, thus placing Methodism in the advance on the great total abstinence reform, which has since been steadily gaining in influence. The cause of higher education elicited general discussion and more liberal support. The Sunday-School Union, with its first distinct editor, the Rev. D. P. Kidder, was creating a literature for the youth of the families; the missionary cause was receiving new impulses, at home in the consolidation and growth of the work among the Germans, through the agency of the Rev. Dr. William Nast and his co-laborers; in the first beginnings of the movement among the Scandinavians, through the pious zeal of Pastor O. G. Hedstrom; and abroad, by the establishment of the first mission among the heathen at Foochow, China.

In all these causes Bishop Janes was active. He was the "perpetual curate" of the General Confer-

ence Societies which centered in New York. In
addition to these, New York city Methodism was
productive of various local movements. The elect
women of the Church, under the leadership of Mrs.
Mary W. Mason, had dared to open a mission Sunday-school in the heart of the infamous Five Points.
Out of this grew the Ladies' Home Missionary Society, which subsequently purchased the Old Brewery,
and on its site erected the first Five Points Mission
building. Through the work of this mission, and
that of others since introduced, a physical and moral
renovation has come over one of the deepest sinks
of iniquity ever known in Christendom. The ladies
had also organized a home for the aged and destitute women of the Methodist Episcopal Church of
the city, and put it into successful operation.
While these general enterprises were going forward
local chapels and churches were springing into
being in New York and in the rapidly multiply-
ing neighborhoods about it. To these Bishop
Janes gave his time, sympathies, counsels, and
means. All workers and works must have his ear,
his advice, his cheer, and his services. Nor did he
ever turn any away. How much his devout and intelligent supervision had to do with this critical
and transitional period in securing wise and stable
results eternity alone will reveal.

I drop here one of his customary epistles to the
children before I hasten to the close of the first

four years of the Bishop's general superintendency.
The children were attending school at Basking
Ridge, N. J.

Your father and mother wish you good-morning. We are
very well. We hope our heavenly Father still blesses you all
with good health and much happiness. We hope, too, that you
are all good children. That you study when your teacher directs you to, and that when you play you do it very pleasantly.

We shall send with this most of the things Charlotte asked
for. I have walked a great way to find the toy Elizabeth
asked for, but I cannot find one. She will have to wait awhile
for it until her papa can find one for her. We send her a nice
book, however, which we think will please her much. Lewis, I
believe, did not ask for any thing, but we send him a book also,
which we hope he will find pleasure in reading. Besides the
two new books, we have selected some others which we
thought would please you. Your names are in them. . . .

Now, my dear children, do not forget to say your prayers.
Always mind your teacher. Be kind to your school-mates.
Love each other. . . .

CHAPTER VII.

1848-1850.

General Conference at Pittsburgh—Annual Conferences—Work in the West.

THE tenth delegated General Conference met in the city of Pittsburgh, Pa., May 1, 1848. The action of the previous General Conference and the events which had followed—particularly the so-called Plan of Separation and the formation of the Methodist Episcopal Church, South—had given rise to intense feeling in the Northern and Border Conferences. In some Conferences, as, for example, in the New York, an issue was squarely raised, and such Nestors of the Conference as Drs. Bangs and Olin were left at home, and younger men, known to be opposed to the " Plan," were elected delegates. It was very evident, as the members came together, that they were in no humor for adhering to its provisions. A general conviction prevailed, that even if the General Conference had a right to provide for the division of the Church and its property, the terms of the provision had been violated by the Southern ministers.

The Bishops of the Methodist Episcopal Church had met in Philadelphia, March 3, 1847, Bishop

Hedding, chairman, and Bishop Janes, secretary, and declared their understanding of the line of division between the two Churches, and their faithful adherence to it.* They also stated, in a report to this General Conference, that in numerous instances the authorities of the Methodist Episcopal Church, South, had infracted the "line." This report, with various other matters relating to the questions in controversy—such, for example, as a refusal of the Annual Conferences to concur with that part of the plan submitted to them—was referred to a Committee on the State of the Church, composed of two members from each Conference, of which the Rev. George Peck, D.D., was chairman.

This Committee reported to the Conference from time to time successive "declarations," which were adopted by the Conference almost unanimously. The fourth declaration comprised eight sections. The seventh and eighth sections of this "declaration" were as follows: "Therefore, in view of these facts, as well as the principles contained in the preceding declarations, there exists no obligation to observe the provisions of said plan. And it is hereby declared *null and void.*" † Yeas, 133; nays, 9.

The General Conference of the Methodist Episcopal Church, South, which met at Petersburgh, Va., May 1, 1846, acting by the authorization of the

* "History of the Great Secession." By C. Elliott, pp. 578, 579.
† *Ibid.*, pp. 646, 647.

Louisville Convention, organized under the presidency of Bishop Andrew, accepted the adhesion of Bishop Soule, and elected two additional Bishops, Drs. William Capers and Robert Paine. The Conference went through with all the routine business of a General Conference, leaving the Discipline substantially as it was, not even changing the article on slavery, except to add an explanatory foot-note. It appointed commissioners to carry out the details of settlement under the Plan of Separation. It also appointed the Rev. Lovick Pierce, D.D., as a fraternal delegate to the General Conference of the Methodist Episcopal Church.

Dr. Pierce very promptly appeared at Pittsburgh, and gave notice of his presence and his desire to know the wishes of the Conference. The reply was, that while the members were glad to welcome him as an individual they could not receive him as a fraternal delegate, for if they did they would thereby be understood to approve the course of the Church South in what it had done. Dr. Pierce was invited to a seat in the bar of the Conference, but he declined all recognition except in his official capacity. He soon after left the city.

It must have been a great personal trial to Bishop Janes to be thus placed with relation to his tried and honored friend, Dr. Pierce; but there is no evidence whatever that he did not fully agree with the action of the General Conference. No man ever allowed personal feelings to affect less his official obligations than did Bishop Janes.

The General Conference, while declaring the " Plan " *null and void*, authorized the Book Agents at New York and Cincinnati to offer to submit the property claims between the two Churches to arbitration, if they could legally do so; and, if it were further necessary, the Annual Conferences should be asked to suspend the sixth restrictive rule, allowing the Book Agents to submit the claims to arbitration.* It is matter of history that this proposition was rejected by the commissioners of the Southern Church, and suits were instituted in the United States Courts, which were finally decided in favor of the Church South, to which was transferred the debts due from persons residing within the limits of its Conferences ; and, in addition, $270,000 were paid to it, with the costs of the suits.

In an article entitled " Characteristic Sketches," which appeared in "Zion's Herald," of Boston, written by the editor, the Rev. Dr. Stevens, is the following pen-portraiture of our subject :

There is certainly but one sense in which Bishop Janes can be said to be the *least* of the Bishops ; he has a diminutive body, but as large a soul as ever filled the lordly bulk of an archbishop. Like St. Paul, his bodily presence is not very imposing, and doubtless many a good Methodist, familiar with his name but not his person, would be egregiously disappointed to find so great an officer in so small a body. . . . If he hap-

* " Great Secession," p. 654.

pens to see, or rather hear, the Bishop in the pulpit or on the anniversary platform, he will soon dismiss all concern for his personal importance. He is really one of the "smartest" speakers in the land. He may yet grow into another Coke. He resembles our first Bishop very much in the smallness of his stature and the defects of his voice ; a little more rotundity will almost complete the similarity, and this old-fashioned episcopal attribute he seems to be fairly acquiring. The countenance of Bishop Janes is habitually serious. . . . His mind is rapid, clear, and highly illustrative ; I know not that it can be called comprehensive or profound, but it is severely accurate, luminous, fertile, practical, and indomitable—and that's greatness enough surely for an eagle thus encaged.

In the July following the adjournment of the General Conference Bishop Janes met the Black River Conference at Adams, N. Y., on the 5th, and the Oneida Conference at Oswego, N. Y., on the 26th. Of the session of the former the correspondent of the "New York Christian Advocate and Journal" says :   –

Various propitious circumstances seem to have conspired to render the present an interesting session of our body. We have the mild, affable, courteous, and yet thorough and energetic, Bishop Janes with us as our president. The preachers seem well satisfied with and encouraged by the action of the late General Conference, and, so far as I have been able to learn, report general, if not universal, satisfaction among our people.

At the Oneida Conference, July 26, 1848, the verdict was that the Bishop discharged all the duties of his office " not only to the entire satisfaction of the Conference, but to the admiration of all."

The correspondent of the " Northern Christian Advocate " writes :

Our sweet-spirited little Janes presides over us with all proper dignity, and yet with great courtesy.   He is never lost in the mazes of business, but in few words will soon make the most obtuse among us see where we are, in the midst of motions, amendments, and substitutes. . . .

I wish I could present you with a correct and full report of the admirable address of Bishop Janes to the young men who are candidates for admission into the Conference. . . . The Bishop remarked substantially :

" We have reached a solemn point in the doings of the Conference.   No more important event in your lives has ever been reached than this.   Entrance upon the work of the ministry, to one truly called of God to that high vocation, stands as really connected with his final salvation as does his conversion to God.   With such a call you cannot trifle with impunity.   Again, if called of God to this work, he will not trifle, with you.   The pillar of cloud and fire will point out your way, and you must, you will, be successful in winning souls to Christ."

The questions, " Have you faith in God ?   Are you going on to perfection ?   Are you groaning after it ? " having been proposed and answered, the Bishop remarked, " I hope that none of you will ever teach after this that justification and sanctification are one and the same thing.   You say that you *have* faith, justifying faith in God.   With this as a starting-point, you are going on *to* perfection, groaning after it, and *expecting* to be made perfect in love in this life.   The two states are, then, distinct ; do not confound them ; and do not teach that there is no middle ground between them.   You are *going on* to perfection.   Both are attainable, and both to be secured by faith."   The Bishop thought that could the framers of these searching questions have known the peculiarities of the present times there would have been given to the eleventh rule for preachers equal prominence with the first, tenth, and twelfth.

That rule requires that we will be ready, not only to go where we are wanted, but where we are wanted most, that is, needed most. Jesus would have acted on this principle, and are not we the ministers of Jesus? The apostles always acted on it, and are not we successors of the apostles? The large villages and cities of our country want pastors. It is well they should not be neglected. But there are localities remote from cities where there are immortal souls to be sought out and saved. Some of these are poor and afflicted, and cannot come to your central points. Others are wicked, and will not come. How shall their case be met? You must go to them. While the residents of your large villages want you, do not those in the adjacent and intermediate points need you more? Visit them at their houses on week-days, and preach in their school-house in the evening. Love them and labor for them, and they will love you and take care of you. Preach in out-neighborhoods on week evenings, and the people will come to the village to hear you preach on the Sabbath. But if you are unfaithful in that which is least, who will intrust you with that which is greater? Do you say your health will not allow of this large amount of labor? Let me assure you that more men die for lack of labor than in consequence of labor. Your health will be promoted by the exercise of walking a few miles every week, and preaching in the evening. Our fathers did not have the dyspepsia, nor should we were we, like them, "abundant in labors." Preach during the week, and you will preach the better on the Sabbath for it. And while walking to these appointments you can muse upon some passage of Scripture, upon which you can enlarge profitably and savingly to your congregation. Sermons thus prepared may have less bone, but they will have more muscle and more soul. It is not your whole work to preach so many sermons, but to do all the good and save all the souls you can.

The importance of pastoral visiting was urged by the Bishop upon the Conference with his usual felicity and zeal. "More preachers are desired," said he, "because they are good pastors than because they are eloquent preachers."

And what Bishop Janes at this early stage of his episcopal career was at those two Conferences, he was every-where. In all places, both among preachers and people, he left behind him the savor of wisdom and piety. The elder ministers regarded him with a parental pride, and the younger men approached him with fraternal affection.

In this year the following touching and teaching incident occurred:

A boy about eleven years of age, a cripple by paralysis from infancy, was being carried by his mother from the cars to the ferry at Jersey City. Just as they were leaving the train a quiet, unassuming gentleman came to them, saying, "That boy seems too heavy a burden for you, will you allow me to carry him?" The mother assented, and the little fellow put his arm about the stranger's neck and was carried to the boat and placed carefully in a good seat, and there left with his mother until the boat had crossed, when the gentleman returned to his charge, and with a smile that lingers still upon the memory, and kind words that soothed and comforted, carried the boy to the waiting-room in the New York depot, where, on being assured he could be of no further assistance, he bade the boy good-bye and left him, speaking cordially as he passed out to an elderly gentleman, who was just entering. The grateful boy beckoned to this elderly gentleman and asked, "Can you give me the name of the gentleman to whom you just spoke?" "That is Bishop Janes, of the Methodist Episcopal Church." That boy had never been taught to venerate Methodists or Methodism, but from that hour was often heard to say he knew at least one good man who was a Methodist. His limbs never received the coveted strength, but God converted his soul, and gave him abundant grace to bear his affliction.

6

Mr. Thomas P. Day, who furnishes this incident as evidence of the influence of an act which has followed him through life, is now a local preacher in the Newark Conference.

In the spring of 1849, after holding his spring Conferences, the Bishop settled his family for the summer and autumn at Mount Vernon Cottage, near Mendham, New Jersey. The air of this hilly region was very favorable to the health of Mrs. Janes and the children. Letters passed frequently between the little group and the absent father and husband. They were the offspring of sweet affections, and strikingly illustrate the characteristics of this wise and good man. I can give only extracts here and there. The quiet pleasure of the grave Bishop may be imagined, as, possibly seated in the chair of Conference, such missives as those which follow were handed to him. He was now on a tour of the North-western and far Western Conferences.

From Elizabeth to her father, Mount Vernon Cottage, July 9, 1849:

I hope you are very well, and have had a pleasant journey back to Rockford again. Porter gave Katy a little kitten that she calls Rosa. She feeds it milk morning, noon, and night. It is very playful. We have a fine brood of young turkeys. Their color is white, black, and a light slate combined. They are eight days old to-day, and are very large. Our chickens are very mischievous—they eat off the cabbages and root up the beans. We have very fine raspberries, black, white, and red, which mamma enjoys very much. I must now bring my letter to a close.

From Charlotte to her father:

We received your two letters on Saturday afternoon, and I am very glad to hear that you are in good health. We are all pretty well to-day, and nearly over our whooping-cough. Yesterday morning's text was, "Continue in prayer." On Saturday Lewis and Mrs. Isaacs went to Morristown and were caught in the showers, as it was a rainy day, but they reached home in safety. On Sunday as we were leaving the church one of "Favorite's" shoes came off, so she could not go to Mendham in the afternoon. Lewy took her down to the blacksmith Monday morning; and yesterday afternoon Lewy, Lizzie, Tilly, Ellen, Katy, and myself went to pick cherries.

From Lewis to his father:

I have received your letter dated June 30. I was very happy to hear from you, and hope that you have recovered from the fatigue of your journey. We are all in good health. Mamma had the headache last week, but is now quite well. Matilda is also improving. Mrs. Isaacs and I went to Morristown on Saturday. We took our feed with us, and fed "Favorite." Mamma thinks that we want a horse-net, so we looked for one, but could not find any to suit us, and we sent to Mr. King to send us one, which he did. It is all white, and looks very pretty. "Favorite" is very well. They are fixing the church at Mendham. I should like to look into Conference and see you this morning.

From Mrs. Janes to Bishop Janes:

It is with a heart overflowing with gratitude to God that I communicate the pleasing intelligence of Matilda's recovery. Her improvement during the past week has been astonishingly rapid. . . . Every thing seems to be prospering among and around us. The little girls are growing stout. They are quite hearty, and enjoy themselves very much. I do not confine them to much study this warm weather. The baby is this moment saying, pa-pa, pa-pa. When we ask her where he is, she points to the door or window. . . . It is now five o'clock in the afternoon, and Lewis and I are going to take a leisurely ride to the post-office, as the weather is quite warm. But we generally find some air up here on Mount Vernon. . . .

From the Bishop to Mrs. Janes, Mount Morris, Illinois, July 13, 1849:

The Wisconsin Conference was protracted and tedious on account of several long trials of preachers. None of them amounted to much after they were investigated.

The Conference adjourned about eleven o'clock last Monday evening with much good feeling. We had very good meetings during the session. The special object of my visit to this place was to lay the corner-stone of a new church on to-morrow. This is the seat of the Conference Seminary, one of the most prosperous institutions of learning in the West. The place was named in honor of Bishop Morris. It is a beautiful village. This place is twenty-five miles from Rockford, the seat of the Rock River Conference. I shall remain here until Monday, and then go to Rockford. I am very thankful that little Matilda was no worse when your letter was dated. Perhaps the Lord will preserve her to us. It is a great comfort to me to know that you are so comfortably fixed this summer. I hope you will all have health to enjoy all your means of pleasure. I am glad to hear so good an account of "Favorite." . . .

My mind has been very serene since the first two or three days after I left you. I have calm religious delight. My devotions are refreshing and profitable. I am trying to do and suffer the will of God with a right spirit and in a proper manner. It is my meat and my drink to do the will of my Father in heaven. I know no higher bliss. The testimony that I am pleasing and glorifying God is the highest good I aspire after in this world. I delight in this greatly. I feel that the smile of the Lord rests upon me. I bless his holy name for his rich grace bestowed upon you, and for all the peace and comfort with which you are inspired. I pray that his grace may abound unto you more and more. I am very desirous that our beloved children should share with their parents in the mercy and grace of God. The only thing concerning them about which I am really painfully anxious is their Christian character. Please to kiss each of them for their father, and tell them he sends them his love and his blessing.

To this reference which the Bishop makes regarding his religious experience the spiritual sense of Mrs. Janes quickly responded:

I feel very thankful to you, my dear husband, that you have written to us so frequently. It is such a relief to my mind to hear from time to time of your health, etc. I prize very highly the brief statement of your Christian experience contained in your last of 13th July. God be praised for giving you right motives and divine approval. My mind continues serene and trustful.

Again, under another date, about this time, she writes thus cheerily:

I feel quite happy in my mind, arising from a sweet and conscious enjoyment of divine things. The few and simple means of grace which I attend are profitable to me. I find the Lord in our little temples, in the class-meeting, at the family altar, and in the closet, and rejoice in those manifestations of his love which he from time to time imparts. I find the yoke of Christ to be easy and his burden light, for love makes all things easy.

To Mrs. Janes, from Iowa City, Ia., Aug. 2, 1849:

I arrived at this place a short time since, on my way to the Iowa Conference. I remain here to-night, and as they have given out an appointment for me to preach I intend to give them a short sermon. I shall proceed to-morrow on my journey. I am traveling now in a covered carriage. The weather is comfortable, and my journey, so far, very pleasant. It is now' near preaching time, and I must be brief. I wish to keep you advised as fully as I can of my movements, health, etc. ; also as frequently as I can to renew my assurances of love and of constant, affectionate, and prayerful remembrance. God has been very gracious to me on this official tour. I have been favored with more than a usual sense of his presence, and also with more than usual divine aid in the performance of my great duties. My mind is mostly in a peaceful and confiding state. I think I have been enabled to do some good. I try to live and labor and preach for this. I have for years daily consecrated myself unreservedly to God. I desire and aim to glorify him in my body and soul, which are his. I am not living to myself. It is a great pleasure to me to know that my wife is a devoted, holy Christian ; that she is a part of God's consecrated property on earth.

From Fort Madison, Iowa, August 10, 1849, to Mrs. Janes :

I am in quite good health. I have had no cholera symptoms for several weeks. The prospect now is that I shall not be exposed to it any more during my tour, as it has left the places where my other Conferences are to be holden. This is cause of very great thankfulness. I hope I am suitably affected by this goodness of our heavenly Father. The Iowa Conference is progressing very pleasantly indeed. My next Conference will be held at St. Louis. Tell Lewis and Charlotte I am very much obliged to them for their affectionate letters, and will answer them as soon as I can. Tell Lizzie I am just as much obliged to her for her good-will to write me a letter as though I received one from her little hand and heart.

To Lewis, from Keosauqua, Iowa, August 16, 1849 :

. . . I have been much pleased with your letters this summer. The composition has generally been good, and the spelling and writing quite commendable. . . . It is a very great accomplishment for a young man to be a good letter writer. . . . Lewis must never forget the kind attentions of his loving and patient mother. He will always owe her a great deal of gratitude and love. . . . There has not been much new or interesting in my travels since I wrote to you last. My travels have again been across prairies, where I have seen prairie chickens, etc., and one evening saw two prairie wolves, but, as there were several of us, they ran away as fast as they could. They are easily frightened, except when very hungry. The Iowa Conference was a very pleasant one. We had the sacrament of the Lord's Supper and some interesting religious services at the time of adjournment. Fort Madison, where the Conference was held, is a small town on the west bank of the Mississippi River. There was once a fort there. . . .

I am now in Van Buren County, about forty miles west of the Mississippi. I came here because it is indirectly on my way to St. Louis, and because it is a healthy and quiet place where I can get a little rest. When in the towns so many call upon me, and I am urged so much to preach, that I get but very little repose for my mind or body. . . . I hope you will seek and find a new heart. Become altogether good. Then you will be happy yourself and make your parents and sisters and all with whom you have to do happy. You will also then be prepared for the heavenly world when you die. I am glad that " Favorite" is so much of a favorite with you all, and that you have so much comfort in your rides. You must continue to take good care of her, and drive carefully.

To Charlotte, from Churchville, Mo., August 24, 1849:

I am not quite certain, but I think it is your turn to receive a letter from papa. . . . I have just arrived here, having come for the purpose of taking steamboat to go down the river, and as I am waiting I improve the minutes to write you a hurried letter. . . . While I was back in the country I spent several days with a very excellent doctor. He had a lame patient, and he desired me to aid him in amputating his leg. As doctors live far apart in that new country I consented to be present and assist what I could. The amputation was well performed, but the poor man was too weak from previous loss of blood and disease to survive it ; he died in three or four hours after the operation. I attended him the day before the amputation, and talked with him about religion and prayed with him, and did the same the morning of the day he died. He prayed very earnestly for mercy. I hope he obtained it. It was altogether a painful case. I am much obliged to Char- · lotte for her affectionate letters since I have been on this tour of duty. They have generally been very well written for so young a correspondent. The last one was a very sweet one. Very good language, pretty good penmanship, and excellent sentiments. I am very much pleased with it. I have read it a good many times.

I am thankful that you are still desiring and trying to be good. I pray much for you, as does also your dear mother. But you must not depend upon the prayers of your parents. You must rely altogether upon the blessed Saviour. Jesus can save you. He can bless and convert you now. I hope you will be able to tell me, when I come home, that you have found him, and that you are happy in religion. That will make me very happy. When I was about starting on this long journey Charlotte said she wished the time of my absence was past, and I was home again. But let me ask Charlotte, Have you not had some pleasures, some delightful seasons, some opportunities of improvement, since I left you ? These you could not have had if your wish had been granted. You did not think of this when you made that wish. So you will be wiser · next time. We will learn to leave things to the order of our heavenly Father, and all will be right.

To Elizabeth, from St. Louis, Mo., August 28, 1849 :

I arrived here yesterday, and expected confidently to find letters from home. So the first thing was to inquire for my letters. A large bundle was handed me, and I soon looked at the handwriting and post-mark of them all, and lo ! none was from the beloved ones. I was much disappointed. So this morning, as soon as the post-office was open, I was there to inquire for letters. The post-master handed me two, and I soon saw they were mamma's handwriting. I broke open the one having the last post-mark, and read enough to learn that you were all well, and then put them into my pocket and walked home pleased and thankful. Though I found a number of preachers in my room on my return, I would not stop to do business with them until I had read both, or indeed all the letters, for there were five in two. I thank our heavenly Father for taking care of you all, and keeping you well and happy. O, how much I desire to come and see you all! I would give a great deal to spend but one day at Mount Vernon. I am much obliged to you for your letter written by your sister Charlotte. It gives a very full and correct answer to my questions. I hope no more of the bipeds are lost. Fifty chickens must make quite a large flock. I hope the kitty has fallen into good hands, where she will be well used, but I hope no one will pet her quite so much as Lizzie did.

Does Elizabeth read her Bible ? Does she think about the Saviour ? Does she pray ? Does she try to be religious ? I hope so. She is old enough now to be a Christian.

PEORIA, ILL., *Sept.* 12, 1849

DEAR WIFE : On last Sabbath afternoon I was taken quite ill with bilious dysentery. This afternoon (Wednesday) I rode out. The doctor thinks I may with safety start to-morrow for Quincy. A preacher goes with me, and takes me in a comfortable covered carriage. If you see accounts of my sickness in the papers you need not be alarmed. I have told you the true state of the case.

To Charlotte, from Quincy, Ill., September 17, 1849.

. . . I left Peoria (from whence I wrote on Wednesday last) in a private carriage, not being well enough to take the

6*

stage. I rode thirty-three miles the first day, fifty the second, and fifty-six the third day. Was not that good traveling for a man who got off from a sick bed to start? But O, they were wearisome, suffering days! When I arrived here, though much fatigued, my health was as good as when I left Peoria. It is remarkable what good care the Lord takes of me. This morning (Monday) my health is quite improved. I feel that I am getting well. I have a very comfortable home, and am taking good care of myself. . . .

At this Conference I have two sets of presiding elders, one German and one English. All the German missionaries for the States of Missouri, Iowa, Wisconsin, and Illinois are connected with this Conference. This will make my duties very laborious. I meet the German presiding elders at half past one o'clock this afternoon in order to make out their appointments, as far as I can, before the Conference meets. It was for this purpose I hurried to get here on Saturday. I am pleased that you are so much interested in preaching. I hope the sermons which you hear will lead you to the blessed Saviour. I hope dear Charlotte and all my children will become Christians now, while they are in their youthful days.

> " A flower, when offered in the bud,
> Is no vain sacrifice."

. . . Tell sister Lizzie I reciprocate her love. Ask her what reciprocate means. If she cannot tell, you can explain it to her. Then you will teach her something that will be useful. I am also pleased to hear that her turkeys and chickens are growing well. Tell mamma I think if you all keep well, and I hope you will, you had better remain where you are until I come home. I would like very much to visit you in your summer quarters. Now be cheerful, be playful, be prayerful, be dutiful, be good, be happy. May our heavenly Father bless you in all things !

Bishop Janes met his last Conference for 1849, the Indiana, at Rising Sun, Ohio County, Indiana,

on October 10. Here he found letters awaiting
him from home assuring him of the eager joy with
which they were anticipating his return. " I am
glad," says one of the children, " that the time is
drawing near when you are to come home." " O,
how glad I am," says another, " that you are on the
journey homeward, and I hope I shall soon see
you ; " while the wife adds, " I rejoice God's hand
is still stretched out over you for good, and that we
may anticipate the unspeakable satisfaction of soon
welcoming you to the bosom of your own lonesome,
family. Be assured that your reception will be
characterized by more abundant joy than perhaps
was ever before manifested, for as the children
grow larger they become more sensible of the privation they sustain in the protracted absence of
their dear and honored father."

The foregoing letters give only the inner glimpses
of the Bishop's work on this long and arduous
journey—for he seldom, even to his own family,
made allusions to his work, especially its difficulties
and triumphs. But from the religious journals of
the day we glean marked proofs of the efficiency
and acceptability of his preaching and administration. The correspondent of the " Illinois Advocate "
writes from the Iowa Conference session : " Bishop
Janes looks as he did three years ago, except that
his face is a little care-worn and his dark hair is
becoming thoroughly sprinkled with the tint that

bespeaks advancing years. . . . In the examination of characters he proceeds with a rapidity unequaled on the bench of superintendents. His processes are both original and successful. No Bishop will turn off more men in a given time than the junior of the apostolic college of the Methodist Episcopal Church." Another, to "Zion's Herald," says: "We had Bishop Janes, who left with us not only the reputation of a Methodist Bishop, but the deep impression of an apostolic minister of Christ. . . . Being the first visit of a superintendent to the Des Moines country, the people were delighted."

The correspondent of the "Western Advocate" writes from the seat of the Illinois Conference: "Bishop Janes was with us in very feeble health, but with a clear head and a warm heart presided over our deliberations as much to the satisfaction of the Conference as any former Bishop ever did. Long may he live to bless the Church and the world with the wisdom of his counsels and the sanctifying influence of his piety and ministry!" At Peoria he dedicated a new, "tasteful brick" church. "The house was crowded with attentive hearers; and though the Bishop was in feeble health, yet he was heard by all the people, and the Spirit of God which accompanied the word seemed to reach all their hearts; and I have no doubt but at the gathering up of the glorious stars to deck his gospel crown he will have some seals to his ministry on that occasion."

The " Indiana American " so aptly characterizes the Bishop and his ingenious, delicate methods while presiding at the session of the Indiana Conference, that I cannot forbear an additional extract:

Bishop Janes presided. He is apparently the youngest Bishop, small in stature, with a pleasant, round face, and a musical feminine voice. He is an able and dignified presiding officer. His manners are easy, his head clear, and his decisions prompt and courteous. This is his first visit to the Indiana Conference, but he has left a favorable impression. His closing remarks to the ministers, who were about to leave and go to their respective fields of labor, were peculiarly appropriate and touching. Could we hope to catch the first inspiration of their beauty and purity, their truth and eloquence, we would give a sketch. We shall not attempt it.

Before the benediction the ministers partook of the Lord's Supper. After this, the most affecting and solemn scene we ever witnessed ensued. The Bishop invited the wives of the ministers to come forward by themselves and kneel at the altar to partake of the sacrament. The wives and companions of Methodist ministers—the companions of their griefs, their journeys, and their labors. O ! it was a solemn scene to see those devoted, cross-bearing, and self-denying wives of itinerant ministers humbly bow at that altar.

A correct estimate of the endurance required on this tour can only be had when it is recollected that almost all the travel was performed by stagecoach or private carriage, over comparatively rough roads, and through regions where the lodgings were uncomfortable, and the fare often unpalatable and unwholesome. Since then what changes! railroads cross the country in all directions! flourishing towns and cities, and beautiful, well-appointed farms invite to their bounteous stores! Then the Methodism of all Illinois was not over 30,000, nor that of Iowa over 10,000, members, and the new Missouri Conference was but in its infancy.

CHAPTER VIII.

1850–1852.

Illness of Bishops Hedding and Hamline—Extraordinary Labors—
The Missionary Cause.

IT does not appear from the General Minutes that
the Bishop had any Conferences assigned him in
the spring of 1850.

An official letter from the stewards of St. George's
Church, Philadelphia, complaining that they were
unequally burdened for the support of their presiding elder, drew from him the following opinion,
March 25, 1850:

> You will please bear in mind that all the rules and regula-
> tions of the Church must be general. It would be unreason-
> able to suppose that rules adopted for the government of so
> numerous and extended a connection as the Methodist Epis-
> copal Church should operate to entire satisfaction under all
> the varieties of circumstances that might arise. This would
> require an exemption from that imperfection which appertains
> to every thing human. The Discipline requires stewards to be
> men of solid piety, who both know and love the Methodist
> doctrine and discipline, and of good natural and acquired abil-
> ities to transact the temporal business. The district stewards
> are to be appointed by the Quarterly Conferences from among
> these men of solid piety, etc. Now it is reasonable to expect
> such Christian and intelligent brethren to act religiously, can-
> didly, and honorably. It is true, the position of a district stew-

ard is not without temptation, but we do not perceive any very strong temptation. The business of a district stewards' meeting requires modesty and prudence in the representatives of the weaker charges, and good judgment and magnanimity in the representatives of the stronger charges. We think these qualifications are generally found in our stewards. Still we admit there may be cases in which the district stewards misjudge, and where their apportionments are unequal and unjust. Possibly such has been the fact in your case. If the district stewards, as you represent, have based their apportionment on "numbers only," they certainly have erred. The Discipline makes "ability" the basis of the apportionment.

Early in the season he located his family in West Jersey, on "Succasunny Plains," not far from the point where they spent the preceding summer. Meanwhile he had purchased a farm in the neighborhood, hereafter known as "Mount Wesley," which became for twenty years the country home. References to this spot, which was the center of so many thoughts and pleasures to the great wanderer over the earth, begin to crop out in the correspondence of this season. It became a green hill to which, when far away over land and sea, his heart wishfully turned and found imaginary rest. Bishop Janes, true to his early traditions and to the instincts of all pure natures, was a sincere lover of the country. He found an inexhaustible pleasure in communion with the varied forms of animate and inanimate nature, and I think, so far as personal ambition goes, could cheerfully have laid down his high office at any time, to take up and pursue the

homely duties of the farm, and to wrest a livelihood
from the stern soil. One clause no doubt he would
have inserted in his release—the privilege of preaching the Gospel to his neighbors, and, especially, to
the poor, wherever within his reach.

The Bishop's first Conference for the summer and
autumn was the Western Virginia, at Parkersburgh,
Virginia.

To Mrs. Janes, from Wheeling, Virginia, June
3, 1850:

I reached this city in safety about eight o'clock on Saturday
evening. . . . My stage ride from Cumberland, Maryland, was
rather uncomfortable, as I was crowded between two large and
aged men. The night in the mountains was quite cold. We
could judge of our altitude on the mountain by the state of the
leaves of the trees. No accident of note all the way. Though
I traveled thus constantly, day and night, in comparison with
the labors of the two preceding months it was rest. I really
found myself rested when I arrived here. My attention had
been diverted, my sympathies had been relaxed, the burden of
official responsibility had been temporarily removed, and my
body and mind had found rest. Yesterday I preached once,
with a good degree of liberty, and, I hope, to some good purpose. To-day I have been hard at work trying to bring up my
correspondence. To-night, at nine o'clock, I expect to take a
steamboat for Parkersburgh.

I have never felt more afflicted on leaving home than I have
this time. The feeble state of your health is the greatest cause
of my anxiety. I know full well from experience, that when our
health is poor and our nervous system deranged, care is a
burden, and kind offices from those we love are very grateful. I wish I could be with you to relieve you of all care, and
to soothe all your sufferings. A divine providence has ordered

it otherwise, and I submit.   Though absent from you in body
I am with you in spirit.   My heart will stay at home.   Wife
and children are before my mind very frequently through the
day and very often in the dreams of the night.

The little winged messengers flew very fast after
the receding father and husband.   Here's a dainty
one from Charlotte, which refreshed him on his arrival at Canton, Ohio:

SUCCASUNNY, *June* 11, 1850.

I was happy to learn in your letter to mamma that you were
in good health, and was rested by your journey.   I hope your
conferences will be short and easy, and will not fatigue you
much.   Last Friday morning Lewis took Lizzie and me over
to the farm, and we brought home four pounds of butter, and
a bunch of peonies, May roses, and snowballs.   This morning
Lewis and grandpapa went to the farm and brought back three
pounds of butter, some asparagus, two dozen eggs, radishes,
the first we have had of our own, and a little branch of cur-
rants, which mamma said were not yet fit for use, but would
be by next week, and a pair of fowls, which Lizzie and I picked
this afternoon.   I wish you were here to enjoy with us our numerous little pleasures, each one of which would be heightened
by the presence of papa.   I am sorry that dear mamma's health
has not improved as we hoped it would.   I trust she will soon
be better.   Matilda is well and happy, and is learning to talk
very fast.   She often runs out on the sand-hill and plays.
Lizzie wishes me to tell you for her that she is well and sends
her love.

Mrs. Janes adds:

I am not able to write much this morning.   Accept the re-
newed assurance of my undying love and gratitude.   I feel
indebted to my dear husband for innumerable comforts and
blessings which, under God, flow to me through him.   I daily

appreciate and enjoy both him and them. Father continues well. He is unceasing in his efforts to make us happy.*

Again Mrs. Janes writes, June 19:

Indeed, I am now enjoying that quiet retirement for which I have so long sighed. We find the house pleasant and airy— my room very agreeable. . . . And O what brilliant sunsets I daily behold sitting by my window! The birds sing all day long, and the flowers are blooming beautifully. I am literally surrounded with bouquets of flowers in my room. And dear little Lizzie invariably presents me with a nosegay of pinks and roses when I come down to my meals. The moonlight evenings this week are most tempting. I sat up till a late hour last night viewing the moon just in front of my window. My thoughts were sweetly soothing and solemn. While alone with God I was engaged in meditation and prayer. I feel that I am indeed encompassed with innumerable blessings, for which I never felt so much thankfulness nor appreciated so fully as at present. But it has always been my experience that

> " Thy gifts alone cannot suffice
> Unless Thyself be given."

And I am glad that it is so. Our blessed Lord, in much mercy, bestows upon me the richer gifts of his love, manifests his presence, and gives the transforming power of his grace. My heart is going out

> " in strong desire
> The perfect bliss to prove."

. . . We think of you, dear husband, and speak of you every day. If we were disposed to forget you, father would not allow it, for he delights to talk of Edmund, and loves to fix in his mind just where you are and what you are doing. May wisdom and might be yours!

---

* The father of Bishop Janes, who was now making his home with the Bishop's family.

The following touches of Charlotte's pen must have affected divers chords in the father's heart :

We would be very much pleased if, at the end of one of your Conferences, you would come and spend a few days with us, and see how all the things are coming on. Yesterday morning Lizzie and I weeded five beds in the garden. I send you a few rose leaves that you may see what various *hues* we have. Caroline [the nurse] says she wishes there was some way to preserve a bouquet of flowers till your return. . . . At eleven o'clock every morning Lizzie, Caroline, and I, and sometimes Lewis, meet together for the purpose of prayer. If at that time your mind is not too much engrossed by other thoughts, think of us as kneeling in the spare room, and meet with us in spirit.

The Bishop, *en route* for Canton, Ohio, the seat of the approaching Pittsburgh Conference, writes to this daughter, June 13, 1850 :

I think if Charlotte knew how pleased her father is to hear from her when he is absent it would make it a pleasure to her to write to him. I have read your last letter over several times. . . . I reached this place [Wellsville, Ohio] last evening. I hurried up the river as fast as I could, because the water was very low and still falling. I feared I might get on a sand-bar and be detained so long that I should not get to the Pittsburgh Conference in season. But I am now passed these uncertainties, as I have no more river travel. I go from here by stage. The Ohio River is a very beautiful one. Many of the villages are delightful. The steamboats on it, however, are not as good as those on the Hudson River. How do you busy yourself nowadays ? Do you work any ? Are you learning to keep house for mamma when she is sick or gets old ? I wish you to know how to do all kinds of woman's work. You are old enough to learn how to do many kinds of work. I wish you to play some for exercise. . . . How come on the flowers? Are any of them growing? Can you make me a bouquet when I come home? We shall see. It is good exercise for young ladies to cultivate flowers. Does it begin to seem like home where you are? I think I should feel at home almost any where, if mamma and the children were with me. O how I would like to drop in and take a cup of tea with you this evening, and read the Bible and sing and pray with you before you go to rest to-night! Well, if our heavenly Father permit, we shall have that pleasure one of these days. Time rolls away very fast. I attended the Sunday-school anniversary at the Western Virginia Conference. Just before I arose to make my speech the choir struck up and sang very beautifully, " I want to be like Jesus," etc. It really seemed for a moment as if I was at home, with my children around me singing one of their favorite hymns. It is a beautiful hymn. After you have read this letter I wish you all to sing it to grandpa. And I hope you will all try to be like Jesus. O what an attainment! To be like Jesus!

A letter to Dr. J. M. Howe, from Wellsville, Ohio, June 14, 1850, lets light upon the Bishop's life of ceaseless toil and the motives which controlled it :

I was very desirous to see you before I left for this long tour of official duty. Indeed, I was very anxious all winter to obtain at least an hour to call upon yourself and family. The past year has been one of incessant toil. My duties engrossed my attention day and night, at home and abroad. I do not recollect making more than three social calls during the season, and those were special cases where I hoped to be useful. I seldom, during the winter, retired until after midnight, generally not until one or two in the morning. For the most part I was obliged to neglect my private business and domestic obligations. What little time was given to these was redeemed from the pillow. Brethren tell me I ought not to take upon me so much labor. Perhaps they judge correctly, but they form their opinion without knowing the circumstances of the case. If they fully understood all the peculiarities of my obligations, and felt them as one feels them in my office, called to exercise a general superintendency over a Church of near 700,000 members and 4,000 pastors, they might judge very differently. The example of one in my position must have much influence upon preachers and people. They cannot understand the private duties of my office. They know little or nothing of my really burdensome correspondence, of my thousand anxious cares ; consequently they can see no good reason why I should not be all the while traveling or preaching. No person can know but by experience the exhaustion of our conference cares and duties ; the amount of intellectual labor to be performed in a few days ; the constant harassing of our feelings by preachers and people; the loss of rest night after night. These things are sometimes very crushing. Yet we must go from one such scene to another, month after month. Still the preachers and people do not see our mental exertions, our cares, our anxiety, our sleepless nights. They, therefore, know no reason why we should not be constant in addressing public meetings and preaching, and especially so with a Bishop of my age. Bishop Hedding they are willing to regard as partially superannuated ; but I am expected to work. Conscious that in many respects I fail in meeting the claims of my office, I am desirous of at least setting my brethren an example of industry. This has led me to take some appointments which under other circumstances I should have declined. I hope, however, that after the next General Conference I may be permitted to labor a little more moderately. I am trying to do right.

After the close of the Pittsburgh Conference the Bishop went to the Erie Conference at Painesville, Ohio ; thence to the town of Medina, where he presided over the North Ohio Conference ; thence to the session of the North Indiana Conference, at Cambridge, Ind. ; thence south-west to Chillicothe, Ohio, the seat of the Ohio Conference. With the session of this Conference, held September 18–27, closed his more public work for the year 1850.

The Church was fast recovering from the depletion caused by the great separation. It reported for the year an increase of 27,367 members and probationers, and 411 traveling preachers.

While the year 1850 closed auspiciously for the work, there were evidences that the hand of God . was resting heavily upon the general superintendents. Bishop Hedding was almost entirely disabled by age and infirmities, and Bishop Hamline, though only in the youth of old age, was entirely prostrated by disease. There was not a really robust man among them. But they were inured to hardship.

The Board of Bishops, at their meeting, December, 1850, apprised of Bishop Hamline's physical condition, made out the plan of episcopal visitation for the ensuing year so as provisionally to relieve him of all the Conferences. Bishop Janes, secretary of the Board, thus writes to Bishop Hamline :

This plan will only require the alteration of the time of two or three of the Conferences one week, and will not burden either of your colleagues. . . . You need, therefore, have no concern about your Conferences for the coming season. I am confident that I speak the feelings and sentiments of all your colleagues when I say we wish you to make your health the first subject of your care and attention. Your work will not be left to suffer, and none of your colleagues will suffer for their attention to it. You may, therefore, dismiss all anxiety on that subject. I hope you will be without anxiety on any subject. "The Lord reigneth, let the earth rejoice." All wisdom, goodness, and power are his. He loves Zion infinitely more than we can. He bought the Church with his blood; he will preserve it by his power.

Bishop Hedding's active official work ended on December 28, 1850. The entire supervision of the Church in 1851, with slight exception, fell upon Bishops Waugh, Morris, and Janes. Bishop Hamline, by slow and easy stages, reached Winthrop, Me., the seat of the Maine Conference, and presided about half the time at its sessions and fixed the appointments. Even this exertion greatly injured him, and led him to the conclusion that he could no longer sustain the cares of his office.

The work thus devolved upon the three efficient Bishops was prodigious. Besides the Conferences at which Bishop Janes assisted he held, from April 2 to September 17, in about twenty-four weeks, twelve Conferences, making a session for every consecutive two weeks, and constituting, with the travel involved, an amount of labor never exceeded, I believe, in the annals of the Church. These Conferences were mostly the older and larger ones of the connection. They embraced not less than 1,500 effective ministers, many of whom were of high standing, and an equal number of Churches, a large proportion of which were of great social importance; these considerations required the utmost painstaking and correctness of administration. It was a year of anxious days and of many, very many, sleepless nights. Yet his spirit never faltered, but rose with the occasion, and bore him on with a steady and sublime energy which overcame all difficulties. "What ought to be done can and *must* be done," seemed to be his motto, and he swept through the land a moral hero. The wonder is that his physical nature could have endured such continuous strain; but he had a single mind, and God was with him.

The first time the writer remembers to have seen the Bishop was this spring, 1851, at the session of the Baltimore Conference, at Winchester, Virginia. Bishop Waugh presided, and Bishop Janes assisted him. I, not having yet attained majority, was there a candidate for admission. He preached the sermon on Sunday morning on Isaiah's vision. Dr. Foster, of New York, now Bishop Foster, preached in the afternoon on " Great is the mystery of godliness." Both sermons made a deep impression on the audience; but I have never forgotten nor ceased to feel the burning force with which the Bishop applied to the preachers the question of the prophet, " Whom shall I send, and who will go for us ?" and the answer, " Here am I ; send me." *Here am I ; send me*, rang in my ears and conscience for years afterward. I was ready, as I thought, to

7

consent on the spot to go to the ends of the earth. Twice subsequently I heard him preach from the same text, and while the effect was always marked, it never reached the power of that occasion. Something, of course, may be due to the most impressible period of a young preacher's life.

Bishop Janes's first Conference this spring was the Providence, at Warren, R. I., April 2, 1851. Then followed in succession the New Jersey, New England, New York, New York East, Troy, Vermont, East Maine, Black River, Oneida, East Genesee, and Genesee. I need dwell no longer on this record of toil. A mark was left on the Church, and marks were left which could ever afterward be read in the junior Bishop. His step was never again so elastic.

But, not content with such herculean tasks of immediate episcopal oversight, his soul was now ablaze with the missionary spirit which Dr. Durbin, the lately appointed Corresponding Secretary of the Missionary Society, was kindling throughout the Church. He had scarcely paused long enough with his family to be refreshed ere he was off with the eloquent secretary on a Western missionary tour. The Pacific coast was pressing for missionaries, and men and money must be raised for the new populations which were pouring in upon it. Ministers and people must be aroused. From Wheeling, Va., Nov. 20, he writes:

We have a missionary meeting this evening, at which I am to make an address. To-morrow morning we take the stage for Zanesville, seventy-five miles from here, where we expect to spend the Sabbath.

Again, Nov. 25, writing from Columbus, Ohio :

We took stage for Zanesville, Ohio, where we arrived at eight o'clock in the evening. It snowed most of the day, and the ride was rather a sorry one. We had in the stage a garrulous old Quaker lawyer, who repeated to us his poetry and told us his history, and enlivened the dull scene by his incessant talk. I had some good religious feelings during the day. Saturday was laboriously employed writing letters to missionaries and others. On Sunday I preached twice to crowded audiences, and made a missionary speech of forty minutes. We took a collection of upward of three hundred dollars. The Lord was with me and blessed me in my labors, but the work was too hard. I went to bed exhausted and restless ; slept some. The next day felt as if I had had a fit of old age. Yet early in the morning took stage for this place. . . . I was favored with a good sleep last night, and feel much recruited to-day. We are to have a missionary meeting here to-night. The preachers say that, notwithstanding the severity of the snow-storm, we shall have a large audience. I am in poor plight to make a speech. I shall try in the name of the Lord, and do the best I can. The missionary cause must go forward, and somebody must push it. I am not very strong, but I have got my shoulder under it and am lifting with my might. If all Christians would take hold with their combined strength we could soon carry out the blessed enterprise.

Further, from Cincinnati, Nov. 29 :

We had a good missionary meeting at Columbus. The weather was very bad, but we had a good congregation, a spirited meeting, and a liberal collection. The next morning, before day, we started for Springfield, where we had a meeting at two'clock in the afternoon and another in the evening, Under the circumstances they were good meetings. The next day we went to Dayton, where we had a large and useful meeting at night. On Friday we went to Hamilton, where we held a missionary meeting in the evening, pretty well attended but rather dull. To-day we came to this city. Thus during the week I have had seven public services, most of them large congregations and lengthy exercises ; traveled more or less every day, and did a good deal of correspondence. A rather hard week's work. Yet my Master has taken care of me, and I hope not to sustain any injury from it. I have the satisfaction of believing the week has been usefully spent.

Also from Cincinnati, Dec. 5, to his youngest daughter, Matilda, then four years old :

Your father loves you very much. He thinks of you very often. He would like to be at home this morning to get a kiss and see your smile. I hope you have kissed your mother good-morning, and smiled in her face very brightly, I expect also you have kissed your brother and sisters, and said good-morning to them very sweetly. Have you talked any to your heavenly Father this morning ? Matilda must never forget her prayers. You must pray for yourself and your absent father. On my return home I hope to get a very sweet kiss from Matilda Palmer Janes for a Christmas present. Will you have one ready for me—a good one, with a sweet smile ?

To Mrs. Janes he writes from Indianapolis a day or two afterward :

. . . I am at the most distant point in my tour. All my movements now will be homeward. Yet I cannot tell how direct or how fast I may be able to make them. Consequently, I cannot tell how soon I may be able to see home and rejoice in your smiles. I still expect to be at home by or before Christmas. My missionary appointments are nearly all to be

made yet. I have been getting information and receiving offers
but have only determined one appointment.   The business of
making missionary appointments is too important to be done
hastily.   I have replied to the letters you sent me containing
invitations to dedicate churches, etc.   I preached yesterday
about heaven, and the way to obtain it.   I enjoyed the subject
myself, but cannot say whether it did any one else any good
or not.   I hope it did.

About the middle of August of this year, between
the sessions of the Oneida and East Genesee Conferences, Bishop Janes was called to Middletown,
Conn., by the illness and death of Dr. Stephen
Olin, the President of Wesleyan University.   With
all the burdens of the year none rested so heavily
upon him as the loss of this eminent servant of
God.   He was subsequently often heard to revert to one of Dr. Olin's dying expressions as of
deep significance and much comfort to himself:
" Bishop, I shall be saved.   I love God.   I love the
good, and I cannot go any where else than where
the good are."   The Rev. Fales H. Newhall, D.D.,
in a communication which appeared years after-
ward· in " Zion's Herald," thus refers, to the funeral
services of Dr. Olin :

What a funeral was that !   On the altar before the pulpit
the fallen monarch lay, and we sat in the pews, crushed, stifled
with the vastness of our loss, too bewildered to weep.   Eminent ministers ascended the pulpit, and spoke and read and
prayed ; but who they were, or what they said, I do not remember now, I only remember that their speech was para-
lyzed—they seemed embarrassed by Olin in his coffin !   Then

Bishop Janes arose, and as he cast one look on the face of the dead, then glanced upward, then looked steadily into our dry eyes, I saw the man for the hour had come, and I trembled for joy—that the Moses who could smite the rock which lay on our hearts and make the waters gush forth had come at last. He lifted his rod and we wept together.

Mrs. Janes, writing to her husband at Penn Yan, New York, under date of August 19, thus alludes to the death of Dr. Olin:

We have just received your letter from Middletown. . . . My heart feels very sorrowful at the removal of Dr. Olin. I felt an interest in him and affection for him deeper than toward any other of our ministers. As I have just heard of his death, my feelings have not yet settled down. I wish he could have lived longer. I was just thinking of Dr. Olin's saying, "The old foundation." I suppose he referred to the verse, "Other foundation can no man lay than that is laid, which is Jesus Christ."

In the administration during the year, Bishop Janes, in the absence of Bishop Waugh in the far West, who was responsible for the Philadelphia appointments, was obliged to fill a vacancy created by the death of one of the ministers. He did so by assigning the Rev. George W. M'Laughlan, who had only that year been admitted on trial, to the vacant charge. The letter he wrote on that occasion to Mr. M'Laughlan is so characteristic that I cannot refrain from its publication. Possibly it may help some other young inexperienced minister.

The decease of our lamented brother, Rev. Daniel Shield, pastor of the Salem Church in this city, has made it necessary to appoint some one to fill the vacancy.   At this period in the conference year we find it extremely difficult to do so, especially as it is necessary to give them a single man, as they cannot provide for a married man and the family of the deceased. We think we can supply your place at Halifax Circuit acceptably and usefully.   We have therefore concluded to remove you to Salem Church, in Philadelphia.   You will come on to the city in time to preach for them on the 19th inst.   In the administration of the Discipline be careful to consult your presiding elder.   You will do well to advise with him about all your plans and arrangements.   I would recommend to you to change with the preachers stationed in the city frequently, probably once each Sabbath.   It is desirable you should give special attention to pastoral visiting.   *Be prudent;* be humble; be modest; be prayerful; be holy.   *Let no man despise thy youth.*   Jesus—holiness—usefulness—heaven.

On his return from the tour for the promotion of the missionary cause, before alluded to, he addressed a letter to the Rev. H. C. Benson, then Professor of the Greek Language and Literature in the Indiana Asbury University, at Greencastle, Indiana, in reference to his transfer to the Oregon and California Mission Conference:

. . . I am pleased with the sentiment and spirit of your letter. . . . In my judgment a short life in that new and rapidly rising country is worth more than a long one in an old-established Conference.   The work there is mission work—hard work—involving sacrifice and suffering, but it has pay for just such service, both while being performed and in heaven.   The man who goes to that country lays the foundation of the Church, he does not build on another man's foundation.   If you conclude to go it is important that you go as soon as possible.   Days here are months in California at this time.   Reasons which I cannot mention make it extremely desirable you should sail at the earliest hour possible. Will you let me hear from you at your earliest convenience; if possible by return of mail.

Mr. Benson writes from San Francisco, December 5, 1877:

I answered the letter, was notified of my appointment to the work in California by telegram, and on January 26, 1852, I left with my family for New York, *en route* for the Pacific. We arrived on February 14, 1852, and have remained to the present in the work here.

CHAPTER IX.

1852, 1853.

Death of Bishop Hedding—General Conference at Boston—The
Far West Again.

IN the spring of 1852 it fell to Bishop Janes to
preside at the Baltimore, Philadelphia, and New
Jersey Conferences. A little incident at the session of the Baltimore Conference, at Cumberland,
March 3–11, showed something of the nervous
decision which so distinguished him. A package
of the New York "Christian Advocate" had arrived, and some one was taking the papers up the
aisles to the tables within the altar rail, and the
preachers, rising from their seats, began reaching
and grasping for the papers. The Bishop springing
to his feet and clapping his hands, excitedly cried,
"Brethren! brethren! this will never do!" His
call quieted them in an instant. He did not preach
at the Conference, but yielded the pulpit on Sunday
morning to Rev. Dr. J. P. Durbin.

About the last of March, in company with the
Rev. George Peck, D.D., he made his last pilgrimage to the bedside of Bishop Hedding. He vener-
ated Bishop Hedding as a father. His admiration
for him was unbounded. If one wished to induce

7*

Bishop Janes to talk, it was only necessary to ask his opinion of Bishop Hedding. He would dilate most enthusiastically upon his excellences—his profound and accurate knowledge of the English language, his full and varied attainments, his judgment of human nature, his statesmanlike comprehension, the tenderness of his sensibilities, the fervor of his piety, and the childlike simplicity of his manners —right along, with a fluency which he seldom indulged in.

He was presiding in the New Jersey Conference, Trenton, New Jersey, when he heard of the Bishop's death. Chained to his seat, unable to hasten to the house of mourning as he wished, he thus addressed Mrs. Hedding:

Most deeply do I sympathize with you in this bereavement. Few women ever had such a husband, consequently few women can suffer such a bereavement. It must be a cause of thankfulness and pleasing remembrance that you were privileged so long to enjoy the companionship of so excellent and so great a man. Fellowship and conjugal intimacy with such a noble mind, and such a Christian spirit, for so long a time, is a privilege few mortals ever enjoy. You have been greatly blessed of God in your domestic relations. . . . I regret most deeply that I cannot be present at the funeral. It would have been a melancholy but great privilege, but such are the circumstances of the Conference that I cannot safely leave. I have telegraphed Bishop Waugh, who answers he will attend the funeral.

The eleventh delegated General Conference assembled in Boston, Massachusetts, May 1, 1852.

There were present Bishops Waugh, Morris, and Janes. Bishop Hedding, the senior Bishop, had died, and Bishop Hamline was detained by sickness. The Church, notwithstanding all its agitations, had increased in the past quadrennium well nigh 90,000 members. The work of conservation and development was going forward throughout all its borders. Here and there little local excitements and divisions had occurred, but nothing to retard the general progress.

The Bishops, in their Address to the General Conference, laid especial stress upon the maintenance of the Episcopacy and the plan of General Superintendency, as essential to the Methodist Episcopal Church, and also advised the re-enforcement of their numbers by the choice of "men who have given indubitable proof that, in addition to deep piety and burning zeal, they both know and love Methodist doctrine and Methodist discipline—brethren who will 'wholly give themselves to the office.'"

The policy of the Church on the subject of "pewed" houses of worship, which came up on an appeal from a decision of the Ohio Conference, was so far changed as to allow the erection of such houses while leaving the rule in favor of "free" churches.

The missions of the Church passed in review, and the celebrated chapter on missions, mainly drawn up by the Rev. J. P. Durbin, D.D., was adopted. This chapter, which makes it the duty of the pastor to supervise, through a committee of which he is chairman, the missionary cause in his charge, first gave organic form and stable success to the great missionary movement of the Church.

Bishop Hamline felt constrained, on account of protracted disease hopelessly disqualifying him for his duties, to resign the office of Bishop. After some discussion the resignation was accepted by a vote of 161 yeas to 10 nays. Two reasons seemed to control this vote: first, it was the opinion of those who knew the condition of Bishop Hamline most intimately, that he must, in order to recovery, be released not only from the work, but from the thought and care, of the office; and, secondly, that the opportunity was a suitable one in which to forever settle, if there had been any doubt, the doctrine of the Church in relation to its Episcopacy, *that it is an office and not an order.* Consequently, when the resignation of Bishop Hamline was accepted, and his parchments of episcopal consecration were returned, he ceased at once to be a Bishop, and he was relegated to membership as an elder in the Ohio Conference. The General Conference thus unqualifiedly sustained the action of its predecessor in 1844, in suspending Bishop Andrew, and declared its judgment as to its plenary power to unmake a Bishop when there may be a disqualification for the office, even though the disqualification may not affect the moral character.

The Rev. Dr. Hibbard, the biographer of Bishop Hamline, in concluding his presentation of this epoch of the Bishop's life, says :

There was a moral grandeur in the act of Bishop Hamline in resigning, of great significance ; and while the Church regretted the fact, they approved the principle involved in it. The right to resign, and of General Conference to accept, was according to the doctrine of Wesley, of Asbury, and of the Methodist Episcopal Church ; and no act simply ecclesiastical has ever occurred in the history of our Church of broader import or more decisive influence upon its polity in the generation to come.*

Bishop Morris writes to Bishop Hamline, July 27 :

I never doubted the doctrine that a Methodist Bishop in good standing might resign his office, that the General Conference might accept it and allow him to return to the ranks of the eldership for an appointment, or for such relation as his health required.†

In the letter of sympathy which the Bishops wrote to Bishop Hamline, evidently composed by Bishop Janes, as his name is signed first in order, is this language :

In performing this duty we take occasion to join with the General Conference in expressing our " profound regret " that Bishop Hamline's health has led him to feel it necessary to tender to the General Conference his resignation of the episcopal office. . . . Be assured, reverend and dear brother, that

---

* " Biography of Rev. L. L. Hamline, D.D.," p. 369.
† Ibid., p. 369.

in retiring from the Episcopacy you bear with you our high esteem, our warm fraternal affections, and our best wishes for your future welfare.

That Bishop Janes himself believed in the privilege of resigning the office subsequently appears in a letter in which he expresses serious thoughts of tendering his own resignation. Writing to Mrs. Janes, from Baltimore, March 9, 1855, after speaking of the imperative nature of the duties of his office, the pain of almost constant separation from his family, of his great affection and concern for his children, he adds:

But, painfully as I regret this, I know of but one way to relieve the affliction, namely, to resign my office. This I have strongly desired to do ever since I became acquainted with its duties and the losses sustained by my family. Poorly as I feel myself qualified for the office, such has been the condition of the Church ever since my election, and such the state of the Episcopal Board, that I have felt I could not resign without doing great injury to the Church. I have, on this point, several times advised confidentially with some of the wisest men in the Church, and they have uniformly assured me that my resignation would be extensively harmful to the interests of the Church. This only has restrained me. The office has no charms for me. I do not love power. I never use any more than I am obliged to. Public life has for me no attractions. Quiet domestic life interests me much more. You know I was unexpectedly, when a comparatively young man, elected to this most fearfully responsible office. I had never had any practical knowledge of the duties of the office. I had never been in the council of a Bishop. I had never been a member of the General Conference. The unsought and unexpected election made me feel that I was providentially called to the office—that it was according to the will of our Lord Jesus Christ that I should serve his Church in this position. This conviction only makes the office to me endurable. I have thought much of resigning at the next General Conference. I foresee that the next session of this body will be a troubled one. It will be necessary for all the friends of the Church to employ all their influence to promote harmony. What I may find consistent at the time I cannot judge now. It would be an inexpressible satisfaction to me to be relieved from the office. But I cannot consent to resign when there is a probability of doing lasting injury to the institutions of our Church. . . . I submit to it as a sacrifice for Christ, as a necessity in fulfilling the ministry I have received of the Lord Jesus Christ.

The General Conference, in accordance with the recommendation of the Bishops, on the twenty-fifth day of the session proceeded to the election of four additional Bishops. On the first ballot, " Levi Scott, Matthew Simpson, Osmon C. Baker, and Edward R. Ames, having received a majority of all the votes, were declared duly elected Bishops of the Methodist Episcopal Church."

Here is the only scrap of a personal letter extant of this long absence from home. It is to little Tillie, written from the conference room, May 31 :

I wish you good-morning. I hope you are bright and happy and loving and obedient this morning. Have you said your prayers ? I hope you never forget your prayers, morning or evening. Your Father in heaven will not love you unless you pray. Have you kissed mamma this morning ? I think all of mamma's little daughters should kiss her, with a smile, every morning and evening. I think papa is entitled to such a kiss also when he is at home ; but he does not always get it. Perhaps a better day is coming, however.

The Bishop's first Annual Conference after the adjournment of the General Conference was the Troy, at Plattsburgh, N. Y., June 16–21.

From Plattsburgh, N. Y., to Dr. Durbin, June 24 :

I have written Bishop Waugh, and advised him to send five men to California and five to Oregon. . . . Possibly more than I have recommended will be needed. One certainly is on his way across the country, Hurlbut from the Iowa Conference, an able minister. I have no doubt others who have decided to go will reach there in a few months. I think we cannot judge so well now as three months' hence. I also approve of sending to China a man to fill the vacancy in our mission there occasioned by the death of Brother Collins.

You will please to write to me just as freely on the subject of missionary interests as though I were still in charge of foreign missions. I shall always feel a pleasure in rendering you any aid that may be in my power.

After the close of the Troy Conference he enjoyed a short respite at Mount Wesley. But with the frequent engagements to preach, to meet committees in New York, and with the mass of correspondence pressing upon him, there was little vacation. Still he made the utmost of the bare opportunity of being at home. By the last of August he was again off to the West. The pleasant message which quickly follows him from Mrs. Janes is, " I freight this little note with a weight of love ; it is laden with anxious tenderness and confiding, grateful emotions."

From Zanesville, Ohio, the seat of the Ohio Conference, he writes, September 3, to his son :

I am sorry my son should ever feel any embarrassment in telling me his mind on any subject. I have always wished that our children should feel that their parents are their best friends. No other person can possibly feel such an interest in their happiness as we feel. . . . We know how great is the danger of their being deceived by the appearances of the world. . . . A good beginning is important to every great undertaking. How all-important it must be, then, that we commence our earthly history aright—that the morning of life be a bright one ! How essential that the great plan of life be well laid, and all our means of prosecuting it properly selected ! We cannot accomplish great things by a careless and irregular pursuit of them. They must be determined upon and pursued earnestly and perseveringly. Neither can we become good by chance or accident, or even by occasional and feeble desire and effort. Excellence of character is an attainment. In view of our depravity and temptations, a difficult attainment. It can be reached, but it must be struggled for, pressed after, aspired to. Real moral excellence can only be attained religiously— through Christ—by the agency of the Holy Spirit. No other power can make us pure and good.

How playful as well as instructive the Bishop could be, and that often in the very midst of the business cares and perplexities of the conference room, the following letters to his children will strikingly show. The first is to Elizabeth, from Chillicothe, Ohio, *en route* for the Cincinnati Conference, September 12 :

Go, little pale-faced messenger, with all the speed of the iron horse, to Mount Wesley, the habitation of my cherished ones, and say to my beloved daughter Elizabeth that her loving, absent father remembers her tenderly, and sends to her paternal salutation and blessing, desiring and praying that she may be good and useful and happy all the days of her life. Further inform her, that her father is in usual health and as happy as he can well be while separated from those he most loves and delights in. Also ask Elizabeth to certify to her mamma that I have received her letter of the 6th instant, and am thankful to her for the same. Also, that my heart is full of grateful, admiring love.

Mr. Messenger, also present to her my compliments, and ask her to give her brother a sweet kiss and a bright smile, and to assure him of his father's love and prayers. Another errand of love, if you please, Mr. Messenger. Elizabeth has two sisters, who, like herself, are very tenderly beloved by their father, and he wishes her to tell them this, and seal the declaration with a really loving sisterly kiss. Now, Mr. Messenger, I wish you to remain and see that all these matters are duly attended to, and then, with the untiring iron horse, return and report to me, bringing also an account of the health and happiness of the loved ones. You will find me, on your return, at Xenia, Ohio. Mr. Messenger, you will now immediately depart.

To Tillie:

Pet! pet! who has so sweet a pet as I? O, you little pet! I wish I could see you this morning. Have you thought of pa this morning? He has thought of you many times already. I would very much like to have you put your little tiny arms around my neck and kiss me. I think you would do it if I were present with you. I hope you have a loving time at home. Indeed, I expect it is all loving time with mamma and brother and sisters. And I guess I am thought of once in awhile, and loved a little, too.

To Lewis, from Xenia, Ohio, Sept. 21, 1852:

MY DEAR ~~BROTHER~~ SON: In the word I have just crossed out you see the power of habit. I am so accustomed to writing fraternal letters that, involuntarily, I commenced this letter as such, though it is intended to be a paternal one. An admonition to be very careful to form good habits. I hope I shall profit by it. It is wisdom to turn every thing, great and small, to good account.

From St. Louis, October 11, to Tillie:

Your pretty letter, with its twenty sweet kisses, was received on Saturday. The kisses are very sweet. I thank you for them. I am sorry the oxen were so naughty as to eat up the cabbages. I am pleased that you have had so many nice dinners from the *Slicer* beans! I hope you have saved some good ones to plant next year. I am obliged to Lizzie for giving you a nice ride in the hand-cart.

I still consider you my pet, and I hope you will always be so good that I shall always be happy to call you my pet. . . .

I would put some kisses into this letter for you, only I am now in the chair of Conference, and I cannot kiss it without having the whole Conference see me. I don't know but they would laugh at me if they saw me packing up kisses in a letter. So you must let me keep them and bring them when I come. They will keep all their sweetness.

From Pittsburgh, October 19, *homeward*, he writes to Mrs. Janes:

A kind Providence has brought me thus far on my way home. I go from here to Bellefont to dedicate a church next Sunday, and shall then hasten home with all the speed I can make. My conference business on the tour has been very satisfactorily arranged. I have no special anxieties about any part of it. I have taken time to do it deliberately, and now leave it with my Master. . . .

Writing to Lewis and Charlotte, at Wilbraham, Massachusetts, in February of the year 1853, we ascertain that he was at home suffering from an obstinate cough.

Your letters of the 28th inst. were received night before last. We were greatly delighted to hear from you, and to learn of your continued good health and continued interest in your literary pursuits. Tillie, especially, was exceedingly pleased with her brother's letter. It made her little eyes sparkle and her laugh ring again.

I am quite unwell. Have been confined at home for more than a week; have my old cough again. I hope to be better soon, if it is the good pleasure of my heavenly Father. His will is always good.

Ten days later:

My health is somewhat improved, though I go out but little. . . . We expect you to come at vacation. We think it will be a pleasure to you, and we wish to see you very much. . . . Hate sin—fear God—love the Saviour. Be prayerful, and improve both heart and mind with diligence.

Bishop Janes began his presidency of the Conferences in the spring of 1853 with the Providence Conference, New Bedford, Mass., April 13. Then followed in succession the New England, the New Hampshire, the Maine, the East Maine, the East Genesee, the Cincinnati, and the Kentucky—the last closing its first session as a distinct Conference under the auspices of the Methodist Episcopal Church, October 17. Not waiting, however, for his own Conferences, he hastened to the assistance of Bishop Morris, at the Philadelphia Conference, Harrisburgh, Pennsylvania, March 23–30. Thence he writes Mrs. Janes:

The Conference is progressing pleasantly. Much difficulty, however, is anticipated in making the appointments. No one but those who have to make these appointments can imagine a tithe of these difficulties, or the cares, anxieties, and mental labors of those who have this work to perform. God loves the Church. He purchased it with his blood. He has preserved it by his power. This is my hope for the Church—"God loves the gates of Zion." Her interests therefore are safe.

With the first swelling of the buds he settled his family at Mount Wesley, and was forthwith off to New Bedford, Mass., the place of meeting for the Providence Conference. Writing home on April 14, he says:

I reached New York on Saturday morning. Gave my first attention to the lost trunks. . . . On Thursday I came to this place by way of Boston. When in Boston I went to see Brother Trafton,* who has lost his little son named "Edmund Janes." He died of scarlet fever. His two little brothers have had the disease and recovered. His only daughter, about twelve years old, was very ill with the fever when I was there. The doctor thought her symptoms better. Brother Trafton himself was also very sick with the fever, but was getting better.

The Bishop passed his forty-sixth birth-day at the session of the New England Conference, Ipswich, Mass., April 27–May 3, 1853. He thus alludes to it and the Conference in a letter to his wife:

Yesterday was my forty-sixth birth-day. In the midst of my many and urgent duties I had some profitable reflections. I endeavored to obtain a few minutes to write you a line, but the incessant duties of the first day of Conference prevented until the adjournment of my council, at one o'clock at night,

* The Rev. Mark Trafton.

when my lamp burned so dim and my eyes were so tired, I could not write, and so I spent an hour in meditation and prayer, and retired to rest. I made an address to the Conference of considerable length this morning on the subject of the ministry. The Holy Spirit gave me utterance. Much feeling was manifest at the time. These Conference sessions are grave occasions. The responsibilities of a presiding officer, who is expected not only to give direction to business, but also tone to sentiment and feeling, and propriety to manner and matter of discussion, is very great. My sufficiency is of God.

On May 14, from Newport, N. H., the seat of the New Hampshire Conference, he writes to his son:

Regular study each day, and not a little one day and a long time the next day, is important. . . . I hope the siren of transient pleasure will not be allowed to divert you from the up-hill and rugged path of science. Flowers are by the way-side, but ripened and luscious fruits are on the summit. Struggle up, then. Disregard present petty indulgences; press after the life-enduring pleasures and benefits of a thorough education, of an enlightened and disciplined mind. These will pay, a thousand times over, all the self-denial and struggle and labor required to make the high attainment.

The following letter from Biddeford, Me., May 25, showing the Bishop's perseverance in making a railroad train, illustrates a trait well understood by those who knew him intimately:

I reached Boston at half past four o'clock P. M. The cars for this place started at five o'clock. I had to cross the city. I went out to a hack and engaged the driver to take me right off to the depot. But when he got me seated he slipped off to find other passengers. I sat uneasily ten minutes waiting for

him. As he did not come I went after him. He then told me
very coolly that I could not reach the train. I said to him,
" I must." I seized my traveling-bag, ran into the street, saw
a cab going off. I chased it a ways, but could not overhaul it.
I then turned almost in despair, when I saw a cab coming
down another street toward the depot. I ran to it and told
the cabman if he would drive me to the Eastern Railroad depot
in fifteen minutes I would pay him double fare. He said he
would try ; he doubted whether he could. But I was in the
cab before he had time to object, and called to him to put on
the whip. So away we went across the city, and reached the
depot just in time.

Sympathizing with Miss Charlotte, who had been
appointed one of the editors of the students' literary paper at Wilbraham, he sends her from the chair
of the Maine Conference, at Biddeford, a motto
which he stated she might be at liberty to publish :

My motto shall be to—
>   Get all the good I can,
>   From all the sources I can,
>   In all the ways I can,
>   By all the means I can,
>   And as long as I can.
>
>   Do all the good I can,
>   To all the persons I can,
>   In all the ways I can,
>   By all the means I can,
>   And as long as I can.

Writing to the same from Portland, Me., June 2 :

The Maine Conference closed its session (at Biddeford) on
Tuesday afternoon. The session was a pleasant one. I was
kept up late but one night. I am now on my way to the East
Maine Conference. . . . I stop at two or three places on the

route to preach. I preach in this city this evening. When the East Maine Conference adjourns I shall return home. . . . To be happy, we must love something higher and better than ourselves; we must hope for something above the things of this world; we must possess more than earth can furnish. In short, real goodness and true happiness can only be found in the religion of our Lord Jesus Christ. This is scriptural, philosophical, and experimental. I have been young. I remember well my sentiments and feelings when at your age. I know how ardently and confidently I expected happiness in worldly things. My prospects, too, were bright. But subsequent experience taught me that when I reached one object of pursuit after another I was just as unsatisfied as before. This is, and must be, the experience of all who seek their happiness in worldly enjoyments. Mind cannot be satisfied with earthly things. The soul must have its appropriate pleasures. These must be intellectual and religious.

Having returned from the East Maine Conference to New York, he cannot pause long enough to run out to Mount Wesley, but writes, August 15, in haste, to Mrs. Janes:

I have just returned from Wilbraham. Left the children well. They are at Mr. Raymond's, very pleasantly situated, and quite happy. I start at six in the morning for Elmira, N. Y., the seat of the East Genesee Conference. I trust in God for a pleasant Conference—a useful time.

From the conference room at Elmira, August 22, he sends the following gem of a letter to Tillie. Think of the man who could thus discourse to his little child amid the excitements and burdens of an Annual Conference!

I hope you are smiling and happy this morning. The sun shines here quite brightly. How is it at Mount Wesley? I wish I could hear the birds around you sing their carols this morning. The honeysuckle at the porch would be to me a very pleasant sight. I expect you have seen it in its beauty. Did you see a little humming-bird there taking his breakfast of honey? What delicious fare he lives on ! Why don't he grow bigger? I suppose because his Maker did not intend he should be any larger. What a beautiful ornament of this bright world he is ! How wise and skillful his Creator must be ! An animate flower, a miniature impersonation of living beauty ! I admire the pretty little thing greatly. I admire the splendid fragrant flower it feeds upon, and I love the Maker of them both. I hope Tillie also admires the flower and the bird, and loves their Maker too. Who made them? God. Who made Tillie? God. So your heavenly Father made the flowers and the birds. Certainly we should admire them then. I thank our kind Father in heaven for having made that sweet flower to grow at our door, and for sending that little beauty to come and feed upon it daily. They make my happy home more attractive. Still there are stronger endearments to bind my heart to its endeared home. There is a vine inside the door that has borne much more beautiful and fragrant flowers than the one at the door. This vine and its flowers are infinitely more lovely and fragrant. In them is combined most richly both natural and moral beauties—a twofold and transcendent loveliness. As divine Providence requires me to be distant from my cherished home most of the time, my heart acts very much like the little humming-bird. It comes several times a day to visit this lovely vine and its bright blossoms, to inhale their fragrance and revel in their beauties. O, I am glad my heart has wings. They are swift wings too. I think my heart, when it is coming home, outflies the telegraph. These visits give me great delight. My heart always returns to duty the happier for them.

8

CHAPTER X.

1853–1855.

The Bishop at Mount Wesley—Central and Western New York—In New England—The North-west.

A N allusion occurs in a letter to his son, written from Mount Wesley, September 12, by which are recalled some of the most pleasing incidents of the Bishop and Mrs. Janes at their country home:

They have but just gotten their plan and specification for the church at the Ridge. I hope it will soon be under way. Mr. Day called on us this morning. I heard him preach a very excellent sermon yesterday. . .

The Rev. William Day, of the Newark Conference, to whom reference is made in the letter, was at this period pastor of the Bernardsville and Basking Ridge charge, within the bounds of which Mount Wesley, the Bishop's country residence, was situated. He has kindly furnished " Reminiscences " of the Bishop at his country home, which may here be appropriately introduced. Mount Wesley was located about eight miles south-west of Morristown, N. J.

During the years 1853–55 it was my privilege to be pastor of the Church at Bernardsville, N. J., the place of the Bishop's

Bishop Janes's Residence at Mount Wesley, N. J.

country home.   Mrs. Janes and the children were regular at-
tendants upon the services of the little church, and the good
Bishop never failed to accompany them when at home.   Young
and inexperienced in my work, and having known the Bishop
only as he had presided at the session of our Conference, it
was with fear and trembling these new relations were entered
upon.   And there remains with me a distinct memory of the
peculiar experience with which I first found myself in the pulpit and the Bishop present as one of the hearers.   But the
prayer with which he closed that Sabbath morning service, his
simple testimony in the little class-meeting which followed, and
the kindly welcome he gave to "our pastor," inspired confidence and love most restful and precious, which repeated and
varied association only strengthened and matured.   It was
surprising to me that the great Bishop could so completely
sympathize with my position, and be so tenderly and thoroughly
fraternal.   I found, too, that amid his multitudinous labors all
the interests of our infant Church were thought of, while to
each member, however poor or illiterate, was given his friendly
recognition, and, if need be, his sympathy and help.   That
large four-seated family carriage was, on the Sabbath, one of
the most democratic institutions I have ever known.   Side by
side with the Bishop and his family were house-servant, farm-
laborer, and poor neighbor.   There was always "room for
one more;" and no way-side traveler to the house of God was
too poor to be invited to ride.   To the pastor the presence of
the Bishop, his friendly communications, occasional sermons,
and living example of consecration to God and duty, became
an inspiration never to be forgotten.

Every Methodist minister and Church, within a wide radius,
was strengthened by his residence, his known interest, and, as
far as practicable, by his service and help.   Respectful and fraternal toward all Christian denominations, by them he was esteemed and honored.   The influence of his great character and
Christ-like life was felt and admitted through all that region by
all classes.   Said an elder of the Presbyterian Church to me one
day, "It is as good as an ordinary sermon to have Bishop Janes

just pass through our village." His clear and strong views respecting the mission of Methodism made him prompt to encourage every opportunity for its extension. Regular Methodist preaching was established in Basking Ridge, an adjoining town, by the Bishop buying a house and devoting it to that purpose. The next year the present church was built, largely through his contributions and personal help.

A peculiar incident in this connection may be of interest. We had only four male members at the Ridge, not one of means, when it was proposed to build the church. The contract for building required that the stones for foundation and basement should be placed gratuitously on the site by the friends of the enterprise. The pastor found it impossible to create sufficient interest in the community to do this. The Bishop, returning after an absence at the Western Conferences, heard the statement of the pastor and said, " I will help you to-morrow." Early the next morning, as the pastor looked out of his study window, the Bishop 'was seen driving a double team of oxen drawing a large cart loaded with stones which with his own hands he had gathered from the top of the mountain more than a mile distant. He invited the pastor to join him. For three days we worked together in this way, carting the stones. Meeting on the road a Christian lawyer, he exclaimed, " Why, Bishop Janes, is that you ! Drawing stones for your farm ? " The Bishop replied, " We don't draw stones for the farm, but we will draw a few *for the Lord* when needed." " What does this mean ? " inquired a wealthy farmer whose sympathies were not in the least with the church enterprise. " It means," said the Bishop, " that the stones *will be drawn*—the church *has got to be built.*" I need not say that the Bishop's example soon secured an abundant supply of stones. The church *was* built. At the dedication the Bishop preached one of his powerfully impressive sermons.

That carting of stones had other good effects. Said a prominent citizen, a keen observer, not a Christian, to the writer : " I have studied the character and life of Bishop Janes for these ten years. He is the best and greatest man I have ever known; but the best thing he has done for this community was the drawing stones for the church, for this reason; all through here men have thought in driving oxen it was necessary to make a great deal of noise, and that they must swear sometimes.   But the Bishop drove a double team—and drove them well—for three days up and down the mountain, only speaking in low and gentle tones.   I want you to tell him that by this he has done more good than he ever did in preaching ten of his greatest sermons."   I was myself much impressed with the Bishop's quiet power over the oxen and the skill with which he controlled them, and observed to him that they seemed "to recognize episcopal authority."   He replied, " Oxen are most tractable creatures."

In the sick room and amid scenes of bereavement his sympathy was peculiar to himself.   Few possessed that almost divine virtue in so high degree ; few, indeed, knew so well how to express it.   Returning to his home after being away many weeks, on hearing of the pastor's sickness, without waiting to take an hour's rest he hastened to my room, and, seating himself by the bedside, talked most tenderly and sweetly, saying, among other things, " You have nothing to do now but to be sick.   I will see that pulpit and church are cared for. Just take a good rest and have a comfortable time.   There is a great deal in knowing how to enjoy sickness.   As soon as you may be moved I will take you to my home."   Each day he was by my bedside ; his look was a benediction.   As soon as might be he took me to his own residence, and, seating me in the parlor, said, " Now all that is in this house is yours." And, with the tenderness of a father's care, each need was anticipated.

It was at home the character of the Bishop unfolded its greatest beauty, so tenderly considerate, simple, and affectionate.   Not much time had he for social entertainment ; but who appreciated a visit of friendship more, or more honored a guest ?   In no home was the pastor more welcome, and in the light of that home he might read, as in few places, the true significance of the pastoral relation.   When the severity of the

Bishop's official responsibilities would permit the full flow of his social feelings he was delightfully genial and communicative, enlivening conversation with pleasing incidents of travel, descriptions of remarkable places and persons, and even with humorous anecdotes.

One of the most pleasant hours of my memory is that in which I listened to an evening discussion by Bishop and Mrs. Janes, almost playful in spirit, on "Scripture teachings concerning the reciprocal duties of husband and wife." It would be as difficult to decide which excelled in the discussion as it would be to determine which best exemplified the true spirit of the relation. The domestic affections of Bishop Janes were remarkably tender ; but here, and always, the religious element predominated, sanctifying and elevating every thing by its purity and love. To be present when he conducted the family worship was a privilege to be remembered, but not to be described. No one who had not seen this inner circle of his being—this home unfolding of his nature—and observed how strong were the ties which centered there, could estimate the self-denial involved in his public life—so little time had he for home, and the most of it wearied by previous excessive labor and taxed to the utmost with official correspondence and care. In these three years of almost constant observation I am confident there were not three days of real rest—I doubt if one —while many of the nights were consumed in episcopal duties. More time, indeed, he spent in prayer than any man of whose private and home-life it has been my pleasure to be acquainted. And for "duty" he was, in spirit, ever ready. " Will you not remain home for a little rest this time ?" I once inquired. True to himself came the answer, " It would be a great pleasure to do so, but duty calls ; *there will be rest enough in heaven.*"

This picture needs no touch from the author's pencil. Letters show that during this July, 1853, when the Bishop was quietly driving oxen and cart-

ing stones for the little meeting-house, he was preparing to lay the foundations of Methodism in New
Mexico and in India.   In letters to Dr. Durbin he
is grappling with the difficulties in the new field in
that remote American territory; and adds, " I will
turn my attention to the finding a man for India."

In the early autumn the Bishop hastened, by way
of Wilbraham, (to see the children at school,) to his
Western Conferences at Hillsborough, Ohio, and
Covington, Ky.   Passing through New York city,
he goes thence by rail to Dunkirk, where he preaches
on the Sabbath, and thence on until he reaches the
junction of the Little Miami and Marietta railroads,
where, while waiting for a train to Hillsborough,
he writes :

Now from " Loveland " I am scribbling a letter to my dear
daughter Lizzie.   I do not know as the name is very inspiring,
for I loved you very much before I came here, and made up
my mind to write you before I knew the name of the place.

The brief account of the session of the Cincinnati Conference he gives in a letter to Mrs. Janes
will illustrate the spirit of his administration and
the zeal which yet survived in this wing of the old
Ohio Conference :

We had an unusually pleasant session of the Cincinnati Conference.   It was characterized by a high degree of spiritual interest.   When I examined the candidates for admission into
full connection, I requested several of the senior members of
the Conference to give a relation of their ministerial experi-

ence—especially of their call and early ministry. We spent nearly two hours in these exercises and prayer. Sunday was a most gracious day. I preached at half past ten o'clock with considerable liberty and more unction than God has often granted me. Deep impressions were made. Bishop Simpson preached in the afternoon. God was with his servant and in his word. The evening meeting was a precious one. Several professed religion and joined the Church. Among those who joined during the Conference were a son and son-in-law of ex-Governor Trimble.

Making reference to having taken through mistake the hat of the gentleman who taught in his family, he says, very humorously:

. . . I know of no answer you can give the·professor—only that his black hat has aspired to the episcopacy, and is making an episcopal tour. It will probably return in a short time, I think fully satisfied with episcopal service.

January 30, 1854, finds the Bishop in Massachusetts, addressing missionary meetings. Under this date, his letter to Mrs. Janes, from Boston, shows him amid sickness and weariness longing, though patiently, for the heavenly rest:

. . . I am sharing the hospitalities of my esteemed Brother Sleeper. I have had quite a sick day. I was very unwell when I left home, and have not found much relief yet. Rather poor plight for three important speeches this week, a very important special sermon next Sunday, and in the meantime to answer almost innumerable disciplinary questions and write letters incessantly. Well, it is all right. God is good. He has a resting-place for me. I trust I shall reach it at last. In the meantime I have to serve him and his Church. It is great pleasure—a high privilege.

Bishop Janes went to the assistance of Bishop Ames at the sessions of the Baltimore and Philadelphia Conferences.

From Baltimore, March 10, 1854, he writes to Mrs. Janes:

I am very anxious to be at home. I know my family interests are suffering—but the Church first. This must be my maxim. My conviction is, that the best way for me to take care of my family is faithfully to fulfill the ministry which I have received of the Lord Jesus Christ. If I meet my obligations to God and his Church, I believe God will fulfill his promises to me and my family. This is my faith. I think it is scriptural. God bless you all! I cannot write more now.

To the same, from Reading, Pa., March 22:

. . . Found the Conference in session. Bishop Ames present and presiding. He is in good health, and it is well for him that he is, for there is so much of him, that if he becomes sick it must be a severe matter.

I have a very pleasant home. Providence has always taken good care of me. I ought to be very thankful and confiding. I think I am. I strive to be. It ought to be very easy to repose on a heart of infinite love. And so it would be if it were not for human weakness and satanic temptations. These make it a warfare. But the "fight of faith" is a glorious one!

While attending the session of the New Jersey Conference at New Brunswick, New Jersey, he was summoned to the death-bed of his father. From South Canaan, Connecticut, he writes to his wife, April 14:

I reached here about two o'clock this afternoon. Our dear father closed his earthly existence at four o'clock this morning.

8*

His end was peace. He was a very affectionate father. His love for his children was more 'than common. I feel thankful I had the means and the disposition to supply his temporal wants in his old age. He will be buried by the side of our dear mother. They will sleep in Jesus until the resurrection morning. I hope to see them again, and to share with them eternal life.

The Bishop's tour of the Conferences lay during this summer and autumn (1854) mostly within the State of New York. I shall not follow him save to give a few extracts from his letters.

From the chair of Conference, Cortland, New York, July 22, 1854, to Mrs. Janes:

Some unpleasant things are anticipated. It would be remarkable if some did not occur. Ministers are good men, but they are men.

I am dreading preaching to-morrow, as I have to preach out of doors, of course to a multitude. I will try to do them good. God must give the increase.

To the same, from Binghamton, New York, July 29:

Yesterday morning held a love-feast at nine o'clock. Preached at half past ten o'clock about our glorious religion and perfected Saviour with liberty and some unction. In the afternoon administered the sacrament of the Lord's Supper. In the evening preached on the subject of personal consecration to God a reasonable duty. A very crowded house and oppressive atmosphere. God blessed me, and I think good was done. It was too severe a day's work. These appointments were made for me, however, before I reached here, and I felt it necessary to try to fill them.

To the same, from Geneva, N. Y., August 21 :

Dr. Durbin is addressing the Conference for a few minutes on the subject of missions. I may not for a little time be called upon to watch a debate or put a motion. I seize this opportunity to send my affectionate salutations. As I cannot use my eyes and countenance to express the tenderness of my heart, I must use the best means in my power to indulge the desire of my heart to sympathize and commune with you. I feel that I can do this notwithstanding the distance intervening. Love has ubiquity : it can be in heaven and on earth at the same time ! It can be in Geneva and at Mount Wesley at one and the same time ! My heart never goes from home. Where wife is, I am. I expect it will be so as long as we live on earth, and I have good hope that, in the fullest sense, this will be the case forever in heaven.

From the same "chair" he thus felicitously discourses about "books" to his daughter Elizabeth :

Do you not find good company in your books ? When you see them in the morning do they not seem like old friends ? almost like brothers and sisters ? Do you not love to sit down and talk with them ? to listen to their lessons of wisdom ? Is it not very pleasant and profitable to spend some hours every day in their good company ? I love good books very much. I never feel friendless or lonesome when I have some instructive, useful books with me. To me they are improving, delightful company.

From Warsaw, N. Y., he writes, September 5 :

I am more honored in my advent into Warsaw than Christ was in his advent into the world. They have found room for me in the *inn*. Myself and all the presiding elders are entertained at the Temperance House, a respectable public house— a very comfortable place.

Toward the close of the year 1854 Bishop Janes thus writes to his three older children, who were attending school at the Conference Seminary at Amenia, N. Y. :

. . . It is a great matter to know how to set ourselves to work ; how to shake off dullness and slothfulness, and not only improve our days but even our fugitive moments ; to seize upon all the little portions of time and turn them to profit. Industry is a cardinal virtue. Without it even genius is useless. An indolent life must be barren of good results. Patient, persevering exertion only accomplishes great things— reaches high elevations. In this wicked world goodness must be struggled for before it can be enjoyed. Wisdom is an attainment, not a gift. Religion is a treasure to be sought and found. So our every interest demands activity—well-directed, appropriate exertion.

I hope you are beginning to feel at home in the seminary. One great advantage of being at a seminary is the living by rule. Education costs money, time, study, and sacrifice ; but it is worth them all. Even when we have to pay for it with home-sickness we do not pay too much.

The Bishop had insisted upon the erection of a chapel at the " Cross Roads," on the Bernardsville charge. In January, 1855, having a little leisure, he sallied forth among the Churches of South Jersey to collect money for the relief of this small Church. It was not an uncommon thing for him to give largely to various enterprises, and also to assume heavy personal liabilities, depending upon his own exertions for raising the money. On this tour he writes, " I have not time to write much this morning, as I am about to start on a twenty-mile ride in a snow-storm."

In February he went to New England to assist the Rev. Dr. J. T. Peck (now Bishop Peck) in the tract cause. If any one thinks Bishop Janes could not appreciate the ludicrous, and was insensible to physical discomforts, let him read the following letter to his wife on hotel fare, dated Boston, February 15:

I reached this city a little after one o'clock this morning. The rain was descending most copiously. I took a hack for the Marlborough House, my old stopping-place. The clerk came to the door and said, "We can do nothing for you, sir; we are all full. You had better go to the Pavilion." So we started for the Pavilion; arrived, rang the bell; clerk came. "All full; cannot accommodate you any way." "Where next, driver?" "There is a house down here where I drive from," said he. "Is it respectable?" said I. "Yes; it is a dollar-and-a-quarter-a-day house." This looked quite suspicious; but I said to him, "Drive there." So there he went. "Can you accommodate with lodgings to-night?' "Yes, sir." Registered my name. "I would like to retire immediately." "Yes, sir. Fifty cents." "What for?" "Your lodging." "Why, I haven't got it yet." "Rule, sir." "What, to pay before we go to bed!" "Yes." Well, I had no choice. So I paid his fifty cents, and he lighted me to a room the regular occupant of which was absent. It looked for all the world like an old bachelor's domestic sanctuary; but it was pretty comfortable. So I said my prayers and went to my repose about two o'clock. Awoke at seven this morning, made my toilet, and went down to breakfast. Such a starve-to-death breakfast—it was a caution! There was food enough, such as it was. Yes, such as it was! and where it was! Dirty, dirtier, dirtiest! Steak almost raw; sent it back to the kitchen to be recooked; came back smoking; so tough I could neither cut nor chew it. There began to be internal signs of revolt; but it was soon agreed that the eyes should only look on the bright side of things, (where one could be found,) the stomach should ask no questions for conscience' sake, steam should be put on, and the masticatory machinery put in motion immediately, and a hard job dispatched as best it could be. With this arrangement I was very successful. The price was moderate ; so now 1 am in pretty good health and spirits, really thankful that I am so much better off than the multitude who have no breakfast, and the many who have no health to enjoy one. . . . I have more concern about the preaching to-morrow, they expect so much on a special occasion, and from a Bishop. Just as if a title could preach ! Well

> "Who does the best his circumstance allows,
> Does well, acts nobly ; angels could no more."

On the 15th the Bishop pressed his way through a fearful storm to Haverhill, and on the 16th preached at the dedication of a new, tasteful, and commodious church in that place. He writes :

This morning the rain has turned to snow. We start in a few minutes for Portland. I trust we shall have profitable meetings there. It would be sorry business to take this winter journey and all its exposures without doing something for God and humanity. The Lord helping me, I will make my impression for good.

The Bishop thus alludes to this New England tour in a letter to Elizabeth :

So you claim a letter a week, do you ? Well, then, I am a letter in debt, and this one is now due. How can I write you every week when I have so many business letters that I must write ? I should have written to you from Portland, but I had the sick headache three days and I had not the strength to write you. I returned home usually well. I had a pleasant visit in Massachusetts and in Maine. I dedicated two churches, preached one sermon in behalf of the tract cause, made two set speeches and several talks, and presided in several meetings. We had a good anniversary.

The writer well remembers some of the incidents of this tour. He, too, experienced the discomforts of travel as he was going from Baltimore to Portland on, to him, a most interesting errand. He had the pleasure of hearing the Bishop preach that one sermon at the tract anniversary. But one other occurrence impressed him much more. It chanced that the Bishop, homeward bound, was spending a night at Lynn, Mass., with his esteemed friend Mr. Jacob Aber, and that on the same night he, then a young preacher, with his bride, was a guest of the pastor of Mr. Aber. That evening the Bishop, notwithstanding all his weariness, made a call with Mrs. Aber on the young married couple, and, after an agreeable conversation of a half hour, offered for them a prayer in which he most feelingly and particularly commended them to God. He had known and loved Professor Merritt Caldwell, of Dickinson College, the bride's father, but the young preacher was a stranger. That a Bishop should take such notice of an obscure young minister on his bridal tour left an impression as to his thoughtfulness and condescending goodness which was never forgotten.

From Baltimore, March 15, (1855,) where he was helping Bishop Waugh with the Baltimore Conference, then very large and unwieldy, he writes:

I cannot yet anticipate the time of adjournment. We are delayed mainly in making out the appointments. This is an immense work, attended with immense difficulties. God has always brought us through heretofore. I expect he will at this Conference.

From the same point to Dr. Durbin:

I expect to be in New York on Wednesday next in time for the evening meeting, ordination, etc. I shall be so jaded that it will be difficult for me to preach. Would it not be better to have some addresses? I presume Dr. Taylor is in New York. He would interest the New York people. Perhaps you can get some one else also. The people are always delighted to hear Dr. Durbin. I will preach if there is an absolute necessity; but wish to be relieved.

Here is a word on Yankee thrift, written home from Newport, Rhode Island, April 5, the seat of the Providence Conference. The Bishop's eyes were always on the alert.

The route from Hartford to Providence was mostly through hills, across a broken and barren country, yet there were all along signs of wealth, comfort, and refinement. The people work themselves, and make every thing else work. Grandfather works and grandmother works; father works and mother works; the boys work and the girls work; and the horse works, and the ox works, and the cow works, and the sheep works, and the dog works, and the cat works, and the hen works. Every animal must earn its living. Yes, and they keep the stones at work, making fence and other things useful. They make the water work; every little rivulet is kept busy turning big wheels and different kinds of machinery. They even make Jack Frost work all winter, in congealing the little lakes and furnishing the immense cargoes of ice sent to distant parts of the world as a valuable article of commerce. Indeed, every thing works. O, this is a very industrious country! hence a prosperous country, and intelligent, too. Few instances are furnished in history of any people becoming so thrifty and wealthy and intellectual under such disadvantages. Their railroads, their factories, their beautiful residences, their schools, their churches, all bespeak their pre-eminent merit.

At Newark, New Jersey, soon after, oppressed with the difficulties of the episcopal office, he utters a well-nigh painful cry to Mrs. Janes:

I anticipate a rather long session. Still I hope for a harmonious one. I need not say we have great difficulty in making the appointments. You know enough of the circumstances of our work and the peculiarities of our economy to anticipate this. God only can enable us to accomplish his gracious designs in raising up our branch of his glorious Church. He can use very poor instruments in doing his work. This is my comfort. I depend on him in this instance, as I ever have done.

From Claremont, N. H., May 4, another cry:

Thus far the Conference has progressed pleasantly. The Church here is not in a high state of prosperity. There is a great want of pastors. I fear also a want of spirit and power in some of those in the work. Politics and secret societies have done them harm. Still Jesus lives and reigns. This is the comfort and hope of his Church.

From the session of the New York Conference, May 14, at Sing Sing, New York, to Mrs. Janes:

We have just received a telegraphic dispatch from Bishop Scott, informing us that he has had a relapse, and is unable to

attend the New York East Conference. The lot again falls on
Jonah : the greatest cross I ever took up, because of the deli-
cacies and difficulties that must embarrass the Bishop who
presides there this year. God can carry me through. No other
power can. The Church is his. He bought it with his blood.
I am his. The work is his. I have no confidence in myself—
I have confidence in God. His wisdom and power are adequate.
My heart is sending up to the mercy-seat its strong desires. I
am sure you will pray for me and the Conference.

From Danbury, Connecticut, the seat of the New
York East Conference, May 16, to Mrs. Janes ·

The preachers have greeted me very cordially. I fear I shall
have great trouble in stationing the preachers. God can enable me to do it right, and then make the preachers and people
satisfied and happy. I trust he will.

In the "chair," his thoughts turn to Tillie, to
whom he writes on happiness, sin, and the Saviour :

Our heavenly Father loves to see us happy.' He would not
have given us so much to make us happy if he did not desire
us to be so. It is right and proper, therefore, that we should
be cheerful and joyful. If we are good we shall have no cause
to be unhappy. It is sin that makes us unhappy. Sin has
produced all the sorrow and misery that are in the world.
. What a terrible thing it is to sin against God ! It makes persons wretched in both worlds. What a blessed thing it is that
we have a Saviour. Jesus can save us from our wickedness.
He can pardon all that we have done that is wrong, and make
our wicked hearts good. O, what a precious Saviour ! How
we should love him and praise him. I hope you love the Lord
Jesus. I hope you will serve him all your days on earth, and
then enjoy him forever in heaven.

From Maine, while attending upon the Conferences, he writes to Dr. J. M. Howe, of New York,

his impressions of the Prohibitory Liquor Law of
the State:

There is a good deal of interest in traveling in this State.
The scenery is very fine. The villages are beautiful, and most
of them thriving. No rum ruins meeting the eye at every turn.
I have not seen an intoxicated man, nor any thing to intoxicate
a man, since I came into this State. You can scarcely realize
the change. O! I hope we shall have a law similar to the one
in this State, soon in every State in the Union. If we could
only be relieved from rum and slavery what a glorious country
ours would be. I have hope in God in relation to these subjects, but not much hope in man. The Gospel must prevail;
the mouth of the Lord hath spoken it. I bless the Lord that I
find my own religious experience an improving one. I find increasing delight in the service and sonship of God. Duty with
me is delight. Self-denial, cross-bearing, and labor for God
are pleasures.

Usually while attending the spring Conferences
the Bishop could run to Mount Wesley in the
intervals of sessions, but the Western and North-
western Conferences of the autumn required a more
protracted absence, during which he was also much
more exposed to malarious influences. Starting
out on a tour of these was fraught with some pangs.
But how heroically, this season, as always, he bore
up under his trials, may be seen by the following
letter to Mrs. Janes, from New York on the eve of
leaving for the North-west:

My business in the city is now about finished, and I am ready
for my journey. I go cheerfully, because it is manifestly duty.
I go for Christ's sake, and that makes it even a pleasure. But
for this motive my life would be intolerable. The love of Christ

"gives even affliction a grace." It makes work a delight and sacrifice a joy. I can neither do nor suffer too much for Jesus. If I could bear all the affliction I would be glad; but I cannot. The sight of one soul in glory, saved through our agency, will be a recompense for a life of trial and sacrifice. I know your heart will respond to this sentiment. You can appreciate this consideration. This religious motive lessens your sufferings in consequence of my almost constant absence from home. There remains a rest for the people of God. The time of labor is short enough. Yes, and the time of rest will be long enough; but how different the length. The former but as a watch in the night, the latter eternal. Momentary—eternal—what a contrast! May it reconcile us fully to our peculiar duties and circumstances. And may we be able to rejoice that we are accounted worthy to suffer for Christ, our divine Lord.

He reached Chicago, August 25, and preached there on the Sabbath following. On Monday he went to Evanston, the seat of the North-western University. "A Methodist college," he writes, "which is in an incipient state; yet I think it is the commencement of a great and useful institution." He then went on to Racine, Wisconsin, the seat of the Wisconsin Conference.

Referring to the session, September 3, he writes to Mrs. Janes:

I was more than ordinarily aided by the Spirit while preaching the unsearchable riches of Christ. On Saturday I had two women call on me, and inform me that the prophecy mentioned in Acts ii, 18, was being fulfilled, that they had received the Spirit, and were called to prophesy, and wanted me to ordain them deaconesses. I saw they were honest women; I conversed with them kindly, but told them I was not authorized to comply with their wishes. They left me disappointed, but,

I think, not offended. One of them insisted on being received into the Conference as a traveling minister. They were English women, possessed considerable intelligence, and I judge were really pious. The Conference so far has progressed but slowly. Rather a restless spirit prevails. I hope it will get moderated before the Conference adjourns. Good men are very frail beings. Even God's ministers are encompassed with infirmities. Unless God preserves his Church there is but little hope for Zion; indeed, but little hope for our fallen humanity.

He finds time to write thus, on early culture:

I hope daughter Elizabeth is cultivating a taste for reading. It is very important she improve, as far as her health will permit, every opportunity for cultivating her mind. Do all you can to educate both head and heart, and to qualify yourself for happiness and usefulness in the future.

Religion—purity of heart, devotion of spirit—gentleness and delicacy of manners, amiableness and meekness of spirit, are essential elements to a lady's happiness and usefulness in life. I trust my dear daughter is cultivating these constantly, especially purity of heart.

To Mrs. Janes after the close of the Conference, from Chicago, September 10:

I thank God for bringing me through it. I pray God to forgive any errors I have committed. The Conference seemed to approve of my administration. By a rising, and, I believe, a unanimous, vote, they passed a resolution thanking God for enabling me to be present and preside with so much patience and impartiality. I was pleased that they thanked God, and not me. I am certain that was in the right direction.

I spend this afternoon in conference with the brethren of the Churches here, about their pastoral interests and also their church-extension enterprises.

To-morrow morning I expect to take the cars for Rock Island, there to renew the perplexities and responsibilities of a Conference session.

I trust you bask in the smile of a complacent God, and exult in the prospect of eternal beatitude. If so, how small are all things else—how transient, how easily dispensed with. God and duty—the favor of the one and the performance of the other—these are all that really concern us.

From the session of the Rock River Conference, at Rock Island, Illinois, September 13, to Elizabeth:

It is a large Conference. So far their deportment has been very amiable and religious, and I think the Conference a noble body of intelligent, spiritual, and faithful ministers. . . . I have not yet received any communication from home since I reached this city. I expect the messengers of love are on their way here. The mail is sometimes tardy; especially when love is looking out for messages from loved ones. Love is a winged angel. But the mail is not yet carried on wings. Perhaps in this progressive age it soon may be. I wish it were so now. I would talk with home much more frequently. How that would sweeten life! It would make absence quite supportable.

To Tillie:

We have here clouds of mosquitoes. O, how they bite! They must work fast, as they have but little time. Jack Frost is after them. He will soon send them into close confinement. Is Tillie learning to read any? Do you ask ma or sister to hear your lesson every day? How about spelling—can you spell all the words in this letter? Suppose you try.

There are allusions to himself in the following letter, at the close of the Rock River Conference, that will be appreciated by any who ever met the Bishop. Even those most intimate with him never heard him refer to his own performances, in a manner savoring of self-glorification. There was one, however, to whom he did speak, and to her but sparingly. Every man must have at least one heart which fully reflects his own, and to which he can at least occasionally unbosom himself. If he was chary of bestowing praise upon men to their face, it was because he did not wish even to seem to expect a return of compliments. Having schooled himself to repress all emotions of self-glorying, he felt obliged not to excite such emotions in his fellow-beings. If his friends might feel at any time that he did not say to them sufficiently appreciative words for themselves and their deeds, they never could complain of a lack of service, by which, as often without their knowledge as with it, they were helped to their true position and influence. "Certainly moderate praise used with opportunity, and not vulgar, is that which doeth the good."

To Mrs. Janes, Chicago, September 21:

The session at Rock Island was one of the pleasantest I ever attended. A very kind and religious spirit prevailed all the time. The business was transacted with great harmony and dispatch. I was specially aided by God in my administration: in all my care and perplexities enabled to be self-possessed. I usually find but little difficulty in presiding when I can keep my own mind calm and deliberate. But when in constant fatigues and strong excitement day after day the nervous system loses its tone, self-government becomes exceedingly difficult. At my last two Conferences, when in the chair, I have been preserved from all hurry and agitation of spirit, and enabled to control my manner more than usually to my own comfort and satisfaction. I have reason to believe, also, to the satisfaction of the Conference to a high degree. At least they so expressed themselves by resolutions. In my addresses to the young ministers—candidates for ordination—I was never so greatly aided before. I am confident impressions were made upon their hearts and minds that time will not efface.

On last Sunday I had a happy season in preaching and conducting the ordination services. In these matters I only speak of myself to my wife. I could not say what I have said except to her. The good that is done God doeth it. Our good is all divine. My correspondence, in connection with my conference duties, has, on this tour, been really burdensome. I am obliged to improve every moment of respite from active duties in answering letters. Dry detail business letters most of them. Still this is one of my crosses.

To Miss Charlotte, from Alton, Illinois, the seat of the Southern Illinois Conference, September 28:

I hope you will not be too earnest in your desires in reference to your standing in the school. I perceive there is not much truthfulness in their rules of merit. A student taking two or three studies, and giving all her attention to these branches, ought to be reported more perfect than an equally meritorious student, who is giving attention to twice the number of different studies. I do not find any fault with the rule. I do not know that they can adopt a better. But I mean to say, it is not a very correct test of merit. Consequently should not control a student in her conduct or feelings. Especially, I hope you will not injure your health in order to be among the first in your standing in the seminary. That would be paying too high a price for such distinction.

To Tillie, from Alton, October 3:

The Conference adjourned on Monday afternoon. . . . My next Conference will be about one hundred and fifty miles nearer home. That is some comfort. Have all the flowers faded and died? Will there be any when I reach home? I suppose the last rose of summer is gone, but, how about the altheas, are they all gone too? Well, if they are, I expect I shall have roses and lilies fresh and fragrant in the countenances of mamma, Lizzie, and Tillie. They will never die there. Those are the most precious ones, too. The diamond eye, the rosy lips, and lily cheeks of my loved ones have a wonderful enchantment in them. I hope to see them soon. That will be a luxury both for my eyes and heart. I rather guess they will be glad to see me by the time I get home. If they are not I will go away again, though I should feel very sad.

A letter from the Illinois Conference, at Paris, Illinois, October 9, to Elizabeth, closes the correspondence on this tour:

After the close of the Southern Illinois Conference I found myself very much indisposed. I remained in Alton three days and then went to St. Louis, where I remained until yesterday morning. Bishop Simpson was with me there, and the interview was pleasant. I heard him preach a good sermon on Sunday morning, from the text, "If a man die shall he live again?" The topics were, the immortality of our souls and the resurrection of our bodies. Grand topics! It is one of my old texts and subjects. Of course, we do not preach alike from the same text. Two minds so unlike each other could not make two sermons alike. This was a very excellent one, and made a deep and good impression on the audience.

The whole country about here is very sickly. In some places there are hardly enough well people to take care of the sick. I am informed that in some counties they have been unable to hold the courts on account of the prevailing sickness. . . .

I have just received a letter from your sister Lottie. I presume a little angel, with words of love, is winging his way here from Mount Wesley. I have a very strong home feeling these days. I want to come and bask again in the beams of the bright blue eyes that are there. The looks of tenderness and

words of love I find there are a very fragrant ointment to my
soul. With me, " There is no place like home." I, however,
have some very important duties to perform before I can visit
my sweet home. I must address myself to them in the name
and strength of God. It makes coming home much more
pleasant when I can feel that my duty is all well performed—
my official obligations all met.

Obliged in December to make a journey westward and to leave Mrs. Janes ill, he writes her:

It made me feel sad, as it always does, to leave you sick
yesterday. But my obligation to leave was imperious. I could,
therefore, do no otherwise than commend you to God, and
prosecute my duties to the Church. I recollect in the days of
our courtship (days of fragrant reminiscences and sweetest
memories) you talked about taking your Maker as your husband. I do not know but you will have to do so yet. Well, I
shall not be jealous of him ; you can love him, and cherish his
society, and seek his most intimate fellowship without objection
on my part. Indeed, I pray that he will shelter you in his
pavilion, that he will cover you with his feathers, that he will
make his abode with you, that he will be the portion of your
heart and your rejoicing forever. If God dwells with you, you
will be happy, whether any one else is with you or not. All
others are inferiors. "Where he vital breathes there must be
joy." May his smile gild with perpetual sunshine the habitation and the heart of my dear wife.

CHAPTER XI.

1856.

Baltimore and New England—General Conference of 1856;
Slavery Agitation—Iowa, Illinois, Indiana.

THE first glimpse which we have of the Bishop in 1856 is in a letter of February 20, in which he recommends to Dr. Durbin a north-western tour of visitation for Pastor Hedstrom, the founder of Methodist missions among the Scandinavians. The " pastor" ever found a wise counselor and sympathizing friend in Bishop Janes, and it will never be fully known how much his success was due to the clear head and open hand of the Bishop.

According to the General Minutes, Bishop Janes did not hold any of the spring Conferences of this year, except the New England. But, as usual, he was present at several of them, assisting those Bishops especially who were in ill health. From the session of the Baltimore Conference, held in old Light-street church, Baltimore, on March 5, he writes to his wife :

Lewis started with me at four o'clock on Tuesday morning and brought me to Morristown in season for the early train. I arrived in Newark in time to take the eight o'clock A. M. train for this city. As you well know, yesterday was a most beautiful day. My early ride was a very pleasant one. It was decidedly one of the most lovely morning scenes I ever saw. The day-break was mellow and rich beyond description. The morning star seemed like a diamond divinely set in the radiant diadem of morning. The earth beautifully robed in emblematic white, the heavens thickly studded with twinkling gems, the gates of day opening wider and wider, and the flood of light spreading farther and farther and glowing brighter and brighter, while all around was serene and all within was calm. I felt truly devotional and happy, having not only the inspiration of nature, but I believe also the inspiration of the Holy Spirit. . . .

This large Conference met this morning. Bishops Waugh and Scott are in somewhat improved health. I do not think they can endure much fatigue. . . . I should much like to look into the bee-hive at home this morning. I wonder if you are all as orderly and industrious and sweet as the honey-making and honey-eating bees. Have you any room to spare? Can you entertain a few angels? They do not require much room, nor are they very particular about their accommodations. They have more respect to their treatment than to their circumstances.

During the session Bishop Janes preached a missionary sermon, made a speech at the Conference missionary anniversary, and also preached a sermon to local preachers. In reference to this he says: " I preached yesterday to a larger number of local preachers and a larger audience, with more freedom and a little less time, than when you heard me preach to the local preachers in New York." In this sermon he not only set forth the historical position of " local preachers," and their importance as an integral part of the Church's organization, but also sought to inspire them with a high ideal of their vocation, and to encourage them to the greatest efficiency by study and application.

The following letter to Mrs. Janes shows how the death of a missionary of the Methodist Episcopal Church, South, returned from China, touched his heart. It was written from the Conference Room, March 18:

I have just received your letter of yesterday, informing me of the peaceful end of Brother Belden. Heaven is enriched. He is glorified. Possibly the militant Church has not suffered loss. For aught we know, disembodied saints may be as useful missionaries as embodied ones. I regret I could not have been present to have witnessed the closing scene. Others were there who could minister to his necessities, and it seems he found the grace of God sufficient for him. May his wife and children ever prove its sufficiency! I am very glad Dr. Stevenson and Brother Cross saw him before he died. Let him be buried in our vault.

From the New England Conference, Salem, Mass., March 31, to Mrs. Janes:

I have reached this place, the seat of the New England Conference. I had a safe passage ; a little delayed by an accident to a freight train. Reached Boston in time to go and hear Mr. Gough. His description of water was very fine—eloquent. The address was well received. But such anecdote-telling, fun-making speeches, will never permanently establish a great moral cause which has to battle against man's cupidity and depraved appetites. As we have all classes to deal with, we need all kinds of agents to act upon them. Mr. Gough has his sphere. The temperance cause has a revived interest in Boston. I hope it will be generous and continuous. It is a blessed moral enterprise ; but needs the influence of the Church to give it a final triumph.

I trust cold, stormy March, as it recedes, like the retiring storm cloud, will be in your sight gilded with the bow of promise, the emblem of hope. As for me, I am determined to hope on, hope ever. Despair, or even despondency, has but one dwelling-place he can properly call his own, and that is perdition. Whenever he visits any one out of hell he is an intruder. No person should despond who is where universal love reigns. Any person who is within sight of mercy's scepter may hope—hope joyfully, hope triumphantly, hope always, hope savingly.

From Salem, Massachusetts, to his three daughters, April 4:

The circumstance of the sisters and brother all being at home next summer will be a very happy one. Mother and her children will make a beautiful circle of domestic love and intercourse. I wish I could be permitted to be with them. But duty—duty to the Church, duty to God, will require me to deny myself this great pleasure. Well, duty before pleasure, always and in all circumstances ; yes, and at all costs, and every sacrifice. But stop—perhaps I am mistaken ; duty before pleasure? To a well-regulated mind and a Christian heart duty is pleasure. Such characters are happy when discharging duty, however painful the circumstances, however severe the sacrifices. Hence the martyrs were happy in the flames— hence modern missionaries, leaving friends and country and home comforts, are happy in going to the degraded and perishing heathen. Duty and pleasure were married in Eden, and God has never divorced them, and never will. This relation will exist both in time and during eternity. Neither in this world nor the next shall we be happy only in the sphere of duty.

Another General Conference was now at hand, and Bishop Janes is found at Cincinnati, at a meeting of the Bishops preparing for the session. While engaged with his colleagues he must step aside to advocate the claims of Irish Methodism upon the benefactions of American Methodism. From the advent of the Rev. Messrs. Arthur and Scott, delegates from the Irish Conference, then in this country, they had received his warmest sympathy and aid. He thus alludes to the Cincinnati meeting, April 28:

Yesterday was a day of some anxiety. The meeting of the Churches in behalf of Ireland was felt to be an important one. To me was assigned the task of the concluding speech and asking for the collection. I was very reluctant to undertake it, but could not well avoid it. The audience was respectable, though not so large as was anticipated. The Irish brothers made good addresses. I spoke only about ten minutes and asked for the collection. We raised about two thousand dollars. More was anticipated. The meeting was not enthusiastic. I do not blame myself, for I did as well as I could under the circumstances.

From Cincinnati, April 30:

I have had no time to look for nature's fresh attractions here. It has been work, work, write, write, all the time. We start now in a few minutes for Indianapolis. I shall probably be so engrossed for the first few days of the General Conference as to be unable to write to you, so I take this opportunity to manifest my mindfulness and regard for my cherished wife and beloved children. So I go from one scene of excitement to another. Well, it is burning out. But I had rather be a candle in the Church than any thing else. I wish my light was stronger and clearer. It is a great privilege to throw even a few rays athwart the reigning darkness of this sinful world.

My health is as good as usual. I expect my ride through the country to Indianapolis this afternoon will do me good. I may see some flowers. I shall doubtless feel the fresh breeze.

The twelfth delegated General Conference assembled at the State House in Indianapolis, Indiana, May 1, 1856. All the Bishops were present. The Episcopal Address was read by Bishop Janes. The Church was again much excited on the slavery question. The advanced antislavery sentiment demanded such a change in the General Rule on Slavery as to forbid slave-holding in the Church. Resolutions proposing this change had originated with several of the Annual Conferences, but each failed of a majority of three fourths of the ministers. In view of which, the address says, "We think it to be our duty to express our strong doubts whether, in view of the restricted powers of a delegated General Conference, any measure equivalent to a change in the General Rules can be constitutionally adopted without the concurrence of the Annual Conferences. As to the propriety of any modifications not of such a character as to conflict with the constitutional economy of the Church, while opinions and views may be various, we can fully confide in the wisdom of this General Conference as the supreme council of the Church."

It cannot be doubted but that this deliverance did much to moderate the spirit and restrain the action of the General Conference, so that at this session no change was made either in the General Rule or in the Chapter on Slavery. The question, however, was the pivot about which the most animated debates revolved and the choice of officers took place. Here and there Bishop Janes's solicitude on the subject crops out in his home correspondence.

Indianapolis, May 3, to Mrs. Janes:

. . . The General Conference is proceeding about as usual. The great questions of general interest have not yet been acted on. I have some fear as to the results. Still I have hope in God. The Lord loves the Church. I believe he loves the Methodist Episcopal Church. With all its imperfections I believe the Church is still useful. I hope and pray and labor for the peace of Israel. I believe this world will be converted yet, but I fear not so soon as I desire and have been accustomed to hope.

May 5, to Mrs. Janes:

On Saturday your husband read the Quadrennial Episcopal Address. It has, perhaps, been acceptable to the majority, but has been very severely criticised by the ultra party and strongly denounced. Still it will do good. We have the prospect of a stormy session. The result I cannot foresee. My hope for the Church is in God.

May 16, to Mrs. Janes:

I have been, to some extent, casting off my anxieties for the issues of General Conference doings. I have been trying to feel that the Church is not mine, but belongs to God, and that his love and wisdom and power are all engaged to perpetuate and prosper it. Still I cannot but feel that a great responsibility rests upon me and upon the General Conference. There

9*

is much uncertainty yet as to the results of the session. The prospect is not encouraging as to the unity or peace of the Church. What may be the position of the Church, or my position when the Conference adjourns, I cannot tell. I must wait the action of the Conference, and then govern my action as wisely and religiously as I can. I am hoping for the best. My hope is in God, and to him I lift my eyes and address my prayers.

To the same, May 19:

The General Conference is approaching its great and exciting questions. I fear, but still hope. The prospect is not cheering. If I did not believe God loved the Methodist Church I should be discouraged. But I believe the Methodist Church was planted by the power of God, has been superintended by the special providence of God, and is still beloved as the purchase of Christ's blood. The Church has defects, many deficiencies, but is still the most efficient branch of the Christian Church. Great will be the loss to our poor, sinful humanity when her force is broken, her efficiency lessened. I hope the Church will come out of these struggles unharmed. If so, I shall greatly rejoice and give thanks. The Conference is now discussing the presiding elder question. It is understood the report on slavery will come up to-morrow. It will be my turn to preside. I expect an excited time.

There seems to be a good religious interest in the Conference and in the meetings. The preaching has generally been excellent. I judge the General Conference is making a good impression on the public mind. The general issues, however, are what create my anxieties. God reigns. That is the joy and hope of my heart.

To the same, May 26:

I have been hoping that by this time I might be able to anticipate the period of adjournment, but I am not able. We are yet a troubled, perplexed body, and no definite conclusions on the great questions are yet agreed upon.   Indeed, I am sorry to say that the prospect of the peace and unity of the Church does not brighten.   But I must leave this to the great Head of the Church.   I still look to him to protect and preserve the Church which he has bought with the price of blood—sacred blood—vicarious sufferings.

To the same, May 29:

There is a probability that the vote on the slavery question will be taken to-day.   If so, there will be a great press of business until the Conference adjourns—no rest day or night. I have hope now that the Church will not be dissevered, though some trouble may arise on the border in consequence of the action of the Conference.   Still I cannot decide positively until after the vote is taken.   If I am disappointed in the vote I will write you by next mail.

The vote, when taken, failed of a two thirds or constitutional majority, and so the Bishop's fears were relieved.

In one of his letters the Bishop makes allusion to the leave-taking of Drs. Hannah and Jobson, the delegates of the British Wesleyan Conference:

Dr. Hannah and Mr. Jobson have just taken their leave of the Conference in a most affectionate and impressive manner.   Bishop Waugh responded most felicitously.   Their visit has been a useful one.   Their memory will be fragrant with those who have had intercourse with them.   They are excellent specimens of Methodist ministers—true embassadors of Christ.

Apart from the slavery question, there is little reference in the Bishop's correspondence to the important measures which came before the General

Conference. His active interest in them cannot be doubted. But it is pleasing to read, during all this season of anxiety, his kindly effusions to the home circle. Only a few extracts can be given.

To Miss Elizabeth, May 9:

I am much pleased that you have hung up my image in the gallery of your memory, so that you can carry it about with you, and ever and anon look at it when we are distant from each other. Every member of my family is most accurately daguerreotyped upon my mind. I have a very beautiful picture gallery in one of the chambers of my soul. I have several beautiful likenesses there. The eye of affection, the hand of love, and the skill of nature were employed in drawing them. I admire them enthusiastically. I look at them very often. Even in the midnight darkness my waking vision is greatly delighted in looking at them.

To Miss Charlotte, under the same date:

Practice is necessary to perfection in any pursuit of industry. You know that practice is necessary in writing, in order to the acquisition of a good style. Learning all the rules in the books will not make a good writer without personal practice. So it is in culinary and house-keeping pursuits. Nothing but practice can make perfect. And skill in domestic duties is necessary to qualify a lady for the ordinary responsibilities of the relations of domestic life. . . . I am highly gratified that my daughter is so interested in her literary pursuits. I do not wish to lessen her ardor in the cultivation of her mind. I shall cheerfully afford her all the advantages I can in prosecuting her education.

May 22, on receiving from Tillie the first letter, written by herself:

It is a very good specimen of penmanship. . . . I am even better pleased with the contents than with the execution of the letter. Bishop Morris was with me when I read it, and I showed it to him. He said, " It is short and sweet." Indeed it is sweet—sweet as love. That, you know, is the sweetest thing in the world. I believe your little heart is full of it. You have a great deal for dear mamma and papa and brother and sisters ; some for the flowers, some for the sweet sunshine, some for the beautiful moonlight, some for the twinkling stars. I think Tillie loves every thing beautiful and good. I hope Tillie has much love for her studies, for her books, and especially for her Testament. And I hope especially that she has a heart overflowing with love to her blessed Saviour, to Jesus. You cannot love him too much. No, indeed, you cannot love him enough, even though you love him with all your heart.

To Mrs. Janes, May 26 :

Reciprocal love from those we deem worthy of our love is an elevated source of delight. Few pleasures equal it. This is the highest joy in religion. The Holy Spirit assuring us that the infinite God we love loves us, delights in us, looks upon us complacently, loves with an unchanging love, with an eternal love. The next highest and purest source of moral pleasure is mutual conjugal affection—the tenderest, the most intimate, the most confiding of human affections. I am very thankful for the large measure of this happiness with which I have been and still am blessed.

This little disquisition was a good preparation for the announcement which soon follows. For a Bishop then to make the tour to the Pacific coast meant something :

I shall feel it my duty to go to California and Oregon. I have resisted the arrangement as long as I could consistently with ministerial obligations or my peace of conscience. It is a severe trial. I should be extremely thankful if my divine Master would excuse me. But the indications of Providence are such that I believe it to be the will of my heavenly Father that I should visit that distant field of ministerial service. If it be his will it will be better for me to go, and also better for my family, than that I should refuse to go. The path of duty is the path of safety. God's will is always good.

The Bishop's autumn Conferences for 1856 were the Upper Iowa, the Peoria, and the North-western Indiana. During the summer an accident had occurred to Miss Charlotte, the eldest daughter, by which her life was endangered, and from which she suffered a protracted illness. From his Western journey, on which his son accompanied him, he thus writes to her, August 22 :

I have been debating in my mind to whom the next epistle belonged. Keeping up the old practice of rotation, it belongs to Lizzie ; but all general rules have their exceptions. As you are the most afflicted one at home I think the law of sympathy entitles you to receive it. I believe suffering has a claim that can only be set aside by more intense suffering. So when Lizzie or Tillie become a greater sufferers they shall receive the same sympathetic consideration. I hope, however, that your severe sufferings are past. The extreme sensitiveness, the indescribable restlessness, the unpleasant apprehension which one in such a state feels, is very hard to be borne. I know more of what you have felt than you suppose I do. Often have I felt it. Even in public sometimes it requires the utmost effort to maintain a discipline over my feelings and my conduct. Certainly it is not to be wondered at that your nervous system should suffer by such an affliction as you have endured. I think that you have exercised unusual moral courage and self-control. I trust your fortitude will not fail you, and that your patience and resignation will continue as long as your affliction shall call for their exercise. I am sure this will be the case if you call upon the Mighty for strength, and upon the Comforter for support and consolation.

From Maquoketa, Ia., another word of cheer to the invalid daughter :

How are you this morning ?   Did you have a pleasant Sabbath yesterday—some good thoughts and sweet devotional feelings ?   I trust so.   Jesus can meet us and smile on us and bless us in the sick-room as well as in the sanctuary.   I preached yesterday to a multitude of preachers and people in the grove.   It was a bright, beautiful day.   I had no thought of a letter from Lottie.   It was a very great pleasure to receive it.   I hope you will live to write a great many more to me and to others.

From Aurora, Ill., to Miss Elizabeth, Sept. 5 :

I reached here yesterday expecting to receive a line from home, but found none.   I hope that the lingering letter will soon come to hand.   I wish I had some way to put spurs to the tardy mail out West.   Certainly it is provokingly slow. But Christians must have patience.   They should never be peevish and pettish, but meek and patient.   I fear the irregularities of the mails have made my letters, like angel visits, " few and far between."   By the by, I do not believe the doctrine contained in this poetic quotation.   To the good it certainly is not applicable.   " The angel of the Lord encampeth round about them that fear him, and delivereth them."   They [the angels] are all ministering spirits to them who are heirs of salvation.   Concerning little children : " Their angels do always behold the face of my Father which is in heaven."   Thus the Bible, *versus* poetry, teaches us the angels have much to do in this world.   I believe the Bible on this subject.   I think they travel with me sometimes.   I also always expect to leave them about my sacred home when I leave to serve God and his Church.

To Miss Charlotte, the same date:

I am pleased that you still have flowers blooming about you. We have many wild flowers on these wide prairies. Some of them are really beautiful. I have always felt a desire to bring mamma out here to look upon these grand prairies. Her admiration of nature, I know, would be highly gratified. If her health had permitted I should have invited her before this time. A love of the beautiful in nature may be successfully cultivated. A journey through the most interesting parts of our country, as Lewey says, "will pay." It would be a source of improvement as well as pleasure, both of which I hope my dear daughters will share one of these days. A good time coming, is it not? Yes, yes, you are not to be always shut up in a sick-room. There is a wide range of thought, of knowledge, of observation, of action, of pleasure, before you. A wide range in this world, and when you get your wings, and wide heaven opens before you its range, I cannot imagine how far you will sail or high you will rise. Eternity spent on the wing will afford a wonderful opportunity to see and enjoy. I hope we will have a fine sail together on those illimitable plains of glory. We will never tire or stop. We will take the family and a few good angels with us.

To Tillie, September 8:

I spend a part of my time with the family where Bishop Simpson puts up. They have a little lady there just about your age. She is a sprightly little miss. She has two pets. What do you think they are? They are two little kittens. One is named Rose and the other Lily. Lily is black and white. Is not that a very singular lily—a black and white one? Did you ever see such a one? I never did before. She is very fond of them, and plays with them very much. Yet one of them scratched her yesterday, and made her cry. I wonder if Tillie would not like a kitten for a pet. She has, however, so many playthings, and so many things to interest her, that I suppose a kitten would not add much to her happiness. Tillie loves to work, too, and that is better than playing with kittens or any thing else. How about the lessons? Do they get some attention? Does Tillie learn them, and dear Lottie hear them? I fancy this is so every day. This is one of the varieties that makes home pleasant, gives Tillie a useful exercise, and Lottie a little change to relieve the tedium of her long confinement.

To Miss Elizabeth, from Peoria, September 15:

I preached yesterday morning with some satisfaction to myself, and, I hope, some profit to the people. The audience was very large and attentive. In the afternoon Dr. Foster preached a most admirable sermon. . . . I listen to the Conference speeches patiently, whether they are pertinent or not. Some of them, certainly, are not remarkably eloquent or direct, but, if they do no other good, they satisfy those who make them; that, you know, is an important point gained.

To Mrs. Janes, from Peoria, September 18:

So far as I can see and learn, the Church in the West is in most respects prosperous. Political agitations are very violent. Speculations are very rife; these disturb, and in some instances even distract, the Church. But still, as a whole, the Church is increasing in all the elements of power and progress. Our Church is exhibiting very commendable zeal in the cause of education. If the present political agitation that is shaking our country passes over without revolution, this western part of our national domain must become very populous, wealthy, and powerful. If it becomes proportionately religious it will be well for them and the world. The Methodist Church has a vast responsibility in this matter. I pray that she may heed it!

From the seat of the Iowa Conference the Bishop writes to Miss Charlotte, September 24:

I hope we may have a short and useful session, but I have some little apprehension, as there seems to be quite a disposition to talk. There are a number of old preachers in the Conference who feel privileged to do this. . . . I wonder how you busy yourself in your sick-room. I do not know but it would be well for you to get up a little mischief—not very bad mischief, you know—but just a little, for the fun of it. Now what kind of mischief can you invent to make yourself laugh heartily? Laugh for exercise—laugh until you grow fat. Let me know what kind you can devise. Perhaps it will do me good as well as yourself. I think it does me good to laugh as well as work. A little play, sometimes, is very desirable for body and soul, for heart and mind. Now, to amuse one's self requires genius. Can you do it?

To the same, September 25:

If I were at home this morning I presume we should talk some. If I did not talk spontaneously I guess Lottie would draw some talk out of me by her questions. I believe mamma thinks I am not a gushing spring, but a deep well, the water of which must all be pumped out. I am sorry it is so. I admire a bubbling spring very much. A gushing, living, limpid fountain is one of the most beautiful and interesting objects in nature. Still, the deep fountains that run under ground and make no gurgling sound or murmuring music, may at least supply to some extent the deficiency of gushing springs and surface fountains, if those who are so unfortunate as to be without these richer blessings will make some effort to render them available. I am afraid that it costs more than it comes to to draw conversation out of me. Still I am so constituted that I fear nothing but pumping can draw it from me. I wish I could make myself different in many respects, but I am growing to be an old man. I apprehend my friends cannot anticipate much improvement in me, except religious improvement. I hope to grow in grace, in moral excellence, in Christian purity as long as I live. Still my purpose to cultivate my conversational powers is as strong as ever.

To Miss Elizabeth, from same point, Sept. 26:

Yesterday Dr. Durbin, Dr. Floy, and Dr. Porter, Book Agent, arrived. Was not that a rich cargo of doctors? We shall have some big speeches from them. They brought me the melancholy intelligence of the early demise of Rev. T. F. R. Mercein. It was astounding and afflictive news. I saw him the day I left New York. "Death loves a shining mark!" It certainly hit a shining mark in this instance. He was a noble youth, a true Christian, an able and improving and promising minister. His loss will be great to the Church.

To Miss Lizzie, from Mount Pleasant, Sept. 29:

I preached yesterday with considerable freedom. The house was densely crowded, and the service interesting. Dr. Durbin preached a very beautiful and effective sermon in the afternoon. His text was, "Behold the Lamb of God, which taketh away the sin of the world." This has not been so harmonious, courteous, and devotional a session as we are sometimes favored with. No serious difficulty, but little irritations and jars. I am beginning to feel as if in point of time I am almost home. It will be a jubilant hour when I reach Mount Wesley. I want a little autumn pleasure with my family before we remove to the city. I do enjoy those rural scenes and pleasures. I grow young when I am amid them.

In a letter to Miss Charlotte the Bishop relates a remarkable instance of liberal giving:

I yesterday dined with a plain family of good parents and children. We dined in the basement. The carpet was spread on the ground. For partitions in the house they had blankets hung up. Yet their center-table had some good books. The gentleman of the house this year supports three missionaries, also gives five hundred dollars to the parent Missionary Society, and five hundred dollars to the Sunday-School Union. Is not that noble? I love to find such spirits. They make me form a higher estimate of humanity. Especially do they give me more encouraging views of the inspiring power of Christianity.

His movements were now eastward. From Crawfordsville, Indiana, the seat of the North-western Indiana Conference, he discourses to Miss Charlotte of himself, of autumn, and on how to amuse the sick. The letter is dated October 6:

Your description of the parting scene of Miss September is very graphic. Her leave-taking of us in the West was more amiable. For two or three days previous she had been fitful and passionate; sometimes weeping, and sometimes even howling. Sometimes she put on a dark and scowling face, and sometimes smiled very brightly. But the closing interview was very agreeable; she was quite complacent. As she withdrew her face for the last time her countenance was radiant with bright, clear, sun-light beauties. Another, bearing her lovely name and resembling very much her person and character, may visit us, but it will not be Miss September of 1856. Her record will be a very interesting and important document. It will make many ears tingle and many hearts quake. I fear she will not tell a very commendable story about me. I did try to be good, and to do right, and be useful while in her presence, but I have so many infirmities, and make so many mistakes! God knows all the disadvantages of our present theater of action. He understands our frailties. He estimates righteously our character and conduct.

To the same, October 7:

By the by, you have not reported to me any new invention to amuse yourself or other sick persons. How about this matter? Are you not going to be the patroness of the invalid world, by inventing for them some new diversion, some yet unknown amusement, some health-giving pleasure? Now, this is a great matter. You know there are a great many invalids; some made such by casualties, some by diseases, and some by morbid imagination. Now to bless all these classes and cases by furnishing them something to make them laugh, or, in the cases of those that belong to the latter class, to even enable them to smile, would be a wonderful kindness to poor suffering humanity. The person who does it will fill a prominent niche in the temple of fame. I hope you have not given up the effort.

To Tillie, Crawfordsville, Ind., October 10:

How is my little pet this morning? Healthy, happy, smiling, singing, talking? Has Jack Frost made you a visit yet? Did you see him before old Sol chased him away? Who is old Sol? Get mamma to introduce you to him. I think you will enjoy his acquaintance. He is a very fine old gentleman. He does a great deal of good in the world. I think you have seen Jack Frost, with his white hair; he is a rather mischievous old personage; he bites little girls' toes and fingers when he can get a nip at them. He also destroys the flowers and sometimes the fruits. Still, he sometimes does good. He makes the atmosphere more pure and healthy. He increases our strength and comfort. He makes our ice. This you know is very useful for household comforts. He gives little girls and boys their icy sliding-places. Without him we could have no sleigh-riding. So you see he is not to be despised or rejected though he occasionally does a little mischief. Little girls and boys must take care of their toes and fingers and ears, and then they may play with Jack Frost, and receive from him many favors.

CHAPTER XII.

1857–1859.

Visits the Pacific Coast—Trans-Mississippi Conferences—The
trouble at Bonham, Texas.

IT was arranged in the episcopal plan for Bishop
Janes this year (1857) to visit officially the Oregon and California Conferences; consequently but
little work was assigned him in the spring on the
Atlantic coast. He held the Baltimore Conference
in Baltimore, March 4–18. The Conference, by the
authority delegated to it from the preceding General Conference, was divided by its own vote into
the Baltimore and East Baltimore, and the Bishop
made out the appointments accordingly. Bishop
Janes at this session, with his two eldest daughters,
was the guest of his esteemed friend, the Rev. William Hamilton, D.D. From Baltimore he went to
the Providence Conference, at Bristol, Rhode Isl-
and, April 1, at the close of which he returned to
New York, and, after settling the family at Mount
Wesley, began at once his preparations for the tour
to the Pacific coast. The " Christian Advocate and
Journal," noticing his departure, remarks :

Truly are our Bishops "general superintendents ;" two of
them are in the Eastern States, one is in the extreme West,

another in the Middle States, one on the way to California and Oregon, and another on the seas for Europe, to look after our missions in Germany, Norway, and Sweden. This is *apostolic* episcopacy, " succession " or no " succession."

The " California Christian Advocate," of June 5, announces his safe arrival at San Francisco :

We announce, with thanksgiving to a gracious Providence, the advent of this devoted and efficient Christian Bishop among us. He came by the " Golden Age." His early arrival contemplates as general and thorough travel and observation on the coast as may be practicable before the Conference sessions. Some six weeks or two months will be spent in California. He will attend the camp-meeting at Santa Cruz, on Saturday and Sunday next, and return to this city by San Jose early next week. His plan of travel is not yet matured. Our friends may expect to be advised of his coming, in different communities, in time to announce public services, as it is understood the Bishop will preach on week days or evenings, as well as Sabbaths. so far as his health will allow.

The work of the Methodist Episcopal Church was rapidly expanding in this distant and extended territory. The Oregon and California Mission Conference was formed in 1848, with the Rev. William Roberts, of Salem, Oregon, for superintendent. " In the spring of 1849 Mr. Roberts had timbers hewed, split, rived, shaved, and prepared for the erection of a new church, and shipped from Oregon to San Francisco. There was not a saw-mill on the coast between Alaska and the isthmus of Panama." The Rev. William Taylor, of the Baltimore Conference, and the Rev. Isaac Owen,

of the Indiana Conference, were appointed missionaries to California in the autumn of 1848, and
the following autumn arrived in the territory, the
one by sailing vessel around Cape Horn, and the
other " overland," by ox teams across the prairies
and mountains.   Already the Mission Conference,
when Bishop Janes arrived, was divided into two
regular Annual Conferences, which comprised 5,598
members and probationers, 131 ministers, 79
churches, and 35 parsonages.   Bishop Janes had
been preceded by Bishops Ames, Simpson, Baker,
and Scott; the first, Bishop Ames, having visited
the coast in 1853.   An anecdote is told of Bishop
Ames illustrative of the pioneer and outspreading
character of the Methodist Church.   " Riding along
in one of the remote valleys lying back from the
coast, he saw an Indian boy coming toward him ;
he immediately said to himself, ' Now I'll have a
chance to preach the Gospel to a soul who has never
heard it ; ' whereupon he spoke to the boy, and
began, with the best English-Indian he could command, to tell him of Jesus.   ' O yes,' said the boy,
' my brother is a local preacher.' "

In a letter to his son Bishop Janes writes from
Oroville, June 31 :

My life here is a very busy one. Never were my time and
strength more fully taxed than they are in this Pacific tour.
There is so much to do and so much to look after ; so many
embarrassments to be removed, so many difficulties to be set-

tled, and so many arrangements to be made, that my mind and time are constantly taxed. But I am not sorry. It is good to be fully employed. I love to work, I feel so much brighter and happier than I do when I indulge in sluggishness and inactivity. I have sometimes wished you were with me, but during the last two weeks I have been glad you were not. The summer is not the season to travel in California. The heat by day, the chilliness of the night, and the terrible dustiness of the roads, make it both uncomfortable and unhealthy traveling. The dust becomes as fine as flour, and is inhaled with every breath. I find it hard upon the lungs. Then the expense of traveling is enormous.

A note from the " Pacific Christian Advocate," Salem, Oregon, of this period, shows the route of travel which the Bishop pursued :

Bishop Janes is *en route* for Oregon, via Yreka, Jacksonville, and Umpqua. He is the first Bishop who has attempted this land trip. His visit will, doubtless, be of great service to the interests of religion on this coast. He will not, probably, reach Salem and Portland until after Conference.

From Yreka, California, he writes to Mrs. Janes, July 9 :

Since I last wrote you I have been traveling on mule-back, and preaching nearly every evening. The sun sets so late, and the people work so long, that our evening meetings commence very late. It makes short nights for me, and I do not get as much sleep as nature requires. It is very trying to be so long without intelligence of your welfare, or evidences of your mindfulness and love. I have handled the letter of the 20th of May until the envelope is so soiled I can scarcely read a word of the superscription ; but it must last me until I receive others. I am now approaching the Oregon line. I shall, probably, reach that territory to-morrow. I am, I suppose, about three hundred miles from the seat of the Oregon Conference. I am traveling on mule-back, with Brother Simonds, the presiding elder of this district, for my companion. Yreka is a large village situated in the Shasta valley, and is the most northern town of much size in the State. I preach here to-night. I hope to speak a word in season. I shall, if God answers my prayer and guides and assists. O how absolutely we need the direction of God in order to do good in our ministry! I do not know what will be the character of the congregation to-night, nor what will be their spiritual wants. I can only draw the bow at a venture. But God knows who will be present, and what truth will edify them and save them. I trust to be divinely guided, and that the word spoken will be so appropriate that it will be as nails fastened by the masters of assemblies. This is a wicked land. The gates of Zion mourn. We have some very able and devoted ministers, and some very good people among the laity of the Church. Still the moral power of the Church is not adequate to control the public mind and the public morals. Some places have been favored with revival influences during this Conference year. This village has been largely blessed. The Church is making some progress; I think is becoming more and more useful and ascendant. There is but little Protestant religious influence in the State, except in a few of the larger towns, but that of the Methodist Church. The mining regions, especially, are almost exclusively left to us. It is a large responsibility, but I hope we shall have grace to meet it.

The Bishop returned by steamer to San Francisco from Oregon, August 25, in "usual health." He finds time, amid incessant labors, for the home pen-talks:

Away off on this western side of the world, all home incidents, however small, have a great importance. Even the little occurrence of nine swallows sitting together on the honeysuckle arbor was invested with real interest, and gave me home pleasure.

I can understand how the little every-day affairs of home affect the sentiments and vary the feelings and influence the happiness of the home circle. My sympathy in all these domestic incidents is so strong that they become almost realities. It really seems as if I heard the swallows chattering, the robins singing, saw little Tillie busily picking her raspberries, and mamma smiling on her when she presents them to her.

From Stockton, Cal., Aug. 29, to Mrs. Janes:

My Oregon tour was an interesting one though wearisome. As I have before advised you, I went up by land and returned by sea. The voyage was somewhat perilous, but not very uncomfortable. I am glad I took the land route up, as it has given me a knowledge of both California and Oregon, and of the state and necessities of our Church, which I could not have obtained otherwise. Knowing, as I do now, the wear and tear of the overland journey, I should very much dread to undertake it again. But it is one of those scenes of exposure and peril and endurance upon which we look back with gratitude and satisfaction. Long and rugged as was the journey, not the slightest accident or casualty was permitted. Every calculation was met. My health has, on the whole, been improved by it.

I found the Church in Oregon in quite as good a condition as I anticipated. We have some noble men there laboring for God. Our Indian missions, since the Indian war, are doing but little. I fear the aborigines of this country are a doomed race. Such is the cupidity and lustfulness of the whites, that I fear, by their knavery, they will destroy them. It is mournful to see them harassed, driven from the graves of their dead, and wasting away. I found it impossible to do much for them. I fear our country will be visited with judgment for its unrighteousness to the Indian and Negro.

From Sonora, Cal., Sept. 3, to Mrs. Janes:

I am deeply interested in this country, especially in our Church here. Humanity as well as Christianity has a great deal at stake in California. This is one of the battle grounds on which liberty and slavery are conflicting. The strife in some places here is warm. I cannot foresee the final result. As yet the prospect of freedom is encouraging. This section of the State is denominated the Southern Mines, and has probably furnished the richest mines in the country. I am thankful that our Church in California is succeeding so well; manifestly God is with his ministers. I hope my visit may be made useful to them. I believe I have been moving in harmony with God's will in my visit and labors here. I intend to do all I can for God and his Church while in this country.

From San Francisco, Sept. 18, to Mrs. Janes:

Since I wrote you I have been traveling and preaching and looking into the state of the Church until the day before yesterday, when I came here to commence my conference duties. . . . I do not like to talk about sacrifice in the service of God. There cannot, to a rightly disposed mind, be any such sacrifice. Our duties may require us to forego some pleasures —to deny ourselves some enjoyments — but then these are compensated by others. I find men out here who have been away from their families two, three, five, and even more years, to make fortunes. O! how small a consideration in comparison to the work of saving souls. If others can endure these privations from such considerations, how much more we, when constrained by the love of Christ, when looking for our reward in heaven, when enjoying the approbation of God! Here is strength, here consolation!

Soon after the Bishop's return to New York in the autumn, he was invited to give the results of his observations in California and Oregon in a popular lecture. An abstract of the lecture was published. The Rev. S. D. Simonds, writing to him from Crescent City, Cal., says of it: " I see the lecture you delivered on California and Oregon is full of statistics. I wonder at your success. The Lord continue to bless you!"

Bishop Beverly Waugh, senior Bishop of the Church, died in Baltimore on Feb. 9, 1858. Bishop Janes preached his funeral sermon in the Light-street Church to a large audience composed of the ministers and people of all Protestant denominations. By request he subsequently repeated the sermon in New York. It was a fitting tribute to one of the noblest men and ministers of Methodism. The Rev. Dr. Hamilton, of Baltimore, writing to him soon afterward, says: "Mrs. Hamilton saw Mrs. Waugh to-day. Your sermon was every thing to her as well as to the public, nor do I think you could have done better had you taken a week to prepare."

Bishop Janes assisted his colleagues at the sessions of the Baltimore and East Baltimore Conferences, March 3-10, and, at the former, in Washington, D. C., took part in the missionary anniversary. The Rev. Dr. T. M. Eddy, editor of the "Northwestern Christian Advocate," who was present and participated, in his correspondence thus alludes to the Bishop:

At nine A. M. the Sunday-school missionary meeting of the charge was held; at eleven o'clock A. M. Bishop Janes preached an excellent sermon. This man is a marvel to me ; he is always in motion—seems never to tire—preaches, plans, delivers addresses, travels day and night. On Sabbath he usually preaches twice, and visits a Sabbath school. Well, perhaps *he* can stand three services a day, *but ordinarily it is next to suicide to attempt it.* His theory is, that preaching does not hurt a man ; that, "judiciously managed," it is a healthy, invigorating exercise. Very true; but I can't manage it judiciously three times a day.

Writing from Baltimore to Mrs. Janes, the Bishop says :

I came here yesterday to negotiate some transfers. The business of both Conferences is progressing pleasantly. The sessions, now the Conference is divided, are very unlike the stormy ones of last year. I am glad for the sake of my colleagues and thankful for the sake of the Church.

To Tillie, from Baltimore, March 5 :

. . . I am pleased that Tillie can sing. This is a very pleasant and profitable exercise. O how I wish I could sing ! I certainly would make some music before I get to heaven. I intend to sing there: indeed I do. I mean to sing there forever. I expect that even *my* voice will be sweet there. And O what a song we will have then and there—the song of Moses and the Lamb ! Have you learned it ? I think I have heard you sing some of it. I hope you will learn it all. Shall we sing it together in heaven ? I think so—with mother and sisters and brother. O that will be joyful !

Bishop Janes's Conferences for 1858 were Kansas and Nebraska, Missouri, East Maine, Erie, Ohio, Cincinnati, Indiana, and South-east Indiana.

To his son, from St. Louis, April 3, *en route* for the Kansas and Nebraska Conference :

I have one hundred and twenty miles more of railroad, and
then I take the steamer on the Missouri River; and then I
know not what—the best conveyance I can find.

Two days later to Miss Charlotte:

This is a bright, beautiful morning. The beauties of spring
are appearing all around me. The birds are singing most
sweetly. The air and earth and sky are uniting in an anthem .
of praise to the great First Cause. Indeed, I never saw nature
seem more devout. All is praise. My mind and heart are in
unison with the glorious *Te Deum* of nature. I feel that if I
were in heaven my feeling would harmonize with the loftier and
holier and sweeter song that fills the spacious temple of God.
Indeed, I feel a strong aspiration to bear a part in swelling
the tide of endless praise to God and the Lamb. Still it is a
blessed service we are permitted to render to God on earth.
This invests our feeble efforts with the grandeur of eternity.
O how inspiring is this consideration ! What a motive to religious activities ! This is worth living for; yes, and worth
dying for '

Bishop Janes preached twice on the Sabbath in
St. Louis, ordained an elder, baptized two children,
and, early in the week, started for Topeka, Kansas,
where he held (April 15-19) what was then the
extreme western Conference. The Kansas and Nebraska Conference, at this time covering such a
vast territory, included but 48 preachers and 2,610
members and probationers.

To Mrs. Janes, from Quindaro, Kansas, April 24:

Since the close of Conference I have been traveling by buggy
and saddle to this place. I have been some out of the direct
course to visit the remnants of the Delaware and Wyandotte

Indians. I remain here over Sabbath and dedicate a new house of worship.

On Sunday, May 16, 1858, St. Paul's Methodist Episcopal Church, on Fourth Avenue, New York, was dedicated, Bishop Janes preaching the opening sermon. This substantial, beautiful, and spacious edifice marked a great advance in Methodist architecture in the city. It was eminently proper that the Bishop, who had been the pastor of Mulberry-street, of which this Church was the outgrowth, should participate in the consummation of so successful and worthy an undertaking.

To Mrs. Janes, New York, May 17:

Preached yesterday at the dedication of St. Paul's with some satisfaction, and, I hope, some success. Dr. Edwards, of Baltimore, preached in the evening one of the best sermons I ever heard. The church is a grand one. Beautiful in its simplicity; commodious. I start at three P. M. for Maine. A multitude of people send their love to you and daughters. I have you all in my heart to live and die.

To his household from Bangor, Maine, May 19:

The East Maine Conference opened this morning. On Monday night, when the train reached Springfield for supper, I was so sound asleep I knew nothing of it until the train started on and the new conductor came and woke me to see my ticket. It was rather rude in him, but I dismissed him quickly and returned to the sweet embrace of Morpheus until the conductor made his last intrusion upon us, as we were entering Boston. I lost a dinner last week in the same way. Sleep was stronger than hunger. The weather is rainy and cold. Miss Spring, of Maine, has but just awoke from her long

wintry sleep. She has washed her face, but is not yet attired
in the vernal beauty or fashion of the season. I fear if she does
not improve very fast she will not be prepared for a matri-
monial alliance with Mr. Summer, who is soon expected to visit
her. Miss New Jersey Spring is much more advanced in her
attainments, and much more mature in her character. I believe her wedding-day is fixed. Let us see, when is it? I believe it is at midnight on the last day of May. So much for
pleasantry. . . .

O, that God would put his Spirit into more of the young men
of this generation and show them that there is a higher, nobler,
happier vocation than the world can propose to them! A work
worthy to employ rational faculties, to engage immortal powers,
to enlist spiritual sympathies. An object worth living for, an
interest worth dying for; results that can only be pictured upon the canvas of eternity, can only be estimated during its endless cycles, and can only be properly celebrated by its eternal
acclaim! How can intelligent young men be so blinded as not
to perceive the glory of such devotion and service?

To Mrs. Janes, from New York, May 30:

I was sorry to leave you this morning. I knew you would
have some hours of sadness. Somehow my obligations are so
stern I cannot fail to meet them. I hope the morning cloud
which passed over your mind has disappeared, or at least has
the rainbow of hope on its receding darkness. Nothing true
but heaven. Nothing reliable but God. Nothing saving but
grace. Nothing satisfying but glory. I believe all these are
yours. Other things are comparatively of little importance.

From the session of the Black River Conference, at Jordan, New York, in which Bishop Ames was presiding, he writes, June 9, to Mrs. Janes:

I am amid the excitements and responsibilities and perplexities and anxieties and sympathies of an Annual Conference.
O, what occasions these are! How they tax the heads and

10*

hearts and bodies of the poor Bishops. Especially when subjects of general excitement and agitation are up in their force and fury. This is a stormy time in this section of the Church. Several subjects of a deeply exciting character have been urged upon the attention of the people for some months past. There is much feverishness and commotion in the general mind of the Church. Some of the ministers are earnest in their efforts to carry out their plans of agitation. Matters have gone so far that it embarrasses us in arranging the appointments. We are compelled to consider every thing that affects the harmony between pastors and people. We must also keep ourselves free from all prejudice and prepossession. To keep one's mind serene and perfectly candid amid all the conflicts and agitations of the Conference and counsel-room requires ceaseless watching and the sternest self-denial, as well as the constant assistance of the divine Spirit. I believe God has never yet on similar occasions deserted me. I trust, for Zion's sake, he never will. I never needed his help more than now. May God grant it me!

To Miss Charlotte, from Dunkirk, New York, June 30:

With two loving fathers, one of them always willing to do you all the good you need, and the other both able and willing to do you all the good you can possibly require, why should you not be happy—perfectly happy? I remember the first year I was in the ministry I visited an aged and poor colored woman. I found her very happy notwithstanding her many infirmities. I asked her, "Are you always so happy?" She replied, "Yes, always happy." "But are you never unhappy?" She replied with great earnestness, "No; I wont be unhappy." I presume I have thought of that visit a thousand times. I am persuaded the will has much to do with our happiness. We may be determined to rejoice in the Lord always, and by grace be able to keep the purpose of our heart. Our peace being as a river, and our righteousness abounding as the waves of the sea.

The Bishops had a meeting at Cleveland, Ohio, in July, 1858. Bishop Janes, in speaking of it, says: "My colleagues, except Bishop Scott, have all been here. Bishop Simpson is present. He is feeble, but improving. We have had a pleasant meeting, and been quite harmonious in our views of the proper polity of the Church." In view of the approaching session of the Erie Conference he writes: "I see the approaching Conference is to be a time of trial to me. Much difficulty has already been presented. Still it is God's service, and I go to it in his name and depending on him for success."

At the session of the Ohio Conference, Marietta, Ohio, August 25–30, 1858, the Bishop is said to have preached one of his most remarkable sermons. Bishop S. M. Merrill, who was then a member of the Conference and was present, stated to the writer that he regarded the effort as not only one of the greatest of the Bishop's, but equal to any thing he ever heard. The text was, " Let him know, that he which converteth the sinner from the error of his way shall save a soul from death, and shall hide a multitude of sins." James v, 20. In the last half of the sermon, after dwelling at some length on the ravages of death, he suddenly changed his attitude, elevated his voice, and *defied death* as the personal foe of the race ; and then, opposing to him the conquering power of Christ, to the close exulted in the victory of the Gospel over sin and the grave. His whole

form, face, voice, seemed to be invested with a su-
pernatural energy.

In November, 1858, Thanksgiving day, the Niag-
ara-street Church, Buffalo, New York, was dedicated. I glean the following notice of the sermons
on the occasion:

> The dedicatory sermon at Niagara-street, by Bishop Janes,
> is described in the "Advocate" as rich and clear in thought,
> and so comprehensible, that at the close an attentive and in-
> terested listener could look back through the whole production,
> and have it presented to his mind as vividly as though it lay
> written before him, in all its purity of thought, its encouragement
> for all laborers in the right, its assurance that God was work-
> ing with them, and that success, through the influence of faith,
> was inevitable. The Bishop's sermon was received by the large
> audience with a keen relish, and with admiration of its descrip-
> tion of true Christianity, as earnest labor for man's elevation,
> conversion, and salvation. At the close of the sermon the
> congregation arose and stood while the Bishop offered a prayer
> consecrating the Church to the worship of God. The house
> was again full in the evening. Rev. Dr. Sewall, of Baltimore,
> delivered the sermon. It is represented as one of the greatest
> sermons ever delivered in Buffalo; beautiful and perfect in
> thought, rich and fertile in imagination, faultless in expression,
> pointed and touching in its appeals.

March 11, 1859, Bishop Janes met the Arkansas
Conference, at Bonham, Texas. This Conference,
lying wholly within slave territory, comprised 20
ministers, and about 1,257 members and probationers. It was the day of small things. A few
persons, mostly Germans, emigrants from the northern States, preferred to be under the care of the

Methodist Episcopal Church.   The Methodist Episcopal Church, South, had stricken from its Discipline the general rule 'on slavery, and thus left itself without a testimony as to the moral character of slavery, and consequently some conscientious persons could not unite with that Church.   To fold these scattered sheep the itinerants from the old Church followed them into the wilderness.   The vast, rich prairies of Texas—the State an empire within itself—was a most inviting field for the husbandman both for tillage and grazing, and the people from all sections soon began to pour into it.

The Republic of Texas when annexed had been admitted into the Union as a slave State; but it was very unfair that men who preferred free labor should not be allowed to settle in it, and to deport themselves in all matters according to their own choice.   The slave power, however, was now uncompromising, growing more and more bitter, and watched with jealousy every apparent intrusion upon what it deemed its rights.   Indeed, upon both sides of the great slavery conflict the forces were becoming more determined, and they were fast closing in for what proved to be the final conflict.   The whole nation was stirred to its depths, and the one issue before which all others paled was that of slavery.   In the border States where mixed labor obtained the excitement was most intense, and the passions called out most violent and destructive.

Such was the condition of the public mind when the little Conference met on Timber Creek, near Bonham, Texas. At a town and county meeting held at Bonham, March 12, in reference to the Conference, a preamble and resolutions were passed which denounced the Conference " as a screen behind which to hide emissaries known as abolitionists, and as dangerous to Southern interests; and determined that a suitable committee be appointed to wait on the Bishop and ministers now in Conference assembled, and warn them to withhold its furthur prosecution : and to secure this result, peaceably if they could, forcibly if they must."

A committee of fifty persons, with Judge Roberts, a Southern Methodist, as chairman, was appointed to carry out the resolutions.

The Conference, as usual, had their love-feast on Sunday, and at the conclusion of it the sacrament of the Lord's Supper. At eleven o'clock Bishop Janes commenced the public service, the house being very full. While he was reading the Scripture lessons the committee were advancing toward the house, with their associates, amounting to some two hundred, on horseback, marching in order, and armed with revolvers and bowie-knives. During prayer they gathered around the house. While the congregation was singing the second hymn as many as could, crowded into the house. When the Bishop began to give out his text, the spokesman of the mob, Judge Roberts, standing half way up the aisle, said, "Do I address the Bishop?" The Bishop continued giving out his text. He repeated, "Do I address the Bishop?" The Bishop replied, "I am a Bishop of the Methodist Episcopal Church." He then said, "I have an. unpleasant duty to perform, and I presume it will be equally unpleasant to you." He then described the meeting which sent him, looked around and referred to the committee, his associates, and called on one of them to read the proceedings of the meeting.

When the reading was ended he resumed his remarks, and concluded by saying that unless our Church should cease to operate in Texas blood would be shed, and the responsibility would be on the Bishop and the Conference. He would not allow any discussion, but two hours would be given them to frame an answer. The Judge was excited, and his address inflammatory. As he began to withdraw Bishop Janes asked his name. He stopped, and said his name was Roberts. The Bishop then remarked that the time was too short; that the topic was not one for Sabbath consideration; that the Conference was not then in session, etc. But the Judge said no longer time could be given, and left the house.

After the Bishop had preached, and the ordination services were finished, the Bishop and preachers and the lay brethren had an informal meeting, at which it was concluded that, as the laity were concerned, the Quarterly Conference should be consulted as to this occasion, and the preachers present agreed to suspend their services till the mind of the laity could be ascertained, and that was to decide their course. This information was conveyed to the mob, and they dispersed for the time being. . . .

On Monday, the 14th, the Conference re-assembled, according to adjournment, finished its business, united in devotion, and adjourned *sine die*.

Bishop Janes, in his modest and truthful account of the mob, goes on to state that he does not attribute this mobocratic outrage to the Methodist Episcopal Church, South, only so far as she or her people have indorsed it. He adds: "When editors or others apologize for such lawlessness and wrong, or speak of them approvingly, they become morally *particeps criminis*, and show that they only need the opportunity to do the like themselves. . . . Or if position or policy should restrain them from the actual outrage, they would at

least hold the clothes of those who throw the stones." . . .
But the following is said nobly and magnanimously, as if
uttered by one of the old martyrs:

"In conclusion, I wish to express my thankfulness that
when the Methodist Episcopal Church, South, has sent her
ministers to the free States to take the pastoral charge of
such as *preferred her ministry*, they have never been mobbed.
I pray they never may be." *

It was objected by the Southern Methodist press
that the "meeting" and "committee" should be
called "a mob," and that the Southern *Methodist*
Church should be held responsible for the action.
It was asserted that the meeting was composed of
the "wealth, the talent, and the best elements of
Texan society," and that the gentlemen went
armed with pistols and bowie-knives simply because it was their custom to do so on all occasions.
The Southern Methodist press, while it avowedly
condemned mobs, yet threw the responsibility of
the whole action upon the presence of the Conference, and never once declared that the proceedings
of the so-called committee were wrong, and sub-
versive of civil and religious freedom.

Unquestionably many good men in the South
regretted the occurrence; but, as I have stated,
party spirit was running high, men's minds were
being blinded by passion, and much was said and
done which a calmer hour would not have allowed.

---

* "South-western Methodism," Elliott, p. 129, etc.   Poe & Hitch-
cock, Cincinnati, O.

I allude to the subject only as matter of history, to illustrate the conflicts of the times—times which tried men's souls—but above all to set forth the Christly and heroic spirit of our Bishop.   Greater self-possession, a better temper, and more firmness and discrimination in a presiding and responsible officer could not have been displayed than he showed in so trying an emergency.   There was no scare, no precipitate fleeing, no rashness of any kind. The sermon and the ordinations of the hour were properly attended to, and the next day—not on the Sabbath, but the next day—the business of the Conference was regularly finished, and the Conference adjourned *sine die*, as is the custom.   Here upon our own soil was as heroic a spectacle as can be found in the annals of Huguenots, Puritans, or Covenanters.

CHAPTER XIII.

1859-1861.

Two New York Conferences—Upper Iowa—Peoria—Michigan—General Conference at Buffalo—Secession in the Baltimore Conference—Western New York and the North-west again—North Indiana, New Hampshire, Oneida Conferences.

BISHOP JANES met the New York East Conference at New Haven, Conn., April 12–20, and the New York, at Kingston, N. Y., May 4–12, 1859. From Rhinebeck, (Wildercliff,) the residence of Miss Mary Garrettson, he drops a word to Mrs. Janes, May 2:

I expect God has greeted you this morning. Permit your husband to greet you in the Lord. His face shines upon me. "I am like a green olive-tree in the house of God." Yesterday was a profitable Sabbath. I preached twice. I am also enjoying my visit to this ancient home of Methodistic piety. The associations are quite inspiring. God's angels and saints have dwelt together here for a long time. I trust they will evermore.

To Mrs. Janes, from Kingston, N. Y., May 5:

Conference commenced yesterday rather pleasantly. I have great trials before me during the session. He can heal the hearts I wound. He can overrule the mistakes I make for the furtherance of his kingdom and even the good of his servants. What is still better, he can keep me from making mistakes. For this I pray and trust. For the sake of my brethren and the

Church for this I am very anxious. In God's name I shall do the best I can and leave results to the Infinite.

From Saratoga, May 17, to Mrs. Janes:

I enjoyed my last brief visit at home very much ; indeed, all I was capable of enjoying any thing. I was so depressed in my nervous system in consequence of the long-continued excitement of Conference, that I was hardly capable of any enjoyment of body or mind. These reactions are terrible. They unfit me for any duty or pleasure. It requires the utmost effort at self-government to maintain propriety of deportment or devotion of spirit. I wonder they have not broken down my health long ago. So it is God takes care of me.

The Bishop was again in Iowa, and from Iowa City, the seat of the Upper Iowa Conference, he writes to Mrs. Janes, August 23, 1859 :

I have just arrived here in safety and comfortable health ; my journey has been a prosperous one. I am hoping and praying for a pleasant conference session. . . . If every thing around us is not bright, there are bright things. The promises are never dimmed by circumstances. The smile of God is always bright and cheering. The hope of heaven is always inspiring and gladdening. There is always some light in the tabernacle of the righteous.

Again, to Mrs. Janes, from Iowa City, Aug. 26:

The season, the past conference year, has been one of great financial oppression. Some of the preachers have suffered want. Still, they are generally in good spirits. We had a most excellent missionary meeting last evening. I talked to them awhile on the great interest. This morning I had a communication from an interesting, pious, educated young lady, offering to go on a foreign mission. In Christianity there is hope for our poor humanity. I see no other agency that can adequately meet a sinful world's necessity.   May God hasten the coming of Messiah's reign !

From Kewanee, Ill., the seat of the Peoria Conference, the Bishop writes, September 5, to Miss Elizabeth :

Providence smiles on me.   I trust he also cheers you with the light of his countenance.   Yesterday was a day of much religious interest to me and the people of this place.   So many attended the love-feast in the morning that they were obliged to occupy two churches.   At half past ten o'clock I preached to a densely crowded congregation.   The windows and doors were open, and many crowded around the house and listened very attentively to the close of the service.   Just as many stood inside the house as could possibly do so.   I believe I never preached to a more crowded auditory.   I had pleasure in preaching.   After sermon I ordained nineteen deacons.   In the afternoon Brother Poe preached an excellent sermon to a full and interested congregation.   After his sermon I ordained eight elders.   I think the public services yesterday made a strong and useful impression upon the public mind.   I hope eternity will show saving results.

From Kewanee, Ill., to Mrs. Janes, Sept. 9, :

The Conference has been to me a very trying one.   We have had some of the most perplexing Church difficulties I ever had in my past experience.   I hope we have disposed of them wisely.   I have had very little sleep for three days and nights—all the time under great mental anxiety, intense study to devise means and measures to remove the difficulties.   The Conference adjourned calmly, and I hope the future will be peaceful and prosperous.   My mind is peaceful.   I feel that God has taken me to his heart.   It is marvelous how he could do it, but it is done through grace in Christ.   I am cleaving to him with full purpose of heart.   My aching body allows no more.   Love to the dear children.

From the Michigan Conference at Marshall, Mich., to Miss Elizabeth, Sept. 14:

The religious sentiments of your letter are excellent and well expressed. There is something sublime in going to heaven as an old, scarred soldier of the cross—one who can recount many conflicts with opposing influences, and triumph over them through grace. Still this is not so weighty a consideration, since we are saved and glorified not by the merit of works, but by the merits of Christ. In heaven we shall give Christ all the glory, and take no praise to ourselves on account of what we have done. Again, is it certain that those who die young will not be engaged in as high and glorious activities as they would have been if they had been continued in the Church militant? If they are, will not the reward be equally glorious? May it not be even more glorious? Is there, then, any loss in an early translation from an earthly to a heavenly sphere of action? In addition to this, while thus employed in heaven should we not be more happy than amid the struggles and conflicts of earth? If so, would it not be gain to die early? After all, is it not best to leave the question with our heavenly Father? Can we be so safe and so happy as when the all-wise God chooses our estate and our sphere of useful and glorious activities? Is it not best to submit the whole question to his love and wisdom? If he gives us earthly and probationary life and labor, shall we not accept it and be faithful and happy in it? And if he says, "Come up higher," and admits us to a diviner vocation and a more ecstatic fruition, shall we not adoringly receive it?

In the autumn of this year Bishop Janes was written to by Mr. John Hurst, a prominent and esteemed layman of Baltimore, Maryland, with the view of inducing him to change his residence from New York to that city, in so many respects the stronghold of Methodism and the joy of Methodist preachers. As will be seen from the correspondence, he declined for what he considered sufficient reasons to accede to the generous proposition:

At the suggestion of some friends I write you in regard to a matter which I have thought of frequently. You know we are without a Bishop in Baltimore since the death of Bishop Waugh. And your friends think we are entitled to a Bishop, and think you are the one they ought to have, if you can be induced to make Baltimore your residence. There would be no difficulty, I think, Bishop, with our people, in manifesting their desire in the right way to have you with us. It is useless to say more until we have your views respecting the matter.

Bishop Janes to John Hurst, Esq., New York, Dec. 12:

I regret that absence from home has prevented an earlier reply to your letter of the 28th ultimo. 1. I concur with you in the opinion that Baltimore should be the residence of one of the Bishops of the Methodist Episcopal Church. I think there are good and sufficient reasons for this. 2. I deem it unadvisable to make any movement on the subject until after the next General Conference for these reasons—As the time of the next General Conference is so near, if any one of us should move before it met our motives would be suspected, and probably our influence impaired: if at the next General Conference one of your own Conference men should be elected Bishop, it would make it undesirable for one of the present Board of Bishops to remove to your city. 3. I presume Brother Hurst will concur with me in the opinion that New York ought also to be the residence of one of the superintendents of the Church, and that I ought not to leave here until my place was supplied. This supply cannot be provided before the meeting of the General Conference. 4. After General Conference I shall be ready to do all I can consistently to effect the residence of one of our number in your city. 5. As to myself, I shall come cheerfully if I am convinced it is my duty to do so. As all my personal and family interests are here, I can only be induced to change my residence from convictions of religious duty. . . . 6. I am deeply concerned for the prosperity of Methodism in Baltimore and the regions round about it. If after the next General Conference no representative of our border Conferences is elected to the Episcopacy, I shall be willing to correspond with you and the Baltimore brethren on the question, and after consulting my family and conferring with my colleagues, to prayerfully consider the question of personal duty in the case. I shall be happy if my views commend themselves to your judgment and meet your approval.

In the spring of 1860 Bishop Janes met the Pittsburgh, New England, East Maine, and Vermont Conferences. From the session of the Vermont Conference he hastened to the General Conference, which assembled in St. James's Hall, in the City of Buffalo, New York, on May 1. All the Bishops were reported present except Bishop Simpson.

The Bishops, in their Address to the General Conference, congratulated the body on the numerical progress of the Church, and the general prosperity in every department of denominational work. The two most prominent measures which occupied the attention of the Conference were the questions of lay delegation and slavery. Certain local excitements connected with the administration of discipline, especially in the case of the so-called

Nazarites of Central and Western New York, were also dealt with, and with such results as in the main to preserve the peace of the Church, and lead the disaffected to leave its communion and to form a new organization, known as the Free Methodists.

The action upon lay delegation was simply to the effect that the General Conference was ready to grant it whenever the ministers and people should express a desire for it. This was a great advance upon the past, and showed that the General Conference was wisely adjusting itself to what it saw to be a growing tendency in the Church.

The agitation upon slavery in both State and Church had now reached its height. The presidential campaign, fairly inaugurated during the session of the Conference, promised to be the most hotly contested ever known in the history of the Nation. It was squarely upon the issue of the admission of slavery into, or its exclusion from, the new territories. The issue was drawn between the free and slave States. The whole public mind was in a ferment; and it was as impossible to keep the excitement out of an ecclesiastical assembly as out of a political one. The moral effects of the question were felt by many to be even more imperative than the political; it had risen above the realm of expediency into that of conscience. As was inevitable, the General Conference was absorbed with it. Delegates had been chosen from many of the Annual Conferences on the single test of a change in the general rules forbidding slave-holding, and constituted a large majority of the General Conference. The Committee on Slavery was composed in harmony with the views of this majority of the delegates, and a majority of the committee reported in favor of so changing the general rule as that it should read: " The buying, selling, or holding of men, women, and children with an intention to enslave them." The resolution failed of a two-thirds vote, and was lost. As this proposition had already failed of a three-fourths majority of the members of the Annual Conferences, and had now failed of a two-thirds vote of the General Conference, further action looking to a change of the general rule was abandoned. The chapter on Slavery, however, was modified so as to read: " We believe the buying, selling, or holding of human beings as chattels is contrary to the laws of God and nature, inconsistent with the golden rule, and with that rule in our Discipline which requires all who desire to remain among us to ' do no harm and to avoid evil of every kind.' "

The General Conference took the precaution to vote, almost unanimously, that the chapter thus altered "was in itself so clearly declarative and advisory as not to need any explanation." It had not, therefore, the force of law. Notwithstanding this it became a ground of offense to many minis-

11

ters and members within the slave States, and was
made the occasion by them of another secession
from the Church. The division was confined chiefly
to the territory of the Baltimore Conference. That
time-honored body, which had stood together so
firmly in the dissensions of 1844, had at last suc-
cumbed under the weight of continued agitation
and supposed grievances, and many of its best
preachers and people left the Methodist Episcopal
Church, some adhering to the Methodist Episcopal
Church, South, and a few forming themselves into
Independent Methodists.

The solicitude of our Bishop for the result of the
slavery controversy at the General Conference of
1856 will be recollected, but at this Conference
there is no word from him. There is every reason
to conclude that his views and feelings were much
the same, and undoubtedly he felt great relief when
the action fell short of extreme measures. There
is but one letter extant from the seat of the Conference, and that is of a purely incidental and friendly
sort.

To his daughter, Miss Elizabeth, May 21 :

I had rather a hard day's work yesterday. I preached twice
to large congregations, and rode ten miles between the services. Yet it was a pleasant Sabbath. I was happy in my experience and enjoyed the services of the sanctuary. I hope
they were also useful to others. I have just returned to the
city, and take a few minutes to say a word to daughter Lizzie.
It seems a long time since I saw you; I hope a shorter one

will intervene before we meet. Was yesterday a happy Sabbath to you? Was it a day of religious edification? Were you made wiser and better by its privileges? Did you go to St. Paul's, or to Greene-street, or to both? I apprehend our pew in St. Paul's will not always find its occupants there for the present. I expect old associations will hold you, however, pretty strongly to St. Paul's. There is much attraction there.*

The Bishop presided in the autumn of 1860 over the Erie, Iowa, Central Ohio, and Rock River Conferences. At the close of the Iowa Conference he went home, and after a few days' respite he returned west, accompanied by his daughter, Miss Elizabeth. It was a gratification in which he could rarely be indulged, to have the companionship of any member of his family on his episcopal tours. When circumstances did allow of it, he reveled in the pleasure.

From Bucyrus, Ohio, the seat of the Central Ohio Conference, he writes to Mrs. Janes, Sept. 19:

We reached this place about ten o'clock this morning. I presume Lizzie will give you the details of the journey. My Sunday service at Poughkeepsie was interesting to me. I think the young minister ordained is one of much fitness for the work of a missionary in India. I visited Sister Hedding. The old lady (seventy-six years) retains her mental faculties remarkably.

---

* The reference here to a possible diversion from St. Paul's to Greene-street Church, in New York city, grew out of the fact that the Rev. Charles E. Harris, to whom his eldest daughter, Miss Charlotte, had been married in the spring of this year, was pastor of Greene-street Church.

On Monday, by rising at four o'clock, A. M., and making all possible exertions, and being favored by the railroad superintendent, who permitted an express train to stop out of its regular order to accommodate me, I reached Amsterdam in time for the dedication. The services of the occasion, I judge, were very acceptable, and, I trust, useful. In order to give Lizzie an opportunity to see Niagara Falls we traveled all night. Lizzie seemed very much interested in her visit to that sublime wonder of nature, that marvelous work of God.

I expect to open the Central Ohio Conference to-morrow morning.

From Bucyrus he ran over to Dexter, Michigan, to assist Bishop Morris with the Detroit Conference. Thence he writes to Mrs. Janes, Sept. 28:

With Lizzie I came to this place at a very early hour this morning. The Detroit Conference is in session here, Bishop Morris presiding. I came with the view of aiding my colleague a little in his conference duties, and to consult him in reference to Church interests. I shall remain until Monday morning, when I expect to go to Chicago. Not having time to nurse myself my cold has to run its course. The Church is generally prosperous in most of her interests. The missionary collections are much increased. I hope time passes cheerily with you and Tillie. I hope you do not feel lonely. I think two who have so much resemblance to each other, and so much love for each other, can keep each other pleasant company. Mamma has as many of the children with her as I have with me. Equal rights equally met. I will return Lizzie soon. I am coming myself also. I think mamma will say her claims are well respected.

From Chicago, the seat of the Rock River Conference, with which the episcopal duties of the year closed, to Mrs. Janes, October 2:

˙ The itinerant part of your family reached this city last evening. Chicago is to-day in great excitement. The Republicans are having a great gathering and parade. It is said there are ten thousand "Wide Awakes" parading the streets. Much enthusiasm. To-morrow morning Conference opens. The beginning of another week of labor and anxiety. No matter, if only the business is done right, the Church prospered, and God honored. This Conference closes my conference labors for this year, the seventeenth of my episcopacy. How soon they have gone, and what a record they have in heaven. Their influence can only be measured by eternity, and comprehended by the divine Mind. The Methodist Church is a most wonderful agency. Its adaptation to educate and influence the world religiously is marvelous. There is no such power in the earth. When this organization is properly worked, and energized by the Holy Ghost, its operations are beautiful and sublime, and their spiritual results stupendous. It is of God.

The following letter from Cincinnati, December 15, to his daughter Tillie, congratulating her on her approaching birthday, was not only emblematic, but alas! all too prophetic of the early blight of her beautiful life :

It would be a great pleasure to see you and congratulate you on your thirteenth birthday. When I left home on Thursday morning the day had not dawned. Soon after, however, the eastern sky began to whiten, then to redden, and in a little time the rising sun filled the whole heavens with glory. It was one of the most charming morning scenes I ever witnessed. But the change from dawn to day was so quick and rapid that, though I was watching, I could not tell when it occurred. The one had passed away and the other had superseded it, but the transition could not be realized. Said I to myself, "Such is the transition from girlhood to maidenhood. It is so imperceptible and so rapid, that even the parent

who is watching it daily is not conscious of the progress."
Thought I, " So it will be with Tillie, whom I have just left,
Before we realize it, she will be passing into womanhood."
Ere noon we ran into a storm cloud. All was dark, and the
snow fell fast and the wind howled through the forest. Soon
the clouds parted and the sun shone brightly. Again the
whole heavens were clouded and the storm was furious. In a
little time, however, the sun appeared bright and beautiful, and
the evening was unclouded, lovely, and serene as was the
morning. "Such," I said, "is human life. It is with none of
us constant sunshine ; all have trouble and suffering." Now,
beautiful as has been the morning of your life, I apprehend
your future will have some clouds—some suffering—but I believe the clouds will pass away and the sun always be in your
heavens.

It fell to the lot of Bishop Scott to preside over
the Baltimore Conference, March 13–25, 1861, at
Staunton, Va. A convention of laymen from the
territory of the Baltimore Conference had met in
Baltimore City in December, 1860, and had taken
strong action against the new chapter on slavery,
and had called another convention to meet at the
time and place of the ensuing Baltimore Conference.
A difficult and stormy session was consequently
anticipated, and all the Bishops looked forward to
it with much anxiety. The following letter from
Bishop Janes to Bishop Scott will give at least a
glimpse of this feeling. It is dated at New York,
March 4, 1861 :

I have just returned to the city, and hasten to reply to yours
of 25th instant. As I understand it, I was appointed to go to
the Baltimore Conference only as your assistant. There is no

other reason for my going that I know of. If you feel that, owing to existing circumstances, you can do better or as well without me, there is no propriety in my going. I have heard nothing from them by way of objection to my being with you, but it would not be reasonable for me to expect to hear it, as delicacy would probably prevent any one from communicating with me on the question. The time required to attend the Baltimore Conference will be valuable to me, and I shall not go on unless you have seen reason to change your mind since you wrote and request me to come. When the arrangement was made for me to accompany you I thought it was to be a confidential matter. I soon, however, received a letter from Baltimore, stating that the writer understood I was to accompany you to the Baltimore Conference, and requesting me to spend Sabbath, the 10th instant, in Baltimore. Since it was known that I was expected to be with you I have said so to different persons. If the report should be started that I had failed to be there through timidity I am confident Bishop Scott will correct it. This is the only delicacy on my part, and this is of small moment. I have no apprehension that violence or even indignity will be offered you. You will have perplexities and difficulties. I shall pray incessantly that God will aid and direct you. I believe he will do it. I now make the following requests: 1. Write me, to Philadelphia, every aspect matters put on and every decision you make. This is very important, that we may harmonize in our administration. It would be very unfortunate if we should decide questions differently under the same class of circumstances. 2. Come to the Philadelphia Conference as soon as your duties and health will possibly admit. I do not wish to do any thing to weaken your administration two years ago.

Bishop Janes did not attend the Conference, but he and Bishop Scott were in·frequent correspondence. Bishop Scott writes him from Staunton, March 13:

I thank you for your prompt response to my letter, and I am gratified to find that we so nearly agree as to the new chapter. It is, indeed, a remarkable coincidence of view that I had already changed the expression of my judgment on the effect of the substitution, etc., to exactly the point you name, " is to place the official and private member on the same platform," etc.

Bishop Scott deported himself throughout these proceedings, during which numerous and most perplexing questions had to be answered *impromptu*, with the utmost wisdom, impartiality, and firmness, and, to the credit of the Conference let it be recorded, as Bishop Janes had intimated, he was treated with all possible consideration and courtesy. And although a majority of the Conference voted to separate from the Church, by his judicious rulings the integrity of the old Baltimore Conference of the Methodist Episcopal Church was preserved.

Bishop Janes met the Philadelphia Conference in Philadelphia, Pa., March 20–30. He had not a very large number of preachers to station, but, under the excitement, the fixing of the appointments required extreme care. The slave territory of this Conference was scarcely less agitated than that of the Baltimore Conference, and heavy local secessions, especially in Lower Maryland and Virginia, took place. Writing to Mrs. Janes, from the chair of the Conference, March 26, he says :

I trust you are this morning exulting in the love of God, and sweetly anticipating the joys of heaven. I am under a great pressure of duty, but am joyful and hopeful in God. I love God, and am seeking to glorify him in my official and private life. This is my highest joy. Yesterday the Conference was engaged mainly with devotional services. There is all the embarrassment I anticipated in the business of the Conference. My health, my experience, my efforts, will be taxed to the utmost in making the appointments. Some secessions will undoubtedly take place. A part of the Conference is violently agitated.

The Bishop next met in rapid succession the North Indiana, New Hampshire, and Oneida Conferences.

From Utica, New York, the seat of the Oneida Conference, he writes to Miss Elizabeth, April 20:

An incident occurred on my way here that it will do to laugh over a little. You know I had traveled all night the previous one to my starting for this place, and was much fatigued with conference labors, consequently was inclined to be very sleepy. I kept awake until I had changed cars at Albany, and then inquired of the conductor when he would wake me for my ticket. He said, before reaching Utica. So I placed myself in the arms of Morpheus for a refreshing snooze. As I took it to be a necessity for the conductor to wake me before he left the train at Utica I felt no care about waking. The conductor, however, for some reason unknown to me, did not ask me for my ticket. The consequence was my nap was not broken until I had passed Utica. Another conductor passed through the cars to examine tickets and awoke me. I at once comprehended the fact that I was going away from the seat of my Conference at the rate of thirty miles an hour. It was not a pleasant state of things by any means. But what was the use of fretting about it? It would not stop the cars or in any respect better the condition of affairs. So I calmly sat me down for a work of supererogation, an extra ride of fifteen miles to

11*

the next station. I waited there, in the depot, two hours for a return train, in which I reached Utica about six o'clock in the morning.

O! how much I wish to get out to Mount Wesley a few days to snuff the mountain air, to drink its pure water, to see its opening flowers, to gambol over the hills and feel a little freedom from cares and official anxieties and the teasings of committees and the pleadings of preachers, etc., etc., etc., etc.

CHAPTER XIV.

1861–1863.

Visits Europe—The Christian Commission—Perplexities at the Baltimore Conference—Spring and Autumn Conferences—Second Visit to the Pacific Coast.

THE General Conference instructed the Bishops to visit the missions in Western Europe during this quadrennial term, and Bishop Janes was designated to discharge the duty; he accordingly sailed for Liverpool, England, June 5, where he arrived on the 16th of the month. He proceeded at once to Bremen, Germany, the seat of the German Mission Conference, and opened its session on the 20th, fourteen days from New York. The Rev. L. S. Jacoby had established the first Methodist mission in Germany, at Bremen, in 1849, and this had now grown to the proportions of an Annual Conference, extending as far south as Zurich, Switzerland, comprising 2,181 members and probationers, and 22 ministers, with a flourishing publishing house, and a Biblical Institute for the training of young ministers, located at Bremen.

From Bremen to Mrs. Janes, June 25:

This Mission Conference opened on the 20th inst. The number of members is small in comparison with some of our large Conferences in the States, but the brethren seem possessed of a good spirit, and some of them are men of high attainments. Our devotional services have had a special zest. Sometimes they have been performed in English and sometimes in the German language. About half of the brethren can understand the English language. From the reports I receive I am satisfied that this mission work in Northern Europe is a very important part of our Church enterprise. It was a needed and is a repaying work. God's approbation is upon it. Brother and Sister Warren are much pleased, and very happy. He is a very good and truly great man.* "The Life of Hester Ann Rogers," which you paid to have translated into the German language, is being circulated in this land, and, of course, with good effect. I very much wish to hear from home, and from my poor distracted country. It is wonderful what interest is felt in Europe on the subject of our war. It is in every paper, and the general topic of conversation every-where. It is a great question. It involves the destinies of millions yet unborn, as well as millions now living. I pray God the right may prevail.

From the same point, two days later, I meet his first allusion to the civil war, which followed so soon upon the inauguration of President Lincoln. In that stern and bloody conflict no man in civil life stood more firmly for the maintenance of the Union, for the vindication of the laws, or more thoroughly supported, in his legitimate sphere, the efforts of the national government for the suppression of the Rebellion. This he did not so much by fierce denunciation of those in rebellion, as by earnest, wise words, and noble, self-sacrificing deeds. Writing to Tillie, he says:

I expect you have heard the drum very often lately. I am sorry men will be so wicked as to make it necessary to fight. Our beloved country is passing through great trials. I believe

* Rev. W. F. Warren, D.D., now President of Boston University.

Providence will take care of our noble, free institutions. I expect the world will sing, "Hail! Columbia!" many generations hence.

The Bishop met the Scandinavian missionaries at Copenhagen, and returning through Berlin went as far south as Zurich, Switzerland, visiting the German and Swiss missions. From Zurich he crossed to Paris. He was a close observer of all that he saw, though indulging but little in minute descriptions. Among the objects on the Continent which especially impressed him, was the mausoleum which the late king, Frederick William IV., and brother of the present king, William, built to his parents at Potsdam, near Berlin.

It is built in the depths of an ornamental forest. As you approach it through the densely shaded avenue, the solitude inspires you with a pleasing solemnity. The mausoleum is built of the most solid and elegant masonry. The main room is circular, the ceiling oval. It receives light from the top, which falls through stained glass so arranged as to create the most delicate blending of shadows and mellowed radiance I ever beheld. The room itself is perfectly plain. The walls have a few costly pictures. Near the center, over the graves of their majesties, is a marble tomb, elevated about three feet, on which are full-sized marble figures, representing the king and queen lying in state. The marble is of the purest and whitest kind that can be found, and the workmanship is most exquisite.

In Paris Bishop Janes stopped only for a few days, where, in addition to all the sights and sounds of that wondrous city, he was refreshed by the companionship of his early and genial friend, the

Rev. Dr. J. M'Clintock, who was at the time pastor of the American Chapel.

To Mrs. Janes, July 18:

You see by the heading of this that I have arrived in this wonderful French city. I am at the house of Dr. M'Clintock. I expect to leave here for London to-morrow morning. I have been out sight-seeing some since I have been here. I am going this morning to see the Palace at Versailles and the tomb of Napoleon. These are all I intend to visit. The rest of the day must be spent in writing. I think more highly of France and the French people than I did before I saw them. I have enjoyed reading some of our New York papers here very much. Dr. M'Clintock has them up to July 11. I am pained at the state of affairs in our beloved country. Still I am hopeful, trusting in God and not in man, or in armies of men. God puts down and puts up who and when he pleases. I believe he has a blessing in store for our nation when we are sufficiently humbled to receive it in a right spirit and ready properly to improve it. I am even more concerned for the welfare of the Church. I fear our missionary treasury will become greatly embarrassed, and our mission work crippled. Still in this, too, I hope in God. His resources are illimitable, and his love to his Church cannot fail.

Dr. M'Clintock, in a letter from Paris, July 27, to his son, Mr. Emory M'Clintock, makes the following brief reference to the Bishop's visit : " Bishop Janes spent three days of this week here . . . he enjoyed his stay highly . . . and I rode about with him all the time showing him the sights." *

From Paris the Bishop went over to England. He was present at the Wesleyan Conference, and

* " Life and Letters of Rev. Dr. M'Clintock." By George R. Crooks, D.D., p. 303.

mingled freely with the Methodist ministers and people.   In his public addresses and private conversations he did not lose sight of the one absorbing topic of the hour with every American, at home or abroad.   He did all he could to promote a correct understanding of the great controversy between the North and the South.   Dr. M'Clintock, in a letter to him after his return to America, thus refers to his work in England:

Your services in England were exceedingly useful both to our Church and to the country.   The appreciation of them in the newspapers is flattering to you, but is not so valuable as that I receive from private sources—especially from William Arthur, whose judgment and sympathy are worth more than any other in the British Conference.   He speaks in the warmest and most exalted terms of your visit and its results.   I am very thankful you were able to go.

The Bishop returned the latter part of August, and presided in September at the North Ohio and Ohio Conferences.   In the winter he made a brief visit to Washington, D. C., and thence went to Springfield, O., to attend the semi-annual meeting of the Board of Bishops.   From Washington, December 9, he writes to Mrs. Janes:

On Saturday I went over to Virginia to see a review of some twenty-five thousand troops.   To-day I have been to see the President, the War and Navy and Treasury buildings, the Capitol, both houses of Congress, and the Supreme Court.   I have also been gathering what information I could on subjects connected with the Christian Commission.

The Bishop refers in this letter to the Christian Commission.   He was connected· from the first with this noble organization as one of the Executive Committee.   His name on the printed list stands, next to the honored President of the Commission, Mr. George H. Stuart, of Philadelphia. But more of this as the war progresses.

Immediately after the meeting of the Bishops at Springfield, O., he ·writes to his daughter, Miss Lizzie, from Delaware, O., Dec. 17 :

We adjourned yesterday, and I immediately took the cars and started for New York.   But when I reached this place I felt too unwell to risk the two-nights' journey to New York and then an all-night ride back to Buffalo, so I stopped here to be quiet and muse a little and get well.   I took a very hard cold in Washington.   I slept better last night and cough less to-day.   I expect a couple of days of quiet in a warm room and a little medicine will restore me.   Now I have told you the worst.   I am stopping with Rev. Dr. Merrick, President of the Ohio Wesleyan University.

I have referred to the action of a majority of the Baltimore Conference at its last session (1861.) The session of the spring of 1862 could not be otherwise than a very critical one.   The breaking out of the war had further complicated the difficulties.   Bishop Janes was assigned to the presidency. There was some opposition to his coming on the part of the seceding element, and there was a slight war of words in the daily papers of Baltimore. But he went calmly forward to the post of duty,

and how well he conducted himself and the business of the Conference the sequel has shown.

Writing to Mrs. Janes from Baltimore, March 4:

I reached this city between four and five Saturday afternoon. On Sunday I preached in the evening to a large congregation. At three o'clock I addressed the class-leaders of
the city and vicinity, who, to the number of five hundred or
more, were seated in the body of the church. They were a
noble looking assembly of men, of most imposing and impressive presence. My address seemed to be well received. I
hope it will be useful. Yesterday, from early morn to late at
night, I was in the company of church committees, or brethren
making calls to state their own cases, or some of the elder
members of the Conference coming to renew their acquaintance and to inquire after my welfare, etc. But all had to
question me on my views respecting the anomalous position
of the Conference and my plan of procedure, etc. Of course
they must be answered courteously. To do this and not commit myself or my plans so as to embarrass me hereafter required me to think twice before I spoke once. We shall have
some very delicate and difficult and very responsible questions
to settle. Party strife is very violent. There is a wall of fire
all around me; go which way I will I must be burned. Or, in
other words, some will be offended and blame me. But that
is one of the kind of burns the balm of Gilead cures. So it is
not a very serious affair. I am only anxious to do right, to
promote the peace and prosperity of the Church, and the honor
of God. If the newspapers discuss me for the next five years
you will understand I expect to survive it and be happy, because I shall try to do right. I should like to have a little
home sunshine on my heart this morning. I am glad you can
look into each other's faces.

The address to class-leaders, which was delivered
in Baltimore and elsewhere, and which was subse-

quently printed in tract form, was a forcible presentation of this important institution of Methodism. The Bishop, impressed as he was not only with the usefulness of the class-meeting in itself, but with its necessity as an integral part of Methodism, especially in its complementary relation to an itinerant ministry, sought most earnestly and intelligently to revive the love for it in the hearts of the people, and to promote attendance upon it. I quote but a single sentence from this admirable paper :

Where else in the Church is found such intimacy, such stated seasons of fellowship, such familiar conversation on Christian experience, such sympathy, so much helping of each other's faith, and such watching over one another in love ? This social benefit of this means of grace is sufficient to give it interest and favor with all who have a relish for the fellowship of saints, and to make it useful in any Church which will adopt it.

From the chair of the Baltimore Conference, March 6–11, he writes to Mrs. Janes :

One day's session of the Conference has passed. Troubles have been initiated, I fear. Still, matters look no worse than they did before the Conference began. The Church belongs to Christ. He bought it, owns it, it is dear to him. He must take care of it. I cannot, only as he directs and uses me. My days and nights are anxious ones. As yet we have had no great excitement. The agitating subject is now up, and how soon we may be in a storm I cannot foresee. I trust in God. I seek his guidance and help.

From the Baltimore he passed in quick succession to the New Jersey, New England, and New

York East Conferences. From Westfield, the seat
of the New England Conference, he writes to Mrs.
Janes, April 2 :

My journey was an uncomfortable one, because I was sick.
The first two hours I had a hard chill, the rest of the way a
high fever. When my fever was raging I made poetry, elab-
orated speeches, and did all manner of things. On arriving
at Springfield I went immediately to the hotel, drank three
tumblers of ice water, and went to bed. After a little the
fever left me, and I began to perspire. I slept pretty well. , I
took cars at six in the morning for here, and have attended to
all my official duties during the day, though quite unwell.

In the month of May the venerable Nathan
Bangs, D.D., died in the city of New York, and
was buried from St. Paul's Church. The Bishop,
who had so long and intimately known this great
man of Methodism, in the funeral sermon, after very
fitly and concisely presenting the outlines of his
character and work, thus beautifully describes his
latest years :

Like the descending sun in the western sky, disrobed of his
meridian splendors and deprived of his noontide fervor, unclouded, full-orbed, with mellow radiance we see him slowly
and serenely descending the horizon of life. Most enchanting
was the moral beauty with which his cheerful old age was
invested.

After the spring Conferences had closed he was
busy with all manner of work, giving as much attention as possible to the claims of the Christian
Commission.

June 7, he writes : "I have been engaged much of my time with the Christian Commission. We have had three sessions, and have another this evening."

On August 28 he bade adieu to missionaries about to sail for India, and then was off again, "a militant necessity," for Conferences in the North-west. Reaching Chicago, after many detentions by the way, he performed there and at Evanston a round of exhausting labors, and then went on to Dodgeville, Wis., the seat of the West Wisconsin Conference. Subsequently he attended the Upper Iowa, North-west Wisconsin, Wisconsin, and Illinois Conferences.

From M'Gregor, Indiana, he thus writes to his daughter, Miss Lizzie, in response to her patriotic feelings :

I am pleased to know that you appreciate our civil and religious liberties, and would be willing to battle bravely for them. Our country now needs gentle influences as well as mighty ones. To preserve the social integrity of the country is as important as to maintain its constitutional integrity. If our social, religious, and moral interests perish, our political condition is hardly a matter of concern. It is quite as high an office, quite as important a service, to preserve the soul of the nation as it is to protect the body politic. The wielding these moral forces is fully as noble and dignified as that of directing and employing its physical agencies. I do not think any lady need envy the gentlemen their mere physical superiority. The æsthetical, the moral and religious influences she may wield so effectively are much more noble. and at least equally potential in molding national character and determining national destiny. I think, too, that here is a sphere in which she can usefully employ all her patriotism. The donning a military uniform and fighting the battles of freedom is perhaps a more imposing manifestation of patriotism than the quiet, delicate moral agency of the maiden who is the charm of the family group, the ornament of the social circle, and the mistress of public taste and manners ; but it is not certain that the exercise of genuine patriotism in the former case is either more real or more useful than in the latter.

A correspondent from the Upper Iowa Conference says of Bishop Janes's presiding :

Bishop Janes was present, and presided with his usual ability. A great many members thought that his address to the candidates for deacon's orders, and his sermon on Sabbath morning, exceeded any thing they ever heard from him. Bishop Janes has presided with us more frequently than any other Bishop ; but, if we judge the future by the past, he will never come without meeting a cordial greeting from the members.

Few men referred less in conversation to their entertainment than Bishop Janes, and no one was ever a guest who was more careful to avoid giving trouble to his hostess. An extract from a letter to his daughter, Miss Lizzie, in reference to his home at M'Gregor, may serve to encourage young house keepers, and will be appreciated for its delicate allusions. It will be seen, also, that he was ready for Mr. Lincoln's Proclamation of Emancipation.

My home at M'Gregor was a small but tasty cottage on a hill-side, simply furnished, as orderly and neat as a Christian sanctuary need be. The table was all I could desire, and as I desired. Never did sweet, light bread seem such a luxury. The simplest article of diet was a dainty, because prepared exactly as it should be. My bed was as comfortable as any I ever occupied. All my surroundings were charming. It was an illustration of how much comfort and elegance and happiness can be enjoyed in a small home, with simple means. Now shall I give you the cause *why* of all this? The lady was from Newark, N. J., the city of your mother's nativity. The gentleman was from Baltimore, and a cousin of our friend, Mr. Henry J. Baker. Are not these sufficient reasons? And now I wish to say I enjoyed their intelligent Christian society even more than their generous hospitality. May God bless them! My home in this place, Hudson, Wis., is a very good one. We have two Methodist churches here, and they are so jealous of each other they could not agree upon a Methodist home for the Bishop. So they settled the dispute by sending me to a Congregational family. We have just received in these ends of civilization the President's Emancipation Proclamation. It is a solemn transaction, a good measure. I hope the nation and God will approve and sustain it. The Lord reigns, let the earth rejoice!

From the session of the Illinois Conference at Bloomington, Ill., October 8, 11, and 13, he writes home :

My conference sessions, so far, on this tour have been very pleasant. No great excitement in the Conferences. All matters have been controllable. I have never preached on conference occasions with more satisfaction. I trust God will give me his gracious presence. I expect to come home with a good conscience. I hope to find you all happy. We must all get to heaven—then, when any of us take an excursion of duty or pleasure, we can all go along. Will we not be a happy family then? Really, for the short time we are in this world the question of our circumstances is not a very grave one. Preached long yesterday. No recommendation to the sermon, but it shows I had something to say.   In the evening I ordained the German ministers in the German church.

The following letter to Mrs. Gov. Wright, (then Mrs. Deuel,) of New York, dated December 31, will show the Bishop's estimate not only of the Five Points' Mission, in New York, but also of the faithful part taken in the mission by this devout Christian lady :

I have long wished in some appropriate manner to express to you my high appreciation of the zeal, patience, perseverance, and skill with which you have prosecuted your arduous and difficult missionary work at the Five Points, in this city.   When in Switzerland, last summer, I saw the accompanying little articles, which were manufactured in Jerusalem out of the wood of the olive-tree, by self-supporting missionaries.   They have no intrinsic value, but I deem their association with the Holy Land, and with self-denying gratuitous missionary labors, make them significant of my sentiments respecting your missionary services before mentioned.   God and duty.   Wishing you a happy New-year.

Early in 1863 the Bishop is found busy dedicating a church near Philadelphia, attending missionary meetings at Baltimore, and engaged with the departments at Washington in the interest of the Methodist missions and the Christian Commission. He and Dr. Durbin officiated in the City Station, Baltimore, and raised missionary contributions to the amount of $2,250, " six times as much as last year." Again, in the depths of winter, he is engaged in a missionary-speaking tour in Central New York.   Writing from Utica, N. Y., February 2, he says, " A full day's work, yesterday. The people will not admit that I am growing old, so they hold me to a young man's work. I start in a few minutes for Rome, where we have missionary meetings this afternoon and evening."

In March and April Bishop Janes met the Pittsburgh, Providence, Wyoming, and Black River Conferences. The Bishop was assigned to the Pacific coast Conferences again this year, and he accordingly sailed from New York June 23. The circumstances of his leaving home for this long and arduous journey were peculiarly painful, because of the illness of his youngest daughter. There was a violent struggle between the parental nature and the sense of official obligation, but, as usual, the latter prevailed. His correspondence while away is full of affectionate solicitude for his darling Tillie. From the steamer "Ocean Queen" his first fugitive note, accompanying a daily record of his voyage, is to her:

I send these little leaves as an evidence that I think of you, and would write if I could. I hope you are daily improving. Especially I hope you are saved from suffering. May our heavenly Father smile on you continually!

Writing to Mrs. Janes the same date, he says:

The captain, indeed all on board, have treated me with uncommon courtesy and deference. On Sunday, at their invitation, I preached twice. The people were attentive. We have two Presbyterian ministers on board, but they excused themselves on account of being sick. So was I, but I could not lose such an opportunity to preach Christ. I intend they shall preach next Sabbath. I cannot write more than one letter a day without making me ill. Hoping it may give an hour of recreation to dear Tillie, as she lies on her restless couch, I cut the leaves from the little memoranda I have kept, and send them to her. I hope it may make a little break in the monotony of the sick-room. I trust she is improving, and will soon be able to go to the concert of the birds and the banquet of the flowers. O how I should relish just four of the luscious cherries from Mount Wesley!

To his daughter, Mrs. Harris, who was also an invalid at the time, he thus playfully describes himself as a prisoner on shipboard, steamship "Constitution," Pacific Ocean, July 10:

I can appreciate your confinement, for I am a more closely kept prisoner than you are. O, if I could only walk out, call on a neighbor, do an errand, any thing to break this monotony! Just the same move of the engine, the same motions of the boat, the same steps to the table, the same place to sit down, the same noise of children, the same sights of novel-reading and card-playing, the same expanse of waters, the same blue sky, the same burning sun, the same bad feelings! A monotony of discomforts! Still every evolution of the engine, every time the vessel rises and falls as she crosses the waves, brings us nearer our desired haven. Every time we pretend to take a meal we leave the number of such occasions less on board. Every diurnal revolution of the burning sun measures off a large piece of the distance that remains of our tedious voyage. So there is a pleasant aspect of the affair. It is somewhat difficult to find it and enjoy it, nevertheless it is a real bright view—a silver lining to the cloud. I try to keep my eye on it.

To his daughter Tillie, a few days afterward:

12

How is Miss Appetite? She is a fickle maid, a good deal
of a coquette. By the by, our captain is a foxy old fellow. It
is the usage for the captain to select those who sit at his table.
He likes his champagne at dinner; he is a jolly old man, likes
wit and jokes and fun. The captain knew I did not drink
wine, and that I would be a little constraint upon the hilarity
and conviviality of the company if I was in their midst, and
yet he wished to treat me with respect. So he sends the steward with the captain's compliments to Bishop Janes, with the
request that he would preside at the other end of the table.
As far from him as possible and be at his table, but still a dignity to be appreciated. So I complacently accepted the honor.
The cunning old man, somehow or other, found just which of
his table guests used wine and which did not, and he seated
those who use it at his end of the table, and those who do not
at my end of the table. So we are arranged as if by elective
affinities. I do not think it was an accident, unless, as the
boys used to say, "it was an accident done on purpose." At
any rate, it has been very pleasant to be in congenial company.
I have the same captain and officers that were on the steamer
I went out in in 1857. They all remembered me, and really
seemed pleased to see me. The doctor told me he remembered the sermon I preached at that time. The steward re-
newed his acquaintance by bringing me some oranges. I
think it is evidence that I behaved pretty well at that time. It
also shows that a minister should always and every-where be
on his good behavior, as he is always a watched man.

The Bishop, after arriving at San Francisco, immediately visited Santa Clara, the seat of the Methodist University, and a few points in California, and
started on July 27 for the Oregon Conference.

To Mrs. Janes, from Marysville, Cal., July 30:

I start at two o'clock in the stage for Oregon. Shall ride
all night to-night; to-morrow cross the Trinity Mountains,

and, by traveling all night to-morrow night, reach Yreka about noon on Saturday. A long, hard ride is before me, but I intend to enjoy it. God lives all along the road, and I expect to converse with him and enjoy his presence and intercommunion. If it was not too familiar and seemingly irreverent language, I would say I expect him to be my traveling companion. Enoch walked with God, why may I not ride with him? Faith gives us some wonderful realizations, marvelous apprehensions, and glorious fruitions. Faith, hope, and love are a trinity of powers adequate to transform and spiritualize and beautify poor sinners here in their probationary state; to make this estate of warfare, of trials and of toils, one of peace and of comforts and of rest; to make time a holy moment of eternity; to make death a sweet passing out of this moment of time into the ages of eternity; a mere stepping out of the ark of safety on to the Ararat of immortality.

The Bishop took the overland route to Oregon and back, wishing to see the state of the country and the Churches, and also desiring the dry mountain air for his health. I give some extracts from his letters on this journey.

From Yreka, Cal., August 1 :

I feel I did right in coming to this coast this summer. As this work was assigned me all the consequences must be right. My mind is serene and hopeful. I preach with full my usual pleasure, and preach short. I try to hit the nail on the head quick. I hope to quarry out, and perhaps polish, some lively stones from these Pacific quarries.

From Salem, Oregon, August 8 :

I find it a trial to be so long without knowing the state of affairs in the East in these times when such great events are occurring. To be a month without knowing what has taken place taxes one's self-control pretty thoroughly to maintain equanimity of feelings. To this time I know very little of the operations of the mob in New York. Still, momentous as are national movements and occurrences, I could wait quite patiently to learn them if I could only get daily or even weekly domestic news. Good is the will of the Lord. I think I am in my place of duty. I find these Conferences here greatly needed a Bishop this year. There are serious troubles in both Conferences—serious, at best, in their results: undoubtedly much more serious if there was no Bishop present with authority and experience to direct and control them. I trust God will make my visit to these Conferences and Churches and States promotive of his cause and kingdom among the people.

From Albany, Oregon, August 11, to the home circle :

We must appreciate and improve the good conferred in order to be qualified to receive and enjoy and rightly estimate other gifts. The martyr in his cell would be unwise to refuse to use and enjoy the few rays of light that struggle through his grated window because it did not, through a broad, bright window, blaze all about him. The mariner would be very unwise to refuse to take his observations from a star because the clouds concealed the sun. So it is error in us to refuse or fail to enjoy the blessings of our lot because they are not more or greater. If we have pleasant sights for the eye do not let us fail to enjoy them because we have not at the same time pleasant sounds for the ear and pleasant tastes for the palate. If we have pleasant rooms and good beds and comfortable chairs and beautiful pictures and fragrant bouquets, do not let us disregard them or fail to enjoy them because we cannot be in Central Park and amid rural scenes of verdure and beauty. If we have at home a Bible and a closet and a mercy-seat we will not neglect to improve and enjoy them because we cannot go to the sanctuary to worship God.

From Yreka, Cal., August 21, to the home circle :

We have traveled most of the way here in large covered wagons; most of the way from here we shall have regular stage coaches. So I consider myself more than half over my staging on my return journey. As I shall not travel on Sunday, I cannot reach Marysville until Monday night—some time in the night. My journey has been a rough one, and some rough fare; for instance, night before last, in the night, the stage stopped four hours. I tried to get a bed, but the landlord said his beds were all full. I asked for a lounge or any thing of the kind, but he had nothing. After much palaver I got a blanket and the privilege of lying on the floor in an open, cold room. I made the best of it, and slept three hours soundly; woke up very stiff and sore, paid half a dollar for the use of a plank and a blanket for three hours, and started off again, thankful for my sleep under disadvantages.

September 1, about to start for Napa City, the seat of the California Conference, the Bishop's yearning heart cries out homeward:

Can't you send a zephyr across the continent to tell me how you all are this morning? O how gladly would I listen to his message! Well, I suppose all I can do is, to pray, and hope for the best.

The following incident connected with the Bishop's preaching in San Francisco at this time is noticed in the "San Francisco Star:"

While Bishop Janes was preaching to a crowded audience, in the basement of the new church now being erected on Howard-street, the gas suddenly went out, leaving the congregation in total darkness. The Bishop, with rare presence of mind, remarked, "The Gospel light shineth in dark places," and continued his discourse; and such was the charm of his naturally weak, but admirably modulated and controlled voice, that none of his large audience moved from their positions, but perfect silence and order were observed until light was obtained. To the ear nothing indicated that any thing unusual had occurred. The effect of listening to a discourse uttered amid darkness was singular in the extreme.

The Bishop returned from the Pacific coast by the overland route, then a long and tedious journey of three weeks. He had written home, before leaving California, that a telegram should be sent as to the health of the family, to meet him at Fort Kearney by a certain date. The wires had only just been laid. On the very day he had named came the message, " Matilda the same. Charlotte still about. Mother and I well." Cheered, he went on his way.

CHAPTER XV.

1863–1865.

Death of his daughter Tillie—Lay Delegation—General Conference at Philadelphia—Loyalty and services in the War—Second visit to Europe.

IN the autumn and winter of this year the Bishop had seen his daughter Tillie gradually and certainly failing. No skill or nursing or solicitude could arrest the progress of the destroyer. The writer was the pastor of the family at the time, and was permitted to minister at the sick-bed of this devout young Christian. In person and mind she bore a marked resemblance to her father. Converted to God when she was fifteen years of age, through the instrumentality of Mr. J. M. Bradstreet, her Bible class teacher, she rapidly developed into a very intelligent, active, and fervent believer. She used to say, "I try to get right in front of Mr. Bradstreet, that I may catch every word he speaks."

During the special revival services held at St. Paul's, in the winter and spring of 1862–63, she was a constant attendant, and no one manifested a closer sympathy with the pastor in his work. Her last illness was painful and protracted, but through it all her faith was unshaken and her unselfishness supreme. She thought less of herself than of others. Her constant inquiry was as to the success of the Sunday-school and the work of religion among her young friends. The pastor quoting to her, on one occasion, a text from which he had preached the previous Sunday, " Whom having not seen, ye love," she quickly responded, " Whom having *felt*, I love." As she approached the dying hour she said, " I have come down to the river; Jesus has me all tucked up in his arms. He will get me over somehow. Love me a little when I have gone." On the missionary day at St. Paul's, the first Sunday after her death, Mrs. Janes sent a note to the pastor saying: " The inclosed ten dollars belonged to our dear Tillie. It was her dying request that it should be given to the Missionary Society through her beloved Bible class." Thus was her heart in its last pulsations in unison with the great missionary spirit.

This bereavement deeply affected the Bishop. There could be discerned under the calm exterior a deep and pensive sadness that indicated how violent was the struggle in his manly breast. But Christian faith and hope triumphed over his natural sorrow. How marked the contrast between his conduct and that of the renowned Cicero under like conditions! No ancient philosopher had written more clearly and plausibly of immortality than the eloquent Roman; but when death snatched away his beloved Tullia he was inconsolable; wandering

from grove to sea-side, he built shrines to her memory, but could not be comforted because she had
gone he knew not whither.   How confidently and
serenely this Christian parent looked up to the great
and merciful Father, and was assured of the immortality and happiness of his dead, is well attested by
the following letter which he addressed to Tillie
soon after her translation:

When it was your turn for a letter from father before, for
reasons I need not name, I did not address you. But as your
turn has come again I feel unwilling to pass you. This will
not be the first letter I ever wrote you which I did not expect
you would read. I wrote you many in your early childhood that
dear mother had to read to you. I have also written you
many I did not expect you would answer, not only in your
childhood, but during your long illness. It was a happiness
to me to write you. I cannot expect you will answer this letter with pen and ink. That beautiful hand—it will not make
you vain to say there never was a more beautiful one—will
never write "dear papa" again. I am not certain but that
you may see this letter, and as an evidence of loving remembrance it may give you a pleasurable emotion. At any rate I
like to continue this habit of love, of writing to you. I am not
sure I have any news to tell you. Have you not been cogni-
zant of all my doings since you left me? Have you not witnessed my travels and services? Perhaps so, and consequently
I can give you no information concerning myself. Though
you may be acquainted with our outward circumstances, I
doubt whether you can read our hearts. You may know from
the tear on the cheek that we are unhappy, or from the smile
on our lips that we are rejoicing, but the cause and character
of our experience probably you may not discern. I do not
think you know how lonely and sad we felt after you left us.
While we had your precious body with us our loss was but
12*

partial. But when in the most delicate, honored, and religious manner possible we had laid that out of our sight, and realized that its eyes would no longer beam on us, its lips no more address us, or face no more smile on us until the resurrection morning, we felt very desolate. There was a great vacancy in our sweet home, an irrepressible desire for the loved presence, an anxious looking for her appearance, and then the painful recollection, she will never come—O ! it was a wonderful experience ! With me it still remains—I think will ever continue until you hail me partaker of your glory. Even if I knew you would read this statement I should not fear it would pain you. I believe all painful experience with you is past. But if you were susceptible of sorrowful emotions, I do not think this knowledge would make you unhappy. In the light that now shines upon you, you understand the reason for this providence, you see how it works for our good. God's ways are all plain and pleasing to you. " Alleluia, for the Lord God omnipotent reigneth," is the song of your heart. And if you know our sorrows, you also know our joys. You know how God comforts us.

You also know how frequent our recollections of you are ; how sweet and strong our assurance is that Jesus will watch your sleeping dust, and bid it rise again like unto his glorious body. You know how we have delighted to think of you as enjoying the beatitudes of the heavenly estate. I have allowed myself to imagine how things occurred with you, and how they seemed to you as you entered the realm of glory. I have thought it not improbable that the spirit of him who enabled you by faith to " Behold the Lamb of God who taketh away the sin of the world," had some agency in bringing you to the open vision of the glorious Saviour. I am certain that vision was not withheld from you. To see Christ as he is, O ! who could turn away from that entertaining sight even to look after loved and loving friends upon earth ? Still I believe such are the powers of the glorified spirits that somehow or other, while they enjoy heaven they are familiar with earth. I can never cease to love Tillie—I do not believe she will ever cease to love me. Because I love you I rejoice in your happiness.

Tillie, I know where you are; you are not lost. I know what you are. This knowledge of your welfare, how it comforts me! I am willing you should be there. I would not call you away. I had rather pass through what remains to me of life without the cheer of your presence than interrupt your enjoyment of your Saviour, or divert you from his praise. I suppose you have seen angels and seraphs—and the spirits of the just made perfect. How glad aunty was to welcome you! Have you not seen grandpapa and grandmamma? You did not know them in this world. I judge they have found you, and rejoiced with you ere this. Have you ever thought, "I wish father and mother and brother and sisters knew how happy I am?" Well, we do know all we can comprehend—thank God for the holy Bible! Let me assure you we are coming to see you; we shall let our heavenly Father set the time, but we are all coming. The time may seem long to us, but it will not seem long to you. We are all coming—we are even going to bring little Guy * with us.

Till we meet thus, I remain your loving father.

The lay-delegation movement was steadily growing in the Church. A call had been issued for a general convention of representative laymen, to meet at St. Paul's Church, New York, on the 13th of May, 1863. The chairman of the committee of arrangements, Mr. Daniel L. Ross, addressed to Bishop Janes, as I presume he did to all the Bishops, a respectful and cordial invitation to give his "presence and counsel" on the occasion. The Bishop saw fit to decline in the following courteous and considerate letter:

I appreciate the courtesy of the committee in the invitation they have extended to me to attend a convention of Methodist

---

* The infant son of her sister, Mrs. Harris.

laymen to be held in St. Paul's Church. Holding, as I do, one of the highest executive offices in the Church, and one which places me in a peculiarly delicate and responsible relation to all the ministers and Churches of the Connection, I judge it inexpedient for me to identify myself with your proposed convention. I therefore feel obliged, in the most respectful manner, to decline your very courteous invitation. I wish it understood that in this declinature I express no opinion, *pro* or *con*, upon the subject which the convention is called to consider. I only state what I believe to be the more expedient and proper course for me in relation to attending the convention. I presume some will differ with me on this point. I avail myself of the opportunity to express the high estimate in which I hold the intelligence, piety, and usefulness of my lay brethren, and the full confidence I feel in their fidelity to God and loyalty to the Church. I thank God that he has moved my heart to the tenderest and strongest pastoral love for all the people to whom he has given me the relation of superintendent, and that he has inspired me with an intense desire in every possible way to contribute to their highest welfare.

Whatever may have been Bishop Janes's opinions upon this or any other question involving fundamental changes in the polity of Methodism, he felt that he could not, in view of the responsibility of his office to all classes of people, be a leader in the movements contemplating such changes. He felt that a definite work was committed to him, and that he was an executive, not a legislative, officer. His function was to obey the behests of the General Conference; to conserve and build up the Church of which he was an overseer under well-defined rules of order. He was by instinct a leader, and had he not been very early in life weighted with such engrossing and consuming official cares, he probably would have always been among the foremost in foreseeing and advocating wholesome modifications. It is certain he was never alarmed, especially in later life, for the safety of the Church when modifications were proposed or adopted. Hence when, in 1869, the laity finally voted to accept the offer of the General Conference composed wholly of ministerial delegates that they should have lay delegation when the people desired it, no one was more eager than he was that the ministers in the Annual Conferences should, by their votes, satisfy the wishes of the laity. He did not hesitate to express himself to this effect with those with whom he was intimate.

During the spring of 1864 the Bishop was as constantly occupied with the work of the Christian Commission as his official duties would allow— planning for the holding of public meetings to arouse the public to its importance and to raise funds for its treasury, speaking in its advocacy, and even going as far to the front of the army as circumstances would allow to preach to the soldiers and relieve their wants. The Rev. W. E. Boardman, D. D., Secretary of the Commission, thus refers, May 28, to a visit the Bishop made with Mr. Stuart to the army of the Potomac:

Mr. Stuart has just returned full and running over with incident and interest of our army work. Of the Camp Convales-

cent visit I need not speak. He speaks of your own morning
sermon there with strong emphasis, as the grand preparation
for all the after services and amazing interest of the day.

No bare outlines, not even *verbatim* reports, could
give an adequate idea of the effectiveness of Bishop
Janes's eloquent addresses in pleading the cause of
the soldiers. He foresaw, as we have all since seen,
the importance of preserving the moral purity of the
army, in view not only of their well-being while under arms, but also of their return to civil life when
the war should close, and so expressed himself.

The General Conference met in the Union Church,
Philadelphia, Pa., on May 2, 1864. With this General Conference Bishop Janes completed the twentieth year of his episcopacy. Referring to this fact
in a letter from St. Johnsbury, Vermont, the seat
of the Vermont Conference, April 14, he says:

This is my last Conference for my twentieth year in the episcopal office. I have great reason to be thankful to my heavenly Father for preserving me and divinely aiding me in such
a series of important and difficult duties.

The Bishops, in their Address to the General
Conference, say:

On a survey of the pastoral work we are moved to exclaim,
"The best of all is, God is with us!" . . . Despite the Rebellion
and the excitements and agitations of the war, it still resounds
in our churches. God has not forgotten to be gracious. His
presence is mightily felt in our assemblies, and he has crowned
the labors of his faithful servants with numerous, and in many
instances powerful, revivals.

Happily the exigencies of the civil war lifted the General Conference out of all its embarrassments on the slavery question, and the General Rule was so changed as to exclude slave-holding from the Church. The feeling was, that the General Government needed all the moral force the Conference could give it in grappling with the Rebellion, whose inspiration was slavery. The General Rule was afterward ratified by the Annual Conferences with equal unanimity. Thus the sword cut the knot which the theologians had tried in vain to untie.

" Lay representation in the General Conference " had been submitted to a vote of the ministers and laymen, and had failed of a majority. From a convention of laymen held at St. George's Church, Philadelphia, May 18, a committee, of which ex-Governor Wright, of Indiana, was chairman, was received by the Conference, and addressed the body in a strong plea for lay representation. The Conference, however, respectfully declined all action, simply adhering to its former position, " whenever it shall be ascertained that the Church desires it."

Three additional Bishops were elected : Davis W. Clark, D.D., Edward Thomson, D.D., and Calvin Kingsley, D.D. By a large majority, the pastoral term was changed from two to three years as the limit a minister could be continued in any one charge. The Rev. W. L. Thornton, M.A., was received as a delegate from the British Conference,

and the Rev. Robinson Scott, D. D., from the Irish
Cônference, and Bishop Janes was appointed to visit
those Conferences as the fraternal delegate from
the Methodist Episcopal Church.

Among the marked features of the General Conference was its thorough loyalty to the United
States Government in the crisis through which it
was then passing. A committee was appointed to
convey to President Lincoln the sentiments of the
Conference, to which. Mr. Lincoln made the following reply:

. . . Nobly sustained as the Government has been by all the
Churches, I would utter nothing that might in the least appear
invidious against any. Yet without this, it may fairly be said that
the Methodist Episcopal Church, not less devoted than the best,
is, by its greater numbers, the most important of all. It is no
fault in others that the Methodist Church sends more soldiers
to the field, more nurses to the hospitals, and more prayers to
heaven than any. God bless the Methodist Church! bless all
the Churches! And, blessed be God! who, in this great trial,
giveth us the Churches.

The Bishop dispatched almost daily letters to
Mrs. Janes. These were often written in the conference room, as " he wrote with one hand and listened with one ear." To cheer her heart and relieve
his own, such thoughts as the following dropped
from his pen:

Who gains the victory over death? Christ, who having laid
down his life took it again.

The dying Christian gains this victory when he meets death
without fear. He can say to death, " I spend the night with

you in sweet repose, but I shall wake and leave your domain in the morning. I only accept your hospitalities."

"We will not plant above thee, O, grave! the weeping-willow, as an emblem of sorrow and despair, but we will plant the evergreen, the symbol of hope; and the fragrant flowers shall shed their perfume around thee. Thou shalt be a thing of beauty as well as a thing of service."

It fell to Bishop Janes to organize the first Conference of colored ministers provided for by the late General Conference, in the city of Philadelphia, in July of the same year. He thus speaks of them, July 20:

I yesterday met my colored brothers—some thirty of them. A very pleasant meeting with them. The colored (Delaware) Conference of the Methodist Episcopal Church is no humbug. It is a grand beginning of good things to the poor colored people.

The Bishop held several of the Western Conferences the ensuing autumn. Extracts from a letter from Keokuk, the seat of the Iowa Conference, to Miss Lizzie, September 12, will suffice:

There has no incident of interest occurred with me unless it be the one I will now relate. Last Saturday a United States Senator said to the Methodist preacher in B., "I hear Bishop Janes is in the city, will he preach to-morrow?" "Yes, sir." "Well, I wish to hear him for a special reason. Fourteen years ago I was traveling on the New York Central Railroad. I entered into conversation with the gentleman occupying the seat with me. I found him ready to converse, and was interested in his remarks. Myself and friends had a flask of brandy with us. When we drank we invited him to drink with us. He replied, 'I have no use for any liquor.' Conver-

sation was continued, and after awhile we took another drink,
and urged the stranger to join us. He declined, saying that
he did not use spirits because he did not need them, and because he wished his example to be in favor of temperance, etc.
As we journeyed, conversation was continued from time to time."

In the afternoon, he said, at a station, several ministerial
looking gentlemen came into the car, and they all recognized me and spoke to me. At the next station more came in,
who in like manner addressed me. At the next station still
more came in and saluted me. Finally, when I left the car,
the ministerial looking men all left with me. His curiosity led
him to go to one of them and ask who I was. He told him it
was Bishop Janes, who had come there to preside at a Conference to commence the next day. He had not seen me since
that time, but he had not forgotten me nor my firm adherence
to temperance principles even among strangers. He was
present Sunday morning, and gave twenty-five dollars in the
collection. I do not think there is much egotism in repeating
this to my daughter. It pleased me to hear that my conduct
had made a good impression. This incident shows how careful we ought to be at all times and in all places of our words
and actions.

Your beautiful white daisy, plucked from Tillie's grave, came
in its perfection. A beautiful emblem of a most beautiful object.
Dear Tillie, how much I think of her! She loses none of her
loveliness to me. My recollection of her is just as vivid and
fragrant as the day after we placed her in her Greenwood home.

In the month of January, 1865, Bishop Janes,
Bishop Lee, of Delaware, and others, were appointed by the Christian Commission, and authorized by the General Government, to visit the Federal
prisoners at Richmond, Va. I give a letter of the
21st, written at Aiken's Landing, Varina, Va., on
board the steamer "Massachusetts," showing his

movements. My impression is, the visitors were refused admission through the Confederate lines. The report they must have carried back of Libby Prison would not have sweetened the temper of the Northern mind.

We are waiting still for a reply from Richmond to our application for admission to the rebel lines, for the purpose of seeing and administering to our Federal prisoners. Colonel Mulford, the flag-of-truce officer, has gone over the lines to receive their reply.

Our sail up the James River was very pleasant. Occasionally on its banks stands one of the old mansions of which there were so many in former times in this rich portion of the State. At City Point, in going in an ambulance to visit one of the hospitals, an incident occurred, which, at the time, was alarming, but proved harmless. As we were descending a very steep hill the reach of the ambulance broke and the vehicle upset. I was on the front seat, and thrown down upon the pole between the horses' heels, and in that way carried some distance. How I kept my balance on the pole I cannot even now understand. I think an angel must have held me up. I did not dare to touch the horses for fear of making them kick. There was nothing else I could seize. After a little the reins came within my reach. I seized one with my left hand and turned the horses up against a sand bank and stopped them. One of the gentlemen ran and helped me to escape from my dangerous position. I was a little strained and bruised. Not enough hurt to make a child cry. It was a marked interposition of Providence. I have felt safe ever since. " He keepeth all my bones—not one of them is broken." I immediately returned and preached.

Our interview with General Grant was a pleasant one. We spent two hours and a half with him. He was very social. Mrs. Grant was present, and their youngest son. She is a lady of good sense, simple manners, and of good conversational powers; talks about country life with a zest. The General gave prompt attention to our business. Wrote a letter to General Lee introducing us. He wrote the letter while conversation was going on around him. It was a well-written document, every word expressive. He immediately put a steamer at our disposal. On reaching this place, Colonel Mulford, in obedience to the order of General Grant, forwarded our papers to Richmond. He then provided us a carriage and four horses, and a conduct of two officers and their orderlies for the day to visit the camps. We visited the several stations of the Christian Commission. The day was one of much interest. It was the first time I had ever seen hostile armies confronting one another; an impressive sight; I hope the world will see but few more of them.

In March, 1865, Bishop Janes held the West Virginia and Newark Conferences, and in April he sailed for Europe, having been assigned to visit the Germany and Switzerland Mission Conference, and to act as fraternal delegate to the British and Irish Wesleyan Conferences, and also having been chosen by the American Bible Society to represent it at the approaching anniversary of the British and Foreign Bible Society.

A letter from London, May 4, to his daughter, Miss Lizzie, gives a pleasant account of his reception in that great metropolis:

At four o'clock Monday morning took the cars for London. Arrived at my hotel at ten o'clock. Went to the missionary meeting at Exeter Hall at eleven. An immense gathering of people and a very enthusiastic meeting. I made a short address. Yesterday was held the anniversary of the British and Foreign Bible Society. As the delegate of the American Bible Society they honored me much. I was seated between Lord

John Russell on my right and the Right Reverend Lord Bishop
of Rupert's Land on my left. There was quite a collection of
nobility. Lord Shaftesbury presided. Lord Radcliff spoke.
Two Right Reverend Lord Bishops spoke. I made an address
which I hope will be satisfactory to the American Bible Society.
Bishop Thomson reached London on his return from India on
the evening of the day on which I arrived here. He sails on
Saturday for New York. I am attending various meetings,
and shall probably remain until next Monday morning, when I
shall leave at an early hour for Paris and the Continent. I
have been very warmly received by the Wesleyan ministers
and friends, and also by the officers and friends of the British
and Foreign Bible Society. The officers and managers are
mostly of the Church of England, and a little formal and dignified in manner, but are really cordial, and show a very hearty
interest in religious affairs in our country. I was last evening
at a select dinner party where they were all Bishops and ministers and members of the national Church; they were very
kindly inquisitive about our national and religious interests in
America. The assassination of President Lincoln seems to
affect the people of England, and, indeed, of all Europe, almost
as deeply as it did the people in the United States.

I have my London home with the same family that I stayed
with when here before, Mr. Lycett. I am to-night to dine with
Mr. M'Arthur. I breakfasted this morning with Dr. Jobson.
I have an abundance of invitations, but I intend to accept only
a few, and those hereafter Methodists. It is very exhausting
to be frequently a guest on public occasions.

CHAPTER XVI.

1865–1868.

Delegate to the British and Foreign Bible Society, and to the English and Irish Wesleyan Conferences—The German and Scandinavian Work in Europe—Centenary of American Methodism—Death of Friends.

IT has been seen that the Bishop, on arriving in London, found the Wesleyan Methodist Missionary Society holding its anniversary at Exeter Hall, May 1, where he was enthusiastically received and constrained to address the audience. Sir Francis Lycett, chairman of the meeting, thus introduced him:

We are very glad to welcome Bishop Janes, of the Methodist Episcopal Church of the United States. We shall be happy to hear him address us this morning, and I have much pleasure in calling upon him to do so.

I give only so much of the Bishop's speech as refers to his reception and to the assassination of President Lincoln, which had occurred just before he left New York:

MR. CHAIRMAN, LADIES, AND GENTLEMEN: Words to be fittingly spoken must be spoken at the right time. I am persuaded that the arrangements for this meeting have been so well made that you can afford to appropriate but a very little time to a stranger, and he an individual who is accidentally with you. The principal consideration which leads me to occupy any part of your time is, a desire which I have to avail myself of the very first opportunity to acknowledge the manner in which I have been affected by the expression of sympathy which I have found in this land for my own beloved country in this the day of her tribulation. When I left America I left a nation in mourning. Our marts of commerce and our temples of worship were literally clothed in sackcloth. And I believe that never has a nation been more sorely grieved than is the United States of America at this present time. Our late chief magistrate was a beloved President—we had found him to be an honest man. We had found him to be a true patriot. He had proved himself to be an earnest philanthropist, and we knew him to be a competent statesman and a faithful ruler. At the time of his death bright hopes were centering in him, and we anticipated speedily the great pleasure of rejoicing with him in the restoration of order, authority, and peace in our land. I will not speak more at length in reference to his character and his office, and the loss which the nation has sustained. But I desire to return to my first remark—the manner in which I have been impressed by the expressions of sympathy and interest on this side of the water.

When on Saturday last the ship "China" reached Queenstown there was an intense solicitude on the part of the American passengers to see the English newspapers; and when we saw them and read them, and understood the feeling which pervaded the public in this country with reference to our country in this hour of her sorrow, there were few American eyes in that ship that were not filled with tears. The impression upon all our hearts and minds was deep and most grateful. And I have no doubt when these communications reach our nation, and are there seen by the people at large, and by our authorities, that there will be made upon our community and upon our Government, an impression which, perhaps, no other event than the sympathy manifested here could have made with reference to your people. This permissive providence of God is to us a strange one. We still believe, however, that "the wrath of man shall praise Him, and the remainder of wrath will He restrain."

I have no report at hand of his address before the British and Foreign Bible Society, whose anniversary occurred about the same time. But the following reference in the minute adopted by the managers of the American Bible Society immediately after his death will show the estimate which the Board put upon his services on that occasion :

Perhaps he was never more happy in public address than when he appeared as our representative before the British and Foreign Bible Society in 1865. It was the last year of our first half century, and his condensed and lucid statements concerning the work we had done produced a profound impression. In this address he spoke of the Bible as "the book that is older than our fathers, that is truer than tradition, that is more learned than universities, that is more authoritative than councils, that is more infallible than popes, that is more orthodox than creeds, that is more powerful than ceremonies — the omnipotent word of God—the wonder of the world—the boon of Heaven."

After spending a week in London the Bishop crossed to the Continent, passing rapidly to Paris and through France, visiting Basle, Lausanne, Geneva, and Zurich, Switzerland ; and thence he went north through Germany to Bremen, where he met the Germany and Switzerland Conference, June 8. He inspected all the prominent missions, preaching almost incessantly as he traveled.

His description of the journey from the time he entered France until he reached Basle is to the life:

After spending a week in London, gaining some knowledge of mankind in general, and of Englishmen in particular, I left Tuesday morning for this place. The country from London to Folkstone, whence I sailed for Boulogne, is very fine : Some of the best-cultivated lands in England. No railroad view in America is so like it as the one between Philadelphia and Harrisburgh. In accordance with my prayer the Channel was smooth. At Boulogne we dined, then started for Paris. Our journey was a very rapid one—fifty miles an hour. We went through the tunnels of the hills as a modern cannon-ball crashes through a wooden ship. We had in my apartment a wine-bibbing English woman, whose tongue was entirely loose at one end, and very limber in the middle; it ran about as constant as the wheels of the car and almost as fast, and there was about as much sentiment in her rattling words as in the clatter of the cars. She teased her husband greatly and annoyed us all.

An English gentleman sat opposite to me, who, when the train started, did as I have been wont to do, closed his eyes and remained for two or three minutes in silent prayer. You cannot think how much safer I felt when I saw that. When I reached Paris I found myself solitary amid a babbling crowd. I stood and looked and listened awhile hoping some one would say a word of English. A gentleman in London had requested me to take a letter with some money to a friend in Paris. A thought struck me. I took out the letter and showed the address to a cabman. He understood, and drove me to the place. The gentleman went with me to the Grand Hotel. At six next morning I left for Basle, which I reached at eight P. M. When I got out of the cars I went about asking, "Speak English?" No one did. I went to a hotel, where the landlord understood me, and sent a servant with me to find Rev. William Schwartz. When I reached his residence I was relieved of my embarrassment.

A letter from Lausanne, Switzerland, to Mrs. Janes, May 16, will be appreciated for its references

13

to Dr. Merle D'Aubigné, and to Nyon, the birth-place of Rev. John Fletcher:

God's mercy still enables me to report my health as good as ordinary. Last Sunday I preached in our Mission Chapel, Basle, to a congregation understanding the English language. About seventy-five persons were present : several of them students from the Evangelical Lutheran Mission Institute—two of them Hindus. The principal officer of the Institute was also present, some English travelers, some American residents, and some learned Swiss. The Spirit of the Lord was upon me. In the afternoon addressed the Sunday-school, the pastor interpreting. In the evening addressed the German congregation, the pastor interpreting. Yesterday came to this place. To-day I have been to Geneva. I first went to the spot where Servetus was burned. I next went to the cathedral where Calvin preached. Sat in the old wooden chair in which he used to sit to lecture. From there I went to see Rev. Dr. Merle d'Aubigné. I wished to see him very much. His residence is an old Swiss house in the suburb of the city. In asking for the doctor a young lady appeared and said, " My husband is in his study, and dislikes to be disturbed." I replied, " Very well, madam, do not interrupt him. I am from New York. I know the doctor well by his writings, and should have been pleased to shake his hand." The lady said she would speak with him, and returned, saying, " My husband will be down in a moment." Soon the venerable doctor appeared, greeted me heartily, and commenced talking about our national affairs. After an interesting conversation I took my leave. He is a tall, well-proportioned man, in his seventy-first year. Conver-. sational powers very fine. His young wife is an Irish lady— smart, talkative, self-complacent, husband-admiring lady. Why he, an old French patriarch, selected her for a bride is none of my business. I judge it is a happy match so long as it lasts.

A few miles from Geneva I saw the *chateau* of Madame De Staël, also her tomb. It is a beautiful spot overlooking the lake, and having a grand view of the Alps. I stopped at Nyon, where Rev. John Fletcher was born. The widow of his nephew still lives here. We had an interesting interview. When I left her I went to the house where he was born, and to the church where he was baptized and where he preached. Went into the pulpit and saw the old psalm book and Bible he used, 1731. It is an old, ill-shaped edifice, but it seemed sacred to me. In the house was a beautiful picture representing him standing with his hand on a human skull, and uttering the words, "Thanks be to God, who giveth us the victory through our Lord Jesus Christ." We have a mission here to the Germans. Held a meeting last night and also to-night.

The Bishop went north to see the Scandinavian work, and in the midst of his constant travel and occupation finds time to remember bereaved friends in the home-land. No man was ever more thoughtful of those he loved, in the times of their sorrow. He writes from Copenhagen, May 30, to Mr. and Mrs. C. C. North, of New York, on hearing of the death of their eldest daughter, Mary, known afterward as " Early Crowned."

I have just seen the "Advocate" of the 18th inst., and learned that your dear Mary has gone to see her heavenly Father, and her elder Brother, and her many celestial kindred and friends. O, how painfully you miss her presence and social influence in the family! You do not complain or murmur—No. God does all things well. You do not repine or grieve—No. You have consolation and calm submission. You have no painful apprehensions for or sympathy with your absent child—No. She is safe and happy, perfectly so, eternally so. Yet you suffer. You can hardly analyze your feelings. You cannot express them. You feel as if you were not entirely yourselves. It seems as if a part of your own being was gone. Something is missing. There is a want—an absence. You look for it, but

the dear face does not show itself. You listen for it, but the
affectionate voice is not heard. O, for that missing presence!
How the heart yearns for it! That vacancy in the heart—what
can relieve it? Nothing in this world. The divine Comforter
can enable us to support this piercing sense of loss, to endure
submissively this keen feeling of absence. Reunion alone can
restore entireness to our bereaved hearts. The meeting in
heaven will make all right.

From Bremen, Germany, to Miss Janes, June 6:

In the afternoon I walked out to the cemetery to visit the
grave of a missionary who died here about two years ago. My
attention was arrested at the entrance to the cemetery by a
remarkable beech tree; it was very large and very old, and the
lower limbs were supported by a frame. The traditional history of it is this: At a time long ago when theft was punished
with death, where this tree stands was the place of public execution. A young girl was beheaded there for that alleged
crime. She protested her innocence, and at the hour of execution took a beech branch, and planting it, small end down-
ward, said, "That will live and grow to be a witness of my
innocence." She died repeating, "I know that my Redeemer
liveth." Many years afterward a man when dying confessed
that upon the girl's refusal to marry him he determined to be
revenged, and, secreting some silver in her trunk, had her arrested and beheaded. He died saying, "O, eternity is so long!"
On one side the entrance to the cemetery is a stone with these
words engraved, "I know that my Redeemer liveth.' On the
other side a similar stone, bearing these words, "O! eternity is
so long!"

While in Germany, and making a brief visit to
Berlin, the Bishop accepted an invitation to preach
a discourse on the death of President Lincoln. It
was listened to by all the English-speaking people

of the city, and was afterward printed and widely
read throughout Germany.

He returned through France, visiting the French
Wesleyan Methodist Conference, then in session in
Paris, and, soon after reaching London, left for the
session of the Irish Conference at Cork.   While in
Ireland he was for awhile the guest of the Rev. Rob-
inson Scott, D.D., so well and favorably known in
America, and from his hospitable home, at Black
Rock, near Dublin, wrote to Miss Janes, July 8 :

I am now enjoying the hospitality of Dr. Scott.   He has a
lovely cottage home called Rose Hough.   They have a great
variety of flowers, especially of roses.   A charming spot.   Mrs.
Scott is an exceedingly pleasant lady.   She has made my stay
of a week very delightful.   I have been writing most of the
week ; leave to-day for the north of Ireland ; preach to-morrow in Belfast.   I have visited the lakes of Killarney ; there is
much of beauty in these lakes ; they are nearly surrounded by
craggy mountains resembling the highlands of our Hudson.
If I had not seen American mountain scenery, I have no doubt
I should have joined with the natives in calling it grand and
sublime ; but you know I have seen the long ranges of the
Rocky Mountains, and the grand conical mountains among
them ; also the majestic, beautiful, imposing, enchanting scenery
of the Columbia River, in Oregon.

To Miss Janes, from Belfast, Ireland, July 13 :

Since I wrote you last I have been journeying with Dr. Scott.
I came on Saturday to this place, preached on Sunday, had a
large audience, heard Dr. Scott preach an excellent sermon in
the evening.   This city is well built—some beautiful residences.
I am enjoying the hospitalities of Alderman William Mullan, a
princely man, who has a princess of a wife.   On Monday I

went to Portadown, to visit an old Methodist family, and preached at night.   On Tuesday I went to Omagh and visited the father and friends of Mr. John Elliott, of New York.   His father is a very venerable old gentleman, venerable for wisdom and goodness.   Dr. M'Clintock's grandfather was buried a few miles from Omagh ; his father was born there.   Bishop Simpson's father was from the same neighborhood.   The next morning I went to Londonderry, and from there to Port Rush, where I visited the Giant's Causeway.   It is a wonder, though not a very sublime one.   I spent the night at Coleraine ; enjoyed the warm and elegant hospitality of an old Methodist family, who used to entertain Dr. Clarke and Gideon Ouseley. At Port Rush is a monument to Dr. Adam Clarke.   I sail for Scotland this evening.

As the previous letter indicates, the Bishop, on leaving Belfast, made a brief tour through Scotland and thence down to Birmingham, England, where he visited the British Conference, which was (July 27) in session in that city, and was most cordially received in his capacity as fraternal delegate from the Methodist Episcopal Church.   On the evening of the second day of Conference an " open session " was held, at which he presented the Address of the General Conference of 1864, accompanying it with a personal address.   On the first Sunday of the Conference he was invited to preach the annual sermon in the place of the ex-president.   Nothing could have been more agreeable to him than to find the Rev. William Arthur, D.D., so highly appreciated by American Methodists, president of the Conference.

An extract from a letter received on his arrival at

home from Bishop Ames, dated August 30, shows
the estimate in which his services abroad were held
by his colleagues :

I congratulate you, and the Church also, on the very satisfactory manner in which you have been enabled to execute your
important mission. We on this side of the water are proud
of you, and I doubt not that those on that side are well pleased.

The Hon. Joseph A. Wright, of Indiana, was re-
appointed Minister Plenipotentiary for the United
States to the court of Prussia by President Johnson
in 1865. Meanwhile he had married Mrs. Caroline
R. Deuel, of New York. The residence of Mr. and
Mrs. Wright at Berlin became the occasion of the
fulfillment of a cherished wish of the Bishop in connection with Methodism in that great capital. A
letter to Mrs. Wright, dated November 20, at New
York, explains the object :

When I visited Berlin, in 1861, I was much impressed with
the importance of our Society having a comfortable and respectable place of worship in that city. On my return I
represented the case to the Board. It was thought the condition of our country and the uncertainty of the future would not
justify the Board in undertaking to build then. While at the
Conference, on my late visit, I conferred with the brethren, and
came home with the fixed purpose to obtain from the General
Mission Committee and Board an appropriation for that object
if I had influence enough to effect it. Your letters, and those
of the Governor, have aided me in securing it. You have
learned from others that an appropriation of $15,000 has been
made to aid in building a Methodist house of worship in Berlin. I am glad you and the governor are there to assist in

the enterprise. I know you will gladly do all in your power
to promote the object. I think it will be important that the
subscription in Berlin should be taken before the building is
commenced.

In the autumn of 1865 the Genesee, Illinois, and
Iowa Conferences were presided over by Bishop
Janes. In the year 1866 he presided over the Troy,
Eastern German,. East Maine, East Genesee, Gene-
see, Central German, and South-east Indiana Con-
ferences.

The year 1866 was distinguished as the centenary
year of American Methodism. A General Committee had been authorized by the General Conference
of 1864 to devise a plan for its due observance, and
the committee appointed by the Bishops under this
authorization met in the city of Cleveland, Ohio,
February 22, 1865. All the Bishops were present
at the meeting except Bishop Thomson, who was
absent in India. Every section of the Church was
ably represented by both ministers and laymen.
The committee defined the objects to which the
commemorative offerings should be devoted, and
created a central committee at New York, and ordered local committees in all the Annual Conferences for carrying out the arrangement. No one
was more active in the counsels of the committee,
nor more incessantly and effectively engaged in the
practical work of creating the funds contemplated,
than Bishop Janes. He was here, there, and every-

where — guiding by his wisdom, cheering by his sympathy and example, and animating by his burning words, the great movement which was to constitute a fitting memorial of the first century of Methodism in the New World, and also form a solid material basis for its progress in the centuries to follow. The Methodists, in common with all the people, had just emerged from an exhausting war, but they rose to the grandeur of the occasion, and exhibited one of the sublimest instances of voluntary giving in the annals of religion or philanthropy. At the ensuing General Conference, 1868, the magnificent total for all objects was reported as $8,709,498 39. And this sum was distinct from the contributions made to all the regular claims of the Church. No one thing more thoroughly impressed the general public with the power and aggregate wealth of the Methodist Episcopal Church than its Centenary Offering.

Persons who were present at the two meetings held in St. Paul's Church, New York, the one on January 25 to inaugurate the movement, presided over by Secretary Harlan, and the other on April 9 to represent the Ladies' Centenary Society in its distinctive aim to aid in the erection of a suitable building for the use of the General Missionary Society of the Church, presided over by Chief Justice Chase, will remember the effectiveness with which Bishop Janes spoke. On the former occasion it

13*

was assigned to him to explain and advocate the Irish Evangelization Fund; and how well he did it let Dr. Robinson Scott, the vigilant guardian of the fund, answer:

I write now not to trouble you with a reply. My first object is to thank you, from my inmost heart, for your noble and generous speech in St. Paul's Church on behalf of Ireland—not the less generous because it was just. I had read a brief summary of it in the " Advocate," but to-day it has come to hand *in extenso.* It says all that the warmest friend of our good cause could have wished on the occasion. That it was delivered, not by an Irishman or by one connected with Ireland by descent, but by an American, and based upon principles that rise above all mere political nationalities and that are common for the kingdom of Christ, will make it all the more effective with the membership of your Church generally.

But it was at the second meeting that the Bishop rose to the full height of his eloquence. It was a great meeting. Chief Justice Chase—the foremost jurist and statesman of the country, then in the acme of his fame—on taking the chair made an address highly appreciative of Methodism. When he introduced Bishop Janes I confess I remember feeling no little solicitude for him. He was before an audience long familiar with him, and it seemed quite impossible for him to awaken any very marked interest in them on a subject the general aspect of which had also become familiar. My fears and the fears of all, however, soon gave way—first to quiet, then to satisfaction—astonishment—ecstasy. Such philosophy, fancy, invective, religious hopefulness, and triumph, all on fire, leaping and bursting over an audience, I have seldom heard. The vast and cultured mass of people and ministers were tumultuous with excitement. For popular effect it was I believe, the crowning effort of the Bishop's life.

The Rev. John Atkinson, D.D., now of the Detroit Conference, thus writes his recollections of the occasion in a late number of the "North-western Christian Advocate:"

I saw Bishop Janes on one of the great occasions of his life. It was at the Centenary Meeting in St. Paul's Church, New York, in 1866.   Chief Justice Chase presided, and made the opening address.   It was able, and well worthy of the man and the theme. Bishop Simpson also spoke.   Then came Bishop Janes, the last of the three.   The intellect, culture, piety, and power of Methodism were represented in that vast metropolitan audience, whose thousands of eyes, kindled to brilliance by the eloquence that had poured from the lips of the great statesman and jurist, and the great pulpit orator, were now turned full upon the resident Bishop.   Before those people he had walked for many years, yet no orator from abroad must send him to the rear.   He must be there and at the front. So the people willed, and on the sympathies of that representative throng he rose to a height of thrilling, masterful eloquence, which none of that assembly can have forgotten.

The abstract of this speech, given in the New York "Methodist" of April 14, will convey a proper notion of its substance, but not of the by-play and passion with which it was delivered. After speaking of the necessity of a building adapted to all the wants of the Missionary Society, among other things a fire-proof room for preserving its records, he proceeds:

"But in my judgment there is a higher interest than this. The records of the Missionary Society are important, not only to the Society and to the Church, but if I have a correct apprehension of the subject, they are important to the public. The history of this world is to be a religious history. It has been measurably so in the past; not sufficiently, however, have God and religion been acknowledged in history. But who can write the history of this country and not acknowledge the influence which Christianity had in its discovery? the influence which Christianity had in bringing the Puritan and the Huguenot to settle it? the influence which Christianity has had in molding and sustaining our institutions? the influence which Christianity has had upon our country the last five years, inspiring its patriotism and sustaining and nerving its patriots for the responsibilities and duties that have devolved upon them? Why, sir, no infidel can write the military history of the last five years and not make Christianity prominent in that record. He might as well leave off its pages the names of our generals, as to leave off the names of our chaplains; he might as well leave off the names of those who are subordinate in office, as to leave off the names of those who have gone out as the agents of the Christian Commission. The action of the Church, the influence of religion in our army, have been so manifest and so happy that, I repeat it, no infidel can write the naked history of the war and not make Christianity prominent in his record.

"And let me enlarge a little upon this thought. Where, sir, are the records of the Sandwich Islands for the last fifty years? The principal records, sir, are not in Washington, neither are they in those islands. The important records of their history are in the archives of the American Board of Commissioners at Boston. There are registered the principal facts in their great history for the last forty or fifty years. Where, sir, is the history of Oregon? It is not at Washington! It is at 199 Mulberry-street! There, sir, are the letters that describe the circumstances of that country at the breaking out of the Indian war, and give information that our missionary drew on our treasurer for the funds to raise the army which went out to meet the hostile tribes, to preserve the population of that land. The most thrilling events, military and civil, as well as religious, relating to the early settlement of the Pacific coast, are in our archives at 199 Mulberry-street. And who could write the history of India for the last twenty-five years and ignore American missionaries and their influence and agency? or of China? or any of the islands of the earth, in fact, in which there has been a history for the last fifty years?"

WORK OF THE MISSIONARY SOCIETY.

The Bishop then spoke of the vice of intemperance, stating that the conscience of the people must be awakened on that question, and asserting that those men who, by their practice, led the young to form habits of intemperance, were guilty of awful crimes.

"Christianity was not that tame and cowering thing that some supposed it to be, but it was the manifestation of the mind and heart of God for humanity. And the Church, with the inspiration of the Spirit in her heart, and with the sword of the Spirit in her hand, is the militant power by which God intends to punish sin and overthrow error, and everywhere bring the wickedness of the wicked to an end, and establish the dominion of the just. And, sir, whoever comes in the way of this will feel its overwhelming influence. This power is rising in the world; it is spreading, it is prevailing, and it is a tide that will never ebb. This stone cut out of the mountain without hands, in its evolutions, has gained such momentum that it will never be stopped in its career; and whoever seeks to stop it, be he King, or President, or Pope, or unfaithful minister, or supple politician, will be dashed to pieces as a potter's vessel.

"And what is the consequence? I say here to-night, standing on the boundary line to which you have referred—I say in this presence here to-night—that the meetings of our board of managers of our missionary societies, our Bible societies, and our Sunday-school and tract societies, are as important, they have in them as much of the weal and the destiny of humanity, as the meetings of the Legislatures of these States; and by consequence their records are as important in the history of the world, and they will be of as much advantage to coming generations of the race, as will be the journals of those State Legislatures. And I would impress upon all men who have the responsibilties of directing these great Christian agencies the gravity of their office and the solemnity of their responsibilities. I call upon the Church to-night to give us the means of providing such a repository as shall securely preserve to all coming time the records of our missionary work."

The Bishop then quoted interesting statistics of the rise and progress of the Missionary Society, and said that in all probability in twelve years from this time that society would administer upon several millions of money annually. The habits of benevolence which are being formed in the hearts of the children, and the increasing facilities which were now afforded for carrying forward the missionary work, were eloquently alluded to. "I wish I had the power to bring before this congregation the grandeur of our position. Why, sir, we have a million of soldiers in the field, and every one of them a devotee to Christ and his cause; we have another million of cadets in our schools training for this office and work; we have thirteen thousand recruiting stations and eight thousand recruiting officers, and we have all this host marshaled. There is not a district or circuit between the two oceans that is not all organized and ready for this work. Why, sir, in this organization there is a power adequate to move the world; and when this marshaled host shall make their stately steppings upon the earth, depend upon it, the vibrations created will shake the very throne of hell, and the powers of darkness must give way before it. I tell you, sir, this missionary work is no trifle! When Jesus Christ said to his Church, 'Disciple the world—preach the Gospel to every creature,' he used no hyperbole. Why, sir, it is an explicit, simple, imperative military order, and we must obey it literally and promptly, or stand court-martial before our God. If the Church wakes up to this sublime thought with all these advantages and facilities to which we have referred, who can calculate the future? I believe it is, as you said, that all great growths in the past have been slow. I prophesy it will not be true in the future. The growth of the Church of the living God, the kingdom of our Lord Jesus Christ, will be in arithmetical progression, and the time is not distant when a nation will be born to God in a day."

In conclusion the Bishop said: " And now let me say to you —and I would I could say it to the whole Church—if you will give to us these mission premises, and then lift up your heart in fervent, believing prayer to Almighty God for a baptism of the mission spirit to come upon us in this year of the centenary celebration, we will accomplish the great avowed purpose of our Church organization — spreading scriptural holiness over all lands; and our monumental offering at our next centennial celebration shall be a restored humanity, and as it comes up in the heavenly realm it shall awaken the most glowing gratitude and praise of the spirits of the just made perfect. Angels shall see it with adoring gratitude, and God shall behold it with infinite and eternal complacency. I intend to be there." Several voices responded, " So do I."

In 1867 the Bishop's Conferences began with the New Jersey, March 20–26, and was followed by the New York, Black River, Erie, Delaware, East Genesee, Detroit, Genesee, Upper Iowa, and Northwest Indiana Conferences.

During the session of the New York Conference, April 3–10, he completed his sixtieth year. On

his birthday he received a thoughtful and affectionate letter from his twin brother, the Rev. Edwin L.
Janes. It expresses the pride and joy which the
brother felt in him, and the quiet modesty with
which he could stand by and see the stronger of
the two perform the mightier work and reap the
nobler rewards. Two brothers were never more
closely joined in a thorough understanding and appreciation of each other:

The tie that binds us in brotherhood is so close and strong
that I feel to be identified with you in your life-history.
Rocked in the same cradle, taught in the same elementary
school, pursuing for years the same educational work, and
laboring side by side for nearly forty years in the Christian
ministry, it is not surprising I should feel an intense interest
and pleasure in your welfare and success. God has been
pleased to endow you with so eminent a degree of mental energy, physical strength, and Christian zeal, as to enable you to
perform a marvelous amount of work in his Church, and with
corresponding success, in which I rejoice, and for which I
thank God most sincerely.

Dear brother, we cannot be unmindful that in passing our
sixtieth birthday we have passed a mile-stone in our journey
that indicates we are getting near its end. Be it so! There
is a glorious rest and reward in the final period. But I
trust that, however bright your prospect of rest and reward
may be, the anticipation will not put you in a hurry to die.
Your position in the Church, as well as your knowledge and
experience of the workings of her machinery, qualify you to
be extensively useful after you shall find it necessary to limit
yourself to the more restricted work of your office. I trust
that, by a timely limitation of your heavy and incessant labors,
and by the blessing of God, your life may be prolonged for
many years.

The Bishop's friends, and the friends of his friends, as life advanced, were ever falling around him. The previous year he had seen the Hon. Moses F. Odell die in the fullness of his powers and usefulness, and now he was called to assist at the funeral services of Francis Hall, publisher of the "New York Commercial." The Rev. Aaron K. Sanford, of the New York Conference, had also been bereaved of his aged father. To him the Bishop writes, February 16:

I sympathize with you most deeply. . . . I know how a loving, filial heart feels when bereaved of an excellent father. . . . I know how worthy of your love your dear father was. I have seen how you revered and loved him. Dear, good old servant of Jesus and his Church—a ripe shock of corn gathered in its season, his life and his death bring glory to God.

On March 11 the Bishop's valued friend, Governor Wright, died at Berlin. He felt this death to be not only a personal bereavement, but a great loss to the Church and the nation. But his views of this sorrow, as of all others, are cheerful. He writes to Mrs. Wright from New York, June 10:

. . . Under any circumstances the loss of your beloved husband would have been a severe affliction, but to be called to the separation in a foreign land, away from most of your friends to whom you could look for sympathy and kind offices, must have greatly enhanced your trouble. But was the death of your beloved a calamity? Surely it was gain to him. Though the honored embassador of the greatest nation on earth to another great nation, and consequently holding intercourse with nobles and potentates, yet to depart and be with

Christ was better.   To wear an unfading crown of glory himself, in the presence of God and his glorified, is better than to
see others wear an earthly diadem here.   He is happier at the
court of Heaven than he could be at the court of Prussia.   To
him his demise has been no affliction, but a glorious triumph,
an eternal benefit.   This is one of the instances in which " 'Tis
the survivor dies."   In your case, however, it is not an unmiti-
gated affliction.   Did you not witness his religious life?   Did
you not perceive his ripening for heaven?   Did you not hear
him declare his faith in Christ?   Did you not see his " hold
on heaven?"   Did you not witness his translation?   Was
there no privilege in this?   Though one aspect excited your
tender and painful sympathy, yet the other aspect is most
beautiful, most sublime—divinely glorious.   O may we triumph
so when our work is done !

The remains of Governor Wright were brought to
America, and appropriate funeral services were observed in St. Paul's Church, New York, August 22.
On that occasion the Bishop paid the following
tribute to his character :

Governor Wright was a man of intelligence, energy, self-
reliance, and perseverance.   His success in life abundantly
proves this.   As a friend, he was affectionate, sincere, generous, and constant.   These characteristics attached his friends
to him with corresponding fervor and fidelity.   He was a true
philanthropist.   He sympathized in all the interests of humanity.   Both in public and private life, human want and woe
ever found a ready response in his heart, and, as far as possible, relief from his hand.   He regarded intemperance as one of
the most destructive vices in the land, and identified himself most
fully with the temperance reformation, and by example and by
public addresses and by personal influence—in every way—he
sought to promote that great reform.

On the Fourth of July, 1861, I had the honor and the happiness of uniting with him, and the American citizens then present in the city of Berlin, in the celebration of our national anniversary. And it was to me an honest pride to see him stand up before the public men there present from this country, and before the learned and noble of that country, and, with his glass of cold water, drink the health of the King of Prussia and the health of the President of the United States. He was a patriot. He loved his country. In all the offices he held in the State and national governments he earnestly and honestly sought the public good. He was incapable of bribery. When governor, a company offered him a bribe of $50,000 if he would give his official sanction to a certain railroad grant. He indignantly spurned the bribe and those who offered it. In his last sickness he said : " If I thank God for any thing, it is that I never received a bribe or did violence to my conscientious convictions of duty in any public position."

Governor Wright was a Christian. When about twenty-six years of age, while in a Methodist meeting one evening, he fully determined promptly to give his heart to God, and become a true disciple of the Lord Jesus Christ. He went home with this resolve fixed in his mind and heart, retired to a private room, humbled himself before God, and implored mercy in the name of Christ. Before the break of day his earnest, penitent prayers were heard, and he rejoiced in the salvation of divine grace. He joined the Methodist Episcopal Church, and immediately entered upon a life of religious devotions and Christian activities. Whatever concerned the cause of God interested him. He was ready in any way to serve his gracious Lord. When the governor of the State he regularly taught a Bible class in the Sunday-school. While at the court of Berlin he had his Bible class in the Mission School of the Methodist Episcopal Church. During his embassy to that court he took great interest in the building of a Methodist Church, in which there might be preaching in the English language for the benefit of the American residents and visitors. To this enterprise he and his family gave their sympathy, their services, their money, and their influence. On the first Sabbath in January a few

Christian friends assembled in his room and united with him in the sacrament of the Lord's Supper. During the services he desired them to sing the hymn commencing " Rock of Ages, cleft for me," and the one commencing, " Lord, I am thine, entirely thine." While they were singing the words,

> " Thy grace can full assistance lend,
> And on that grace I dare depend,"

he looked up, beckoned his wife to him, and exclaimed, " He floods my soul with light and love. ' The great transaction's done.' ' Jesus is mine and I am his.' " From that hour until his death he had not a doubt of his salvation. An infidel friend was present at one time conversing with him on the subject of Christianity, and expressing to him his disbelief in the claims of the holy Scripture, the governor, smiting upon his breast, said to him with great emotion : " I know I am right ; I would not take ten thousand worlds for this inward consciousness of eternal life through Jesus Christ. Nothing can destroy my faith in God." To the young ministers who visited him he said, " Preach Christ, and only Christ." To Dr. Jacoby he said, " I am not excited, I am very quiet ; but I am very happy. I have the full assurance of heaven and glory."

As yet but little reference has been made to a branch of Church work in which the Bishop heartily entered—the camp-meeting. At this period the institution, if I may call it such, was recovering much of its primitive vigor, and by a widening out of its uses and adaptations was entering upon a new career of usefulness. To a man of the Bishop's temperament no scene could be more inspiring than a sea of upturned eager faces amid the hush and sweetness of the forest. On such occasions he preached some of his most effective sermons. A large and beautiful grove had recently been dedicated to divine worship at Denville, near Morristown, N. J., and in the summer of this year he was among the preachers. The following correspondence between Mr. Jacob Aber, of Lynn, Mass., and himself, is valuable for its allusions to the sermon then preached, and also for the sound words the Bishop uses about himself.

Mr. Aber to Bishop Janes:

We have had several letters speaking in the most flattering terms of your sermon preached at the camp at Denville, N. J. Last Saturday the "Methodist" of the 7th inst. came with your sermon in it in full. I read it in the afternoon; in the evening we talked it over. Sabbath morning I was not well enough to attend church, so I read your sermon. Read it again in the afternoon, and in the evening my wife read it to me. So you see we have about devoured it. O, it reads so good! It is the same doctrine that was taught us by the fathers in our youth. Ten thousand thanks to you for it.

Bishop Janes to Mr. Aber:

Yours of September 9 reached me duly. I am much obliged to you for it. It brought vividly to my mind experiences of my early official life. What a life of care and toil and exposure mine has been! I regret nothing but my unfaithfulness. I have lived and labored for Jesus. The motive has made all service and all suffering a religious pleasure. I have not sought happiness, I have sought goodness and usefulness. I judge that is the surest way to obtain happiness. My life has been a happy one.

I have seen much of the goodness of the Lord in the land of the living. I appreciate your commendation of my sermon at Denville camp-meeting. That is a good sermon which is approved by the spiritual children of God, that edifies and encourages believers. I pay no attention to literary criticisms. I have always preached to save souls. My office does not allow me to do much pastoral work or preach as often as I desire. I love to preach; it is an unspeakable delight to me to hold up Jesus to my sinful fellow-men, and to say to them all— through him you may be saved. Hallelujah to God and the Lamb!

The Indiana, North-west Indiana, and South-east Indiana Conferences held their sessions simultaneously, September 11, and had a reunion at Indianapolis. Bishops Janes and Ames made addresses. In Indiana Methodism has won some of its greatest victories, and the occasion was one of sincere congratulations.

At the close of the year the Bishop was the recipient of a high mark of consideration from the Irish Wesleyan Conference, in the presentation of a set of the reprint of Minutes of the Conferences since 1851. The Rev. James Tobias, Secretary of the Conference, accompanied the gift with the hope that "you will receive it as a recognition of the kind and generous interest which you have taken in our affairs."

The last General Conference had created the Delaware Conference for the people of color, and authorized the Bishops to organize in the South, as the territory might open and the circumstances might require, Mission Conferences, which should

extend the pastoral care of the Methodist Episcopal Church over those wishing to adhere to it.
During the four years the Washington, South Carolina, Virginia and North Carolina, Georgia, and
Texas Mission Conferences were formed. January
2–6, 1868, Bishop Janes met the Virginia and North
Carolina Mission Conference at Richmond, Va.
He appointed 22 preachers to charges. Thence he
went on to Charleston, S. C., and met the South
Carolina Mission Conference, February 26–29, where
he assigned 40 preachers to the care of 18,200
members and probationers. Thus the work among
the people of color in the former slave States, since
productive of such wholesome results, was fairly
begun. The freedmen in large numbers left the
communion of the Methodist Episcopal Church,
South, and gave in their adhesion to the old
Church, believing, as they did, that the Church
which had been the ally of the Government in the
war which had freed them was their truest friend
and their best spiritual home. Bishop Janes es-
poused the cause of this people with his customary
zeal, and in all the measures which contemplated
their relief no one of the Bishops was more sagacious, earnest, and active than he.

On returning North the Bishop met the Phila-
delphia and New York East Conferences. The
New York Conference convened at Harlem, New
York, April 1, and the New York East, in Brook-

lyn, on the same day. The two Conferences had not met together since they were divided in 1848, and it was thought the present time, after the lapse of twenty years, was a fitting occasion to do so, and a reunion was, accordingly, determined upon, and held in St. Paul's Church, April 3, presided over by Bishops Janes and Clark. I give a portion of Bishop Janes's appropriate address as reported at the time:

My feelings incline me to refer a little more distinctly to the lists of those brethren who were with us at that time, but whose bodily presence is now lacking. What a company of men! what a ministerial power! The patriarchal, wise, good, long-honored Nathan Bangs; the profound theologian, the able minister, Peter P. Sandford; the loving and beloved Bartholomew Creagh; the courteous, practical, useful Martindale; the intellectual, scholarly, self-reliant Floy; the eccentric, but intelligent and really godly Phineas Rice; the eloquent, the popular, the successful Kennaday; the majestic, mighty, learned, but humble Olin. But time would fail me to refer to Seaman and Jewett and Matthias and Hagany, and a multitude, or many, at least, of others of eminence and worth, whose record is on high, but whose memory should be cherished on earth. And then another class—Mercein and Foss and Law, who were in the morning of their ministry, who were yet blossoming, and passed away before their maturity, and upon whose memory rests the fragrance of the Rose of Sharon. O! many of our brethren who then stood with us in these ranks, whose names we have not even called, will be stars of the first magnitude in that beautiful cluster which these Conferences are placing in those spiritual heavens where they that have turned many to righteousness shall shine as the stars for ever and ever. I express it as my conviction that we have in the ministry at this time, in the fathers, in the brethren, and in the young men, as much wisdom, as much qualification for the work, as much devotion to it, as there was at that period ; and I believe that there is no backsliding in the Churches either; that the present day is as good as the past, and I look forward to our future with the highest hopes, with the liveliest anticipation.   I will conclude by saying that I trust these two New York Conferences will appreciate their position, and will feel the peculiar responsibility that rests upon them from their geographical location in this great city and the surrounding cities—this center of many influences, and this place of general power.   But—I cannot enlarge ; the watch will not stop for me to talk.   I have you in my heart, to live and die with you.   I received my natural and my spiritual birth within your Conference bounds.   I commenced my public Methodistic career, also, within your limits, and I shall be happy, if God so order, to die with you, and to have my grave with you.   And yet I feel, from my position, that I am just as likely to die in China or India, or, like Coke, on the ocean. But wherever I give up my spirit, I intend to have a union with you in heaven, at the throne of God.

The new, capacious, and beautiful St. John's Methodist Episcopal Church, Brooklyn, E. D., was dedicated on April 23, Bishop Janes preaching in the morning, and the Rev. William Morley Punshon, of England, in the evening.

14

CHAPTER XVII.

1868-1870.

The General Conference at Chicago—Summer and Autumn Conferences—Opening of the Work in the South—Twenty-fifth Year in the Episcopacy—Eminent Dead, Bishops Thomson, Kingsley, and others.

THE fifteenth delegated General Conference met at Chicago, Illinois, on May 1, 1868. All the Bishops were present at the opening session but Bishop Baker, who was detained by illness. The Bishops say in their address:

Never in the history of the Church has a General Conference convened under circumstances more favorable than those which attend this session. . . . The place of its assembling— this city so recent in date, of such wonderful growth, located on the shore of a beautiful inland lake, yet reaching its arms of commerce to distant parts of the globe—seems in harmony with the progress of the Church, to which God has given such rapidly extending boundaries. It has not only kept pace with the advancing columns of population on this continent, but, claiming the world for its parish, it has organized its Conferences in Africa, Europe, and Asia.

Bishop Janes, in response to the request of the Conference, delivered a report of his visit to the British and Irish Wesleyan Conferences. A few extracts only can be given; from one of which it will be seen that his sagacious and comprehensive mind had already forecast the Ecumenical Council of Methodism, which occurs this year (1881) in the city of London.

I was most profoundly impressed with the wisdom and dignity and spirituality of the Conferences.

My examination of Methodism in different countries has convinced me that it can live and operate in almost any condition and despite almost all embarrassments. It is simply consistent truth and divine grace working together, by chosen and sanctified instrumentalities, for the salvation of men. Its spirit is the spirit of Calvary, its power is the power of Pentecost, its glory the glory of the Cross. Yet the less incumbered it is, and the better adapted its instrumentalities, the greater will be its success. I have also been impressed with the importance of the connectional character of Methodism as essential to the fullest accomplishment of its great mission. Its direct action is to convert sinners, and to spread scriptural holiness over all lands. Its indirect, incidental influence is, in connection with other free evangelical Churches, by the moral effect of the voluntary principle, to separate all Protestant Churches from the State. This end, in my opinion, draws nigh. And, when this is done, then it will be our work and mission to antagonize a non-political and spiritual Church to a political and ceremonial Church. When these antagonisms meet, as meet they must, we shall need the connectional power. In those times, how it will encourage the hearts and strengthen the hands of those who may compose that great General Conference —and I believe there are men here who will be there—to have present corresponding sympathizing members from England, Ireland, France, Germany, Turkey, India, China, Africa, South America, and the islands of the sea! What a representative prayer-meeting they could hold! Where that General Conference shall meet—whether in Chicago or New York, or San Francisco or London, or Rome or China—I do not know. But meet where it may, it will be a grand power for the transformation of the world. This may seem chimerical to some, and perhaps to most, but I think I see it, and it is no chimera to my mind. It has not yet fully taken shape in my mind, but its outline is there; and I trust you will see it when it has taken shape and is established. But I submit whether there is not sober truth enough in it to show the importance of maintaining our connectional character inviolate, and fraternizing with the other branches of the Methodist family more closely.

The Rev. William Morley Punshon, M.A., had been appointed by the British Conference fraternal delegate to the General Conference of 1868, and his advent in America, not only because of his official character, but because of his pre-eminent position as the foremost pulpit orator of Wesleyan Methodism, excited a very profound interest. His sermons and address before the Conference, and, indeed, the sermons and lectures he delivered at various times and places while resident in Canada, as President of the Wesleyan body in the "Dominion," were listened to by large and delighted audiences. He became greatly endeared to Bishop Janes, and to all the Bishops, ministers, and people of the Methodist Episcopal Church, as well for his sterling personal qualities as for his transcendent eloquence.

"Lay Representation in the General Conference" was the absorbing topic of the session of 1868. A hotly contested debate finally resulted in the adoption of a report re-affirming the positions of 1860 and 1864, and providing for the introduction of lay delegates into the General Conference of 1872 on condition that a majority of the people above twenty-one years of age present and voting, and three fourths of the members of the Annual Conferences, and two thirds of the delegates to the next General Conference, should so decide.

The Church Extension and Freedmen's Aid Societies of the Methodist Episcopal Church, which had originated during the interim of the sessions of 1864 and 1868, were fully authorized by this Conference, and adopted as General Conference societies. After a session of twenty-seven days the Conference adjourned, Bishop Janes making the closing address and offering the closing prayer.

A fragment of diary, in the Bishop's hand-writing, for the month of August, shows how he usually whiled away his time through the dog days, when no Conference sessions were on his hands:

Sunday, Aug. 2. Dedicated Tompkins Avenue Church, Brooklyn.

Sunday, Aug. 9. Dedicated a Church at Long Branch, N. J.

Tuesday, Aug. 11. Preached at the Sing Sing camp-meeting. God helped me.

Wednesday, Aug. 12. Dedicated a church at Rondout, New York.

Wednesday, Aug. 19. Dedicated the church at Summit, New Jersey.

Thursday, Aug. 20. Dedicated a church at Mount Kisco, on the Harlem railroad.

Friday, Aug. 21. Laid the corner-stone of a church in Perry-street, New York.

Sunday, Aug. 23. Preached at Bernardsville, from "He shall be called Wonderful." A pleasant meditation.

Wednesday, Aug. 26. Preached at the Morristown camp-meeting from James v, 19, 20. Loss of sleep and close application to letter-writing left me poorly qualified to preach.

Thursday, Aug. 27. Spent day in business in New York. Took cars in the evening for the West.

From the sermon at the Sing Sing camp-meeting, on the peace of God, Phil. iv. 7, in the preaching of which he says, " God helped me," there occurs a passage on the right of a believer to shout, and what it is that should shout :

Shall men be full of joy and utter it with music, with dancing, with singing and with shouting, in their wild revelries of sin and folly, and shall not men and women, when they come together in the name of God, and engage in his most holy worship? When He comes down and manifests his presence, reveals his glory, dispenses his grace, supplies their every want, and makes them exultant in the divine and joyous experience of his grace, shall they have no utterance, no testimony? " Cry out and shout, thou inhabitant of Zion : for great is the Holy One of Israel in the midst of thee." Let the world hear our joyous noise ; let the whole earth be full of the praise of God, and from the lips of his people. It is just as orderly and as proper to shout here as it is in heaven ; it is just as proper to lift up our voices like many waters as it will be in the day of our triumph in glory. Let your conduct and your shout have an affinity. You may not only send them to heaven, but you may send them to the ends of the earth ; not only shout at your family altar, and in your sanctuary, but in your store, and in the street ; but, remember, it must be *character* that shouts. And when you have this experience, when you have this peace of God in your souls, the life will be such as will justify the wisdom of God's children in all their rejoicings and in all their trials. There will be a great deal of religious noise in this world before it is converted ; there will be a great deal more when it is converted. I hope you will have here, before this meeting closes, the shouts of converts that will ring through all this congregation and fill all this space; and God will be honored by it. If any are so precise in their religious character as that they cannot enjoy it, let them go to their closets, and in answer to prayer, get power, and when they get the taste, they will relish it as much as we do, and as much as angels do, and as much as God does.

In the summer and autumn the Bishop met the Delaware, Iowa, Illinois, and Central Illinois Conferences, concluding his official work on Sept. 28.

Among the earthly havens into which the Bishop loved to put, if he could find a leisure day to furl his sails and lie at anchor, was Wildercliffe, the residence of Miss Mary Garrettson, near Rhinebeck, N. Y. This beautiful home, bequeathed to Miss Garrettson by her venerable parents, overlooking the Hudson, and commanding a distant view of the Catskill Mountains as well, was ever open to Methodist ministers, and none were more welcome guests there than Bishop and Mrs. Janes. The peaceful rural surroundings, the play of light and shadow upon water, valley, and mountain, to say nothing of the high and holy thinking and converse within doors, constituted it a thoroughly attractive and restful spot to the weary sojourner. Yet it was seldom the Bishop could indulge himself in its luxurious rest.

To Miss M. Garrettson, August 20:

May grace, mercy, and peace be multiplied unto you abundantly. I received your letter very kindly inviting me to visit you at the time of the dedication at Rondout. It was in my heart to do so, but official obligations did not permit. My public duties become more and more engrossing every year. Every advance of the Church increases the care and labors of the General Superintendents. It is sweet to work for Jesus. It is deeply interesting to labor for humanity, especially for the spiritual welfare of the race. To be workers together with God in saving souls is a sublime and blessed privilege. I am sorry I have not appreciated it more highly. My sun has passed its meridian. I am in the afternoon of life. I am resolved that my evening time shall bring good to man and glory to God. I trust you are in comfortable health. I doubt not you enjoy as keenly as ever the remarkable and almost redundant natural beauties with which your heavenly Father has surrounded you. Though your eye may become dim,* they will never fade from your mind. In childhood you looked upon them when your father and mother enjoyed them with you. To you they are sacred. O how your heart must cherish them! But there are sublimer, sweeter, and more sacred visions for us to behold. To see the King in his beauty, to see Jesus as he is, to see those beloved parents in their beatitude, and to be with them and like them—O what ravished visions heaven will afford! What a blessed hope is ours while here on earth we stay! We will not be concerned if our bodies fail, if time flits by. Death is gain. To depart and be with Christ, when life's work is all done, is far better. Glory be to God for the assurance! I intend to visit you just as soon as God will permit. Mrs. Janes loves you very much.

Among the burdens which pressed upon the heart of the Bishop this autumn was the work in the South Carolina Conference, solicitude for a new church building in Richmond, Va., and also the

* An allusion to the fact that at this time Miss Garrettson was threatened with blindness.

urgent growing demands of the City Sunday-School
and Church Extension Society in New York city.
The Rev. T. Willard Lewis writes him from Charleston, S. C.:

Baker Institute opened Monday last with eighteen promising
young men, but how I am to get through the year without
more aid I know not, and I feel sad at the condition of our
missionary treasury, but trust God may open some way for our
relief. If Grant is elected I think we shall have passable protection, and can push forward our work if we can only have
the men and the means.

And the Rev. Dr. J. A. Webster, of Charleston,
further says:

We shall greatly need an increase in our appropriation here.
Think of one presiding elder district with nearly, or quite,
20,000 members.

Mrs. General Canby writes to the Bishop from
Richmond, Va.:

I am glad to hear you favor the idea of keeping up a Northern Methodist Episcopal Church here in this very heart of
rebeldom. The need of a good Union Church in this city is
far greater than even you imagine—a Church where loyal
people can feel they are among friends.

The above reference to the election of General
Grant may appropriately introduce a letter of the
Bishop making mention of a visit to the General at
Washington. The great captain had just been
elected to the Presidency, and was, if possible, more
than ever the center of all eyes. The Bishops had
united in a congratulatory address to the General
14*

on his election, and Bishops Janes and Ames were deputed to bear it:

General Grant received us very courteously. Bishop Ames briefly stated our object in seeking the interview, and I read to him the official letter of the Bishops. He seemed considerably affected by it; thanked the Bishops very earnestly for their consideration of him. After the official transaction was ended we entered into a free conversation. He was very easy and unreserved in the expression of his views of his position and of public affairs. The leave-taking was expressive of reciprocal regards.

How like the rich, sublime beauties of an autumnal day the portraiture here of growing old! These beauties, alas! the harbingers of approaching winter; but with him even winter shall be gladdened with the fruits of holy living.

To Mrs. Janes:

It is true the autumn of life is on us, but its frosts will only purify our spiritual atmosphere, and its cool days only invigorate our souls. The winter of life with us, you know, is to be very pleasant. Even

" On the cold cheek of death smiles and roses are blending,
And beauty immortal awakes from the tomb."

Religion makes flowers bloom every-where, and its ripe and luscious fruits are always plenteous and within reach.

The fiftieth anniversary of the parent Missionary Society was held in Washington, D. C., on January 10 and 11, 1869, at which the Bishop was one of the preachers and speakers. Standing in the cap-

ital of the nation, surrounded by scholars and statesmen, and looking back upon the half century's
work of the society, he says:

Who sympathizes with the heathen world to-night? Where
is there any interest on this question except with God and his
Church? Who are laying plans, forming schemes, devising
measures, and giving money to meet these circumstances and
to relieve these wants? The governments of the earth are not
directly doing it. England and the United States are the two
most enlightened and most powerful Protestant nations in the
world; and yet this question has never come up in the cabinets
of either of these governments. I do not say that it ought
to. It may not be the legitimate function of government; at
any rate, perhaps the minds of neither nation are prepared to
sustain the government in doing this. Well, infidels do not
do it. There never has been, and is not to-night, an infidel
missionary society for sending the light of God's truth and the
institutions of God's grace to the benighted, perishing heathen
nations. Infidels do not send help; on the contrary, they seek
to rob us of our God, of our Saviour, and of our heaven. Philosophers do not do it. We have scientific associations—historical, geological, astronomical. These philosophers are interested in the study of the stars, and in the discovery of those
which have not before been observed; but who of them ever
talks to the world about the Star of Bethlehem? These philosophers are most deeply and proudly interested in the triumphs of science, and are engaged heartily and earnestly in
forming electric currents of thought through the ocean, from
continent to continent and kingdom to kingdom, but which of
them ever thought of sending a current of God's love to any
one of those distant and barbarous climes? Commerce is not
doing it. Commerce has aided in providing facilities of inter-
national communication—and they are advantageous to our
Christian enterprise; but commerce does not seek to evangel-
ize the nations: on the contrary, many of its agencies are the

most embarrassing circumstances which we have to contend with in propagating the Gospel. I repeat it, the only sympathy which the heathen world has is in the heart of God and the heart of his Church, and the only influences which have been exerted for the recovery and salvation of the nations is God and his people—his people working with him in this work of evangelism, of sending his word and his grace to the ends of the earth.

In our missionary work we embrace the domestic as well as the foreign. We are looking to our own country as well as to distant lands ; and my impression is that we are wise in doing so. I think in these United States is to be the seat both of civil and religious power ; that our institutions must be preserved in order to the bringing in of those happy days which have been referred to by both the previous speakers. For this purpose we have been, as a Church, seeking to follow emigration as it has gone westward, and to give to the border populations of the country the institutions of religion, and God has aided us in doing it. We have also sought most earnestly to meet, with our religious institutions and agencies, the immigrant populations that have come from the Old World to this. As one result we have at this time some three hundred pastors, native Germans, preaching to their countrymen in their native language, and some twenty-seven thousand communicants in our Church who are natives of that foreign land. We have also several presiding elders' districts among the Scandinavian population that has come to this country.

I say here, in the presence of these eminent statesmen, that there is no power which can denationalize this immigrant population that is coming here, and assimilate it to our American character and make us a homogeneous people, but the religion of our Lord Jesus Christ, the truth and spirit of almighty God ; and in this divine evangelism, this gospel power, is the hope of our country as well as the redemption of our world. And we must see to it that all the peoples of this country have these institutions, agencies, fellowship, and sympathy displayed to them as they come among us. When we do this.

with God's blessing upon us, we shall succeed in the two purposes of blessing the nation and saving the people.

Again it was the lot of the Bishop to meet the South Carolina Conference, which held its session this year, Feb. 11–13, 1869, at Camden, S. C. Thence he writes to Mrs. Janes:

I had a prosperous journey, and reached Washington Tuesday A. M.; left immediately, and reached Wilmington, N. C., at five A. M. Wednesday. Now I think if my march was not as wonderful as Sherman's in some respects, it certainly was more rapid. I arrived at this city about six and a half o'clock, tired and dusty, not having washed or brushed since I left home. I slept well last night, and am quite naturalized today. By to-morrow I shall be thoroughly reconstructed. We had a very interesting session of Conference this morning. The work has prospered largely during the year. Our Church is rooted and grounded in South Carolina. God is with the people, and our cause cannot be overthrown.

In March he met the St. Louis, Missouri, and Kansas Conferences, and in April the Nebraska Conference. Writing home while on this tour, such expressions as those which follow fell from his pen. The reference to the completion of the twenty-fifth year of his episcopal service is very touching.

Conference commenced pleasantly yesterday. Some serious difficulties to be adjusted; anxieties, of course; they abide with me every-where and all the time—"the care of all the Churches."

Another busy week before me. All right! Working for God and his Church is the highest privilege in this world.

Conference times are seasons of hard work and great anxiety. The Church is growing in this section. I am without anxiety about our temporal affairs. I have left them, for the present, in the hands of my heavenly Father.

The telegraph reports the death of Brother James Harper. A sad termination to a long and useful life. I am very thankful the meetings in St. Paul's are so interesting and successful. I pray their power may increase and extend. This is the last Conference I expect to preside over in the first quarter of a century of my episcopal office. Next month will end that quarter. How soon it has passed away! What a history it has made! What events have occurred in Church and State in that period! Eventful times, indeed! I have in that time seen much of the goodness of God. What protection! What assistance! What encouragement! What manifestations of his love! I am thankful. A few years more must end my official career. I hope to finish my course with joy, and the ministry of the Lord Jesus Christ.

On the first Monday in June following the Bishop chanced to be at home, and attended the devotional exercises of the New York Preachers' Meeting. In response to an invitation he briefly addressed the meeting, saying substantially that he had always found pleasure in preaching the Gospel, and he preferred the pastoral relation to any position in the gift of the Church. He mentioned, also, very affectingly, that on this day he had reached the twenty-fifth year of the office he was then filling. At the close of his remarks a congratulatory resolution was offered by the Rev. Dr. (now Bishop) Foss, and unanimously passed by the meeting.

As far back as at their meeting at Erie, Pa., in 1865, the Bishops of the Methodist Episcopal .

Church took initial steps looking to a closer union between all the Methodist bodies of the country, especially those whose separation had been caused by slavery. The General Conference of 1868 appointed a commission of eight members of that body and the Board of Bishops to promote this object. Accordingly the Bishops, at their spring meeting in 1869, addressed a letter to the Bishops of the Methodist Episcopal Church, South, and appointed Bishops Morris, Janes, and Simpson to bear it. In May Bishops Janes and Simpson, Bishop Morris being unable to accompany them, went to St. Louis, where the Southern Bishops were in session, and presented the letter. Bishop Janes's letter to Bishop Clark, from St. Louis, May 8, will explain his connection with the matter:

We had an interview with the Bishops of the Methodist Episcopal Church, South, this morning ; were courteously received. After a little social conversation we presented our letter accrediting us ; then, Bishop Morris's letter of apology for not being present ; then a communication stating the points in the text presented to the Board at Meadville. They were all read. Each of us then said a few words, stating they were not official, but personal. Bishop Paine replied that they appreciated the object contemplated in our communication ; were glad to see us ; they would consider the subject and forward a reply. We then had prayer together, and parted in a very friendly manner. The reply will be sent to Bishop Morris.

The Bishops of the South met the overtures of our Bishops by affirming that they must stand by the words of their rejected delegate, Dr. L. Pierce, of 1848, and entered their objection to "slavery as the cause of the separation" between the two great Methodist bodies. Nothing was appreciably accomplished by the interview beyond a courteous, kindly interchange of personal good feeling; and yet it was a beginning, however slight, of a closer approach between the two Churches. In view of ·the asperities which grew out of the war, it is not surprising that more was not effected. There are some wounds which time alone can heal. As the events and controversies of the past recede, and the men who participated in them are gathered to their fathers, and new men and new issues arise, it can be confidently hoped that all that Bishop Janes so earnestly desired and sought will come of itself. His heart yearned for it, and he felt it to be one of the happiest acts of his life to be the first to go forth with the olive branch, even at the risk of finding no solid ground for his feet.

In the summer and autumn his Conferences were the Delaware, East Genesee, North Ohio, Central Ohio, and Ohio. From the sessions of these he returned wearied, but not to rest. Some claim for special service was ever at his door.

November 3 the venerable Dr. Heman Bangs died at New Haven, Conn.; and, according to his request, the Bishop delivered the address at his funeral, which was "a beautiful tribute to the memory" of a strong and useful minister.

December 12–14 the Bishop participated in a missionary anniversary at Boston, Mass. On Sunday evening the great gathering of the Methodists was at Music Hall, and before it he delivered one of the addresses. The Rev. Dr. Warren, President of Boston University, writing to him a few days afterward, says:

I wanted to thank you for your splendid missionary speech Sunday night, but being in a distant part of the hall it was impracticable. It will not soon be forgotten. Some tell our students that, after all, a missionary life is a very easy and comfortable calling, that they need not fear its hardships, etc. I would rather have them go out expecting to be scalped and roasted, or, at least, prepared to be.

The Bishop is next found at the national capital, possibly on some errand to preach the Gospel, or to look after some interest of missions in connection with one of the departments. Through the courtesy of the Rev. Dr. J. P. Newman, then chaplain of the United States Senate, he was invited to offer prayer at the opening of the session of the Senate, December 16. The record of the year may be appropriately closed with the insertion of this prayer:

Most gracious and most glorious God, we hallow thy name; we reverence thy majesty; we acknowledge thy authority. Thou art God over all, blessed for evermore, and we worship thee. We desire at this time to render to thee our praise for our being and for our well-being, for our happiness and for our hopes. From thee cometh every good and every perfect gift, and we do bless thee for thy many and great mercies which we have shared. We confess ourselves unworthy of thy regard, for we have sinned; we have strayed from thy ways; we have greatly failed to meet our obligations to thee, our Maker and Redeemer and God. We have not loved thee and worshiped thee and served thee as it was our duty to have done. Have mercy upon us. O, for Christ's sake, have mercy upon us and forgive us all our sins, and grant to us the transformations of the Holy Spirit, that we may be made partakers of the divine nature, be restored to the divine fellowship, prepared to walk with God on earth, and qualified to reign with thee in heaven.

We invoke thy blessing, O God, upon our nation, upon the people of this great country, all classes of them, all conditions of them. We invoke thy blessing upon the authorities of the land. Bless thy servant, the President of these United States. We pray that his life and health may be continued, and that he may be providentially and graciously aided in the administration of the authority which is intrusted to him. We pray thee to bless thy servant who presides over this branch of the legislative department of the government, and every member of this Senate. May their lives and health be precious in thy sight. May they receive favor from God, and be guided by thy Spirit in such a manner that they will perform their official duties here in accordance with thy will, and in such a manner as to promote the best interests of this nation. And in their absence we pray God to take care of their families. Preserve them from disease and from death and from all afflictions, and grant unto them all the temporal and spiritual benefits which are needed by them.

We pray God to bless the other branch of this legislative body. Guide them by thy wisdom, and control them by thy power, and bring them to right conclusions upon all questions. We entreat thee to bless the judicial department of the government and all who are in authority. May our public affairs be so ordered as to secure the intelligence and virtue and religion of the land, to preserve and perpetuate our institutions, and to make our example as a nation a blessing to all the kingdoms of the earth.

We pray God to hear us in these our supplications at this time, and continue to each one of us thy grace and mercy through future life, and when we shall have served thee in our generation upon earth, grant to us a peaceful egress from the world, and an abundant entrance into thy eternal kingdom and glory, through Him who has taught us, in our devotions, to say, " Our Father," etc.

In January, 1870, the Southern sea-board Conferences were again assigned to Bishop Janes. He writes to his daughter, Mrs. C. E. Harris, from Charleston, S. C., January 18 :

My tour so far has been decidedly pleasant. Flowers are in bloom in the gardens. Next week I expect to see figs and oranges and lemons, and all sorts of bloom. Our Church is making some progress, mostly among the colored people. Social and financial improvements are very slow. Some of the people do not know how to do any thing out of the old rut of slavery. Some have not become good-natured enough to try to do any thing. I spend the Sabbath here, and expect to preach in two colored churches. One of the congregations is really colored, dyed in the wool. The other is a faded congregation, all shades of black and brown and yellow and white. They are pretty intelligent. Some noble men and women. Reconstruction has been accomplished in this State. I visited the Legislature. One third of the senators and two thirds of the lower house are colored men. It was a novel sight to see in the proud Palmetto State such a mixed body of men filling the legislative halls.

The Bishop's spring Conferences were the Wilmington, Pittsburgh, Wyoming, and New York. But the cares of these Conferences were the least of the cares which oppressed him this season. Death was abroad, and his darts fell upon some of the great and wise men of the Church—men who were the Bishop's chosen friends and compeers. It was a season of sorrow. First died the Rev. Dr. John M'Clintock, President of Drew Theological Seminary. The loss of no prominent minister since the death of Dr. Olin so deeply affected him. Over his lifeless form, in the presence of a dense and weeping multitude, he said :

God has smitten, and his stroke is heavy upon us. O how heavy! Gracious Parent, sustain us under it. . . . How we loved him—how worthy he was of our love! How we trusted him, and how true he was to our confidence! So ready to sympathize, so wise to counsel, so willing to help, so charitable to our faults, so loving, and so loved.

To the death of this great preacher and scholar quickly succeeded that of Mr. William W. Cornell, one of the choicest and most benevolent laymen of New York city. To him, also, the Bishop was strongly attached. He had scarcely recovered from these strokes ere the telegraph bore the news " Bishop Thomson is dead," and " Bishop Kingsley is dead." Both had fallen at their posts. Bishop Thomson died of typhoid pneumonia, in the city of Wheeling, W. Va., on March 22, after only a few days' illness ; and Bishop Kingsley died suddenly of heart disease, at Beyroot, Syria, on April 6. Great as this blow was to the Church, it was even heavier for the surviving Bishops. Bishop Janes's personal grief at the loss of his younger colleagues was very acute; and their death added, in connection with the protracted illness of Bishop Baker and the extreme feebleness of Bishop Morris, greatly to his official labors. The painful and consuming cares of 1850–52 were now repeated and even intensified. Such was the unwisdom of the General Conference in not re-enforcing the ranks of the Episcopacy, but keeping it down to the *minimum* working capacity.

Bishop Janes to Bishop Morris, Wilkesbarre, Pa., April 14:

How greatly God has afflicted us! Our two youngest, and, perhaps, most cherished colleagues have been taken from us so suddenly, so unexpectedly, so mysteriously! "It is the Lord, let him do what seemeth him right."

A letter to his daughter, Mrs. C. E. Harris, about the same date, better shows his personal feelings:

O what scenes and experiences I have passed through since we parted! If I were to measure the period by its events, excitements, and duties, it would be a full year. Rarely do so many important events and deep experiences occur in the life of even a public man in a year. The death of my own dear sister, of my cherished friend Dr. M'Clintock, of my very valuable friend W. W. Cornell, of my two dear colleagues, Bishops Thomson and Kingsley, the youngest and most hopeful of our Board. Beloved colleagues! dying so suddenly, so mysteriously, away from their families! O it is very, very sad. I feel this loss most deeply. Then, in these few weeks I have presided in six Annual Conferences, stationing about a thousand ministers, preaching, and dedicating churches, etc. They have been wonderful weeks ! Excessive labors and frequent colds taken in my night travels very much impaired my health. For about ten days I was really ill.   But I am quite recuperated again. My cough has not entirely left me, but I am able to sleep quite well at nights.   I expect to come home from this Conference quite restored.   Yet we have been impressively taught that life and health and all sublunary things are very uncertain.

The following extract of a letter to the Bishop, from the Rev. Mr. Punshon, dated at Toronto, C. W., April 28, on the death of Dr. M'Clintock and Bishops Thomson and Kingsley, is a noble tribute :

I have very profoundly sympathized with the great losses which your Church has recently been called, in the providence of God, to sustain, in the deaths of administrators so wise, scholars so ripe, and preachers of the truth so eminent, as Dr. M'Clintock and Bishop Thomson and Bishop Kingsley. The ways of God are surely past finding out, and we must wait for the solution of the mystery until the stone is rolled away from the mouth of every sepulcher.

CHAPTER XVIII.

1870–1871.

Letters to absent members of his family—The routine of Conferences
—Third visit to the Pacific—Conferences in the South-west.

DURING the summer of this year the members of the Bishop's family were separated. Miss Lizzie Janes accompanied Mrs. Ridgaway and myself to Europe, and Mrs. Janes availed herself of the opportunity to visit Mrs. Luqueer, at Pittsfield, Massachusetts, and also Mr. and Mrs. Henry J. Baker, at Sing Sing, N. Y., while the Bishop, as usual, was passing hither and thither through the land.

To Mrs. Janes, from New York, July 13 :

Good morning to my beloved bride. Our honeymoon is still waxing, so I conclude your bridal days are not over. I believe we agreed to make the journey of life our bridal tour, so it is not ended yet. True, we have each of us traveled much of the time by ourselves, but still we have met now and then, and the luxury has so delighted us that we could go in the strength of it many days. I have never been in solitude since I was married. If my bride was not by my side she was in my heart. If I could not speak to her I could think of her. If I could not pray with her I could pray for her. As we have gone up the hill of life in sweet sympathy, so we will go down the hill, if not hand in hand, heart in heart.

To Mrs. Janes, from Middletown, Conn., July 19:

I went last evening to hear Senator Willey's oration. A grand one it was! I went not as a matter of pleasure, but as a matter of duty; yet it became pleasant duty. . . . I have been in the chair all day, and weary enough; still I must go to hear an oration to-night. I judge the college has been prospering this year. A fine class will graduate.

The Bishop scarcely ever failed to attend the commencements at Middletown. The commencement this year was one of much rejoicing among the friends of the institution. On the occasion Bishop Janes addressed them in words of encouragement and cheer. "The president," he said, "had alluded to the fact that he (the Bishop) was an old man. Physically speaking, that was so; but his feelings were as young as ever. Still, he was apprised that his day of active service was already in the evening time, and as its close approached he looked with increasing interest upon every thing that related to human destiny. The subject came up before him with a solemnity, a sublimity, and an interest which he did not perceive in it years ago. He was sure if he had seen it in that light when in youth, he would have been more given up to the one great service of benefiting his generation and glorifying God. It would not be egotistic in him to say that there was no man who had seen so much of the fruits of the Wesleyan University as he had. He remembered well its organization, and was pretty

well acquainted with its history. His duties required him to traverse the entire country, and wherever he went he met some one who had been connected with the institution, whose education and
character qualified him for usefulness in the Church,
and usefulness in whatever sphere he was called to
act.   At the present time the great educational
work of the Methodist Episcopal Church was more
in the hands of the graduates of that university than
of any other.   There were more of the associates
of those whom he addressed at the head of institutions of learning, professors in them, than were
furnished by any other of our institutions. This
was more especially true of the theological institutions, the majority of whose teachers were
graduates of Wesleyan University. What a
great moral power and religious agency was this!
He expected that the young men educated by
those teachers would soon reach the ends of the
earth, for he believed that God was in earnest to
convert the world. Hinderances and embarrassments would come up, but God intended to make
them all subserve the great result of the evangelization of the world; and this institution was an
efficient agency in bringing about that most blessed
result."

To Mrs. Janes, while visiting at Pittsfield, Mass.:

I have just returned from New Jersey. I yesterday attended
the temperance mass meeting at Denville camp-ground. The
15

morning was cloudy and threatened rain ; still there was a gathering of several thousands. Six speeches, and then your husband was called to the stand. A late hour and wearied audience ; still they stayed and listened and cheered, and we had an interesting forty minutes. Neal Dow spoke for one hour and thirty-five minutes. A good speech, and a good deal of it. The speeches were all good, not excepting my own. There! is not that a fine specimen of egotism ? Well, I really think it ; and if you and I are one, why should you not think it too ? It was a plain, honest, earnest talk on the great subject of temperance. I was glad to be able to telegraph you of Lizzie's safe arrival at Liverpool. I had been a little anxious for two days.

I spent last night with our friends Mr. and Mrs. Baker, at Sing Sing. I was anxious about him, so I went up last evening. He has been sick, but is improving. He is meet for the inheritance of the saints in light. I start in a few minutes for Newark, where, you know, I spend the Sabbath.

I inclose a newspaper report of the commencement at Middletown, that you may learn how the occasion passed, and also see how absurdly they can write about your husband. It may amuse you a little.

I spent yesterday at Mianus ; dedicated their beautiful church ; ordained one of the missionaries who sails for India on Wednesday. I am trying to get my correspondence straightened out. I wrote all day on Saturday, and am doing so to-day. I have over seventy yet to answer.

You have not been from home so long since we were married. It must seem strange to you. Well, I have no doubt it would be a sore trial if—yes, if—if you were not among angels. Cannot be unsatisfied in their society. Now, after all my sympathy, perhaps you have gotten so weaned from us, and so fascinated with your new home characters, that you will not be willing to come back. Who knows ? What shall I do in such a case ? It would be an ugly thing to send a constable to bring the household god. And then you are out of the State. I should have to apply to the governor of New York for a requisition on the governor of Massachusetts. O what a fuss! Well, I will not borrow trouble. I apprehend business will allow me to try my luck the last of this week or the first of next, and see if I can get you home again. Excuse this nonsense.

To his daughter Miss Janes, while in Europe:

How I wish I knew where you are, and how you are. I suppose you have sniffed the air of, old Ireland before this. I presume you were much surprised on reaching England to find a state of war on the Continent. It is a very sudden, and, I fear, a very disastrous war. . . . Learn all you can of the world; make the acquaintance of all the good people you can; fill your memory with lovely visions.

We sent you in our last letter the notice of the death of Mr. George T. Cobb and Mr. Theodore Stout. Yesterday I attended the funeral of Mr. Stout. I am pleased you met Dr. Robinson Scott. I am delighted Bishop Simpson made so good an impression at the Wesleyan Conference.

I go to Sing Sing to-morrow to preach at the camp-meeting. I also expect to preach at the Morristown camp-meeting on Friday. I keep pretty well. My hard work and sympathy with the sick and bereaved have been rather trying to my strength.

The Church was called upon in this month to give up another one of its choice ministers—the Rev. Thomas Sewall, D.D., died in Baltimore, on August 11. No one in all Methodism more highly estimated this polished and eloquent man than Bishop Janes. He is found under the pressure of the arduous summer turning aside to write to his friend, then in the extremity of the last conflict. The letter reached the dying saint just before the angels bore his victorious spirit home:

Yesterday I saw Rev. Brother Buckley, who informed me you were very feeble, and, perhaps, growing weaker. I wish I could come and see you. O how much I wish to greet you once more in the flesh! I do most affectionately salute you in the Lord. The great affliction I feel at the prospect of not seeing you again in this world shows me how greatly I love you. I should feel very sad did I not turn my attention to your beatitude—to your glorification. O, how much better to depart and be with Christ!

When Brother Buckley told me of your prostration, my first thought was, Is he to be gathered with M'Clintock and Foss and Nadal and Kingsley and Thomson? What a select circle of noble spirits! So like each other, and so associated on earth as to seek each other in heaven. To be one of that circle will be blessed indeed. O how rapturously they will hail you on your approach! How tender and congratulatory will be their greeting! You will not be a stranger in heaven. There are many there whom you will recognize when you meet them. Jesus will recognize you, and I am sure you will instantly distinguish him. How I wish I could see you enter the golden gates, and witness your first sight of "Him, as he is." I fancy I have a pretty clear idea of how you and M'Clintock and Nadal* will act on your first interview. I think you will all want to speak first. Possibly you may all shout together. Then, too, that excellent, godly father—I know how much you loved him. I know how eminently worthy of your love he was. How you will delight to be again in his company. Verily, you have a great amount and a great variety of treasure in heaven. I know you loved to preach Christ when you had health and could do so. I know it is a trial to lay down that silver trumpet. I know, too, it is a severe trial to leave your beloved wife and little ones. You are not responsible for these consequences. You have not decided the question of life or death. God has done that. He will look to

---

* The Rev. B. H. Nadal, D.D., Professor in Drew Theological Seminary, who died June 20, 1870.

the consequences. He will carry forward his work. He will be a husband to your widow, and a father to your children. How do you know but that you can minister to them as kindly and as usefully out of the body as you can in the body? If God calls you to himself, without anxiety leave your loved ones to him. Confide all their welfare to him. He will care for them. I am coming after you. I am determined to keep the faith and lay hold on eternal life. I shall want to see you very soon after I get there.

I commend you to the love of God, to the mediation of Jesus, and the comfort of the Holy Ghost. With much love for your family, and much prayer for yourself, I am your affectionate brother in Jesus.

The Bishop's fall Conferences began with the Cincinnati, August 24, and concluded with the Rock River, October 11.

From Piqua, Ohio, to Mrs. Janes, August 24:

In thirty-eight hours and forty-eight minutes after I left you I reached my lodgings here. The journey was very dusty and warm. I hope you reached your second heaven in great comfort. 107 East Twenty-fourth-street* is the first heaven, Brother Baker's is the second heaven, and Paradise the third. Well, we have shared the two first, we must see to it that we shall share the last together. We cannot afford to come short of that.

I hope our dear friends, Brother and Sister Baker, are comfortable in their health. I see nothing else to detract from their felicity. Their resources of happiness are so varied and rich I expect the good Lord saw it necessary to give them a thorn in the flesh. So happy in their circumstances and friends and each other, perhaps they needed something as a remembrancer of their mortality. After all, a thorn in the flesh

---

* The residence of the Bishop in New York city.

is not a very grievous thing. We can bear the pain of the body, but "a wounded spirit who can bear?" If the balm of Gilead makes our souls whole—if we share the nature and partake the joy of the Lord—all is well. That is the supreme good, the highest attainment.

. . . I have several times, when sailing on the ocean, seen a little bird which had been driven out to sea by the storm, light on the vessel panting for breath, all exhausted, and just ready to perish. Poor little spent thing! it could not sing to please an angel. It could only put its head under its wing and say, "Let me be quiet." O! how often has my condition been similar. Fatigued with labor, wearied with travel, oppressed with cares, teased by dissatisfied preachers and Churches, perplexed with questions of administration day after day and week after week, until, all exhausted, hardly alive, I reach the ship of love called home, and every part of my body and every faculty of my soul says, "O, let me rest—rest! Don't disturb me—let me rest!" How sweet is home then ! Quiet home! To please a friend—no, not to please a wife— can I sing or even talk.

To Mrs. Janes, from Cedar Falls, Iowa, Sept. 9:

God's blessing is upon me this morning; I am comfortable in body and serene in spirit. Conference is progressing pleasantly and I think profitably. The weather is now pleasant. We have had two terrible thunder showers. During the first a Methodist church in this vicinity was blown into widely scattered fragments. Several dwellings also were demolished. The prairie storms are wild and grand and awful. I desire to be spared the sight of a first-class storm at sea and a first-class storm on the prairies. They are both sublimely awful scenes.

. . . I trust we shall spend our eternity together. Stop. Possibly our blessed Lord may have some mission on which to employ us then. If so, I am sure we shall respond, "Here am I, send me." I am of the opinion that one element of our heavenly felicity will be found in our employments. These capabilities of ours, restored and perfected, will be employed in some service worthy of their highest exercise, and which will afford the purest pleasure. The rest of heaven will not be found in sleep. It will be found in exemption from all annoyance, and in adequate power to sustain the vision of God and all the fruition of the spiritual world. Nothing will exhaust our power, but every thing increase our strength and energy. To work without weariness—will not that be blessed! To worship without fatigue—O, how glorious! To be with God uninterruptedly and eternally—how infinite and exalted the bliss! "Forever with the Lord." That is my heaven.

At the session of the Upper Iowa Conference the Bishop preached a sermon on Christian holiness which was afterward fully reported. I give an extract, which shows how clearly he recognizes this doctrine as taught and maintained by Methodism :

Another element of Bible holiness is spiritual power—an appreciable measure of which we felt when we repented of our sins and received pardon. This power raises one to a higher plane than the one on which we stood in justification. Being cleansed in the flesh and in the spirit takes away all the friction of the soul. It moves in its sphere smoothly and harmoniously, just as a piece of machinery which is perfect in its construction does its work in a quiet and satisfactory manner. The source of this power is found in the devotion of that whole being of which we have already spoken.

... I am not prepared to say that in this new experience, this holy change, your experience will be more rapturous than when God first converted you; but you will have a peace that is deeper and more constant than you had before. I do say that you will have a serenity of spirit that you had not before, and could not have. You will have a truer conception of God. You will taste more of the power of the world of happiness to come. You will have more of the spirit of the eternal, of the divine, glory, than you found in your lower religious experience and life, and this joy of the heart will be increased in proportion to your strength—it will grow more and more.

The year 1871 is memorable as being fraught, if possible, with more constant, responsible, and certainly more extended labors than the year 1851. His travels reached from the Atlantic to the Pacific coast, and from New Hampshire to Texas. The sessions of seventy Conferences devolved upon four effective Bishops! In the spring Bishop Janes presided in the Baltimore, Central Pennsylvania, New Jersey, Providence, New Hampshire, Vermont, East German, and Black River Conferences, eight in about as many weeks. Yet from the sessions of all these he found time to send cheery letters to the family circle. I can give an extract only here and there.

To Mrs. Janes, from Carlisle, Pa.:

I adjourned the Baltimore Conference a quarter before twelve o'clock to-day. Immediately took cars for this place, and arrived safely this evening, though a good deal fatigued. From five o'clock Monday morning until two o'clock Tuesday morning I was intensely engaged. Then, from six this morning until this present time, I have had no rest. I am expecting a good sleep to-night, and to be bright in the morning. The public attendance upon the Conference at Baltimore was enthusiastic. Ladies, by scores, stood in the aisles four to five hours at a time—the house in every part of it filled to the utmost.

I hope you and Lizzie are both as bright as angels, and as happy. Why not? Do you not belong to the family of God?

So do the angels. They are in the upper room and you in the lower one. But the Lord is in both rooms. Perhaps the upper room is a little more richly furnished, and there may be more of the family there; they have no imperfections or sufferings; but we belong to the same family, and are soon going to see and enjoy their beatitudes.

This, you know, is my birthday. Sixty-four years old to-day. Sixty-four years of varied and deep experiences—years of activity. My boyhood was spent in work; my manhood has been spent in labor, responsible, difficult, anxious labor. I have been the recipient of many great mercies from God, and many favors from men. My family are endeared to me by thousands of kindnesses. I am grateful for them all.

To Miss Janes, on her birthday:

I congratulate you that you have been preserved to see another anniversary of this great event. To me it was a great event, full of interest, filling my heart with joy, and giving my paternal love a new pet to cherish and an additional child to train up for usefulness, for heaven, and for God. I have often tried to realize somewhat the vastness of the consequences to follow the birth of a human being. An interminable existence —eternal happiness or eternal misery. Who can appreciate these interests? How wonderful the event that ushers a rational being upon an endless career of life, of duty, of experiences!

To his little grandson, Charles E. Harris, from Norwich, Conn., March 23:

How I wish I knew how my darling little missionary is to-night! I am so sorry to learn he has been sick! I hope he is getting better very fast. My time was so short, and I was so tired, I could not go to visit him when in New York. I hope to be able to take a peep at him next week. . . . If I were with you I would try and tell you a story. I will tell you
15*

a few things about this place. It is a city of some seventeen or eighteen thousand people. It is the residence of ex-Governor Buckingham. The wicked traitor, Benedict Arnold, was born here. Mamma will tell you about him. This place used to be the head-quarters of two Indian tribes, the Narraganset and the Mohegans. Each had a celebrated chief. One was called Uncas, the other Miantinoma. Uncas killed Miantinoma with a tomahawk after taking him prisoner. They each have a monument in this neighborhood. It is now so late, and my eyes ache so bad, I believe I must kiss you good-night.

To Miss Janes, from the German Conference at Poughkeepsie, March 31 :

I am enjoying the Conference. Business is proceeding pleasantly and rapidly. I like to hear the brethren express themselves in earnest broken English. I enjoy their singing very highly. They turn their faces upward, and open their mouths wide, and give a full, grand volume of sacred music. Mr. Wesley would say they sing lustily. I enjoy it greatly. You know I have not a cultivated musical taste. I like the noise and unction. Earnest devotional singing is what takes hold of my heart. These Germans sing after that manner. They report considerable progress in Church interests.

I have received from the Rev. D. E. Miller, of Vermont, some account of the address of Bishop Janes to the candidates for ordination at the Vermont Conference this spring :

He was trying to impress upon them the importance of relying on divine aid for success rather than on human help, and in his own inimitable way he exclaimed, " Send off for an evangelist ! No, send up to Heaven, and get the Holy Ghost to come and help you ! " The effect was most thrilling, and will never be forgotten.

On May 14 the Bishop preached at the dedication
of the new and beautiful St. James's Church, located
at Harlem, New York city. Within a few days he
hastened to the bedside of Bishop Clark, at Cincinnati, and was present with him in the closing hours
of his life, on the 23d of this month. He remained
and delivered an address at the funeral services.
Among other fitting things, he said :

The death of Bishop Clark is a loss to the world and the
Church. He was a true philanthropist. He desired and
sought the welfare of the race. His efforts to promote the
welfare of society were put forth mainly in connection with the
agencies of his Church. His holy life was a blessing to the
community. His prayers and intercessions were fibers in the
cord with which Christ is drawing all men unto himself. His
ministry was one of sympathy, of instruction, and of power.

A brief word from Mrs. Bishop Clark will show
the high estimate in which she held his visit to her
dying husband :

I shall always be thankful, dear Bishop, that you have been
with us in this season of deep sorrow, especially that you were
with my dear husband during that last hour. I never shall
forget your prayer. Its influence has been with us every moment since.

In the midst of this summer what was known as
the " Book Concern trouble" reached an issue
which involved the official action of Bishop Janes.
A trial was had before the Book Committee and
Bishops Ames and Janes, looking to the suspension
of the Rev. John Lanahan, D.D., the Assistant

Book Agent at New York, for alleged misconduct in his office, particularly in applying to the civil courts for a mandamus giving him possession of, or access to, the account books of the Concern. A majority of the committee voted to suspend him, but it was necessary, in order to effect the suspension, that the two Bishops should *concur*. Bishop Janes voted to concur, and Bishop Ames to non-concur. The measure, therefore, failed, and Dr. Lanahan remained in his position until the ensuing General Conference, when all the Book Concern matters involved were investigated by a General Conference committee, composed of ministers and . laymen. The findings of this committee were generally satisfactory to the public, and gave quiet to the Church on the subject.

It again fell to the lot of the Bishop to visit officially the Pacific coast. He was accompanied by his daughter, Miss Lizzie Janes, and this time crossed the continent on rail, in marked contrast with his last stage ride. He held successively the Colorado, Nevada, Oregon, and California Conferences.

From Denver, Colorado, to Mrs. Janes, July 21:

We reached this city on Wednesday evening, having had a prosperous journey by the will of God. We are both in as good health as when we left our sweet home in New York, some two thousand miles distant. We are the guests of Governor Evans. I wish you could have come with us. I should have insisted upon it if your health would have allowed you to enjoy such a journey. I am sure you would feel an enthusiastic pleasure in beholding the wonderful works of nature which meet our vision on every side. As you know, I am not sight-seeing; I am here on most important business for the Master; I hardly give attention to any thing else save official obligations. God is with me graciously and consciously. I know he is your chief joy. In the radius of his smile you find joy and gladness. His presence makes a paradise. I hope you greatly enjoyed your visit at Brother Dikeman's lovely home at Basking Ridge.

To Mrs. Janes, from Portland, Oregon, Aug. 7:

We are now at the extremest distance from home to which our journey will take us. We have traveled about four thousand miles since we left " Lovedom." I am stopping with my old friend, General Canby. From my windows I have a view of the snow-covered Mount Hood, and the snow-clad Mount St. Helen's is seen in the distance, some fifty miles away. It is eight years since I was here. The Church and the country have made great advance since then. Truly this is a magnificent and most glorious country. Any citizen who does not admire it, love it, is not proud of it, is a stupid blockhead, who ought to be banished from it. To think of its advantages, its institutions, its glorious liberty of being good in your own way, and being happy because good—and not have an enthusiastic love for it, is outrageous.

From St. Joseph, Missouri, to his daughter, Mrs. C. E. Harris, Sept. 7:

You will see from the heading of this that we are again on the eastern slope of the continent. We expect to reach New York by the 24th inst. I am anticipating great joy in seeing the faces of my dearly beloved ones, from whom I have been separated so long. My stay, however, will be short—only a visit. I have no abiding place—no continuing city. A pilgrim and a stranger. I trust all my meanderings are heavenward. I cannot think of going in any other direction. All my wanderings must end at the golden gate. I do feel that I am on my way thither. I also feel that I am ripening for that divine estate. I seem to get nearer to God in prayer, to have more constantly a consciousness of God's gracious presence. I feel that I am walking with God, and that I please him. Nothing else is worth living for. Life more and more seems like a dream when one awaketh—so short, so uncertain, of so little consequence, only as it draws interest and importance from eternity. The immensity of future interests to be shaped and determined by our conduct here makes life a great solemnity. O that we could always measure things by the calculus of eternity!

The Bishop reached home toward the last· of September, taking the session of the Michigan Conference on his way. He almost immediately turned back, and met the Genesee and Ohio Conferences in October. After another brief respite at home, he proceeded to the extreme South-west to hold the Texas, Louisiana, and Mississippi Conferences.

To Miss Janes, from New Orleans, La., Nov. 29:

I reached this city at noon to-day. Have had a prosperous journey by the will of God. Chaplain M'Cabe met me at Humboldt, Tenn., as we arranged when he was at our house. The cities and the country are very unlike any thing you have seen in Europe or in this better land. I have sublime anticipations of the future of our country. Nothing has given me so much confidence as the overthrow of slavery in the South, and the overthrow of the official banditti of robbers in New York. These events both show how mighty are the virtuous people when aroused and combined. Great exigencies will combine them. They will stand together when the public weal really demands it. Then, united and moving in solid phalanx, nothing can resist them. I take steamer in the morning for Galveston, Texas.

To Miss Janes, from Austin, Texas, Dec. 4 and 6:

You will see by the heading of this that I have arrived at this most distant point of my journey in safety and season. I had a very hard journey after I left New Orleans. The last night we traveled in an open hack over a very rough road. I yesterday preached in the Presbyterian church. Enjoyed the service myself. I hope others were profited. At night I heard Brother M'Cabe. He preached a good sermon and sang three songs. He interested the congregation. Dr. Rust preached in the Southern Methodist church in the forenoon.

The prospect is that we shall have a pleasant visit to this State. I hope it will be with advantage to the Church and to the cause of Christ. I dreaded to start, but as I have reached the extreme point in safety, and have turned round, and my look is homeward, I feel cheerful and hopeful. I feel the privation of being absent from my charmed circle over Christmas and the holidays. But to spread the name of Christ is perhaps the best way of celebrating his advent. The angel who first announced his appearance was gloriously employed, and, I judge, as sweetly employed as an angel or man has been before or since. To echo his voice in the ears of perishing men is the next best employment for men or angels.

I am in the chair of Conference in the State Capitol. A dignified place, a dignified Conference before me, at least, they have dignity enough to make it necessary for me to look after it. Business with a mixed Conference of white American ministers, German ministers, and a majority of colored ministers is awkward and slow. My traveling companions are full of pleasantry and cheer. So my days glide sweetly as well as swiftly away. Though the Conference is small, yet it is not without care and labor. To me it was of great interest. I look upon it as the germ of evangelical Christianity.

The allusion of the Bishop to his traveling companions suggests some pleasing incidents by the way. He was accompanied by the Rev. Dr. Rust and the Rev. C. C. M'Cabe. On the steamer from New Orleans to Galveston, Texas, there was an old gentleman who had in his possession the parchments of Bishop Asbury, which he wished to present to Bishop Janes. He did not know the Bishop, and supposing from Dr. Rust's appearance that he must be the Bishop, he approached him and handed him the parchments. The reverend doctor at once corrected the gentleman's mistake, and, introducing him to the Bishop, felt content to have enjoyed, even for a brief moment, the dignity of an *episkopos*.

When the party arrived at Austin, on Sunday morning, weary and dusty, Dr. Rust and Chaplain M'Cabe supposed that none of them would be expected to preach that day, and they were anticipating a day of rest. Looking toward the Bishop they saw he was very carefully preparing his toilet; whereupon they said, " Bishop, what are you doing?" He immediately responded, " I have an appointment to preach here to-day." And preach he did; and they all preached. One afternoon, during the session of the Texas Conference, when Dr. Rust was about to preach, the Bishop requested the chaplain to sing a hymn, supposing he would give them one of his own favorite spiritual songs. But the chaplain struck up one of the colored people's songs, with the chorus,

"My Lord, will you stand by me?"

Very soon the colored preachers and people were shouting all over the house. When they had got fairly through with this song, a colored brother extemporized an additional verse and the chorus followed, then a colored sister improvised one, the chorus again followed, and last, the chaplain himself improvised another, and the chorus rang out stronger and louder than ever. The Bishop, becoming at this point somewhat uneasy, reached over, pulled the chaplain's coat-tails, and very gently asked, "Chaplain, how long is this piece?"

These are specimens of the pleasantries of the tour. The Bishop could enjoy a little humor in his quiet way; but possibly he never felt more profoundly the importance of his great mission than on this same visitation. One night when these brethren were with him in the State of Mississippi, either going or returning, they were all lodging in the same room. Dr. Rust and the chaplain had retired, leaving the Bishop on his knees. They both fell asleep. After some time they chanced to awake—how long they had slept they did not know, but looking toward the Bishop's bed, which was near a window, there he was still on his knees, his face uplifted toward the open window, and the moonlight gleaming in upon it. Says the chaplain, "We could hear his groans, and his face shone as it were the face of an angel." Such was his preparation for the work in the South. God's lowly poor lay upon his heart with a weight which found its only adequate relief in groanings which could not be uttered. Nothing could exceed the sense of responsibility he felt for the religious and social culture of the Freedmen; and in these official visits he believed he was planting seeds which would grow into ever-widening harvests.

To Miss Janes, from New Orleans, La., December 11:

We finished the business of [the Texas] Conference Saturday evening. Sunday morning I preached in the hall of the House of Representatives. A large audience. The chief Justice and all the Judges of the Supreme Court were present. I mention this because the last time I was in Texas a mob interrupted my preaching and undertook to drive me and the Conference from the State. The papers then warned me, that if I was ever caught in Texas again I should never leave it alive. But now I was treated with courtesy and respect every-where and by every body. At the hotel in Galveston several ministers of the Church South called on me. I left Austin on Monday morning; rode twelve miles in a carriage, then took a construction train six miles; waited four hours on an open prairie, took another construction train twenty miles. Reached a small town of shanties, went to a shanty hotel, got a shanty supper, went to a shanty bed, and slept as best I could until morning. I arrived in this city Tuesday evening at six o'clock. Went to a restaurant and got some supper; then went to the church and opened the Conference. The first time in all my episcopacy when I commenced a Conference in the evening. I did it this time to meet my reaching the city and to save my time.

My Texas trip was a tiresome one, but pleasant. I have a beautiful home here. I am entertained by General Bussy.

The Conference has just adjourned to give place to a Sabbath-school *jubilee*. The house is filling up with bright children with as many hues as there are in the rainbow. They are not so arranged as to imitate that supreme beauty of creation. It is, nevertheless, to the philanthropist or patriot or Christian a grand sight. There is future citizenship, church membership, statesmen, ministers, and all sorts of public men. I presume, also, some vagabonds. The whole is managed by colored persons. Not so very orderly, but all will come out usefully. A little six-year-old orator is now displaying himself. We have four hours of this rich entertainment — interesting. "The Bishop must see and hear it." He is speaking the "Six Hundred." Is it not appropriate? Now we have a hurrah with feet and hands. The marshal forbids any more slapping or stamping. They had a love-feast this morning. It was heavenly.

Then after meeting the Mississippi Conference, December 21–25, he returned home about the close of the year, having held since the first of March twenty-one Conferences, and traveled about thirteen thousand miles. "God's care," he says, "has been constant and tender."

Again he was called upon to mourn the loss of one of his colleagues. Bishop Baker died at his residence, Concord, N. H., on December 20, and on January 7th following Bishop Janes delivered an address at a memorial service for the Bishop in the Bromfield-street Church, Boston.

CHAPTER XIX.

1872-1875.

Parts with Mt. Wesley—General Conference at Brooklyn—Assurances of Love from his Brethren—Boards of the Church—Fraternization Camp-Meeting at Round Lake.

IN January, 1872, after having just closed his official visit to the South-west, the Bishop successively held the Washington, East German, Troy, New Hampshire, and Maine Conferences.

Among the letters of this period is one written to a returned missionary. Omitting the personal allusions, I give an abstract or two as showing the estimation in which he held the calling of a missionary to the heathen. Men and women animated by the spirit he describes would indeed soon take the world for Christ:

I do not believe that any thing but the question of life or death should induce a missionary who has qualified himself to labor in a heathen country to quit it. This matter of evangelizing the world is a great and solemn duty. It cannot be done without sacrifice, without suffering. Many will have to take a short route to heaven. But it must be done. The world must be restored to holiness and God. O, how I wish I was young enough to go with you and be among those to whom it is given not only to believe on Christ but also to suffer with him—to suffer with *him!* O what a thought, to bear with

Christ a part of the sufferings by which our world is to be saved !

It is one of the most precious memories of all my past life that when young I offered myself for the mission work.   I was not accepted on account of my health, I believe, mainly.   I would not have that act of my life blotted out for the wealth of the Indies.   I can now only cheer on my younger brothers, do all I can to raise the means for sustaining the work, and pray.

I repeat, God helping, you must go back.   Your life there is a hundred times more precious than it is here.   An inch of missionary life, after you have acquired the language and are prepared to work to advantage, is worth a mile of ministerial life here.   Life there and life here, in God's service, are not comparable in their interest.   I can scarcely refrain from envying a missionary when I see him starting for a foreign mission field.   Tame men can work here in this Christian country; but it wants do-or-die men in heathen lands—men who would rather die than fail.

The fifth anniversary of the Freedmen's Aid Society of the Methodist Episcopal Church was held in the Hanson Place Church, Brooklyn, Feb. 8, 1872. Bishop Janes was one of the speakers on the occasion.   He said, among other things, as he claimed what should be done for the freedmen :

. . . And as this cause comes up before the eyes of our rich men, they will see a draft in the handwriting of Providence they must honor.   These men must meet their obligations; there must be no trifling with God.   We have the money; it is in the Church, and the love of Christ and the conviction of duty must bring it forth; we *must carry out this work.*   If we do not do it, it is a crime, and nothing short.

I look beyond our own country on this question.   I have the conviction that Africans must redeem Africa; and we have in

our schools the men who, in five or ten years, will be missionaries to Africa, will go out and light the fires of salvation in
that dark and gloomy continent. They can live there; they
have a sympathy for their own race that others cannot have,
much as we are interested.   Nevertheless, we cannot go with
the same feelings that they will go with. We must have these
educated men for this work. I do not want to make a wrong
impression here upon this question. When we speak of men
educated for the ministry, we speak of men educated appropriately for their work. When we first went down among that
people we found old men who had been Christians for many
years, who had taught these people, who had been accustomed
to pray with the people, who had preached and exhorted the
best they could, and had been acceptable and useful, and they
are grand old patriarchs now; but the children of these people
began to go to school, and learned the proprieties of speech,
and correctness of utterance; they began to have some educational taste and feeling, and they are not satisfied with their
style of address in the pulpit, and we are now giving them
ministers in advance of them. When another generation comes
up we shall have more extended and general education in the
congregation, and we must have an advance in the ministry.
The ministry must be kept ahead of the people. That is what
we mean by this educated ministry.

And now, in behalf of these millions, their present and their
future, their temporal and eternal good, I appeal to you for
help; I appeal to this nation, to the people of this Republic,
this "land of the free and the home of the brave." I appeal
to all to help educate these dependent millions. For Christ's
sake, help; for God's sake, help; and help now, and help largely, and continue to help, until the work is done.

From the Washington (colored) Conference, at
Baltimore, March 2, to Mrs. Janes:

It is spring by the almanac, but is stormy winter according
to the weather. . . . You and I will see but few more of the

storms of life.   The perpetual spring of heaven, the songs of angels, and the beauty and blessedness of paradise will ever feast us.   The title to this inheritance is written on my heart by the finger of God and sealed by the Holy Spirit.   I am rich in prospect; yes, and in possession.   Religion and a happy home make any person rich.

It will have been observed that for several years there have been no removals for the summer to Mount Wesley, and indeed scarcely a reference to the charmed spot.   For judicious considerations the Bishop had sold the property.   It is now owned by Mr. A. V. Stout and Mr. George I. Seney.   These Christian gentlemen, so well and favorably known in the business and Methodist circles of New York, have capacious and beautiful summer residences near the humble "Mount Wesley."   Still, as the following letter will attest, the great and good man's heart was in the country, and had his engagements allowed, its scenes and pursuits would still have been his delight.

To Mrs. Janes, from Bristol, N. H., April 5:

I expect you hear the chattering of the little chirpers in the park every day.   I am thankful these little sparrows have been brought to our cities every time I hear them or see them.   I shall always be a country boy.   I can never lose my love of country scenery and employments and life.   The flocks and herds, the flowers and fruits, the labors and amusements of the country always charm me.   But I am doomed to a city life so far as my home life is concerned.   All right.   No one in city or country has a sweeter home than mine.   It really matters little where I am so my family are with me and God is with us.

The General Conference convened in Brooklyn, N. Y., on the first day of May, 1872, Bishops Morris, Janes, Scott, Simpson, and Ames were present.

It having been ascertained that three fourths of the ministers of the Annual Conferences had voted to change the second restrictive rule so as to allow, in conformity to the avowed wishes of a majority of the people, the admission of laymen into the General Conference, it was resolved by the Conference at its first session, " That we do now admit to seats in the General Conference, and to a participation in all its rights and privileges, the laymen provisionally elected by the several Lay Electoral Conferences and properly accredited."

Bishop Janes presided the first day. The session was unavoidably one of great pressure, owing to the careful rulings which had to be made in adjusting the body to its altered composition. He was taken violently ill at the close of the session and had to be carried home, and was not able to again attend upon the proceedings for about two weeks. During his illness the Conference unanimously adopted a resolution of sympathy, and on his recovery and re-appearance in the Conference received him by a rising vote of welcome.

The Bishops, in their quadrennial address, in view of the death of four of their colleagues and the feebleness of Bishop Morris, the senior Bishop, and the constantly enlarging demands of the work at home and abroad, recommended the election of from five to eight additional Bishops. The Conference finally fixed the number at eight, and Thomas Bowman, D.D. ; William L. Harris, D.D. ; Randolph S. Foster, D.D. ; Isaac W. Wiley, D.D. ; Stephen M. Merrill, D.D. ; Edward G. Andrews, D.D. ; Gilbert Haven, A.M. ; and Jesse T. Peck, S.T.D., were duly elected and consecrated to the office of Bishop. Thus the wasted ranks of the Episcopacy were re-enforced by eight efficient superintendents. The General Conference voted that the Bishops, in arranging the work, should, as far as practicable, relieve the senior Bishops. So we shall find Bishop Janes for once trying to take a vacation. It will be seen it was hard for him to learn how to play—work had become the habit of his life.

From Saratoga, to Miss Janes, July 20:

I propose to spend the Sabbath here, and on Monday go on to Sheldon, Vt. Yesterday was the first time in my life that I felt I was traveling without an object. On my way to Middletown I was going to meet the trustees of the university ; on my way to Canaan I was going to see and comfort afflicted relatives ; but when I left there and started off, I could hardly tell why. True, the professed object was to benefit my health, but that seemed so much of a myth I could hardly recognize it as a real object. I never before traveled a day in pursuit of health or recreation—always on some of God's errands. It was breaking an old mental habit to travel for any other interest. I seemed to feel I was "doing nothing," as the boys sometimes say. Perhaps I shall get over the feeling ; I want to grow old and useless gracefully, if I can.

16

From Bernardsville, N. J., August 9, where he was resting awhile, he writes : " I am doing well in health, and am happy in all respects. Mother has her celestial sunshine, and is basking in its glory."

Early in the autumn he was again off on an official tour, meeting the North-west Indiana, Chicago German, and North-west German Conferences, from September 4 to 30. As he travels along he represents himself as an aeronaut who, when he rises and moves away, sends out frequent parachutes, with some little notices of the progress of his voyage. I open a few of these.

A few minutes after seven P. M. I started for the depot at the foot of Cortlandt-street. It rained, and was very dark. Going down Cortlandt-street a man stepped up to me and said, " Your satchel is too heavy for you to carry, old man ; let me help you." I said, " No, I thank you." " Ah, yes, let me help you, old man," he repeated. I said, " No !" with emphasis, but he seized hold of one handle and walked along with me. I just kept my hold, but let him carry it. When we got to the ticket office I said, " Put it down." He did so, but when I had gotten my ticket he quickly caught it up and walked on the boat. As I knew he could do no mischief I let him carry it, and went and sat down beside him, intending to take the valise and let him know I was not a greenhorn as soon as the boat stopped. But before we got over a gentleman came along and accosted me, as Bishop Janes, and soon after my generous stranger withdrew. If I had been an inexperienced traveler I might have lost my baggage ; as it was, I only had a little amusement.

My health is quite comfortable. Dr. Eddy is now addressing the Conference on the missionary cause—witty, pleasant, and useful. We also had a speech in favor of the Freedmen's

Aid. Society. So we are well supplied with sacred rhetoric and religious elocution. These conference orators relieve the tedium of routine business. They are generally spicy, lively, pathetic, and even rousing. These Annual Conferences are really great institutions.

To Miss Janes, with regard to the infant school at St. Paul's :

I am sorry you could not spend more time in the country with mamma. I suppose those human or angelic kittens gathered about you yesterday. Have they grown any since you left them? Grown mischievous, I dare say, not much wiser. Well, that is why they need a teacher. It is no great task to enlighten their understanding, but it is a difficult thing to stop the leaks in their memory. If your patience strengthens, like the blacksmith's arm, by hard using, you will soon be made perfect in that grace. I 'spects old children tries it too, sometimes.

To Mrs. Janes :

God smiles on me to-day. The future looks very hopeful. I think national matters look encouraging. Church interests are cheering. God reigns.' I do not preach to-morrow; two ordinations ; besides, I judge a German preacher will be more edifying to the German congregations than I should be. Our German work is doing well.

I closed my Conference last night. I am to-day doing up my writing, after which I hope to get a little rest. I start to-morrow morning for Galena. I expect the old nest was quite attractive and comfortable to you. Association is a very considerable part of home. I will peep in at you in a few days. Shall I find my nest feathered? If the old bird and young bird are there, we will not think much about the feathers.

To his grandson :

Few boys of your age have received such careful, loving, religious instruction as you have been favored with. Few boys of your age have had such opportunities to see people and the world as you have enjoyed. You have seen something of your own country and something of foreign countries. You have also been the child of Christian parents. Now, with all these advantages, ought you not to be a very manly youth— a good, wise, gentle, loving, praying youth?

The Rev. John L. Smith, D.D., of Indiana, referring to the Bishop's presidency of the North-west Indiana Conference, at Thorntown, this year, says:

In his address to the candidates for full membership in the Conference he excelled even himself in one of the most searching and exhaustive addresses ever listened to on a similar occasion. On the subject of pastoral visiting he repeated and emphasized the declaration, "*I would rather it should be said I was a poor preacher than a poor pastor.*" His words are not forgotten.

After returning home he hastened, in October, to the assistance of Bishop Peck, at the Central New York Conference, Palmyra, N. Y. Bishop Peck was just recovering from a protracted illness, and was barely able to resume his official duties. Bishop Janes writes of him at the time, " He is getting well, and I judge will be a strong Bishop for years to come."

The year may appropriately close with a letter to Mrs. Gov. Wright, who was traveling in the far East:

In my pastoral reviews and solicitudes this Christmas-day I have been thinking of the scattered sheep of the fold. I find some are entirely beyond my personal watch-care, so I can only speak to them with my pen. I am sure your journey will be a source of exquisite pleasure to you until you reach your heavenly home. How much to think of! how much to speak of! How richly you can entertain others! No solitary place, no sick-bed, no social hour, will find you without abundant resources of enjoyment. I doubt not but that, like the busy bee, you are storing up honey from every opening flower, from every beautiful landscape, from every mountain prospect, from every beautiful work of art, from every monument of human greatness, from every architectural triumph, from every contact with different peoples. Something to remember and reflect upon all the time. And how will the pleasure and edification be increased as you enter the Holy Land! When you begin to walk where Jesus walked, and to see what Jesus saw, and to be reminded continually of what Jesus did! What a privilege it is to visit the places Jesus hallowed and rendered sacred and precious by his presence and works! O, that one place where he trod the wine-press of the wrath of God alone, for me and for mankind! No spot on earth so sacred, so melancholy, and yet so sweet and so inspiring as that. There my soul was bought with a price, even the precious blood of Christ. There my hope was born. There my resurrection was secured. With what mingled emotions I think of it! How I would like to see it! Still, the great interest would be wanting. Jesus is not there now. It is only the place where he lay. O how happy it is for us that he has gone away! Yes, that he has gone to the mercy-seat, and there ever liveth to intercede for us. I am going to see him there— to see him as he is. I am on my way thither, longing for the beatific vision. Still, I have no desire to be dismissed from his service here. If I can only spread the savor of his name among perishing sinners and bring them to behold the Lamb of God that taketh away the sin of the world, I can joyfully wait a great while before I sit down with my Master on his throne. The pleasure of advancing his kingdom on earth is only second to the felicity of his presence in heaven.

January, 1873, the Bishop was assigned the Mississippi and Louisiana Conferences.

From New Orleans he writes on the 14th:

I have seldom been as much exhausted with the labors of a Conference. We have had several very troublesome questions. Last Friday and Saturday I was very anxious. I prayed hard, and God brought me out of the difficulties. I think the interests of the Church are safe in this section for a time—I hope, permanently. Satan never seems to tire of his mischief-making.

He next held the Washington Conference, at Washington, D. C., February 26–March 4.

To Mrs. Janes:

God's blessing is on me this morning, and I doubt not is also upon you. Our heavenly Father has been very kind and gracious to us for a long time. He will not fail us in the autumn and winter of life. Perhaps we shall have a tropical winter, flowers and fruits to the end. Indeed, I expect this life will be all spring-time, and the next life all summer-time; December as pleasant as May. The Sun of Righteousness never removes to the north or the south. His meridian is always over our heads. A shining way to heaven.

You will read in the morning paper how Congress settled the Credit Mobilier matter yesterday. A small result for so much storm. The inauguration is the subject of every body's conversation. I expect it will be a grand pageant. If a good administration follows all will be well.

Conference business is progressing pleasantly. We are having a funny debate on the question where the Conference shall hold its next session. Some first-class spread-eagle eloquence. I wish you could hear it. They are ready to vote, and I must stop.

The Bishop's next Conference was the Vermont, at Richford, Vermont, April 23–28.

To Mrs. Janes:

I reached this place in safety yesterday, though wearied and more feeble than usual, and Conference has opened very nicely. I hope for a pleasant session. Already some troublesome questions have arisen which will give me some labor, but, I hope, not anxiety.

Says Mr. Miller, of Vermont, in connection with the close of the session:

The Conference was about to close. It was just before dinner, and the train which was to take the Bishop and most of the members away was to leave at an early hour after noon. Some one respectfully suggested to the Bishop that there was little time for unnecessary delay, and, moreover, that he, the brother, wished sufficient time to get some dinner before starting for home. "Yes, yes, brother," said the Bishop, in his peculiar voice, "yes, but let us get a little bread from heaven first." Then he turned to the Bible, and then to prayer; and all felt they would rather be thus fed than to have the bread that perisheth.

It was very refreshing to the Bishop in his advanced years to receive assurances from his brethren of their respect and esteem. Especially was this the case when such assurances came from unexpected sources. The Rev. W. H. Wilson, of the Baltimore Conference of the Methodist Episcopal Church, South, having occasion to address him a letter, commending a colored minister to his attention from his neighborhood, Port Republic, Virginia, thus takes occasion to express his warm personal affection for the Bishop:

And now, my dear Bishop, I cannot forbear greeting you in the name of our divine Master. When a youthful preacher in the Baltimore Conference I learned to love you for what I regarded so eminently worthy of my confidence and love. National, ecclesiastical, and social upheavals have made time itself more exacting on our natural feelings and affections. But, Bishop, there is a province unaffected by these rude influences—it is the domain of Christian affection. I feel toward you to-day the strong affections of other years asserting themselves with irrepressible emotions. How I would love to greet you once more in the flesh.

Here are two more expressions of affectionate consideration, this time from his colleagues.

Bishop Foster to Bishop Janes, from Berlin, Prussia, June 27:

MY DEAR BISHOP: I seize the first spare moment to write you a line, both to thank you for your kindness in seeing me off, and to gratify my desire to communicate with you. Your parting benediction has sweetened all my journey, and lingers with me yet. How many times I have prayed that the good God would give me a measure of your spirit for the great work he has laid upon me, and I am comforted with the thought that you also pray for me. I know with what yearning interest you regard the work in these regions, a work that has had both your care and prayers for many years. I will, therefore, devote this letter to the matter of chief interest, the work which I am sent here to look after. This I know will best meet your desires. . . .

From Bishop Ames to Bishop Janes, from Ypsilanti, Michigan, Sept. 6:

I have this moment signed my name, with Bishop Wiley, to a telegram addressed to you, saying I would attend your Central Ohio Conference, at Van Nort, and also, that I would attend your Conference at Albion, N. Y. Now, my dear brother, I pray you do not suffer one moment's uneasiness about your episcopal work. God, who has so long and so graciously watched over our beloved Church, will still take care of it when we are all dead.

As expressive of the tender recollection in which the Bishop held all his early friends and associates, I insert a letter written July 18, to the Rev. James H. Dandy, of Philadelphia, Pa.

I am very thankful to you for your kind remembrance of me. I am not yet a very aged man, but most of my early friends in the Church and my early associates in the ministry have ascended to their God and our God. Those that remain are very precious to me. I have very few opportunities of meeting them and but little time to correspond with them, but I think of them much and love them very tenderly. My life is a very busy one and a very responsible one. I am obliged to forego to a great extent social pleasures, yet the fellowship of my Christian brethren is a great luxury to me. The fellowship of God is my chief delight and joy. I am thankful that you are resting in the love of Jesus so peacefully. Our refuge does not fail us when the storm beats on us. God does not leave or forsake us in old age, nor even in death. He loves his own unto the end.

Among the most important duties of the episcopal supervision are those arising from the official connection of the Bishops with the various Boards of the benevolent societies of the Church. The meetings of the General Committees on Missions and Church Extension are fraught with great responsibility. The relation of the Bishops to the general appropriations and to the administration
16*

of the several mission fields is very close, and gives rise to questions both delicate and difficult, and which require the utmost caution and courage. At the meeting of the Committee on Missions, in 1872, an advance on the appropriations of about $190,000 was made, and the receipts of 1873, on account of the financial panic, fell short, leaving the society in debt. At the meeting this autumn (1873) there was a strong effort made for retrenchment, and it was seriously proposed to recall missionaries already under appointment. The proposition called Bishop Janes to the floor, and thoroughly aroused him. In a speech of half an hour he electrified the committee. After he concluded nothing more was said about receding from any position already taken, but the cry was rather for an advance all along the line.

From the meeting of the Mission Committee, in company with his colleagues, as is the custom, he went to Philadelphia to attend the annual meeting of the Church Extension Committee. The work of this Society also enlisted his deep sympathy, and received on all suitable occasions his judicious counsels, liberal contributions, and eloquent advocacy.

To Mrs. Janes, from Philadelphia, Nov. 20:

In company with several of my colleagues I left New York at five P. M. yesterday. Reached my home, at Mrs. Peterson's, at 8:35. Mrs. Peterson prepared me a good warm supper. I partook of it with zest, as I was cold and hungry. Bishops

met at 8:30 this morning, and remained in session until ten
o'clock, when the Church Extension General Committee commenced its session. As senior it fell to me to occupy the
chair. I cannot yet judge of the state of the Society, but think
there has been some increase in its funds. The Church is
generally prosperous, but still very deficient in zeal and devotion. God would do much more for us as a Church if we
would do all we could for him.

Middletown, New York, to Mrs. Janes, Dec. 28:

So the last Sabbath of 1873 is gone. How rapidly time flies!
How soon we shall reach our final home! Thank God, we
have a home to go to when this pilgrimage is ended—"a house
not made with hands, eternal in the heavens." O happy destiny—forever with the Lord! Amen.

The Bishop's colleagues were very considerate of
him in making out the Plan of Episcopal Visitation
this year, as the Minutes show but four Conferences
presided over by him. In March, April, and May
he met the East German, New England, New
Hampshire, and East Maine Conferences.

The Bishops held their spring meeting at Columbus, Ohio, May 16. At that meeting the Rev. Al-
bert S. Hunt, D.D., who, with C. H. Fowler, D.D.,
and General Clinton B. Fisk had visited the General Conference of the Methodist Episcopal Church,
South, as fraternal delegates from our late General
Conference, called upon the Bishops and reported
the highly satisfactory results of their visit. Thus
the cause of " fraternization " was progressing.
Another step was to be taken the ensuing summer
which would still further advance it.

The conception of holding a Methodist fraternization camp-meeting at Round Lake, N. Y., had been formed the preceding year, and Bishop Janes had been unanimously requested by the presiding elders and Mr. Joseph Hillman, President of the Round Lake Camp-meeting Association, to take charge of all the devotional exercises. The aim was to bring together representative men from all the several bodies of Methodism in the United States, Canada, and the British Provinces, and also any English and Irish Methodists who might chance to be in the country. As far back as December 3, 1873, Mr. Hillman wrote the Bishop, " Every thing looks very favorable. I am highly pleased with the prospect of having a grand, glorious, old-fashioned camp-meeting."

Bishop Harris, then making a missionary tour around the world, writes the Bishop from Rustchuck, Turkey, May 18, 1874, making reference to this camp-meeting :

Allow me, from my heart of hearts, to thank you for the noble Christian utterances of your letter consenting to take charge of the approaching camp-meeting at Round Lake. I have read them with profound satisfaction, and with devout thanksgiving to Almighty God. I cannot but regret that other duties will prevent me from personally enjoying the privilege of your feast of tabernacles.

The camp-meeting was accordingly held, beginning July 8. Bishop Janes presided throughout. The meeting was well attended and highly successful. It was, however, not so successful but that it was felt another such might be even more so. It was, therefore, resolved to hold another fraternization meeting in 1875. It was thought, that with the earnest of the present meeting, and the longer time which would be afforded for preliminary arrangements, greater results might follow.

The Hon. J. F. Simmons, in a communication to the New York "Methodist," June 26, 1875, referring to the first meeting, says:

I feel *and know* it was a happy time—a perfect Pentecost, in which the Spirit came like "a rushing mighty wind," and filled the whole vast multitude of God's people. It was no time for recurring to old differences or new differences, or any other differences. No, no; in the language of good Bishop Peck, "*Then we were one Methodist Church.* Thus we felt and thought and spoke." And God poured out his Spirit and his blessings abundantly on all.

I wish every Methodist, North and South, East and West, could have been there.

The meeting, which was held beginning July 1, 1875, was more largely attended than that of the preceding year. Bishop Janes was again present and presided. His sermon and addresses were full of freshness and power. At the opening service, after a brief sermon, he followed with a few remarks, in the course of which he said:

I presume most who are present worshiped here a year ago. Some have gone to worship in the sanctuary above. The year has been one of varying circumstances with me. I have been very ill, and, as it seemed, near the spirit world. It was not a time of doubt and darkness, but one of peace and hope, and even of joy and love. I desire to live and labor and die with holy charity as the controlling power of my being.

Such was the atmosphere of "holy charity" which his spirit and words diffused throughout all the intercourse and services of this memorable meeting. Thus the social and devotional feelings were gradually and surely dissolving party differences, and men were being brought to see, in the light of the religious affections, their truer and better natures as superior to the ecclesiastical variations which separated them. There is a realm where, with us all, charity reigns; and when we emerge into its holy light we instantly recognize the unity which, while it may exist even with differences, is yet stronger and better than them all.

The charity which ruled in the Bishop's heart shows itself on this occasion in the hopefulness with which it led him to regard the Church. He rejoiced in the belief that Methodism was not retrograding but progressing; that in the present it was essentially the same as in the past. In one of his addresses he says:

It is now thirty-five years since I began to travel extensively through the connection. It is my clear, honest conviction that we have not retrograded during those thirty-five years. I believe that our preaching is just as spiritual and practical as it was thirty-five years ago. I believe our conference sessions are seasons of as much spiritual enjoyment, of as much devotional pleasure and profit, and that our conference work is done as much in the immediate presence of God, as it was when I first began to visit the Conferences. I think our love-feasts and prayer-meetings are not only as spiritual, but they are as spirited, as they were in former times, and our revivals are as numerous and as gracious as they have been in any period of my ministry in the Church ; and I think there is as much hungering and thirsting after God, that there is as much coveting the rich gifts of divine grace, as there ever has been. I think the only reason why this has been questioned by observers whose views have been limited, and whose examination has not been careful and thorough, grows out of these circumstances : first, that our membership has greatly increased, and it would be wonderful if in this increase of members there should not be an increase of those who are worldly, and who are partially devoted, and who do not exemplify very fully the spirit and power of the Gospel. They do not consider the increased number of spiritual and holy members ; they only look at the increased number of those who are less consistent. Another reason is, we have been building another class of church edifices, and a large number of men have the idea that simplicity and spirituality can only dwell in very plain and simple houses of worship. To some extent, perhaps, these convictions are just. But I must declare here, that when I go into these better edifices, in most cases—I cannot say in all—I find the same fervent preaching and the same fervent prayers for the cause and kingdom of Christ that I do in any other. The truth is, that spirituality and simplicity and devotion can dwell any where—with the humble and the high, with the poor and with the rich—and God can manifest himself to his people under any circumstances.

Then, referring to his own personal religious experience, he thus expresses himself :

I want to say that I am saved from sin through Jesus Christ ; that I have an increasing nearness to God and a more intimate fellowship with him, a greater sense of his gracious presence with me continually, by day and by night; if I have a title to any thing, it is to heaven; if I have a hold upon any thing, it is on heaven. I know my probation is drawing to its close. I have had great opportunities to serve my Lord and Master, and to do good service for him. I have a very solemn account to render. I appreciate it more and more, and yet through God's great mercy in Jesus Christ I meet it without fear, for I believe that all my imperfections of service and devotion are forgiven for Christ's sake, and that he is the Lord my right-eousness, and that through his mercy I shall give up my ac-count with joy, and enter into the presence and beatitude of God. Blessed be his name!

The Bishop, it will be seen by one of the above extracts, refers to a severe sickness in 1874. Dur-ing the months of August and September of that year he was extremely low. While ill he received very constant attention from the Rev. Dr. Thomas M. Eddy. The Bishop had scarcely recovered when Dr. Eddy himself was stricken with the dis-ease of which he died on the fourth day of October. I well remember the sorrow of the Bishop at the loss of this able and devoted servant of God. I and my family were his guests at the time. Only that very Sunday morning the same hospitable doors from which we had gone forth to wander over sea and land to distant parts, opened again to receive us. And there the joy of our " welcome " was sad-dened by the death of one of his favorite sons in the Gospel.

Only a month before, while the Bishop was ill,

the venerable Bishop Morris passed to his reward, full of years, honor, and usefulness.   Bishop Janes's attachment to this truly wise and good man was very sincere and ardent.   For long years they had counseled, prayed, wept, and rejoiced together.

Bishop Scott to Bishop Janes, from the " Lodge," (near Middletown, Del.,) October 9, 1874 :

I am grieved and shocked at the death of Dr. Eddy.   At the Central Illinois Conference he preached a noble sermon.   The Church loses a very efficient laborer in Dr. Eddy.   The circle still contracts. Bishop Morris, Dr. Eddy ; who next?   You say nothing about your own health.   I assume that you are better.   I have been much disturbed with accounts of your illness.   My prayer is that you may be restored, and that you may be continued with us yet many years.

One of the most pleasing offices which Bishop Janes performed after his recovery is referred to in the following letter from the Rev. Alexander M'Lean, of Hudson, N. Y., September 26 :

The erection of the East River Bridge may necessitate the removal of the Sands-street Methodist Episcopal Church, under the altar of which the remains of Revs. William and John Summerfield have lain for these forty-nine years.   Mrs. Blackstock,* of Portchester, has thought best to see personally to their re-interment, and a plot at Woodlawn has been selected. In a letter received from her she says : " It is my ardent desire that our venerable and beloved Bishop Janes, if this be possible, should honor us on this occasion with his presence.   It is thought the time would be opportune as to the demands of approaching Conferences upon him.   I can think of no one to substitute in place of Bishop Janes."

---

* Mrs. Blackstock is a sister of Rev. John Summerfield.

CHAPTER XX.

1875, 1876.

Illness of Mrs. Janes—General Conference of 1876—Episcopal Address—Fraternization with the Methodist Episcopal Church, South—Last Conference—Death of Mrs. Janes—The last sermon —Final illness, death, and funeral.

IN the spring of 1875 the Bishop was assigned but two Conferences—the Wilmington and the Delaware.

To Mrs. Janes, from Wilmington, Del., March 22 :

I had a pleasant Sabbath yesterday. I did not preach. Conference is proceeding pleasantly. Dr. Curry is here ; preached yesterday. Mr. Phillips, of the Book Room, is here : also Dr. Rust and Dr. M'Cauley, President of Dickinson College. Dr. Dashiell has been here. Bishop Scott is still here, and Bishop Haven is expected to-day. So you see wheresoever the carcass is, there will the eagles be gathered together. This day is pretty much given up to speech-making ; some excellent speaking.

The great men here named might be the eagles, but who or what was the carcass ?

In the month of April Bishop Janes participated in two exercises, both highly interesting, but also with what different emotions ! The one was on the occasion of the Centennial Sermon, by Father Boehm, on the 2d, in Jersey City, and the other the

funeral services of the Rev. J. B. Wakeley, D.D., at Sing Sing, N. Y., on the 29th.

On the former occasion the Bishop said :

I have stood in the presence of kings and nobles, of scholars and divines in other countries, but I never have felt, in all my experience, such an interest and so profound a reverence as I feel in the presence of our revered and beloved father in God, this aged servant of our Lord Jesus Christ. It is forty-three years this month since I made his personal acquaintance ; and, having been intimate with him from that time till now, I say in this presence I have never known a fellow-man in whom there was so little moral infirmity as in this our father before us to-day. I venerate him for his associations. He was associated with those names that are dearest to us in our Church history—Asbury, Whatcoat, M'Kendree, Jesse Lee, Freeborn Garrettson, and Nathan Bangs ; names that we hold in the highest regard ; they were his associates. And then he has been associated with a great multitude of godly men and women who have composed our Church from that early period until now. What fellowships he has enjoyed !

Dr. Wakeley had offered the prayer at the Boehm celebration, and on the 29th he was dead. His ministerial life and that of the Bishop had been closely associated from their youth. Though stricken by the fall of his beloved comrade, yet it was with joy he could repeat over his grave the victorious words of his dying friend, " When you go to the grave don't go weeping. Death has no sting. The grave has no terror. Eternity has no darkness. Sing at my funeral."

In May the Bishop met the Board of Bishops at Chicago, and, after returning, met the Delaware

Conference, in July. In August he availed himself
of the waters and medical treatment at Clifton
Springs, N. Y. A few words gleaned from his not
less frequent, but now much briefer, epistles to Miss
Janes will be enough :

I reached this place about nine o'clock this A. M. I am not
settled yet, have not made many observations, and am not
prepared to express any opinion about men and things. I hope
you will find contentment in indolence. They do not often
keep company, but I do not see any good reason why they
should not in dog-days. I hope in your case they will not have
a falling out until Jack Frost shows himself. I am trying to
coax them to be friends. There is no trouble in keeping Indolence quiet, but Contentment is a chary nymph, and inclines
to a roving life.

I would like to have the privilege of a bird, to hop among
the branches in Vineyard Grove, and light down upon Mrs.
Wright's sweet cottage, and look and listen an hour this morning. It pleases me to fancy myself there. God bless the loving circle, especially mamma—the central figure in my eyes.

I suppose you and the mother bird are in the old nest again.
It is good to have a place to return to from our wanderings,
especially a *home* to go to. There is no place like home, if it
be small and unfashionable. A big house and rich furniture
and fashionable appointments never made a home. I have
been so much of a pilgrim and a stranger that I appreciate a
home—only one in all the world. The more the doctors examine my case the more hopefully they speak. I see no change
yet, but they say it will come. I hope so. I preached in the
Methodist Episcopal Church on Sunday morning, and heard a
Congregationalist minister in the evening. I attend family worship every morning. Is not that a good example ? The morn-
ings are getting shorter. Breakfast hour comes quick. Must
be in time. The bell for prayers rings at a quarter to eight,
whether through breakfast or not.

One more *billetdoux* from the Sanitarium.   The next I expect to date at 107 East Twenty-fourth street, New York. You know it does not matter with me where I am, or how I am, if I only know I am where I ought to be and doing what I ought to do.   I have felt, since I have been here, that I was in the right place and doing the right thing.   That settles every thing.   Unquestionably now it is my duty to be somewhere else, and I go with cheerfulness.   No conferring with flesh and blood if I know I am right.

In September the Bishop met the North-west Indiana Conference, at Greencastle, and the Southeast, at Indianapolis, Indiana.   Dr. Smith, before quoted, speaks of an incident of the session at Greencastle :

On the Sabbath Dr. Dashiell preached for the Bishop in the university chapel, from the words, " He that believeth and is baptized shall be saved ; but he that believeth not shall be damned."   Although the doctor's sermon was able, clear, and scriptural, he evidently felt obliged to close, for want of time, without dwelling on the last part of the text.   When the doctor was about to take his seat the Bishop spoke out in a very decided manner, " Doctor, we want you to finish that sermon." Doctor Dashiell proceeded, and made a stirring appeal to the unconverted.   When the Bishop was about to commence the ordination service some one said, " Bishop, we want to hear you exhort."   And he did exhort for twenty minutes.   It was an inspiration and a benediction.   Like peals of thunder and flashes of lightning the truth fell upon the audience in bursts of eloquence that made the strongholds of unbelief tremble. Believers rejoiced, many of the preachers shouted aloud, and all felt that a master in Israel was there, and the mighty power of God had come upon them.

The Indiana Conference, Bishop Foster presiding, convened in Indianapolis at the same date with the

South-east, and, by previous arrangement, a convention in connection with these sessions was held in the interest of the Indiana Asbury University. "Bishop Janes, at this convention, endeared himself to all. hearts by his well-chosen words in the reunion, and his admirable address on the subject of Methodist education."

To Mrs. Janes, from Indianapolis, September 20:

I preached yesterday morning and ordained a class of deacons, and in the afternoon ordained a class of elders. I suppose this is my last day of conference service for this season. I am thankful I have been equal to all my official duties during the year. I hope I shall be able to perform them until the General Conference shall meet. God's will is my will.

While an invalid at Clifton Springs he could not resist the impulse, ever strong in him, to send a word of cheer and guidance to a brother minister who was struggling to raise a Church debt.

To the Rev. T. Morris Terry, of Brooklyn, N. Y., August 10:

I am glad to learn that you are making an effort to relieve the Flatbush Church of a part, or the whole, of its burdensome debt. I have felt for years that it ought to be done and could be done. The Churches of Brooklyn cannot afford to let it be sacrificed. I am sure they will not let it be lost. If you approach them lovingly, and represent the case fairly to them, they will aid you. Do not depend on committees, on collections, on preachers. Rely on God and the people and yourself, and, for Christ's sake, do the hard and disagreeable work of going to the brothers and sisters and making personal appeals. Pray all the time that your faith fail not, and that the hearts of the people may be opened to help. God will give you the victory.

While on the point of sympathy with Church-debt paying and church building, it may be well to give another letter, at a little later date, in the same general direction.

To the Rev. J. W. Hamilton, Boston, Mass.:

I am glad to learn that you are holding on to the idea of a church for the masses in Boston—a church of such dimensions as will make it a great rallying point for the people. Every great city needs such a church, I mean such a Methodist church. It should not be a costly edifice, but substantial, commodious, neat, well lighted and well ventilated. Such a church, well located in Boston, would be a great evangelistic power. It seems to me our intelligent men and women in the Churches and in our congregations will appreciate and aid such an enterprise.

Soon after his return from Indiana the Bishop went again to Clifton, where he hoped to be still further benefited. While there he received the sad tidings of Mrs. Janes's sudden prostration by sickness at the residence of their son, at Madison, N. J., an illness which proved not only protracted, but finally fatal.

At the close of the year there came from across the water a breath of tender sympathy from the noble-hearted Dr. Robinson Scott, of Belfast, Ireland.

The Rev. Robinson Scott, D.D., to Bishop Janes, December 18:

During dear Mrs. Janes's protracted and serious illness I looked for the "Advocate" weekly with prayerful solicitude, and could not but rejoice with you when I learned she was likely to be spared a little longer to you and to the Church. I trust the hopes now so fondly cherished will be realized. It seems to me that it has been only by the specially sustaining hand of Providence that you have been able to get through the amount of labor with which I have seen your name connected from time to time. Your address to the Preachers' Meeting in Boston did me special good.

In the winter of 1875–76 the Bishop was closely confined by the continued illness of Mrs. Janes. He did not go from home on long journeys, but in and around New York he preached and worked as his strength would allow. His only Conference in the spring was the Newark, March 29–April 5. On leaving his invalid wife for this official duty he bears testimony to her unselfish devotion to the work of God.

To Mrs. Janes, from Newark, N. J., March 29 :

I am at my post of duty. You have never prevented me from going to my work. Whether sick or well, you have always told me to go—sometimes when I knew it subjected you to cares and discomforts of a serious character. I can also testify, that in all possible ways you have aided me in my public duties, and added much to my efficiency as a minister and Bishop of the Church. God knows it all; will understand whom to recompense. I hope and pray that you may have a comfortable day !

The seventeenth delegated General Conference convened in the city of Baltimore, Md., on the first day of May, 1876. All the Bishops were present except Bishop Wiley, who had been detained by sickness, but afterward, on the tenth day of the session, appeared and took his seat with his colleagues.

This General Conference, apart from the measures which were brought before it, was of great interest as occurring in the centennial year of American Independence, and in the city where the Methodist Episcopal Church was organized, and where it is still noted for the numbers, piety, and zeal of its adherents.

It was very hard for Bishop Janes to be absent from Mrs. Janes, but he regarded his official duties as imperative. As the senior Bishop he felt that the Church, at such a time, needed his most watchful care. Daily, however, except he went in person, missives of cheer were dispatched to the sick-room in New York, and Mrs. Janes looked as regularly for the sweet morsel from her husband's pen as for her breakfast. I give extracts from these letters from day to day.

Pausing at the Book Room after he had left his home, he writes, April 26:

Good cheer to you! I have not taken Jesus away from you. Though he goes with me, he abides with you, and will do so evermore. I am sorry to leave you in your weakness, and would not do it but for the great obligations that are on me. God smile on you!

17

From Baltimore, April 27:

Sixty-nine years ago to-day a great event took place. A little boy baby cried. They named him Edmund. He grew to be a man, and is now gray-headed. About forty-one years ago he asked you a certain question, and you were so kind as to say " Yes." A few days after the minister asked you a question, and you answered, " I will." These are the great events in my history. I don't remember much about the first one. The others I remember all about. I know just the spot on which each occurred, the manner of their performance, all the little incidents attending them. I have never ceased to be thankful for them. I send you my sixty-ninth birthday kiss.

April 28 :

I have been shut up with my colleagues and have seen nobody as yet. To-day is our fast day. We spend a part of it in a prayer-meeting: special prayer for the divine blessing on the General Conference. I offer special prayer for my beloved ones at home all the time.

April 29:

My draft of the Episcopal Address has been read to my colleagues, and by them approved. I intended to read it to you and have your sharp criticisms upon it before I left home, but you were not able to bear it. My colleagues modified it very little. I have added to it a little. As soon as it is published I will send you a copy.

April 30:

I hope you will have a comparatively comfortable Sunday to-morrow. I hope you will eat angels' food. I am sure you would if you could hear Dr. Chapman preach one of his sweet sermons. Prayer can bring the celestial banquet to you in the sick room if it is offered in fervency and faith. God's presence makes a sanctuary every-where.

May 1 :

This morning our General Conference opened. It falls on me to preside. The organization of the Conference is always more or less trying to the presiding officer. I hope, by God's favor, we may have a peaceful and useful Conference. I wish I knew just how you are this morning. I feel sure that your trust in God is unfailing, and that your peace and spiritual joy continue.

May 2 :

My burden of organizing the Conference is gone. It looks now as if the session would not be so long as sometimes, but we cannot tell what debates may arise. I wish I could kiss you good morning.

May 4 :

The Address has been read. It took me about an hour and a half to read it. The resolution adopted immediately in relation to it will show with what great favor it was received. No one but the Lord knows, or can know, how much study it cost me. Nothing but my interest in the Church could have induced me to perform the labor. It is the last Address of the kind I shall ever write or read. I am thankful God has most graciously aided me in preparing and delivering this one.

May 5 :

The Conference is now discussing the Indian question, in some respects, in my judgment, unwisely—more politically than religiously. General Fisk is now cooling them down. I wish you could be here and hear them. Nature is putting on her spring dress, green and red and blue, very gay, but very lovely indeed. God's pictures are the most beautiful we ever see, or ever shall see, till we look at the beauties of heaven.

May 6 :

The first week of Conference is passed. To-day we had the Address of the British Delegates—very good. This afternoon Bishop Ames gave me a drive to the park and to his farm, five miles from the city. The park is very fine; its natural beauties, I think, are greater than our Central Park, but it is not much improved as yet. The Bishop's farm is a very nice one. The fruit trees were in full bloom. I wish you could see them. I know how pleasant a sight it is to you to see an orchard in bloom. I presume the picture of last spring has not faded from your mind.

May 8:

Another Sabbath is numbered with those before the flood. Another Monday morning has dawned, bringing its activities and responsibilities. So life is being measured and passing away. No matter how fast it goes if it is well employed, or how soon it ends if God calls us to a higher sphere, and brings us nearer to himself. I went to church but once yesterday. Heard Bishop Bowman preach a good, earnest, practical sermon from Esau selling his birthright. After it I administered the sacrament to a very large number of people. It was a devout and spiritual service.

May 9:

I wish you were able to enjoy your former activity out of doors. Perhaps that time may come by next autumn. I am thankful you have so many indoor pleasures—sweet flowers, sweet friends, sweet prayers. These mitigate confinement and suffering, though they may not remove them. God can give relief. I entreat him to do so.

May 10:

We can afford to travel a long, weary road to get to heaven. A very short experience of its joys will well repay all the struggle and pain endured on the way. Heaven will be cheap at any cost to us. Jesus did not pay any more for it than its true value. If it is worth the price of his sufferings and blood, certainly it is worth all we can endure in its pursuit. I know that your enjoyment of the divine nature and divine presence here and now, give you a richer apprehension of the heavenly world than we can put into words.

May 11:

I awoke this morning with the hymn running through my mind which has in it this expression, "Rivers of delight." The thought never arrested my attention before. " Rivers of delight!" what an expression! · Celestial delight—rivers that never dry. "Who shall make them to drink of the river of thy pleasure, O Lord!" The pleasure of God—a river of God's pleasure. You have long tasted this bliss, it has been to you a satisfying portion. I doubt not you feel its power this morning. God bless you more and more!

May 17:

I was surprised when you told me that the nine months you have been on a bed of languishing and pain seemed so short to you. I supposed they seemed long, tedious months. Eternity will be without pain; will that seem short? No, it will neither seem short nor be short. We shall never fear to enter into any pleasure because it will take a portion of our eternity. Eternity has no portion or parts.

May 18:

I awoke this morning with this passage in my mind, "He brought me to his banqueting house, and his banner over me was love." God's banquet—spiritual food. You have been sitting at this table of spiritual luxuries, of heavenly dainties, a long time. It is a royal banquet. None but God could furnish it. "His banner over me was love." Not an ensign of authority, not an emblem of power, but a banner of love. Who but Jesus ever floated such a banner? Who but Jesus ever invited men to a standard he had stained with his life blood? "I, if I be lifted up, will draw all men unto me." The cross is his ensign. Following this banner we shall find our latest foe under our feet at last.

May 19:

The elections are mainly over. The great excitement of the Conference is probably past. There will be some earnest debate on questions of change in the Discipline. It does not look now that any radical changes will be made in our church polity. The Bishops and delegates had a reception given them last night by Brother R. Stockett Matthews. It was a very pleasant, and I think profitable, occasion.

May 21:

I preached this morning to a large, intelligent congregation of colored people. I enjoyed the service. I preached on " Walking in the fear of the Lord, and comforts of the Holy Ghost." It is a hundred years to-day since the first Methodist Conference was held in this city. They have a centennial celebration this afternoon. I am too weary to attend. God has made a wonderful history for himself since that first little Methodist Conference was held. I trust you are having a Sabbath of much spiritual comfort. You worship in the "Queen's Chapel." God is with us in the closet, especially when that closet is a furnace of affliction.

May 24:

Yesterday a friend took me to Mount Olivet Cemetery, where Bishops Asbury, George, Emory, and Waugh are buried; also, Dr. Robert Emory and a number of our distinguished ministers. Strawbridge and Jesse Lee are likewise buried here.

May 25:

Is the loving-kindness of the Lord new to you this morning? Has the Sun of Righteousness risen upon you with healing in his beams? Is it a bright, beautiful day-time with the soul? I trust so. The Conference to-day takes an excursion to Annapolis. I shall not go. I do not believe in the thing; and if I did it would be too wearisome for me. I have work enough to employ me usefully.

May 27:

I am thankful that grace enables you to sustain your long-continued afflictions. Christ was made perfect through suffering. If we suffer with him, we shall also be glorified with him. "There remaineth, therefore, a rest to the people of God." Not the rest of sleep, but the rest of exemption from all suffering and all liability to sorrow. To be separated from all evil, and removed beyond the reach of it, will be a wonderful salvation. But the Christian's heaven is not a mere negative one. It is also the possession of all perfection and all bliss. With God—like Jesus—that is heaven.

May 29:

Another holy Sabbath is passed. I preached in the morning in Bethany Church, an Independent Methodist Church. To me it was a profitable service. I preached Christ crucified. The Conference on Saturday voted on the Presiding Elder Question. The conservative men were found to be in the majority. This was satisfactory to me and the conservative portion of the Conference. I do not think there has been so important a vote in any General Conference since 1844.

June 2:

I once more greet you from the head-quarters of the army of Methodism. The forces are scattered in every direction. The chief officers are planning for the campaign : I pray that it may be one of signal success. I expect to be at the domestic head-quarters to-morrow.

It was well understood by the members of the Conference that the Episcopal Address was chiefly the production of Bishop Janes. Rarely has any document in any assembly been listened to with more profound respect and attention. All felt that it was likely the last authoritative utterance of a

Bishop who had studied and loved and served the Church for so long a period, and with an absorption which knew no bounds. The document was worthy of the man and of the Church of whose polity and mission it was an exposition. Never had Bishop Janes stood higher with his brethren than at the conclusion of its delivery. It was conceded to be equal to any effort of his life. Though he was now threescore years and ten, it was evident that his eye was not dim nor his natural force abated. The record contained in these pages would be far from complete unless the concluding paragraphs of this noble deliverance, into which his soul was wrought, should have a place:

The true Church has always preached the Gospel to the poor. This has been characteristic of Methodism throughout its history. It is not only Christ-like, but it is expedient. The Church which preaches to most of the poor of this generation, other things being equal, will preach to most of the rich in the next generation. While we have not been inattentive to the pastoral and spiritual interests of the more wealthy of our congregations, we have been especially desirous to provide for the religious necessities of the poor; hence the new and more needy parts of the work have received our especial consideration and care.

While it is proper that every government should, in its organic law, make provision for changes which may become necessary, and prescribe the method of effecting the same, yet it appears to us a monstrous absurdity that any government, civil, military, or ecclesiastical. should allow men to whom the administration of its affairs has been intrusted to use their office, or executive authority, or opportunity, to overthrow or modify the same. We, therefore, have resisted the pressure brought to bear upon us since the last General Conference, which sought to induce us to restrict our labors and administration to Episcopal districts, and have continued to meet the explicit requirement of the Discipline to travel through the connection at large. We regard it a very gross solecism to say that a districted Bishop is an itinerant general superintendent. On this subject the Bishops, in their Address to the General Conference of 1852, spoke more at length.

Perhaps our office and work lead us to think more about the future of the Church than we would do but for our special duties. Be this as it may, whenever we meet for consultation, it is a subject of intense interest, of earnest and prayerful consideration and study. When we contemplate the great number of her ministers and members, the perfectness and power of her organization, her vast resources of men and money, her educational and publishing facilities and arrangements, the vantage ground she occupies by her strategic positions in so many of the nations of the earth, the gracious manner in which God has blessed and prospered her in the past, his infinite readiness to bless her still more abundantly in the future, and the grandeur of her possibilities in the time to come, we are overwhelmed with the weight of our responsibilities in superintending such immense interests. At the same time, this glorious prospect of the advancement and achievements of the Church in her coming history is an inspiration to us to call mightily on God to help us, and to go forward in the faithful discharge of our important duties.

For the reason given before, we have judged it due to ourselves, to the General Conference, to which we are amenable, to the whole Church, indeed to the Christian public, that with the utmost frankness and candor we should make this declaration of the principles, sentiments, and purposes which have constrained, and guided, and governed us in our official duties, and in meeting the grave responsibilities which have rested upon us.

You will infer from this statement, and the Church will infer
17*

from it also, that your Bishops have not considered themselves Church architects employed to examine an antiquated and dilapidated edifice, and to show how it can be remodeled and modernized and improved ; but that, on the contrary, they have understood themselves called to be general superintendents of a glorious temple, its walls salvation and its gates praise ; a temple built by God ; built on the Rock of Ages, and built for the ages ; that it is their office and work to see that its doors stand open night and day ; that its light is shining clear, and strong, and afar ; that its voice of instruction, and admonition, and invitation, and entreaty, is breaking upon the ear of humanity every-where and all the time ; that its altars are all aglow with the fervors of love and the fires of devotion, converts flying as a cloud and as doves to their windows ; all nations flowing into it, and the glory of Immanuel filling it.

The correspondence of the Bishop from Baltimore shows the intense interest which he felt in the " presiding-elder question." This was the principal issue before the Conference. The question of a readjustment of the presiding eldership has, from time to time, agitated the Church from its origin. The agitation for change had been going forward for the preceding four years, and culminated at this Conference in a proposition so to modify the office as to give the Annual Conferences power to nominate the men whom the Bishops should appoint. Many members of the Conference were of the opinion that such a modification would be wholesome, and would in no sense impair the efficiency of the appointing power. It was well understood that the Bishops were averse to the change. Bishop Janes, in common with his colleagues, deprecated it. We have seen how well satisfied he was with the failure of the proposition.

The next most absorbing matter with the Bishop was that of fraternization with the Methodist Episcopal Church, South ; and few hours of his life gave him more pleasure than that in which he introduced to the Conference the Rev. James A. Duncan, D.D., and Landon C. Garland, LL.D., fraternal delegates from that Church.   Thus the chasm between the two great Methodisms of America, which had yawned for thirty-two years, was spanned, and he who was the only surviving Bishop elected by the two sections of the Church before the separation, was allowed to preside at the happy consummation.

By resolution of the Conference a commission of five, three ministers and two laymen, was appointed to meet a similar commission from the Church South to adjust all existing difficulties between the two Churches.   These commissioners subsequently met at Cape May, August 17, and adopted a plan of settlement which has done much to promote actual as well as formal fraternity between the two great bodies.   Bishop Janes lived long enough to rejoice in this result.   A tradition floats in my recollection that one of our commissioners said to the Bishop, in speaking of the difficulties in the way of settlement, " What, Bishop, if we can't agree ? "   " You must pray until you do agree," was the quick and emphatic response.

Upon the adjournment of the General Conference the Bishop hastened to his invalid wife. After a week or two he is found for a few days at the Round Lake camp-meeting.

To Mrs. C. E. Harris, from New York, July 2:

I had a pleasant time at the Round Lake camp-meeting. I returned on Tuesday night. Dear mother continues about the same. God's ways are indeed mysterious. Why your precious mother, one of the most devoted, godly Christian women, should be called to such great distress in the last period of life is wonderful. If we looked only at the outward and present circumstances of God's children we should be led inevitably to inquire, " What is the Almighty, that we should serve him?" etc. But we have further knowledge. We know that God is love. We know his wisdom is absolute. His reason for cleansing his people in the furnace of affliction will not always be a secret. I have no doubt when it is clearly revealed we shall shout "Hallelujah!" with all our immortal powers. Eternity will not be a struggle of faith, but a fruition of vision. How your dear mother has been divinely supported! She could never have endured her sufferings but for her spiritual comforts. God does not leave nor forsake those that trust in him.

To the same, from New York, July 9:

Your mother is fully ripe for heaven. She longs to depart to be with Jesus. Though filled with the anticipation of heaven, indeed with the realization of heaven, she does not repine at her protracted sufferings. She repeatedly says, " Good is the will of the Lord." His time is her time.

The Bishop met the Delaware Conference at Philadelphia, July 20–24. Thence he writes Mrs. Janes, on the 21st:

Another day's work is done. It has been a day of trial and care, and, I hope, of some usefulness. I wish I knew how you are to-night. I hope you will be able to get some good, refreshing sleep. I hope the worst of the hot season is past. The atmosphere of heaven will always be perfectly delicious. No excess—no lack—just right.

This was the last Conference the Bishop held. His official work of "fixing" the appointments was to close with the poor and lowly brethren of color. He had met the Washington and Delaware Conferences more frequently than any other Bishop, and none of the board felt a kindlier and more tender sympathy with these bodies than he. The Rev. J. Emory Round, A.M., who was present at this Conference, thus speaks of it:

This Conference, as is generally known, consists entirely of colored men. He attended to all his duties with the same patience and carefulness as ever. I remember the occasion the more clearly because it was the first time that any of my own sons in the Gospel (from the Centenary Biblical Institute) were set apart to the ministry. Very few suspected him to be in physical distress until just before the close of the conference session, when he asked the presiding elders to call on him the next morning that he might sign their drafts on the missionary treasury, adding, "I cannot attend to it to-night; I am in too great pain." Yet on that very afternoon he had been present with the Conference to have a photograph taken of the body, enduring a long and most vexatious delay, at which he was probably the only one that did not utter a word of complaint. After making the above request, all of the concluding exercises of the Conference were likewise conducted with no more haste than usual. After adjournment I exclaimed, "I wonder what Bishop Janes will do when he is *compelled* to stop work," adding, after a moment's reflection, " I think when he cannot labor he will be unable to live;" a prediction that was very speedily fulfilled.

Bishop Janes's most intimate friends knew that, so far as any part of the work of the Church could be regarded as an object of *especial* interest by him, his specialty was the work among the colored people. He usually, however, escaped eulogy on this account, as his interest in *every* department of Christian effort was so great that his especial devotion to this one never attracted general attention.

A great change was fast drawing nigh in the Bishop's household. Mrs. Janes was perceptibly failing, so that he rarely left the house. Once he went down to the Jersey sea-shore to dedicate two churches, one named in honor of himself; where besides, I know not, but certainly not often nor far did he go from home. On Sunday evening, August 13, his saintly wife entered into rest. Her funeral services took place at the residence, in East Twenty-fourth-street, on the afternoon of the 16th, conducted by the devoted friend and pastor of the family, Rev. J. A. M. Chapman, D.D.

These pages have given evidence from first to last of the pure conjugal love which subsisted between the Bishop and his wife. Through forty-one years they had cherished an unfaltering and ever-deepening affection for one another, and were helpful of each other's faith and usefulness. The amount and character of the service he was enabled to perform was not a little due to her. The Church saw his work, much of it at least; but did not see,

save the few who intimately knew her, the life of.
faith, zeal, and self-sacrifice at home, which in its
wealth of gentle and untiring service gave the leisure and supplied the resources of the great worker.
Though always of feeble physical health, she never
detained her husband from his official duties either
to nurse herself or to care for the children. She
exemplified in the family circle the homelier virtues which rendered that circle the charm of her
itinerating husband and the delight of her children
and friends. And if any who were only distantly
acquainted with her supposed she was reserved and
severe, they greatly misunderstood her nature. A
more genial, playful disposition was never possessed than hers. Evidently her original sportive-
ness had been much repressed by her earlier, strict-
er views of religion ; but later in life the virgin
spring would bubble up, much to the joy and sometimes even to the entertainment of those about her.

I doubt if there ever was a more truly religious
woman than Mrs. Janes. Her insight into spiritual truth was more clear and correct than that of
any lady whom I have known. Her own consciousness, in which she had sounded the depths
of the perfect love of God, threw a flood of light
on every subject of which she spoke. This was
true of her public exercises, in the social devotional
meetings, but eminently so of her private talks. I
was accustomed, when her pastor, often to call on

her on Saturday afternoons, that I might be enlightened and inspirited by her judicious and elevating conversation. I think all her pastors felt much the same. Her incisive, subtle intellect would lay open the most abstruse question of the Christian life; while her faith, always supreme, would lift the discouraged out of the shadows of doubt and fear. Her calm and wide views of God and his ways afforded anchorage for the weary and tossed believer of every degree of culture; the high and low could alike find a haven of spiritual rest by her side.

And no one appreciated so highly the vigor of her intellect, the fullness of her mental resources, and the delicacy and purity of her taste, as her husband. We have seen how he wished to submit the Episcopal Address to her judgment: "I intended to read it to you and have your sharp criticism upon it, but you were not able to bear it." But how often such processes had taken place, especially in the earlier years of the Bishop, is not known. It is fair to infer they were frequent, and possibly systematic, and that they account in no small degree for the uniform fertility and adaptation with which he met all occasions. While, therefore, accepting as the suitable sphere for herself, her home, and the religious and benevolent work of the Church, she might equally have excelled in the more conspicuous walks of life.

The following graceful and loving tribute to Mrs. Janes was written by her friend, Mrs. Mary Lowe Dickinson, soon after Mrs. Janes's death :

A PICTURE.

Just as sweetly as fades the light
  After the sun is gone,
Just as gently as through the night
  The steady stars shine on,
Just as softly as spring leaves come,
  Or snow-flakes whiten the sod,
Passed she out from an earthly home
  Into the home of God.

Never the rays of moon or sun
  Fell on her face that day,
And only a heavenly artist's hand
  Could have left such light on clay.
We knew that angel hands had wrought
  Each day at the soul within,
With loving touches of prayer and thought
  Hiding each trace of sin ;

Sweeping the heavy shade of pain
  Over the smile of her face,
And leaving the gleam of a Father's love
  And the light of the cross in its place.
And so it was—their sweet work done—
  When the Master bade them cease
There was left for our eyes to gaze upon
  This beautiful picture of peace.

The Bishop never seemed fully the same after she was taken from him. He went about attending to the claims of his office as strength and circumstances would allow, but there was a subdued, pen-

sive tone and manner in all that he did.   Evidently
the spell of his earthly life was broken.   The presence which made home had fled, and to find home
he must follow it.   And very quickly he did.

The last sermon he preached was in the little
church at Maplewood, N. J., of which his son, the
Rev. Lewis T. Janes, was the pastor.   He was the
guest, at the time, of Mr. D. H. Carpenter, to whom
I am indebted for an account of the services and
some of the attendant circumstances:

A few days before the Sabbath above mentioned the writer
received a note stating that the Bishop would be present with
us, and would preach in our little church on the next Sabbath,
August 27.   He came to my house on Saturday afternoon,
and with his son, our pastor, spent the Sabbath.

On Sunday morning, at family worship, I read for our Scripture lesson the Ninetieth Psalm.   I did not purposely make this
selection, but remember full well, as I read the verse, "The
days of our years are threescore years and ten," the quiet
glance—cheerful, peaceful, happy—which met my eye, as for a
moment I looked up from the sacred page.   At the service in
the morning he read and prayed with much fervency, and his
sermon was listened to with the deepest attention.   On his
return from church he seemed quite fatigued, and after dinner
lay down awhile.

My little girl had, from the first, made friends with him, he
bidding her call him "grandpa."   While he was in his room
she slipped away from her mother and must have crept up to
the room of the Bishop, and, before she was missed, he came
down-stairs with little Mabel riding on his shoulders "a la
pick-back," and it was hard to tell which was most pleased, the
Bishop or the child.   At this time, seemingly referring to our
morning psalm, he said : " I am not yet quite threescore and

ten. I preached in this church in 1832, and have traveled thousands of miles since, yet have never forgotten my early days on this circuit and the rides through this beautiful valley." His memory seemed very good, and he apparently recalled these scenes of his early ministry with a great deal of pleasure, albeit acknowledging that they were days of physical hardship.

At the evening service in the church he made the opening prayer, and was so much affected that the tears coursed down his cheeks. One of the audience afterward said to me, that that was the grandest prayer he ever listened to. He then took the large Bible from the desk, and, holding it up before him, read, in clearest tone, the fifth chapter of second Corinthians, " For we know that, if our earthly house of this tabernacle were dissolved, we have a building of God," etc., taking for his text the fourteenth and fifteenth verses of the same chapter. Of this sermon I will only say, had Bishop Janes known that this was his last opportunity " to preach Christ crucified," I doubt if he could have preached more earnestly, more feelingly, or with greater eloquence.

He returned to New York on Wednesday morning, stopping at the Book Room, as was his custom, to get his mail. After reaching home he was taken suddenly and violently ill with a recurrence of the disease with which he had several times before suffered. For more than two weeks the disease continued without abatement, baffling all medical and surgical skill. All the while his pain was so excruciating that he could not converse, paroxysm following paroxysm, so as to preclude connected conversation. Once, while lying on the couch and there was a moment of comparative ease, as his daughters knelt by him, opening his eyes he said,

"My angels!" Frequently, when all was still in
the room and he was thought to be asleep, he might
be heard breaking forth into ejaculatory prayer.
He asked for the reading of the Scriptures and of
hymns, and would listen with rapt attention. To
the prayers of Dr. Chapman he would fervently
respond, and, taking him by the hand, would say,
"Pastor, I thank you." Beyond this he spoke but
little.

On Sunday, at midnight, his son-in-law, stooping
over him, said, "Bishop, say something to us—
some parting word." His brief reply was, "I am
not disappointed." On Monday morning a letter
was sent to the Preachers' Meeting communicating
the fact that he was dying. Several of the ministers came to the house, and the Rev. M. D'C. Craw-
ford, D.D., offered prayer by the sick-bed. By
noon all was over. Bishop Janes had ceased from
his earthly toil and suffering, and was present with
the Lord. He died September 18, 1876, in his
seventieth year. He was for forty-six years a minister, and thirty-two years a Bishop, of the Methodist Episcopal Church.

The funeral services took place from St. Paul's
Church, on Fourth Avenue, on Thursday, the 21st.
The large church was thronged with a multitude of
weeping people. The prayer was offered by the
Rev. C. D. Foss, D.D., and addresses were delivered
by Rev. J. A. M. Chapman, D.D.; the Rev. R. L.

Dashiell, D.D.; the Rev. Bishop Scott; and Rev. Bishop Simpson.

Dr. Chapman spoke as follows:

The character of Bishop Janes was so full and round, so symmetrical and harmonious, its diverse elements and powers so well balanced, he carried himself in such perfect equipoise, was so completely the master of himself, that we are not fully aware of his real greatness, the rare wealth of his mental and moral endowment and attainments, until we attempt an analysis of his character. He possessed an intellect of a very high order, capable of grappling with the profoundest and most abstruse subjects, of the broadest generalization, of the most subtle analysis, logical in its processes, clear in its perceptions, thorough in its mastery of subjects, which, together with a varied and accurate scholarship, enabled him to present his thoughts with great transparency, and made his impromptu deliverances almost as chaste and finished as his more carefully prepared efforts. His mental furnishing was so thorough and complete, his memory so tenacious, and his versatility of talent so great, that he was able to meet any emergency or respond to the demands of any occasion, however sudden or unexpected, and to do himself, the subject, and the occasion ample justice. His ability to see and master subjects thoroughly made his statements of truth so clear and accurate and sharply defined, that the hearer or reader found no difficulty in apprehending his views of any theme he discussed. While never undervaluing the aid of oratory, rhetoric, and elocution, constantly using them with great skill and force, and while his style was not wanting in the ornaments of a chaste and fertile imagination, culled from the varied fields of learning and thought, yet he depended chiefly upon the truth and spirit of the Gospel for success in the ministrations of God's word. His intellectual conceptions of the great doctrinal truths of Christianity, and his deep, rich experience of their power and blessedness, rendered him impatient of that so-called liberalism that is giving to the world a diluted theology, a superficial experience, and a powerless religion. He believed that the Gospel, as announced by Christ and his apostles, constituted the best theme of pulpit discourse ; and, while not unmindful of the bearings of theology upon the great speculative and practical questions of the age, he, nevertheless, was pre-eminently a preacher of the word. To him the Christian religion was something more than a creed, more than a system of ethics, more than a ceremonial, more than a sentiment. It was a divine life, and took hold of the very springs of his being. It was a revelation of Jesus Christ to and in the human soul ; and so he held, with a tenacity born of the most intelligent conviction and the deepest and richest experience, to the old fundamental doctrines of Christianity, believing that the hope of the world was wrapped up in them.

Bishop Janes was endowed with a peculiarly warm, tender, sympathetic, loving nature, that shone out in his whole official and private life, shedding a soft, mellow, beautiful light over it all. He carried his Conferences upon his heart, listening patiently and with the profoundest sympathy to the grievances' hardships, and sacrifices of pastors and people, doing all that careful thought and earnest prayer could do to lighten the burdens of the itinerancy and relieve the feelings of the itinerant and his family. I am safe in saying in this presence, that Bishop Janes never read the appointments at the close of a Conference over which he presided, which had not been conscientiously and prayerfully made, not only with reference to the interests of the Church and the work of God, but with the tenderest and most brotherly regard to the feelings and welfare of each minister and his family. Who ever came to Bishop Janes in trouble for sympathy and counsel, and was repulsed ? Who ever came to Bishop Janes with any burden, and did not go away with a lighter heart, at least, because of his tender, considerate, loving sympathy ? Bishop Janes was the preacher's friend ; he was the layman's friend ; he was the friend of man, every-where and always. Who was in sorrow and affliction, and his heart was not touched ? How many homes, and how many hearts, in the dark night of sorrow and bereavement, were cheered by his saintly presence, or by those tender, loving letters of sympathy and condolence which he alone could write! His quiet, kind, loving nature contributed much to make his own home one of rare beauty and attraction. There, as every-where, he was the perfect gentleman, courteous, high-toned; but in his own home there was a freshness and simplicity of affection that neither the burden of public life and high position, nor the weight of increasing years, suppressed or even chilled. . . . It was my privilege frequently to visit him during his sickness. Almost always he would request me to pray with him, and on such occasions he would respond with a hearty "Amen." His sufferings and weakness were so great that he could converse but little. He said to me one day, between his paroxysms of pain, "The mission of life seems to be to work and to suffer." At another time he said, "I do not know what I should do without Christ." And Christ was a great deal to him.

When asked if Jesus was precious, he replied, "O yes;" and when the beautiful words of the psalmist were repeated, "Though I walk through the valley of the shadow of death, I will fear no evil: for thou art with me; thy rod and thy staff they comfort me," he responded, "Beautiful," the full significance of which he was then triumphantly realizing. So passed away one of the noblest men God ever gave to the Church, and so ended one of the most perfect lives that has ever blessed the world. I have a fancy—it may be only a fancy—that when Christ called his original college of apostles he unfolded his Gospel, analyzed it, and let each disciple represent an element. But when he called Paul, the great Apostle to the Gentiles, he put it together, and gave it to us in him embodied. In the first he spelled Christianity to the world, in the last he pronounced it for the world; and in the character and life of few men in the history of the Church has the Gospel—the whole Gospel—been so clearly, fully, and distinctly pronounced as in the life and character of our lamented Bishop. He was as practical as James, as intense as Peter, as tender and loving as John, as many-sided and comprehensive as Paul. Truly " A prince and a great man has fallen in Israel." And the great heart of the Church beats sadly, sorrowfully, at the portals of his grave.

In his address Dr. Dashiell spoke of Bishop Janes in his relation to the missionary work:

Bishop Janes, in his relation to the Missionary Society of the Methodist Episcopal Church, embraced almost its entire history and work. The cause of Christian missions was always first upon his heart; and long before he became one of the Bishops of the Methodist Episcopal Church, he sought every opportunity to plead for that Christian charity; and when he was made a Bishop he became more immediately identified with the active work of the Society. One fact will sum up the relations of that great and good man to this Society. He carried in his loving heart, and in his great, comprehensive mind, not only the whole field of missions in its entirety, domestic and foreign, but was minutely acquainted with all the particulars of that work. He was, indeed, a walking encyclopedia of the missions of the Methodist Church. It was almost an impossibility for any of the secretaries to make an inquiry of Bishop Janes, with reference to the mission work at home or abroad, that he was not found to be as familiar with it as with the appointments of the last Conference. When a letter would come to our office from some brother at a distant point on the frontier, asking for aid, it was only necessary to wait until Bishop Janes came in, and to lay that letter before him, to see that he was as familiar with the personal condition of the ministers of the Methodist Church scattered all over this vast country, as he was with those immediately near him in the city.

I shall never forget the majesty and the solemnity which combined in his voice, as he shook my hand for the last time on that morning when he left my house. I had been lamenting the condition of the missionary treasury. Holding on to my hand with a grasp that told the deep feeling of his soul, and looking into my eyes as his own almost flashed with fire, he said to me, "Doctor, *the Church of the Lord Jesus Christ must sustain the work of the Lord Jesus Christ.*" And these were the last words that fell from his sainted lips upon my ear and upon my heart. And they have been as the inspiration of a new life to me, as I have thought of them since that hour, and as I have stood by and seen his eyes closed in death. My heart yearns to say some tender words of his loving personal relations in the homes which he has visited. That gentle, loving voice greeted children and domestics with a kindness that at once seemed to take possession of them. You remember when he entered your home, how he would have felt he had neglected some great duty and pleasure if he had permitted himself to enter without putting his hands on the heads of the children, and asking God's blessing upon them. I now have rising before me the memory of the last sight I had of him as he stood upon my porch. The members of my family, including my old colored help, came out to bid him good-bye, and he shook hands with, and gave a blessing to each one. When he had crossed the street he remembered he had not said good-bye to the little child, the youngest born of the family, and he walked back again, though pressed for time, and said, "O, I haven't said good-bye to my little daughter!" then, taking her hand, he left a benediction upon her little head, and upon her little heart. It was this tender, loving spirit that made him always welcome in our home; we greeted him with a doxology, and we felt that he left a benediction with us all.

After a short address from Bishop Scott, Bishop Simpson said:

Bishop Janes's character has been analyzed to-day very beautifully—and all his characteristics existed in force—his clear and vigorous intellect, his very quick perception, his logical powers, his vivid imagination, that gave him grasp of all surrounding circumstances, and his deep piety, bringing all to the foot of the cross. But I believe, after all, the grand and strik-

18

ing feature in Bishop Janes's character was the strength of his will. He had one of the most indomitable wills that I think ever was placed in a man's bosom, fitting him for any work, or for any enterprise. If he had been a general he would have been like Charles the Twelfth or Napoleon, sparing neither himself nor his army. As a statesman he would have led this country forward without regard to health. But the manifestation of his will was modified by his loving spirit, his deep devotion, his tender regard for the feelings, the reputation, the interests, and the honor of his brethren; and only occasionally did you see its outbursts, at some moment of decision, some moment requiring energy. Then, just as if from the bosom of some placid flood, when you never suspected winds, or lightning flash, or thunder blast, there came an outburst that almost startled you, his whole nature would rise at once, and you knew you were in the presence of a master-mind when Bishop Janes was aroused and displayed the power of his will. He controlled his feelings; he was naturally quick and impulsive, but in all perplexity and trial he was affectionate and tender. This strength of his will made him consecrate his whole powers to the Church. I never knew a man who spared himself so little, and was so determined to meet all engagements he had made. Dr. Chapman has spoken of his resemblance to some of the apostles. In a sermon I heard him preach, in his peroration, Bishop Janes used language which I shall never forget. After showing how workers with Christ would be sharers of his glory, he urged upon the ministers a holy ambition; he urged them to set their mark high, and, among other things, said he intended, God helping him, if he could, to get as near the throne as the Apostle Paul. It was strong language, and yet such was the ardor of his soul he seemed to feel it all. It was a holy ambition. For depth of emotion, for perfectness of consecration, for dedication of the whole life and power to the service of God, especially in the Church of which he was a member and an instrument for good, I have never known his superior. My belief is, that few wiser, holier, more consecrated, and more successful ministers have ever gone up to glory.

Bishop Janes was buried in Greenwood Cemetery the next morning. Seldom has a man been borne to his grave amid deeper grief. There, in scarcely more than one short month, he was laid by the side of his sainted wife—"they were lovely and pleasant in their lives, and in their death they were not divided."

From all the different societies and bodies with which he had .been connected, and from many of the Annual Conferences and Preachers' Meetings, and many great and good men in both hemispheres, resolutions and letters expressive of respect for his memory and of sympathy for the living were received by his family. The secular and religious press every-where took note of his death, and spoke of his services in terms of high appreciation. "The entire Church will sorrow over this afflictive providence, something as a household mourns when the father is removed."

CHAPTER XXI.

Character and Work.

WHAT most of all must impress the reader of the foregoing memorials, is the completeness of Bishop Janes's life and character. He averaged well, and the average was high, as man, thinker, patriot, preacher, ruler. Far from being deficient in any one, he excelled in them all, and it is difficult to determine in what capacity most to admire him. At this distance he looms up in his individuality; a distinct figure, clear-cut and grand in outline, as some tall peak lifts itself from the general level of the mountain range. And as the hour of his translation from the Church militant to the Church triumphant recedes into the past, more and more will his relative pre-eminence be seen and acknowledged. The lapse of time is necessary for the full estimate of a character which combined such an assemblage of good qualities; touching all men so easily as to obscure somewhat, by their very naturalness, their true worth. For tenacity of purpose, knowledge of men, and ability for work, he may be compared with Asbury; for legal acumen, he was the equal of Emory; for statesmanlike sagacity, he was a second Hedding; as a Christian gentleman, he was the peer of Waugh; and as a preacher, he combined the sententiousness of Morris, the unction of George, and the eloquence of M'Kendree.

The background of the whole of this was prayer. Piety was Bishop Janes's element. He lived in an atmosphere of prayer. It will be recollected that while a very young preacher, when asked why he prayed so long in the public services, his answer was, "Because I love to pray." The members of his family testify, that not unfrequently when at home he would spend much of the night in devotion. He would write letter after letter, until the usual bedtime approached, when the family would retire, and leave him with the understanding that he would quickly follow. When he did not come, his daughter, Miss Janes, ever so watchful of him, knowing how weary he was, would call to him, " Papa, do come; you need your rest." "Yes, my dear, directly." To each call, the answer was, " Directly." And there, in the back parlor, with the lights turned low, as the small hours tripped in, might the man of God be found, alone and wrestling with the Angel of the Covenant. His work was among men, but the roots of this activity penetrated to those depths whence flow the perennial springs which supply the life-giving power and freshness of all saving work. Writing to his wife on one occasion, he says, " I have for years daily consecrated myself

unreservedly to God." He maintained not only the
frame and habit of devotion, but his practice was
to precede every duty of importance with especial
prayer. Like the divine Master, who spent the
whole night previous to the calling of his disciples
in the solitude of the mountain with the Father,
so thus his humble and devoted servant uniformly
prepared himself for every great event by personal
heart-searchings and by communion with God.

On the point of his personal religious experience,
whether in private or public, he was rather reticent
than otherwise. He spoke sparingly of his attainments; nothing of his sacrifices and labors; but
much, very much, of Christ and his salvation—of
the yearning desire he possessed to spread the Redeemer's kingdom. If there be such a thing in the
future life as a mission to preach the Gospel to
other worlds, the language of his heart will be, "I
want to go on it."

If there was ever any appearance of narrowness in
Bishop Janes, it was in his impatience of any thing
which interfered with this same preaching of the
Gospel. With him, both for himself and for others
engaged in the sacred vocation, it was the matter
of supreme importance. In this he shared the views
of Mr. Wesley—"Getting knowledge is good, but
saving souls is better:" and he believed implicitly
in the preaching of the word as the great agency
for saving men. He said of himself, that he had

not turned aside "to write books or to deliver lectures," but had kept to the one work of preaching.
This seeming intolerance of time and energy employed otherwise than in the direct pastoral function, was not that he appreciated other work less,
but that he appreciated this work more. He was so
convinced of the indispensableness of the proclamation of the Gospel by divinely appointed and qualified men as the one constituted method of saving
the race, that he felt for a man so called and furnished to step aside for any thing else, however
good, was a waste of resources. "Let the dead
bury their dead; but go thou and preach the kingdom of God."

Still, it must not be thought that he in any sense
undervalued learning. He was from the first the
patron and promoter of schools and colleges. He
spoke the most pronounced and encouraging words
for the education of both men and women, of both
laymen and ministers. No one had a greater regard for the more cultivated and scholarly men of
the Methodist ministry. He deferred to them; he
sought in every way to accord to them all possible
honor and means of usefulness and advancement.
If in the first beginnings of theological schools he
was indifferent to their establishment, it was not
that he undervalued an educated ministry, but that
he dreaded the artificial and spiritless methods of
preaching which he had known to result from the

drill, or want of drill, in such institutions among other denominations. Hence, in his address at Drew Theological Seminary, he exclaims, with warmth and tremendous emphasis, "If there comes to you a lion, don't take away his roar; and if a tiger, don't extract his teeth or cut off his claws." He wanted the learning from books, but not at the expense of original genius: first, that which is natural; afterward, that which is learned. No one knew better than he did, that "it is not by books alone, or by books chiefly, that a man is made a man" and a preacher.

This leads me to speak of him as an educated man. His early school advantages were very limited, but we have seen how he read law and medicine; and his whole career discloses the fact that he was an habitual and close student. The number of his books was small, but these he pondered well. It is said that he read and re-read the orations of Daniel Webster every year of his life, regarding them as the best models of good English. He possessed to a remarkable degree the power of abstraction: he could think subjects through under very unfavorable circumstances; compose sermons and speeches, improvise verses, frame decisions, write long and choice letters, in the turmoil of Conference sessions and while seated in the chair. He was a man of wide and close observation, nothing escaping his attention, and by a rapid assimilation he made all that he either saw or heard his own. Thus his mind became stored with all manner of information, so that a judge so capable as Dr. Stephen Olin remarked of him years ago, "Of all the distinguished men with whom I have been acquainted, I have never known any one whose practical knowledge of men and things exceeds that of Bishop Janes." There is not a doubt, but if he had in his early career been directed into professorial lines of work instead of into the more practical fields of employment, he would with application have become as exact and thorough in scholarship as in his knowledge of affairs. The same original insight and patience of research which made him eminent in the department to which the allotment of Providence assigned him, would have rendered him great in any other one sphere of investigation to which he might have confined his faculties.

First of all, Bishop Janes was an orator. From the beginning of his public life he thought, felt, and spoke as an orator; eloquence was the medium of his communications and the instrument of his power. "Beneath the philosopher's brow there was the warrior's eye." It was this divinely-endowed gift which first gave him access to men's minds and ascendency over their wills. Upon eloquence as a basis his fame and power arose. As a speaker he was equally at home on all occasions; always possessed of a quiet repose which invariably put his

18*

hearers at their ease, and prepared them to expect
a just, sensible, and thorough treatment of the sub-
ject-matter on which he spoke. They seldom failed
to get what they expected—and at times more
than they expected—for with instruction and argu-
ment for the groundwork of what he said, he would
rise with his theme, his voice and person expanding
as he proceeded, until, not unfrequently, he would
conclude with a burst and blaze of impassioned
thought and appeal which would arouse the deepest emotions. At such moments, he would utter
truths well-nigh inspired, that would burn into the
hearts, and sink with astonishing weight upon the
minds, of his hearers. Once, addressing a crowded missionary meeting in Boston, after arguing,
coaxing, pleading, and inveighing, because of the
want of adequate comprehension of and giving to
missions, he exclaimed, "We must stop talking
as a Church about so much per member. We cannot convert the world by *poll-tax!* We must appeal to the conscience. This small talk gives small
collections. We must give as God has prospered
us!" The effect was electrifying, and men went
to their homes ashamed of their petty " my-propor-
tion " giving.

But most of all, the orator was himself in the pulpit. Here was his strong tower. He felt himself
invested with an authority and clothed with a responsibility, when he arose before men as the em-

bassador for Christ to speak to them the word of reconciliation, such as he realized at no other time. As I have intimated, he had the highest possible conception of the sacredness and grandeur of the preaching function. The vocation of a Christian pastor, of which preaching the word is the principal element, was not adopted by him simply as a profession, but accepted from God as an imposed necessity. The same Will which saved him from his sins also set him apart to proclaim salvation to sinners as the one great and indispensable work of his life.

As a preacher, therefore, he had the first and highest qualification—a thorough personal experience of the power, and an equally thorough conviction of the importance, of the Gospel. Only a powerful persuasion can make a powerful preacher. He knew that the Gospel had saved him from sin, and he fully believed that it, and it alone, could save other men. This conviction made him a very earnest preacher. He could not trifle in the pulpit. He could not go into it without preparation —"beaten oil for the sanctuary" was his ideal. He could deal but little, if at all, with any other than the saving or evangelical themes of theology; he must feel each time that he left the sacred desk that he had spoken to spiritual edification, and with such distinctness and fullness that every unconverted sinner would see the way of salvation.

He used plain language. His words were as few as possible and as simple as possible; not, indeed, few to paucity nor simple to baldness, but they were as few as would consist with the copiousness which properly belongs to the richness of the Gospel, and simple in the sense that they were so familiar and vivid as to be easily understood by. even the most illiterate hearer.

As to the manner of Bishop Janes in the pulpit it was naturalness itself—look, attitude, voice, gesture —all answered to the man. There may have been art, he may have studied the rules of elocution, but certainly no one thought of it in his public exercises. There was the farthest remove equally from the tricks of oratory and the stolidness of a so-called preacher-tone and delivery. His manner was the manner of a man who has something important to tell men, and tells it. He seldom used a manuscript in the pulpit. Sometimes, on special occasions, when there were facts to be stated, figures to be given, or extracts to be quoted, when he wished to be accurate and could not trust his memory, he would read; but he was rarely known to deliver a sermon or address throughout other than in the extempore style. And of this style he was one of the best examples our times have known.

While Bishop Janes thus highly estimated the preaching element of the pastoral calling, he did not the less esteem what is commonly known as the pastoral branch of the calling—the work of visiting and personally caring for the members of the congregation. When he was himself the pastor of a Church he was very attentive to this department of his duties; and, indeed, he never ceased to visit and to feel a personal solicitude for those persons in New York city to whom he had borne this sacred and endearing relation. When they were in trouble or sickness, or upon the return of the great festivals, such as Christmas or Thanksgiving, or the recurrence of anniversaries in their families, he would be found snatching a few moments and dropping in upon his former parishioners. His gentleness, tenderness, and devotion rendered his coming to the house of mourning like the ministry of an angel; whoever else might be wanted at the funeral, Bishop Janes must be there, and speak or pray; and this was not because he was the resident Bishop, but because, as a sympathizing pastor, he was known and loved among the people.

It was never of his seeking that he became other than the Christian teacher and pastor. He was often heard to say he preferred that position before any office in the Church. It is not surprising, therefore, that when elevated by the suffrages of his brethren to the office of a Bishop, there ever remained with him such a close sympathy with the pastors, and that there was always in him

such an utter absence of the assertion of prerogative as he mingled with them. He loved to be
with them, to preach for them, and to assist them
in all manner of work. Many a time when his
whole body was aching for rest, and his well-nigh-
starved home affections were crying for the converse of his family, he has been known to go out to
some little village church in New Jersey or elsewhere
to assist a young and struggling preacher with a
protracted meeting, or in the desperate effort to
raise a little money for the liquidation of a church
debt, or the payment of arrearages on the slender
salary.

The grandest preparation of Bishop Janes for the
Episcopacy was his heart. He was a man of deep,
refined, even exquisite, sensibilities. It may, at
first blush, seem absurd to speak of the heart preparation in a man called to an office the discharge of
whose duties so frequently hurts the feelings of the
best men and women, but it must be insisted upon.
A Methodist Bishop without deep and tender affections would be a human monster. There is no
office, in State or Church, so completely founded in
the confidence and love which men bear one for
another as the Methodist Episcopacy. It requires
in its exercise a very delicate and sincere appreciation of the holiest rights of the most conscientious persons. These commit themselves to its
keeping and commands. The whole of what con-

stitutes the highest usefulness of a pastor, as well as the well-being of himself and family, the health, education, and settlement of the children, is involved in the appointment which he may receive from the Bishop; and what the preacher wants to feel most of all, in his assignment, is, that back of the power which appoints him, there lies, first of all, not the highest knowledge, but the truest manliness. This Christian manliness—real love of the brethren—is the conservative element of our Episcopacy, and not eloquence, learning, and statesmanship. In it Bishop Janes excelled.

The unwearied patience with which he listened to the statements of preachers and people was proverbial. Interviews, interchange of letters, the representations of friends, all were considered in the effort to understand all the conditions which should affect an appointment. And just so long as any thing could be done which might possibly render an appointment more acceptable or less grievous, he would not abate his efforts.

Years ago, when the guest of Dr. Eliphalet Clark, of Portland, Maine, at the close of a session of the Maine Conference, in the evening the doctor said to him, "Bishop, you are weary, and had better retire." "No," said he; "I will throw myself on the lounge here. Some of the brethren may feel aggrieved with their appointments and may wish to see me; I want to be convenient for them." And there he would lie, although he was obliged to leave early the next morning. He was known to sit up night after night with his cabinet of presiding elders canvassing the case of one preacher. "It was his motto that 'No appointment was good enough while it might be bettered.' Often he would rally an exhausted and sleepy cabinet, saying, 'Never mind your sleep; you can lose that better than this brother can endure a mistake for a year or longer.'"* He would pour into the ear of his wife such a plaint as this: "We have a great stress of ministers; I know not how to station them. I shall do as well as I know how, looking continually to God." Again: "I will write to Brother ———, when Conference is over, as wisely as I can. It is a delicate and difficult case. A large family and large expectations, with good but not very popular talents. A very good man. I wish I could meet his views. I will do the kindest and best I can with the case."

While there was this love of the pastors which constrained him to do every thing within his power to place them eligibly, his sympathies did not override his judgment. Wisdom ruled in his counsels. There was a love for God and his Church above all human feelings, and to its test he brought every decision, whether it involved the destination of others or himself. The divine will was author-

* "Memorial Discourse," by the Rev. C. H. Fowler, LL.D.

itative; and when, with the best light he could obtain, he discovered this will, he bowed to its behests, even though personal preferences might be invaded. We have seen how he surrendered his home delights to duty; he could not, therefore, hesitate when his friendship for any man stood in the pathway of the higher obligations of conscience.

Undoubtedly the source of his power in the great office he filled so acceptably and efficiently for so many years was this same conscientiousness. He was controlled by a scrupulous regard for the right. He would spare no pains to discover it, and when he had, he was immovable in his position. "Here I stand, I can do no otherwise." This gave him great singleness of purpose and entire simplicity of method in dealing with men and measures. It also gave him an ascendency over men. Nobody ever questioned the motives of Bishop Janes. All believed him to be honest and unselfish. They may have differed with him in opinion; they may sometimes have thought him a little too much imbued with the Methodist churchly idea; but they could not doubt that it was the Church, and God in the Church, and not his own interest or glory, which governed him.

This same conscientiousness made him a man of decided convictions in his Church relations. It repeatedly appears in his correspondence that he would cheerfully have resigned the office of Bishop could

he have done so as a good Methodist. No man
would have endured such hardships as he did unless
he were convinced that the good of the Church
which had been the means of his salvation, and
which he believed to be the best form of Christianity for saving the world, required it. He could
have retired at any time to the pastorate of first-
class charges, or to a snug secretaryship; but no,
he must continue in the laborious work of a Methodist general superintendent, where the decision of
the Church had placed him, and in *it*, with all the
experience which time had given him, serve Methodism, and maintain its doctrines and usages by all
the power with which he was endowed and invested.

If Bishop Janes had grown rich, instead of spending a good fortune and dying comparatively poor, in
his long career in the Episcopacy; if he had used his
power for himself or his friends, there might be a
little possible room for saying, " Men are seldom
known to surrender power, and he was like the
rest." But do we not see that he pursued his work
at the expense of his worldly affairs? " I did not
stop to look after this business; if it suffers I cannot help it. I left these things all with God when
I gave myself to this work." Such, substantially,
was what he wrote when his affairs were suffering for
lack of personal attention. It was no unusual thing
for him to give away in charity, in some years, his
whole salary. For the duties of his station, for the

grand services to Methodism, humanity, and Christ which those duties involved, he laid all upon the altar, and counted not his life dear unto him.

Thus far but little has been said of the abilities which he showed in the Episcopal office. He was wise, tender, and conscientious; this much has appeared; but these attributes were associated with a genius for administration. His mind combined comprehensiveness with a rare knowledge of details. He knew each particular, and knew it in its relation to the whole. No department of Church life, and no man who was active in any department, escaped his attention. A young minister in a remote Conference was once invited to make an address at the anniversary of the American Bible Society in New York. He could not imagine how he came to be invited. Years afterward, expressing his surprise to the Bishop, he quietly replied, " I suggested you." His acquaintance with the preachers, their adaptations and circumstances, and with the Churches and missions, was marvelous. His eyes were over the whole field, at home and abroad, at once; with a lightning glance he surveyed all its possibilities and dangers. Not only did his eyes go, but his feet went every-where. It was a principle with him to be an ensample to the preachers of constant and useful employment. His motto was " Come," rather than " Go." He rejoiced that he had once offered himself as a missionary among the heathen. His determination was to commend his office, not by the exercise of its authority, but by making it out-work and out-sacrifice any other position in the Church, and so prove itself the most useful and indispensable office of the Church.

It is not surprising, therefore, that Bishop Janes's administration was highly successful. His appointments of the preachers at the Annual Conferences usually gave satisfaction. He was always acceptable as a presiding officer—a model of dignity, courtesy, self-control, and dispatch in the conduct of business. He rarely seemed in haste—only the least so when his Conferences crowded one upon another so fast as to compel him forward. He was never known, while in the chair, to use his position to wound a preacher by holding him up to ridicule or censure, but was considerate of the rights of every one. No law decision he made was ever overruled by a General Conference. Some of his chosen enterprises may have fallen short of becoming all he wished or anticipated for them, but it must be remembered that he was obliged oftentimes boldly to throw himself forward in the advance in order to inspire a following at all. Bishop Janes was never afraid of undertaking great things for God, because his faith in God knew no bounds other than His own promise. It may take the Church a century to fill in and complete the picture outlined by his daring, masterly genius — in educational institutions, the conversion of the heathen, church extension, home evangelization, African colonization, the regeneration of the colored race, systematic beneficence, and such like causes—but it will do it. His faith was, that through all dangers "God would take care of his Church," and finally plant it in all the earth.

While a stanch Methodist and a Methodist Bishop, Bishop Janes never lost sight of his relations to all true believers. He was eminently catholic in his views and sentiments. There was a serene height to which he often ascended, where he much delighted to linger, and whence he looked down upon a scene in which all denominational distinctions were dissolved in the entire oneness of the great body of Christian believers. He was in kindly sympathy with all institutions and movements which sought to express Christian unity, and to combine the energies of believers in the extirpation of sin and the advancement of the human race. He loved all the denominations, and rejoiced in their prosperity. Writing to the Rev. Dr. M'Cosh, of Princeton, in answer to an invitation to attend a commencement of the New Jersey College, he says: "Princeton College and the Presbyterian Church have each a noble record on earth, and I am sure they have a glorious one in heaven. . . . I greatly delight in my beloved Church, but I have no denominational jealousies." In the same free spirit we have seen him joining hands with the evangelical Churches in the work of the Christian Commission during the civil war. Despite the weighty stress of his office, he was one of the most active promoters of that noble organization.

But this characterization, inadequate as it is, would be more so if there should be no special mention of his domestic virtues. In the home, more than any where else, his beautiful nature showed itself. His coming was a benediction to the family. And though often too weary to talk, too bur‑ dened with official care to have leisure for the pas‑ times of the house, yet his quiet smile, his heartfelt response to the attentions of wife and children, his fervent prayers at the family altar, rendered his presence at home the source of richest enjoyment while it continued, and of fragrant memories when he had gone.

Who that was ever so favored as to be a guest at his house, can forget the cordiality of his welcome, or the high talk, gentleness, and affability with which he was entertained? "True friends make all the sweetness and all the bitterness of life." So felt Bishop Janes; and if he suffered much bit‑ terness in the long separation from his family, the sweetness he enjoyed when in their society was all the intenser for the privations. Hope was ever carrying him forward to the infinite sweetness of the reunion in heaven. When far away in jour‑

neyings and at Conference sessions his heart was ever turning homeward, and the best cheer for his pilgrimage was the letter from some one member of the family. "These letters from home are bright gems glittering along my pathway ever and anon."

"Marriage," says Clement of Alexandria, "is a school of virtue for those who are thus united, designed to educate them and their children for eternity. Every home, every family, must be an image of the Church." So thought Bishop Janes, and such he sought to make his own home. No man was ever better fitted to perform the duties and to enjoy the amenities of the family; and yet, by the behests of his office, he was obliged to live more in the houses of others than in his own. But everywhere he stayed, or even lodged as a wayfarer for a night, he left the memory of a cheerful, familiar piety, which uniformly inspired in the breasts of all, adults and children alike, the earnest desire for his speedy return.

It is yet too early in history to assign the comparative place of our Bishop among his contemporaries, or among the holy worthies of the past. Nor is it important to do so. His position is somewhat unique. No man certainly since Asbury has made a stronger or a more distinctive impress upon American Methodism; his wise sayings, holy example, heroic services, sweet charity, and self-denying piety will be treasured by generations to come.

"Who is that aged gentleman?" asked one of the most noted generals of the late war of another gentleman, as they were hurrying into New York one day on a New Jersey train: "I see him quite often on the train and have wondered who he is; I have seldom seen such a head and face."

"Why, that is Bishop Janes, of the Methodist Episcopal Church."

"Ah! I thought he must be a remarkable person."

He was a good and great man. We have had but one Bishop Janes, and we shall never have another. "Brief is the span of life given us by nature; but the memory of a life nobly rendered is immortal."

THE END.